The PICKERINGS' LAST Tango

Published by River Grove Books
Austin, TX
www.rivergrovebooks.com

Distributed by River Grove Books

Design and composition by Greenleaf Book Group
Cover design by Greenleaf Book Group
Cover images used under license from ©Adobestock.com

Publisher's Cataloging-in-Publication data is available.

Print ISBN: 978-1-966629-80-1

eBook ISBN: 978-1-966629-81-8

First Edition

The PICKERINGS'

A Very DIFFERENT LOVE STORY

LAST Tango

JOHN GRAYSON HEIDE

River Grove
BOOKS

The Pickerings' Last Tango is dedicated to Janice,
the author's late wife, who listened to his retelling
of a movie-like dream one fateful morning
and said, "You ought to write that."
John lost her to cancer in February 2022.

Prologue

A fine day for a once-in-a-lifetime flight.

Five thousand feet above the Atlantic's blue-green waters, an aging but stalwart Beechcraft Bonanza four-seater jittered through the air as an imposing Navy Seahawk helicopter popped up out of nowhere and began jockeying at an aggressive distance—a nervous mackerel beside a shark.

"Shit! What the—" Guy glanced sideways out his cockpit window and recoiled at the chopper's alarming roar. The helicopter's pilot maintained a menacing span between the weaving aircrafts while glaring back at the Bonanza from behind dark wraparounds and jabbing a finger at his headphones. Guy winced at the grating directive in his own headphones. "November Niner Niner Seven Zero Two, do you read me? Repeat! Do you read me?"

Guy reached for the microphone button, hesitated, and instead shut the radio off. "Shit!"

From the passenger seat, a bony, pale fist punched him on the shoulder. "Sweetie, one escort wasn't enough for you?"

"What? Where?" He squinted past the woman's enigmatic grin and her outstretched finger.

Trailing two hundred yards behind them flew the WFYU *On-the-Spot News* Bell 407 helicopter with the distraught, yelling faces of his daughter and grandson squeezed into a circular side window. No need to hear their words—Guy already knew the message.

"Unbelievable! You have to be kidding me." He thumped his forehead.

"So, Guy! A flying parade. You keep surprising me." She wagged two fingers at the Navy helicopter pilot, who only tilted his head in confusion.

He turned to face his wife, Dorothy. Her left brow arched high, and random tufts of gray hair stuck out from under her headphones. On her forehead, a lopsided red blotch showed how hard she had pressed against the window in a vain attempt at making sense of any-thing below. After an entire lifetime with this woman, Guy gulped hard, recognizing his time was running out.

"What now?" She waited. He didn't have an answer.

The Beechcraft Bonanza's thin metal skin rumbled and vibrated as the impatient Navy pilot, hell-bent on recognition, maneuvered even closer.

"Well, dear, I'm so glad you're in complete control of things," she said in that mild caustic tone that always tightened his jaw. She settled back into her seat, pulling the shawl tighter around her shoulders.

Guy swiped the sweat from his brow. "Don't worry. I got this. . . ." His faltering voice dwindled under the steady thrum of the Bonanza's engine while he stared straight ahead in the distance. The hazy horizon between sky and water mirrored the murky threshold between his intent and reality.

Dorothy coughed and grimaced at a spasm of pain; then, her eyes softened. With a strained smile, she reached across and laid a hand on his thigh.

With innocent wonder, Guy beheld the face he had loved for so many years. He sat transfixed and confused by his pounding heart. For a brief moment, the intense presence of the Navy helicopter and the Channel Seven newscast helicopter faded away, right along with the whole damn plan.

1

**ORLANDO, FLORIDA
JUNE 2007
FIVE DAYS EARLIER
MONDAY**

*Keep the doctors away?
Don't eat the apple; throw it at them.*

Dorothy squinted through the glare on the Ford Fairlane's windshield at the whitewashed walls of the Orlando Medical Outreach office, shimmering in the early summer heat. She coughed and cleared her throat. "I don't want to go." Her flat, resolute tone sounded final. "I know what he's going to say. Same old poo-poo, right?"

"We should see what the doctor says. C'mon, honey. You promised," Guy said, reaching over and unbuckling his wife's seatbelt. He sighed, rubbed his chin, and scanned the parking lot bordered by squat, dull buildings emanating a distinct sixties aura—modern in an outmoded manner and cheap to build. Dusty green-brown juniper bushes laced with spiderwebs amid scattered clumps of defiant weeds revealed minimal efforts at landscaping maintenance.

With the engine and air conditioning off, the Ford's interior was stifling hot in the Florida sun. Dorothy sat, muttering with considerable displeasure. Her same fierce, sparkling eyes that so often had nailed him to the wall now appeared distant and rimmed with tears. Her ill-looking frame bordered on skeletal. A wrinkled floral print blouse with a white collar curled upward over mismatched buttons hung like a deflated balloon on her thin body. She had retrieved it this morning from a seldom-used dresser drawer, but despite her clothes appearing well worn, the skin on her face maintained a smooth beauty that seemed to defy the ravages of age. *Typical Dorothy-style rebelliousness*, he thought.

She dabbed at the moisture around her upper lip and began speaking in a high, lilting voice: "Besides, I don't know if he remembers. I've told him I'm married. I think he just wants to get in my pants."

Guy grinned. "Well, I can't blame him with such a babe like you." Allowing a moment of silence, he swallowed and patted her knee—this would pass. He tapped the steering wheel as she scowled into the depths of her purse, at last fishing a semidesiccated lipstick from a tiny pouch. She painted her lips with a slightly out-of-bounds smear.

"You look wonderful, honey," he said, checking his watch again. "We're late."

With Dorothy finally settled into one of the medical center's wheelchairs, Guy guided her up to the front entrance. He smoothed down an errant wisp of her silver hair.

"Okay. Here we go."

The automatic glass doors swung open with a whoosh and a burst of antiseptic smell. A woman dressed in crisp nurse's white pushed a wheelchair holding a bone-thin figure past them, out of the air-conditioned interior, and into the sun. Guy pulled his wife out of the way and drew back at the stark sight of the man slumped against the armrest. *At least Dorothy doesn't look that bad.*

"Thank you, sir." The nurse nodded, but her countenance faced straight ahead. As the gaunt patient glided by on silent wheels, his watery gaze reeled upward, looking for something—anything. The exiting pair rolled on, the attendant guiding her cargo toward an idling van parked at the curb. Guy gulped as he witnessed this shifting of John Doe to wherever someone had designated for the old man to die. *I hate this place.*

A gaunt display of discomfort and resignation permeated the reception area, where every seat was occupied. Guy dismissed the stares of others as he guided Dorothy's wheelchair through the crowd and up to the check-in window.

He bent down and spoke through the hole in the glass. "We have an appointment with Dr. Berger."

"Do you have your card?" The woman on the other side waited with her hand over the metal pass-through slot on the counter. Guy pulled a bulging leather lump from his hip pocket, wrinkled his nose, and began fumbling through the stack of plastic cards and paper bits.

"I'm not going!"

Heads spun in the nearby chairs. Guy, still searching through his wallet, glanced sideways and spoke in a strained whisper, "We're already here! Come on, you promised."

"You keep saying that." Dorothy glowered back.

The receptionist tapped on the glass. "What's your name?" She peered over the top of her glasses while a half dozen lights on the phone console in front of her blinked.

"Pickering. It's Pickering, just like all the other times . . . Sasha." *Three years we've been coming here.* He shifted from one foot to the other until she confirmed the data on a screen.

"Please wait. Someone will call for you." She pointed an immaculate finger toward nonexistent seats. "Orlando Med Center," she mono-toned into her headset and listened to an incoming medical plea.

———

Twenty minutes later, Guy pushed the wheelchair along a fluorescent-lit corridor, trailing a nurse who smelled of industrial-grade soap.

The expressionless woman opened a door and motioned them into a cramped but spotless examination room, then crossed over to the room's one window and adjusted the venetian blinds to subdue the sunshine. She unfolded a plastic chair for Guy. "The doctor will be right with you."

Dorothy tapped the nurse's sleeve. "Would you mind grabbing me a beer?"

"Behave yourself, dear." He glared at Dorothy. Then, with a more softened voice, he swiveled to the nurse. "Sorry, you can go."

She looked back and forth between them, sighed, and disappeared into the hallway.

Dorothy suppressed a chuckle. Guy shot her an admonishing frown and settled onto the chair. "You don't even drink beer."

She studied him for a moment. "You need a haircut. And it's getting kind of thin up top."

"Thanks for that." He turned his attention to the stark walls, the biohazard waste bin, then frowned at a side table piled with months-old smiling-face magazines touting weight loss breakthroughs. *What parallel universe is that from?* He patted Dorothy's knee "Hmm . . . I don't think we've been in *this* room before, honey, have we?" When she didn't respond, he stretched out his long frame.

His fingers massaged the nagging pain in his left knee, and like creeping sundown shadows, the silence pulled him into memories of a different day in a similar room. That had been six months ago, the worst of all the appointments. Dr. Berger had held Dorothy's hand and delivered the diagnosis. "The treatments are not working. The cancer is still progressing. I'll mix up the dosage, and we'll try another round. It might work," he had said. The hollow promise did nothing to buffer the blatant news. The hand of death had reached out to them—Dorothy was the first summoned.

"It's natural, don't you know? We're all falling off the conveyor belt sometime," she'd responded that day with characteristic nonchalance. But Guy couldn't accept this, and soon afterward, he found himself holding a grudge with whatever forces bulldozed a human being's destiny. *How could this be?*

Guy was no stranger to death. He'd witnessed it firsthand during his Army piloting days in Vietnam. Every flight could have been his last, but as life goes on, luck has its limits. To die before Dorothy was assumed. But in these past few months, dreaded visions would occasionally strike: waking up alone in bed; wandering in an empty house; a table set for one.

Ever since that worst-news day, Guy had struggled with this new reality while maintaining his duties as attendant and witness to Dorothy's slow descent. Yet even today, a flicker of hope battled with his sporadic bouts of denial. *The treatments might give us more time.*

Footsteps and voices filtered in from beyond the door. "Hold my calls." Dr. Berger swept into the examination room.

Guy liked this man. He was tall, forty-something, with a serious demeanor, but always showed kindness when he talked to Dorothy and served as a faint beacon in the high seas of fading hopes.

Dr. Berger smiled at his patient and took one of her hands in both of his.

"You again." Dorothy peered up, amusement in her voice.

The doctor raised a clipboard that held a few sheets of paper. After studying the numbers and graphs, he laid it on the counter, gave a heavy sigh, pushed his glasses up, and studied his patient.

"How have you been feeling, my friend?" Dr. Berger leaned forward and peered into her face.

"Really horny." She winked with an arched eyebrow.

Guy chuffed. "Yeah, we ran out of lube a month ago."

The doctor suppressed a grin. "Well, that's healthy. Better than the last visit, when all we discussed was pain."

Dorothy lowered her head and stared at the floor. "The truth? Everything hurts. I go in a diaper sometimes. Can't think straight. No way to live. Wouldn't you say, Guy?" At this, she looked straight into his eyes. The intent burned behind her pupils, and Guy swallowed hard at her meaning.

After a few seconds of confused silence, Dr. Berger gestured to Guy. "How would you say her pain level is these days?"

He winced. "Not good."

The doctor sat and listened as Guy detailed the worsening symptoms. A constant discomfort cut into Dorothy's body and Guy's emotions, deep as a bayonet. There were occasional spells of nausea and incontinence.

Dr. Berger kept his attention on Dorothy but tilted toward Guy. "And how is her mental cognizance?"

Guy sighed. "Well, as you can tell, she's as feisty as ever. Comes and goes. Opinionated and difficult, and the morphine clouds things for her. She gets mixed up." He wiped a Kleenex across his forehead. "She walked off last week, and I found her a couple blocks away. All she had on was a bathrobe. I felt awful. . . . It scared her."

The doctor asked no more questions. Instead, he reached back to the counter and picked up the stark clipboard again, contemplating the row of checkmarks as if searching for an alternative conclusion. His eyes misted up. "I love my work, my patients, but moments like this are by far the hardest. I'm so sorry, but it looks like one month, maybe two."

Guy sucked in his breath and peeked over at his diminishing wife, wondering if she had heard any of the conversation.

Dorothy glowered at both men. "I heard you! Trying to be so

secretive and such. It'll be a pleasure not listening to you two nincompoops anymore." She pointed at a plastic laminated poster on the wall—a graphic depiction of the human body's entire musculature, sans skin. "And what about this poor sucker? They skinned him alive and made him pose like an underwear ad." She shook her head in disgust.

Both men paused and pondered the patient.

"I see," said the doctor.

"Nothing we can do?" Guy inquired.

"Nothing but keep her comfortable. It's time to up the prescription. I'll add liquid along with the patches. Be careful with it, though. For now, just measured doses."

Guy shrugged with consent. *What's to lose? Might as well give her the good shit.* He listened with care as the doc gave him instructions on how to administer the increased dosages.

Dr. Berger reached into his white coat pocket and pulled out a vial of pills. He paused, his eyes darting over the crammed writing on the labels. "Two of these a day ought to help. They're new. I've read up on this one in the journals. In a number of cases, it has aided with brain stimulation."

"Any side effects?" Guy asked.

A shadow showed on his face. "Erratic behavior, perhaps somewhat unpredictable. But at this point, anything feels worth a try, doesn't it?" He reached over with tentative fingers and placed the vial in Guy's hand.

With his head still spinning, Guy blinked at the pills, an outerspace object in his hand.

"You understand, we have *your* health to talk about, too."

"Later, Doc. That can wait."

"Guy, let's leave now!" Dorothy rasped as she struggled to back up her wheelchair. She peered around the room with wide eyes. Her breath quickened.

Dr. Berger caught his arm. "Call me anytime with updates or if you have any questions."

Guy stared at the doctor for a long second, remembering the need in Dorothy's eyes. He opened his mouth to keep pressing but reconsidered and merely nodded. He pivoted and pushed Dorothy into the hallway, then set the handbrake again.

He bent down to Dorothy's ear. "Honey, I forgot something in there. I'll be right back."

He nudged the door open again to a surprised Dr. Berger. "Doc, there's a matter I need to talk to you about." He paused, gritted his teeth, and blew out a long breath. "She wants to go," he said while staring at the floor.

"What's that?" Dr. Berger asked.

"This is so awful. She wants to go. You understand? Not be here. The suffering and all. She's talked about it and wants me to help her. I don't know what to do. What can I do? She made it clear long ago what she wants when the time came. Can you help?"

Dr. Berger folded his arms and studied Guy. "If I understand you correctly, you're talking about euthanasia. Assisted suicide . . . yes?"

Guy's jaw clenched in response.

The doctor sighed. "The short answer is no. I cannot help you in any way. I could be prosecuted and lose my license for even consulting you. And, by the way, you could go to jail too, for years. It's tough, but my advice is to get this out of your mind and let nature take its course. I'm sorry. I wish I could do more."

"Figured as much." Guy's shoulders slumped.

Without another word, he hurried into the corridor and rushed the wheelchair toward the exit. As they passed through the waiting room's stale air, Dorothy leaned over to a stone-faced elderly lady. "Run! Get out of this place!"

Guy pushed her faster.

That's it for the clinic. Guy eased Dorothy into their car. *No sense in coming here again.*

"Thanks for everything and nothing, Doc. Guess I'll take it from here." Guy scowled at the nondescript building that hid so many stories of pain and rampant despair. "This is the very last time." He slammed the car door behind him.

At least these drugs will ease the pain for her a bit. But now . . . Shit, the promise!

— **CHAPTER** —

2

7501 WILLOWSIDE ROAD
ELEVEN MILES NORTHEAST OF ORLANDO, FLORIDA

In a perfect world, cats plant trees.

The journey back home took twenty minutes, but to Guy, time vanished in his trance. He drove on autopilot, with arms extending robot-like to the Fairlane's steering wheel. A honk from behind jerked his head to the rearview mirror. A line of five cars followed him, all going at the same snail's pace. He coasted through the last stop sign two blocks from their house, then cut the corner too close into their driveway, jumping the curb, sounding a groan from the front right shock absorber.

Dorothy startled awake in a momentary panic. She blinked with discomfort and dug her fingers into the armrest. "Uh . . ."

"Sorry, honey. We're back." Guy grimaced at his lack of attention.

"Oh . . . good." She searched for her words. "Help me upstairs? I want to go to bed." She reached a thin blue-veined hand across the seat and grasped his sleeve. Her arm was as light as a child's.

"Of course, it's been an enormous day already. Let's get you inside." He turned his gaze to their home's second-story window. *What the hell is next?*

The Pickering home, built decades ago, featured a weathered canopy spanning the entire front porch. Guy called it the "grand veranda." When they had first viewed the house forty years ago, the old farmhouse appearance reminded them of their rural Tennessee roots. Their son, Mitch, and their daughter, Heather, were still in high school when they refused an offer from a developer that was well above market value. As if to spite the Pickering holdouts, the developer greased a few local council members' palms and slammed through a rezoning.

Soon afterward, a brand-new neighborhood sprouted up and surrounded their wood-shingled home with dozens of six-thousand-square-foot low-maintenance lots and a sea of tile roofs tucked behind stucco archways. After exiting the car, Guy once again silently lamented the choice of the young New York architect hired to design the homes in the subdivision. He had aimed for an innovative Southwestern/Mediterranean style, but to Guy, he had missed the mark.

The Pickerings' house, a two-story plain Jane with faded paint and a vegetable garden instead of a pool, did not blend at all with the surrounding five different floor plans and stuck out like a dusty farm truck amid a fleet of shiny sedans. Not that Guy would have wanted anything but his old farm truck of a building. His face relaxed as he surveyed the house, the one they had made a whole life in—their home. For years, Guy and Dorothy had declared their presence by maintaining two rows of corn along the front sidewalk. Today, he gazed with satisfaction at the tall green stalks. *We've always done things our way. Why stop now?*

After Guy got Dorothy comfortable in bed, he pulled the window curtains inward, careful not to block the plastic air conditioner grille as it pumped its monotonous whine and cool breeze into the darkened bedroom. The light from the tarnished brass lamp angled across Dorothy's forehead and cheeks, accentuating the inevitability of age. The sight transfixed him. Despite the fading smear of pink lipstick from earlier, she had never looked so colorless or tired.

Guy finally broke his gaze and turned toward the door. "Don't leave yet," she said, her lips taut with effort. She stretched out a hand. "Talk to me."

He sat on the bed's edge to the familiar sound of creaking springs, feigned a puzzled face, and scratched his head. "Well, let me think. What shall we talk about?"

She lay as expectantly as a child, yearning for the soothing voice of a storyteller.

"Remember that afternoon at Dee's Diner?" Guy prompted.

Dorothy's gaze roamed the room, as if the answer were hiding behind a dusty piece of memorabilia. "Oh . . . yes."

He knew she loved the story, having told it many times at family dinners. "I'd been back in Perryton for only a day and a half. On my first leave from the Army." Guy leaned on one arm and gazed over to the nightstand that held a brass picture frame—two young, laughing faces beside a lake. "You walked into the diner wearing that pretty dress with all the flowers on it."

A trace of a smile tugged at Dorothy's face. He chuckled.

"You didn't see me at first. You sat there in the booth, all prim and proper. More beautiful than ever. Damn hamburger got stuck in my throat. I wasn't hungry anymore anyway. That Marvin Bailey was late, of course, drinking himself silly over at the Lucky Aces. You had just noticed me when the bastard staggered in and . . ." He clenched his fist. "I got so angry at that son of a bitch."

Dorothy grinned in anticipation while Guy sighed.

"I couldn't help myself. You and everybody else in that place knew how foolish I looked. But didn't *somebody* say the word gallant, though?" He sounded a bit defensive as he recalled marching over to the chrome dinette booth and demanding that Marvin have better manners toward the lady. "Sucker punched me. That's what he did. I never saw it coming."

"I took you home." Dorothy's voice was fragile and dry, but her eyes glinted with delight.

"Yes, you did. You came by the next morning, and we walked out by the cornfield and talked for hours. Yes, ma'am."

A muted light filtered through the window shades, and the memory of that timeless moment, the day they had glimpsed the future, washed over him. He wiped a tear away.

Pedro, their twelve-year-old tabby cat, traipsed in through the doorway and jumped on the bed.

Dorothy reached across and petted the length of the cat's body. "My God, Pedro, soon you'll have to look after Guy when I'm gone. You know he can't cook anything worth squat and couldn't tell the difference between a teaspoon and a tea bag."

The cat purred in response.

"Honey. No need to talk about that."

She grabbed his wrist and squeezed. She took a shallow breath and raised her chin an inch toward Guy's face with eyes that penetrated deep.

He balled up his fists, dreading what he anticipated she was going to say.

"That was the beginning. Now it's the end." She coughed and trembled with the effort. Her eyelids fluttered and drooped. "My thoughts are slipping, too much pain. It's time, while I can still decide on my own," she said. "I need you."

"Honey, I know what you're getting at. And don't think I didn't remember. I've been really fretting about it." He paused and looked away. "I want to help you. You know I do. But . . . this is not like putting an animal down. This is drastic."

"You'll have Pedro put to sleep at some point. And I'm an animal . . . you want me to bite you? I could turn into a real bitch. Maybe make it easier."

"Dorothy!" Guy groaned and rolled his eyes. "Be serious. By the way, it's illegal."

"Illegal? So what?" She winced at the effort. "There's a better place for me." Her voice lowered to a whisper. "I want to go. I need to go. Please get off your high horse and kill me. Will you?"

Guy gaped at her, then broke into a smile. "Certainly, ma'am. Would you prefer our soulful sendoff party with wine and hors d'oeuvres? Or the more adventurous eaten-by-bears weekend in the woods?" Guy kept as straight a face as he could, hiding his true feelings.

Dorothy cracked up. Then, she coughed, and her laughter faded away. There were no more words, only hand holding.

He sat with her for another ten minutes. Her breathing soon took on a slow regularity, and he carefully smoothed a morphine patch onto her hip. She drifted off to sleep. He rose, paused at the bedroom window, and, for a moment, gazed through the gap in the curtains at a peaceful, now somehow irrelevant outside world.

Downstairs in the kitchen, Guy peeled open a can of sardines and devoured the contents. After pulling a beer from the refrigerator, he pushed through the kitchen's screen door out to the revered front porch. The planks squeaked under his feet, and for a second, he glared at the loose nails that had long ago given up any capability of securing the floorboards. The east side of the house also needed some repair and painting. He snorted a soft disdain for chores that had dropped away from his mind like falling leaves.

This porch was where he did his best thinking. Guy stood behind a stained cherry wood rocking chair and stared at the well-worn cushion. He ran his fingers along the high back. "I *could* sit my ass down here again and just worry about it. But it's all history now. The doctor appointments, the therapies, the ambitious optimism. All done."

He crushed the beer can and whirled it Frisbee style over the railing, across the strip of lawn and into the mouth of a garbage bin leaning open against the garage. "Two points," he said, smirking at the previous day's missed shots, which lay nearby on the grass.

He plopped into the rocker with its familiar rhythmic wooden squeak and extended his long legs. Reaching over to a small table, he picked up a plastic information packet that Dr. Berger had slipped into his hands that morning.

First out of the bag was a brochure from North Orlando Hospice Outreach. The high-gloss cover, multipage foldout featured a picture of a plaque mounted at the entrance to the rainforest section of the New York City Central Park Zoo. Guy put on a pair of reading glasses and tilted the page toward the light.

"ON THE LAST DAY OF the WORLD, I WOULD WANT TO PLANT A TREE." —W. S. MERWIN

"Humph!" He frowned at the paper and cast it aside. "Why in hell would that matter?" The offending pamphlet with the cryptic phrase only added another pin to the cushion of his heart. Unforeseen but damn predictable, cancer lived and thrived in Dorothy's frail body. He wiped away an errant tear.

I'm not letting a bunch of strangers take over. They don't know her at all.

The alarm clock buzzed to life on the kitchen counter. Guy rose, stretched his back, and strode inside to switch it off. It was four o'clock, time for the oldies radio show.

He crept up the creaky steps and peered into the bedroom. It was customary, every afternoon, for him to flick on the ancient stereo set beside Dorothy's bed. For an hour, the tiny speaker blared the tinny sounds of fifties and sixties rock and roll from a local AM station. Fats Domino, Bobby Darin, Little Richard, Elvis Presley. The best music of all time.

Today brought sleep, a temporary peace treaty between the tissues and the tumors, like sunshine between violent storms. The golden oldies would wait for tomorrow.

Guy left the door open a crack and retreated downstairs, where he pulled another beer from the refrigerator. He hesitated over the unwashed dishes in the kitchen sink, holding the can a few inches from his lips. Two years ago, he would have been swaying behind her, pulling her from the dishes as they danced to the croon of the radio. A year later, she could only sit at the table as he cleaned up and shimmied around the kitchen to her peals of laughter. Now, she couldn't even make it downstairs. The exhaustion of her decline flowed over him in a wave of emotion that spilled over into tears.

He'd known this day would come. He'd felt it coming—an overdue train. Today, indecisiveness squirmed on the chopping block, and he realized that something had to change. His stomach churned with sordid thoughts. He *needed* to be different for his Dorothy. *She made me promise, damn it. If there's a way for a peaceful exit, that's what she deserves. If doctors cannot deliver that, and God can't either . . .*

He cast a glare upward as a twinge of righteous anger rose in his gut. Finishing off the can, he crumpled it. The ever-narrowing choices made it simple, but he couldn't even allow himself to think the words.

He shook his head, breaking the trance. The sun was low in the sky, and a breeze lured him to the porch.

Pedro lay on the rocking chair's cushion, and as Guy approached, the tabby cat arched on his back in a full twisting extension. The late afternoon rays glittered in Pedro's amber-colored eyes. Guy slumped onto the couch beside his favorite chair and stroked the gray stubble on his chin. He leaned forward, searching the cat's presence for any shred of empathy, but Pedro only blinked and stared back with the impassive gaze of a haughty concierge.

"You know, you could be of immense help if you morphed into a man-eating tiger." He grinned at the cat. But seconds later, his expression sank into a frown as an unspoken obsession settled on the moment like a chilling mist.

He took a deep breath and whispered the words that had come to haunt him. "How the hell *do* you kill your wife?"

PERRYTON, TENNESSEE
A SUNDAY IN OCTOBER 1938

Time and innocence don't dance together for long.

Dorothy intently studied the landscape from the backseat as her father maneuvered their spotless new Chevrolet down a pot-holed dirt driveway. Ahead, the quaint farmhouse, with its peeling paint, dusty drive, and overgrown gardens, made the car stand out like an exotic object.

"Here?" Dorothy's father leaned over the steering wheel, honked the horn, and scanned through the windshield. "Honey, can't we just buy eggs in town?"

"Of course we can, Cecil, but I hear that these are the finest. And besides, it wouldn't hurt to meet some folks around here. Let's give it a minute." Dorothy's petite mother adjusted the glasses on her nose and laid a hand on her husband's knee.

Dorothy squirmed in the backseat, ready for a new adventure. She had always liked how elegant her parents dressed, but Dorothy's

Sunday best felt foreign, and she longed for play clothes so she could properly explore this farm. She pressed up against the rear window and jabbed a finger toward a corral. "I see a cow!" Behind the fence boards, the bovine chewed her cud in a lazy oval motion. "I want one. Can we get a cow?"

"We're not getting a cow today, sweetie." Her mother straightened her daughter's hair, and Dorothy turned to sit down again, pouting.

From around the back corner of the house, a woman in overalls finally appeared, her beanpole stature rising above a cluster of tomato plants. She dropped a garden hose, squinted in the sedan's direction, and strode forward.

"You folks lost?" She bent down to peer through the driver's window.

Dorothy's mother leaned against her husband and boosted her voice above the engine rumble. "Hello there. We're new in town and got your name from our neighbors, the Williamsons. Clara told me you sell the best eggs in Perryton."

"Clara, huh?" The woman's abundant eyebrows shot up as she scanned the car's interior. "Her apple pie beat mine last year at the county fair."

There was a pause in the air, and Dorothy wasn't sure if they were getting in trouble for being there.

"She's a good woman, but I'm still not convinced she's a better cook. The name's Molly Pickering," the woman said with a broad smile.

Cecil leaned back as Molly's arm thrust across his torso and grasped Dorothy's mother's hand. "Come on up to the porch. I'm sure my husband, Lloyd, is ready for more coffee. We'll have some and then talk eggs."

Dorothy popped out of the rear seat and caught a wide-eyed Guy peering at her from a kitchen window. She recognized him from school and gave him a pert wave. Now it made sense why he would come to school with dirt on his pants sometimes.

A minute later, the grown-ups settled onto chairs, and Molly instructed Guy to "go fetch the eggs."

He grabbed a basket, Dorothy grinned, and the young duo headed toward the outbuildings.

"Huh?" Guy swiveled to better hear his new friend while continuing to slide his hand over the screen and pluck out the eggs, one by one. The slanted lid covering the chicken coop's nesting box rested on his head. "What?" The squawking chickens made it hard to hear.

"I said I've never seen a peepee." Dorothy Benson fiddled with her long blonde hair and lowered her eyes down to her spotless dress and once-shiny shoes, now layered in dust. She glanced at their folks chatting away on the farmhouse front deck, a hundred yards across the barnyard. Then, she swiveled and zeroed in on Guy. "That's what she calls it."

Guy paused and stared back at her with a blank expression.

"Sally Hagerman. You remember . . . in class? She's got this three-year-old brother, and when he takes baths, she sees his peepee all the time. She told me."

She remembered Guy being shy and avoiding girls in general. She waited while he seemed to struggle to recall his schoolmates. After a few seconds, his eyes lit up. "Oh, yeah. Her?"

Dorothy lowered her voice. "I've never seen one. I'm just wondering." Her lower lip jutted out. "I don't have a brother."

Guy continued to stare at her, confusion written all over his face.

She stamped a foot and traced her hands down the pleats of her dress. "Oh, never mind." She looked away, ran her fingers along the aged gray wood and chicken wire structure, and moved a bit closer. "You do this every day?" She wrinkled her nose.

"Yeah." Guy nodded in her direction.

"Why?" She blinked at him.

Guy blinked several times as he pulled out the last egg. "I don't know." He held up a pale green one and offered it to her. "Hold this one. It's still warm."

She cradled the object in her hands and studied it with a new-found fascination. "These come out of a chicken butt." She giggled with delight.

Guy frowned at this comment but, after a pause, brightened up. "Hey, you want to see my horse? His name's Ol' Blue."

Dorothy perked up. "Yes!"

Guy wasn't sure why he was smiling, but with considerable effort, he pushed the barn's tall sliding door to one side, just enough for them to slip through. He strode down the hay-strewn center aisle like a confident tour guide, and Dorothy walked beside him, her nose crinkling again as it sniffed the leather and manure and dust.

Surrounded by walls covered in cobwebs, bridles, saddles, scythes, and other farm implements, they ventured further into the musty shadows. On the right side, Ol' Blue snorted behind the stall's wooden planks. The sound made her jump back and land on Guy's foot. She righted herself and stopped short.

"He's okay. He won't hurt you." Guy set the egg basket down, reached into his back pocket, and pulled out a limp half carrot. "Here, you give it to him," he said, expecting her to take the offering.

Dorothy hesitated and turned to peek in between the stall's boards. Her eyes widened at the sight of the stallion's immense flanks, and she stumbled backward. "He's a big one, isn't he?"

"It's okay," Guy assured her, feeling a little proud that he was braver than Dorothy. "He won't do nothing. He's a good horsey. Here, just poke one end into his stall."

With shaky fingers, Dorothy took the half-dehydrated vegetable and nudged it into the opening. After a moment, Ol' Blue decided it was worth paying attention to the short newcomers and extended his nose up to the railing. He snatched the carrot with nimble horse lips and munched it with a loud crunching sound.

Dorothy shrieked with delight.

"Give me another one." She thrust out her hand.

Guy searched his pocket and frowned. "I only had that one."

"That's okay," she said, and sauntered over to a saddle slung over an ancient wooden sawhorse. She stroked the burnished metal buckles and straps. "Ol' Blue is a boy horse, right?"

"Yeah, they call him a stallion," Guy announced, puffing his chest out.

Dorothy pirouetted around and leaned a few inches closer. "You've got one of those." She pointed a finger to his waist like an accusation and shot a quick glance below his belt before avoiding any eye contact.

Guy's mind clotted to a halt. His outside world ceased to exist. "What?"

Dorothy chewed her lip and kicked a soft mound of hay, further covering her shoes with another coat of dust. She shot a quick glance toward the empty doorway. "I'll show you mine if you show me yours." She spit out the phrase in rapid fire, so Guy barely had time to process the words. "They're different. I just want to see," she said in a softer tone. She flopped her arms down at her side as if these protracted negotiations had worn her out.

Guy raced through a list things to say, but none of them felt right. "My birthday's tomorrow. I'll be six years old."

"I turned six a long time ago." Dorothy swatted away the comment like a bothersome fly, then crossed her arms. "Well?"

Guy gaped at her. A sudden numbness extended from his fingers down to his feet. *Dang!* A glimmer, a ray of faint understanding broke through. His gaze lowered down to his pants. *Oh . . .*

He sensed he should respond in some manner. His mama had

always hammered in to be polite to people and be willing to help them, so at last, he nodded. "I guess, we—"

"Okay, I'll go first." All traces of hesitancy disappeared from her voice. In quick succession, she hoisted her dress, pulled her underwear down, and lifted her eyes toward the hay loft above. "One, two, three, four, five, six, seven, eight, nine, ten!" she proclaimed in a steady, even order. Having satisfied her half of the deal, she spun away and tucked all her clothes back in order.

This unexpected circumstance was over before Guy had comprehended anything. But the curiosity seed had been planted—a yet-unidentified stirring in his gut.

"Your turn," Dorothy called over her shoulder.

Her words slapped him in the face. He gulped, shifted his attention to the open doorway, and didn't move a muscle.

"Guy?" she prodded, as if offering a hand to help him over a creek. "C'mon." That was all she said, but her voice, the curious arched eyebrow, and penetrating gaze tipped the scales.

Like a determined soldier under fire, he unbuckled his belt. He managed to unbutton his fly and pull the front of his Levi's down, along with the lip of his jockey shorts. Back in there, hiding like a turtle's head startled to see the light of day, lay Guy's fledgling manhood. He couldn't manage words or speech, so he endured the agonizing wait. Dorothy bent down for a closer look; somehow, he held steady.

"Huh!" she snorted, sounding like an Ol' Blue imitation. "Well, I guess that's it. No big deal."

To Guy, this sounded like a mixed message.

Just then, Frieda Benson's face appeared through the barn door's narrow slit. "Dorothy! Time to go." Her eyes popped open. Guy's face flushed red as he stood there with his pants down and her daughter inspecting his terrain.

"Oh, my!" She clapped a hand to her chest and bustled toward them.

Guy spun around while fumbling with his buttons, lost his balance, and landed on his butt.

Dorothy greeted her mother with a quivering, innocent face. "It's okay, Mom. I asked him to show me. I only wanted to see."

Frieda bit her lip while she looked from one to another. "Dorothy, this is not ladylike behavior, and you are not to do this ever again. Do you understand?"

Dorothy glowered at her mother but bowed her head in submission.

"And you, young man, just because someone asks you to do something doesn't mean you should do it. Understand?"

An already-trembling Guy nodded.

"Now, we shall not speak of this again to anyone else! Understood?" More nods.

"I'm sorry, Mama, but when you were little, didn't you ever want to see? Did you?"

Frieda's head jerked to the side. Her mouth dropped open, and her gaze drifted somewhere . . . else.

An instant later, she clapped her hands, and the moment was over.

"Children, we are leaving!" She herded a speechless Guy and Dorothy in front of her toward the door.

Within minutes, Guy watched Dorothy bound into the Chevy's rear seat and wave goodbye as the Chevy bounced down the driveway, trailing a cloud of dust.

For the next half hour, Guy wandered around the yard, taking longer than usual strides, wondering what it all meant, and somehow feeling older than before.

ORLANDO, FLORIDA

2007

~~MONDAY~~

TUESDAY

Neighbors—the bane of civilization.

A streak of morning sunlight streamed through the kitchen window, highlighting several spaghetti-smeared plates and Chinese takeout remnants. Guy stood beside the sink wearing a once-white T-shirt with "Daytona Beach Week" emblazoned on the chest. He remained motionless as the incoming light and the mounting delinquency of undone chores neutralized all thoughts of action.

After a restless night with little sleep, he longed for the comforting blanket of mundane ritual, so when his trance faded, he pressed the electric coffee grinder into service. The piercing whine did little but ricochet off his consciousness. With uncharacteristic sloppiness, he poured the grounds into the drip coffee maker, spilling some down the outside. *Who cares about a few grounds?* He filled the coffee pot halfway full with water and dumped it into the reservoir. After pressing the *on* button, he gazed out the window for a minute until the first black drops fell into the pot, then leaned over the rising aroma. *Ah, that's wonderful. I wish it was for two of us. Like it used to be.*

The telephone hanging on the kitchen wall rang. He scowled at it, not wanting to talk to anyone.

The ringing persisted until he gave up and snatched the receiver from its cradle. "Yes. Who's there?"

"Guy, this is Dr. Berger . . ." Guy stayed silent. "Hello? Are you there?"

"Yeah, I'm here. What do you want? We're a little busy here."

"I want to say how sorry I am to be the one who delivers awful news about Dorothy." The doctor paused as if to let his message soak in. "I've grown fond of her. She's quite a feisty and special character. She will be missed."

Guy said nothing but cleared his throat to choke down the somber feelings rising in his chest.

"But we must go on living, and my job is to keep you healthy. To that point, I wanted to inform you of your test results."

Guy could barely bring himself to care, but he wanted to hurry Dr. Berger off the phone. "Yeah, yeah. I suppose."

"You're basically in good shape. Your blood work shows elevated risk for arthritis—not too bad, though. And your triglycerides could be improved. We can control that; for instance, you could—"

"That's okay, doc. Can we talk about it later?"

"Sure, but one more thing: your prostate biopsy. The results aren't back yet. I expect them soon, but the enlargement concerns me, so we'll have to jump on that if—"

"Thanks, doc. I've gotta run."

Guy hung up the phone and stared at it for a minute. *Hmm . . . Funny how the things you care about change.*

He filled his mug, shrugged off the lack of creamer, and then started for the new day just beyond the screen door. After settling into his favorite chair, he wiped his tired eyes, yawned, and stretched. Within minutes, his eyelids drooped, and his chin sank to his chest. The warm sun engulfed him and lulled him into a sleepy depth.

> *People mill about, distant and uninterested. Tall trees, a velvety green park and music coming from beyond.*
>
> *"Dorothy! Dorothy! Where are you? There you are! I can see you now." She looks radiant.*
>
> *"I have to leave!" Dorothy calls.*
>
> *She's walking away. Running . . .*
>
> *"Honey! We should stay here."*
>
> *She's ahead somewhere.*
>
> *Go to her. Go with her. Go with her.*

"Mr. Pickering. Oh, Mr. Pickering." An invasive chatter jabbed Guy's forehead with the force of a blunt mop handle. "Are you asleep?"

A rotund figure in a shiny daisy-patterned spandex halter top and matching shorts stood at the base of the stairs, wriggling her fingers. Izetta Tooney had something to say. Guy's body jerked to attention, his head snapping up with an audible *pop* as he clawed his way back to front porch reality from the depths of that most engaging dream.

"What?" He blinked into the sun. "Huh?"

"Mr. Pickering, sorry . . . I didn't imagine anyone would still be asleep at this hour." Mrs. Tooney's voice picked up with a tittering lilt that both teased and admonished. After dubbing herself the neighborhood monitor, Guy had witnessed her derive an unmistakable pleasure from giving demerits to offenders of homeowner's association rules with the precision of a dentist's drill.

Today was no exception.

"Your hose is running again," Izetta said with a shake of her head, causing her jowls to jiggle.

Guy stared at her, still waking up with snippets of his dream. "Must have drifted off . . ."

"Your garden hose, you see, it's going and going and come all the way across the street to my yard." She pointed a pudgy finger toward her split-level Montenegro model. Indeed, a steady stream of water ferrying bits of leaves and lawn clippings snaked over the asphalt and sank into a gutter on the far side. "Could you take care of that, please?" She pasted on a wide smile. "You remember our association does not allow water to be—"

"Guy! What are you doing?" Dorothy's electric-knife voice sliced through the kitchen screen door. A second later, with a light blue bathrobe draped around her slight shoulders, a matted gray hair halo sprouting from her head, and eyes riveted on her husband, she hustled onto the front porch.

"You need to move. I must clean up this mess." Dorothy rushed toward him, arms waving with an orchestral conductor's passion, shooing him from the "filth." Never mind that Dominga, their stern and ancient Guatemalan housecleaner, came in every two weeks and cleaned the house top to bottom (including the grand veranda). Dorothy swiveled and glared at the bulging, flowery figure standing at the foot of the steps. "And *you*?"

Their wide-eyed neighbor inched backward.

"Mrs. Tooney's only paying a visit, honey. Everything's okay, I just forgot about the water. Mrs. Tooney, please stay a second. I need to explain a situation to you."

With neck and back muscles taut as bridge cables, Guy labored to get up from his rocker. In contrast, Dorothy glided across the planks with the grace of an Olympic ice skater and grabbed his head, pulling it to her chest in a warm and exuberant cuddle-hug.

As she rocked Guy back and forth, Dorothy's robe ties came undone, and her limp left breast peeked out from under the folds.

He glanced down and registered the slip just as Mrs. Tooney gasped.

"Oh, Guy," Dorothy intoned with an easy, singsong affection.

"Honey! Stop!" he shouted from his bent-over position.

Dorothy sprang her arms apart, releasing Guy, and fixated on Pedro, who returned her steady gaze from his perch on the railing. A puzzled expression crossed her face as she snapped the robe around her body. "That cat knows something!"

Before either Guy or Izetta could react, she spun around, slipped through the screen door, and disappeared—the only remnant of her presence being the soft shuffling of slippers on linoleum.

"Where'd she get all this energy?" he mumbled. "Old age, morphine, and little pink pills. What a party!" He rubbed his neck and turned to the speechless Mrs. Tooney. "Sorry about that, uh . . . we have a situation we're dealing with here."

Trying to improvise a disclosure, he descended the steps and leaned his haggard, unshaven face toward the neighbor. "I've got to tell you—she won't be here much longer."

Izetta Tooney wrinkled her nose and abandoned the smile. "Mr. Pickering, I don't really want to get involved. I have to get back to my gardening. You understand: the weeds, of course. Please, if you'll just turn off your water." She retreated a step.

"Mrs. Tooney, our situation. I mean, give me a chance to explain."

But he spoke only to her backside, which was already wobbling toward the safety of her own yard.

Guy limped over to the garden faucet and twisted the handle till the water squeaked to a stop. The hose stretched from the nozzle, across the walkway, and disappeared down a hole in the lawn fifty feet away. He often stuck a hose running at full blast down a gopher tunnel in a vain attempt at rodent control. He'd gleaned the technique from a yellowed issue of *Rodale's Organic Gardening* magazine he had once found at a garage sale.

Today, six wet and muddy but otherwise robust gophers crouched behind the flowerbed's tangle of stems and leaves, peering out at the familiar two-legged creature. Guy just turned away; these maintenance actions were old habits. With each passing day, he was becoming more indifferent toward the gophers and, in fact, all mundane matters.

He retrieved the hose and absentmindedly trained the water stream over the weed-choked flower bed. Dorothy had always maintained her flowers like she was out to win awards. Now, he gazed at these grounds as if they were someone else's, observed from behind tourist bus glass. A begrudging sense of acceptance for the dead and drooping foliage's fate soon took over, and after one last glance toward Mrs. Tooney's house, he returned to the porch and collapsed into his rocking chair with a sigh.

The recent unprecedented toll on his body and mind mandated two more ibuprofen from a nearby bottle.

Guy was uncomfortable with the unknown, awkward with disorder, and miserable without hope. A grounded purpose in life had always been a guiding principle.

"I have to do something," he said aloud while continuing to rock, unable and unwilling to accept this unchartered tide of indecision. He scowled at an annoying squeak emanating from his chair's seat, jumped up, and marched to the garage. After gathering a screwdriver, a plastic bottle of white glue, and a long bar clamp, he returned and stared at the chair like it was a naughty dog. Five minutes later, the long-suffering loose joint was smothered in glue and tightly secured. He breathed a little easier and settled onto a nearby stuffed sofa.

He listened to the nearby palm tree leaves rustling in the wind. Then, in his mind, his "something" quite unexpectedly occurred. All external sounds receded to a distant murmur, leaving only a mesmerizing image in his mind's eye. He neither accepted nor rejected this engaging vision. Not a thought, not an idea or a forced decision—instead, the specter revealed itself as if in a painting. He *and* Dorothy walking together in a field, hand in hand.

His body stayed rigid, but his eyes darted around to see if anyone had caught him with his outrageous thoughts that somehow started to feel perfectly logical. *I want to be with Dorothy.* He sat dumbfounded by the revelation. *If she needs to leave . . . I can go with her.*

"Of course. Why didn't I think of this before?" He leaped from the chair with an energy he hadn't felt in weeks and paced in a tight circle. Hell, he wasn't working anymore. He was older than most folks. Nobody really needed him. He eyed their bedroom window. "I've always been chasing that woman. Why stop now?"

Guy tried to imagine a day, an hour, a single minute without Dorothy by his side. It simply seemed unreal. There was no way he would want to live like that. His mind's eye went back to the vision. He wouldn't let Dorothy walk that field alone. That wasn't the type of love they had; theirs was much longer lasting.

A weight lifted from his chest, and he misted up at the poignant image of lasting love, mixed with honorable dignity and a hint of relief.

. . . For only a second.

As his initial bravado fell away, a storm cloud grew in his consciousness, and he turned his gaze skyward with an angry voice in his belly. *They claim it's a sin to take a life, even your own. Well, God, I say it's a friggin' sin for her to suffer so damn much! What do you have to say about that? Huh? To hell with it. I accept the risk.* He spun and, with a defiant grunt, plopped onto the glued-together rocker, ignoring the discomfort of the bar clamp in his back. He rocked back and forth at a frenzied and clumsy clip, as if sheer energy could outpace the tentacles of a long-ago-spurned church.

He grabbed the armrest with a fierce grip. *Your little grim reaper dance. Ha! You don't scare me.* He spread his arms wide. *This is how I live up to my promise.*

A moment later, the blood drained from his face as a decade-old minivan pulled into the driveway. Heather was arriving for her almost-daily visit.

He froze as his daughter shoved the Toyota into park, waved toward the house, and flashed one of her trademark grins.

"Oh, yeah." His tone mixed love with chagrin. "I forgot a few things."

Are lies forgiven when offered with pure heart?

"Papa." Heather bounced up the pathway, her raven hair framing a broad smile above a trim figure. She threw her arms around her father. "How are you? I worried about you and Mom all night. How is she?"

She held him at arm's length and looked up into his face. The corners of Guy's mouth drew up as if hanging from hooks.

Guy loved these drop-ins. The familial bonds of love tugged at his heart as they had every day since she was born. *Damn, look at her.* At forty years of age, the mother of two active boys still turned heads when out on the town. She'd always been her father's jewel. Now married for twelve years to Richard, she lived only minutes away.

Guy's head and stomach got in an argument—his head fighting for his brand-new fantasy of himself and Dorothy, pain free at last, sauntering into the promised land, and his stomach roiling at the thought of leaving Heather. This complicated scenario didn't fit together in any acceptable manner, so he stood with a wooden stance and teeth bared like an amateur comedian mounting a stage for the first time. Instead of speaking, he grabbed her and hugged tight.

She furrowed her brow and cocked her head, a hint of suspicion behind her stare. "Is everything okay?"

Uh-oh. Guy recognized that face. *She sees right through me.*

"It's Mom, isn't it?" Heather's voice dropped to a tender tone. On her tiptoes, she peered past his shoulder into the dim kitchen interior. "Is she up?"

"Yes, yes, that's it." His voice gushed relief. "I mean no, she's sleeping." He ran his fingers across his bald spot. "She had a hard night. The doc gave us a sack of drugs for pain, with this new one to help her head. I think they're good. I'm sure they're helping . . ."

"This situation is so horrible." Her arms slipped off his shoulders in an exasperated fall to her sides. She stepped back. "Come sit with me a minute," she said, and gestured to the couch.

Guy followed her like an exhausted puppy dog.

Once seated side by side, Heather's brow furrowed in concentration. "I see what I've got to do. I will move in and be here twenty-four seven. You need me."

"But—"

"Hold on. Just hear me out." She held up a finger to keep Guy from saying anything. "I called Dr. Berger yesterday, and he told me about—" A catch in her throat stopped her cold, and she looked away.

The wire harnesses in Guy's cheeks yanked upward again. "Oh no, Heather." His mind raced for excuses. "You can come over whenever you want, but your kids need you. Richard needs you home. Don't worry, everything's *fine*." Realizing he'd blurted the last word out with too much emphasis, he froze.

"Papa," she said, drawing out the word.

He saw the hint of suspicion in Heather's expression, poking with searchlight intensity into his brain's murky depths. He all but collapsed in a heap of writhing confessions—unsavory deeds contemplated and grand endings. His stomach would calm down if he could just talk it all out with her, or anyone for that matter, who could sympathize, share his frustration, and help him sort out details.

"Are you okay? What is it?" She fixated on his face.

Get it together, Pickering. To confide in anyone was out of the question, especially with his half-baked plan and emotions teeter-tottering on a fulcrum made of Jell-O.

He took a deep, soulful breath and began, "Please understand. We both love you very much, and I appreciate what you are offering, but you can't leave your family, and I'm doing just fine taking care of your mother myself." If his intentions had any chance of being realized, privacy would be a must in the coming days.

Heather fell silent and tapped her fist against her chin. A minute passed; something was no doubt bothering her. She turned, commanded his eyes to meet hers, and reached out for his hand. "On one condition. You need someone here, and I have the perfect person."

She paused and stared at him to ensure that Guy was listening as intently as she was speaking. He knew his daughter was like her mother. She would not back down. "Your grandson, Alex."

Guy opened his mouth to object, so Heather raised her palm. "He's coming to Orlando for two weeks to stay with us. Poor Mitch, it's hard for him to handle Alex for even a little while by himself."

She blew out a breath at the mention of her older brother. Guy and Dorothy's son, Mitchell Pickering, was a midlevel Miami attorney currently mired in a nasty divorce. Guy recalled her description of a forty-five-minute conversation she'd had last week with Mitch, slurring his bourbon-fueled, expletive-laden update on his latest relationship status. Sharon, the soon-to-be ex-wife, had taken off for a Jamaican vacation the previous Saturday with her boyfriend, Mitch's prior drug-trafficking client.

"Ah, Mitch, he's dealing with loss in his own way." Heather pursed her lips. "Poor Alex is often left alone, and he was great when he visited last summer. He's a sweet kid. He's just going through a read-justment period and doesn't play with my kids, anyway. They're too young for him. Why not have him stay with you guys? The timing is ideal. He's fifteen now and won't be any trouble, and he can help you around here and . . ."

She studied his face. Guy knew what Heather *did not* say. It was obvious: She also wanted someone to keep a watch on *him*.

He glanced sideways, seeking an escape. This complicated matters, but he couldn't see a way out of it. "All right. All right. Okay. That's fine."

Brightening up, she dropped the bomb. "Great! He'll be here tomorrow afternoon."

Tomorrow? Guy's head snapped up. *That sure speeds up my timeline.*

He took a hard gulp and swallowed his worry. "It will be nice to spend some time with my grandson."

A few minutes later, with a wistful stare, he watched the Toyota back out of the driveway. *I'm doing what's needed,* he declared in his most powerful inner voice. *Heather, I hope you can understand and forgive me. I promised your mother.*

He was resolved; the deed would happen before Alex arrived. Guy could not imagine carrying out this deadly scheme with people around, much less his grandson.

Guy squinted at the upstairs bedroom. *Tomorrow morning! We've got to do this tomorrow morning!*

He paced the porch's length, wringing his hands and brainstorming.

Guns? No. I can't do that to her. Not dignified enough; too messy and violent. His contract for glory focused on a hazy but delightful image of a healthy, disease-free Dorothy awakening with her husband at her side in paradise, or on a cloud, or whatever. No drama, no trauma. Besides, he didn't even own a gun.

He plopped down in his porch chair, mumbling phrases of lethal intent, and scowled at a wall clock reminding him of the pressing time.

Jump off a bridge? Yeah, that might work, if there were tall bridges around here. He remembered that was a remark Dorothy had said to him years before on a New Year's Eve when she'd brought up this gloomy subject. *Despite what she thinks, there are no cliffs either.*

He leaped up and strode to the refrigerator, needing a moment of distraction from his gruesome thoughts. His hands were shaking as he pulled out a beer and swigged a healthy pull on the can. He heaved a sigh and kept thinking as he returned to the porch.

Pills? He visualized the cramped medicine chest in the upstairs bathroom containing a few half-empty bottles—no lethal doses of anything. *Dorothy hates pills. Won't even take her damn vitamins. No way. Morphine? No, it wouldn't be enough for both of us.*

He continued to pace up and down the length of the veranda.

Suddenly, another aspect of the plan thumped him in the chest. "What do I say? How do I tell her we're going out together?" He set aside the empty can.

As he contemplated, the lengthening afternoon shadows gave way to dusk, and two more beers later, Guy's chair stopped rocking. "Okay, that's it," he declared. The grueling machinations and painful deliberation ceased. "Now, to get the cast of characters on board." He rose and trudged inside.

When he got to the bedroom, he halted at the door. Dorothy was awake, staring at the ceiling.

"Everything hurts. I'm all worn out. Never wanted to be like this." Her red-rimmed eyes wandered around the room. "I'm confused . . . except, I haven't forgotten. Do you have a bomb or something?"

He shook off the sarcasm—focusing on frying bigger fish—and lowered himself onto the bed. He'd never been able to lie to Dorothy, so he was counting on a bit of drug fog to help convince her of his intention. "Yes, I promised. You've always been one to know what you want, honey. I get it, *and* I've been dreading this moment. But I have news. Something came along, and it's better for both of us."

She concentrated on his face but said nothing.

"Dr. Berger called me this afternoon." He hesitated, gauging Dorothy's curiosity. "He had test results to tell me. It's bad. Real bad. Remember I had a biopsy on my prostate? Well, I've got cancer down there, and it's spreading fast, and it's going to kill me real quick. So I don't have much time, and it's only going to get worse, and . . ." He stopped and bit his lip.

Her mouth fell open, and she teared up. "Oh, Guy. That's terrible. I had no idea. I wanted you to live your life and be happy, you know . . . after."

He struggled to find the right words despite the snakes of guilt writhing through his insides. "Yeah, I understand, honey." He paused and exhaled slowly. "But here's the deal. We're going to do this together. You and me. Think about it. After you go, what happens to me? I'd only lie around for another month or so, moping and suffering on my own. You wouldn't want that for me, right?" He placed a gentle hand on her thin shoulder. "I'm old, anyway. No thanks! I'm going with you!" He rushed the last sentence like he'd reached a finish line. In his mind, he crossed his fingers.

"What do you mean?" Dorothy's expression was pure shock. She shook her head from side to side, disbelief on her face. A spasm of pain interrupted the moment. The way her cheeks hollowed when she winced just steeled Guy more toward his task. When it had passed, she took his hand. "I don't see you suffering. Doesn't seem the same."

"Well, I hide it pretty well. It's my tough guy act and all that." He put on his most sincere face.

She blinked and covered her mouth. "You mean . . .? No, this can't be right." Her voice faded.

Guy leaned forward. "I understand this is hard to accept, but crummy things happen sometimes. Like this cancer. I figure ending together is the best way."

She fell silent for what seemed like an endless moment, then pulled him closer. "Are you sure? You can be such a bird brain."

He bobbed his head with as much conviction as he could muster while his gut twisted.

Dorothy's expression turned to amazement. Her eyelids drooped, and she lay back on her pillow. "This is so terrible. You and me?" A minute passed. "Okay," she whispered.

———

Later that night, as he lay in bed listening to Dorothy's labored breath, Guy stared through the ceiling, into an awaiting abyss. The peace of mind that accompanied his strategy was a meager consolation prize—but a mission and a plan were in place.

Dorothy and I are going to die tomorrow.

PERRYTON, TENNESSEE
SEPTEMBER 1942

To jump or not to jump—that is the question.

Guy emerged from Simner's Market carrying a bulging brown paper bag and headed toward his bike, a rusted Davis Twin-Flex scorching in the noonday sun. It was rare when he got permission to ride into town alone on his bicycle, but he was ten now, after all. On this hot late summer day, he had ridden the mile and a half with instructions to bring home sugar and baking soda.

Across the shimmering asphalt lot, a Chevrolet coupe slid into a parking place. Mother and daughter Frieda and Dorothy Benson had arrived at Simner's for their usual Saturday grocery shopping.

Guy was kneeling, securing his paper sack to the bike's rack with twine, when he spotted Dorothy bouncing out of the car.

"Come, dear," Mrs. Benson called after her daughter—but she was already sauntering toward him.

Dorothy called over her shoulder to her mother. "I'm going to play in the park for a while. I'll walk home."

Guy pretended not to notice her until she stopped three feet in front of his bicycle. He squinted up at her, then leaped to his feet.

A coy, confident smile spread across her face. "Guy Pickering," she said in a leisurely, somewhat accusing manner. "What are you doing?"

Guy got the feeling she already knew what he was doing and didn't much care. "I . . . I was just . . . uh . . ."

"Want to go to the park with me?"

His body tensed. He regarded the paper sack. Remembering his mother's warning to get home, he clenched his fists and jerked his head in the farm's direction. "I can't."

"Oh," Dorothy muttered, spinning on her heel and marching up the slight slope toward the park. She stared straight ahead, not checking to see if he was following.

Guy watched the bouncing ponytail for a moment, then grabbed the handlebars and did his best to catch up. *Okay, just for a while.*

———

Four blocks away, a thirty-foot stone pillar with an inlaid metal sign bearing the year 1908 marked Fennington Park's entrance. A custodian stood atop a ladder leaning against a bronze statue of General Fennington, the seldom-remembered Civil War–era town legend. Every fall, the custodian would chip away at the crusted pigeon droppings in the gentleman's generous hat brim. Guy had always liked the way it looked like a mottled turban. The custodian turned to the kids and saluted them with a gap-toothed smile. A row of shrubby dogwood trees behind the statue hid a baseball field, now emanating the excited shrieks and howls of a game.

"Hey, some boys in our class are playing today," Guy called out.

Dorothy shook her head, motioning him forward. "I changed my mind. Let's go down by the river. You know the place." She shaded her eyes and pointed across the road, past a line of dilapidated buildings with boards where windows used to be.

He *did* know the place. He'd been there once with an older cousin who was visiting from Texas. Beyond the decrepit structures, down a steep brushy bank, lay a hard-to-get-to swimming hole, untouched on most days. Above the spot where the river collected into a deep pool was a daunting rock face. They called it Luke's Rock because of the creepy old man who supposedly camped down there in the rugged brush. To Guy, Luke was scarier than the infamous jump. The old man was more of a myth than anything else, only sighted by a few people. But he had a reputation. He once hurt a kid with a rock. Or that's what Guy had been told.

He considered the brown sack tied to his bike, imagined the river ahead, then peeped up at Dorothy. "No, I should get home."

She stood, rocking up and down on her toes, looking at him, and chewing her lip. Another cheer rose from behind the dogwoods, and his gaze went off to the trees.

She still waited.

Maybe she likes me. "Uh . . . okay," he said at last, propelled by a vague notion about not wanting her to go to Luke's Rock by herself.

———

A rotting wooden door tilted and sagged open on one of the moss-covered buildings. Guy wheeled his bicycle inside and leaned it against the wall of the musty former tavern, abandoned during Prohibition and now filled with cobwebs and busted furniture. He hurried out to join Dorothy, who was eyeing the steep bank that fell away toward the river.

The pair skirted around a mound of rusted cans and dirt-encrusted bottles and pushed forward along a path through the thick branches. Guy's pulse quickened with every step as realized he was breaking the rules. He kept checking over his shoulder, back up the trail, as if his mom and dad were following them—or old Luke.

They skidded and slid through the alder and willow sprigs, the chokeberry and hedge bush, down through the last steep section of path, until they arrived at a cleared, flat spot in the dirt beneath an immense gnarled oak tree. To the right, bathed in bright sunlight, was the infamous rock knob.

They inched up to peek over the edge at a wide turn in the Perryton Valley River. The green waters swirled below them with the beauty of an unhurried song. On the far side, only dense foliage hung, giving the river a sense of privacy, an enclosed grotto. In his gut, Guy felt the anxiety of a leap. Guy's cousin had made the leap years ago and had dared him to take the plunge. He never had.

"No way you're jumping, right?" He backed away from the edge.

Dorothy only giggled, and they both retreated to the safety of the oak tree. She lingered, fidgeting with the rubber band at the end of her pigtail, and scanned the surroundings. Guy listened for signs of Luke or anyone else. "Guy," she said, then paused and studied him once again.

He grinned at her. "What do you want to do? We could head back and watch the game." *I could buy her a hot dog or something.*

"Guy," she said again, her voice soft and shy. "Have you ever kissed a girl?"

"What?" His spine jerked to attention.

"Yeah, I heard girls were supposed to wait around." She got up and took a few steps toward the massive oak trunk.

"Well, everybody kind of waits around." He curled one side of his mouth.

"Ethyl Stedmeyer thinks you're cute. She told me so. I was wondering if . . ." Dorothy's words faded. She tossed a small piece of bark into the air.

Guy didn't move an inch. Unsure of what she was saying, he tried to connect the dots. "Ethyl gets good grades." He swallowed and tugged at his ear.

"So, you want to kiss Ethyl Stedmeyer?" she drilled him.

He imagined this fate and shifted his approach. "But you're the cute one," he said with sudden inspiration, as if he'd just made an unexpected base hit.

"Do you want to kiss me?"

This time, she angled away—all he could see was her profile. While his head reeled, he faked confidence and managed to say, "Okay."

Guy watched, fascinated, as she turned to him with both eyebrows raised in heightened anticipation. He hesitated and a vague sense of early manliness grew. *This might not be so terrible.* His hand trembled. He hoped she didn't see it.

Without hesitation, Dorothy bridged the distance between them. "Okay, then, you sit here." She pointed at a flat shady area where kids often waited for courage to jump from the knobby rock. "And I'll sit here." She brushed away a few leaves next to Guy's spot. She sat beside him with an expectant grin. "Well?" she said, glancing in his direction.

Despite her show, Guy sensed the nervousness in her tone. He sat cross-legged in the dirt, and while his mind tumbled the unknowns, he bought time by picking the stickers out of his shoelaces. With the same farm-boy determination that he brought to his chores, he gulped, threw an arm around Dorothy's shoulder, and, in one abrupt motion, planted a kiss on her cheek.

She stiffened and drew back. "That's not a kiss!" her words rang like a long, drawn-out accusation.

"Yes, it is." Guy said. He had seen his mom do the same on his dad's cheek a hundred times.

"No, it's not." Dorothy frowned and stared at him in disbelief.

"But—"

"No, it's not," she repeated.

He leaned back on his palms and glanced around the clearing for an escape route. That's when she took action. She reached over and grabbed Guy's face with both hands, squeezing hard enough to poof out his cheeks and lips. Without a second's hesitation, she drew him closer while she zeroed in on the target. Lips collided, then lingered. Breath mingled with a shock of hair from her bangs that tickled his left eye. And then it was over.

Dorothy sat back, a satisfied grin. "*That's* a kiss!"

Guy wiped his mouth. He looked over at her and grinned. "Yeah, I guess you're right. You want to do it again?"

"No. I just wanted to do that." She rose and brushed the dirt from her backside.

He sprang up beside her.

Blushing, she pointed her thumb toward the trail to the outside world beyond the green oak umbrella that had served as the setting for this awkward, time-honored rite of passage. "I should go," she said, just above a whisper, and took a step to leave.

She stopped mid-stride at sounds coming from uphill—a snapped stick and the dull clatter of rocks rolling down the bank in front of hurried feet. Up the slope, behind the foliage, someone was rushing downhill toward them.

She swiveled to Guy with a gasp. "It's Luke! What do we do?"

They both shot looks in all directions. The sounds in the brush stopped, then resumed. Whoever it was, they were getting closer. That was clearly it for Dorothy. She rushed past Guy to the very edge of the rock face and, stopping only long enough to wave him forward, disappeared over the ridge.

Guy heard the splash and the voice behind him at the same time. "Hey!"

Whether it was survival instinct or simply a desire to follow Dorothy, he reacted. He did not stop at the edge to contemplate the leap; he bolted from under the tree and ran full speed ahead, legs churning over the lip, arms flailing.

It was over in an instant; he hit the water with a smack, and the impact of his awkward landing stunned him hard. Submerged in a cool green otherworld, his body went limp.

He tried to focus on the thousands of gurgling bubbles. Soon, a growing and familiar need in his lungs gripped his consciousness. He thrashed against the heavy water. A ferocious panic raced through him, leaving him oblivious to the slender hand that reached through the murk.

They broke the surface, both gasping and coughing, with Dorothy still holding on to Guy's shirt.

On top of the vertical rock, Marvin Bailey frowned at the two figures floating downstream. He reached up and rubbed the angry red welt over the left side of his face where his father had cuffed him that morning. He had run to the park, as he often did, where he'd spied Dorothy and Guy stepping past the abandoned buildings. With a streak of shadowy envy, he had followed them—he was in the mood for a fight. A year older and standing three inches taller than Guy, Marvin knew he could have taken him.

Now, he grunted and squatted on the edge of Luke's Rock. "I'm not jumping like those dummies. No way," he said to no one.

He watched the two swimmers disappear around the bend in the flowing river.

They floated to a sandy bank partially obscured by river willows. With his heart beating like a *Titanic* survivor, Guy followed Dorothy as they sloshed onshore and dropped onto the muddy sand.

Guy clasped his arms tight around himself and stared at the ground. "I coulda made it, you know. I was okay." His shivered words broke the silence.

"Yeah," Dorothy said. "I was just helping."

They sat, looking at anything but each other.

"We'd better keep going. Get back to the park." He rose to his feet, visions of Luke still pounding in his brain.

The two created their own trail, muscling their way up through the thick vegetation, and soon stood again in front of the deserted buildings.

Guy squeezed through the wrenched doorway and a moment later emerged, pushing his bike ahead of him. "Wow, we made it. I think he almost got us."

With the familiar now reestablished, he wore an open-faced grin. He had escaped from old man Luke, dared his first jump, and even had his first kiss. He couldn't have felt happier.

But Dorothy, as the adrenaline subsided, stood at a stiff angle. Wet locks of hair framed her face, now pale and drawn. She spun away. "I have to go," she said.

"Yeah, me too. But hey." He was brimming with excitement about their escape. He only saw the back of her head, and his grin faded. "You okay?"

She did not speak or move. This was not a place or time to talk, Guy realized.

Guy pushed his bicycle while she followed back up the incline to Fennington's entrance gates. The baseball game was over, and parents and kids shouted their goodbyes while filtering out of the park.

Dorothy closed the short distance between them and grabbed his shirt sleeve, tugging at it in a desperate grip. "Guy Pickering! If you tell anybody about this, I'm going to get you good!"

Guy froze, surprised at the anger in her voice. He hadn't realized that she had been crying. For him, it was already a secret.

"Boys talk about girls. This is between you and me."

"Sure. I won't."

Dorothy studied his face, eyes narrowed, as if searching for a lie. Something in his tone must have reassured her. She loosened her grip on his shirt and drew a breath. "All right, then," she said. She fiddled with her wet hair and chewed on her lower lip. "See you at school, okay?" She turned and hurried off toward her neighborhood.

With soggy shoes and clothes still damp, Guy grinned at the fleeing figure. "Yeah, between you and me," he said as he watched her disappear around the corner. A seed had been planted years before and had now grown into something he clearly felt. He stood still for several more minutes, alternately grinning, then shaking his head. "I want to live in a nice house with her someday," he muttered to himself. "Yeah."

He knew he was in trouble with his mom and dad, but that was not what he thought about as he pedaled home.

ORLANDO, FLORIDA

2007

~~MONDAY~~

~~TUESDAY~~

WEDNESDAY

Being dead's okay; it's getting there that's no fun.

Alex Pickering sat in the passenger seat of his father Mitch's black Mercedes sedan as it idled a block away from his Aunt Heather's house. His father flicked a half-burned cigarette out the window and turned to him. "Alex, listen. Heather told me they could use your help around here. A couple of weeks with your aunt and your grandparents isn't going to kill you. Right? C'mon."

Alex continued to stare out the side window. "I suppose it would kill *you*, though, huh?" He disliked the tone in his own voice, but at the same time, he felt his father deserved his pushback.

"We've been over this before. I wish I could stay, but you know

I'm up to my ass in work. There's a corporate meeting at one o'clock, so I've got to book it back to Miami right now. My future with the firm is at stake." Mitch's pressed business suit and well-knotted tie were a deep contrast to the black slack-legged jeans and metal concert T shirt Alex wore. Just another reminder of how far apart they were.

"Yeah, and after that, there's the blonde, right?" The words blurted out with an edge that surprised even Alex.

"Okay, I get this is a tough period for you." Alex tried not to roll his eyes. "It's tough for me too."

"Yeah, yeah." Alex waved his hand forward, preferring to be anywhere else at the moment, even if it meant hanging with his young cousins. "Let's go."

———

Three miles away, Guy began his morning by peering at an overcast sky. "Passing squall," the meteorologist promised from the tiny TV perched on the kitchen counter corner. "No rain in sight. This will blow over in no time, and we'll have ourselves another sunny afternoon in Central Florida!"

Guy reached out and punched the *off* button.

He walked out the front door and leaned on the porch railing. "As good a day as any," he said as he tossed his mug's last dregs of cold coffee onto the lawn.

Beyond the porch, along the sixty feet to the sidewalk, a flower bed overflowed with untended roses, hydrangeas, daisies, and succulents. A crooked wooden trellis lay hidden under a tangled mass of morning glory vine. Tall weeds and dried, unpicked flowers sagged into the first row of struggling corn. Guy scowled as he studied the neglected yard. *Not what it used to be.*

Near the lawn's far edge, a fresh dirt mound caught his attention. "Shit! Another damn gopher." He glared at the new brown monument and shook his head.

Who the hell cares anymore? He broke into a grin. *I wonder if the gophers will miss me.*

———

"Dorothy, wake up, honey." He stroked a caring hand on her cheek. "We're going on a picnic."

She lay dozing in the dim morning light after a difficult night of much-interrupted sleep.

Her eyes fluttered open as Guy squeezed her hand and stroked her forehead; he waited for her to gather her wits. Beside the bed, crowded around the lamp on the nightstand, stood a variety of framed pictures of young Mitch and Heather. To Guy, the array of smiling faces beckoned from a receding shoreline. He and Dorothy were on a departing boat.

"Picnic? What are you talking about?"

"That's what I'm calling our plan."

"Plan? What plan?" She glared at her husband, coughed for a few seconds, then collapsed back on her pillow.

"Honey." Guy scooted closer and took her hand. He had learned many years ago that his ideas had a better chance of success if he personified the patience of Job and the silky voice of Nat King Cole. "You know . . . you and me. Together."

Dorothy stared at Guy, who held his breath. The silence felt overwhelming. A tear rolled down her cheek. "Oh yeah. I remember. But are you sure?"

Guy didn't hesitate. "Yes. Yes, I am. We're doing it this morning. Our last picnic, and we're taking the Olds."

Dorothy chuffed a soft chuckle. "You've always loved that car."

The huge automobile was a classic. Right out of the military, when Guy and Dorothy were just starting their family and buying their first house, this had been Guy's dream car, but he hadn't been able to afford it. Only on his retirement day, eleven years ago, had he gone out and bought it.

Dorothy, of course, had encouraged the purchase. She'd phoned Mitch and Heather and told them how handsome their dad looked sitting behind the wheel.

Guy knew that random snippets of memory and snatches of her well-lived life wove through Dorothy's consciousness like detours these days. He began again. "Let's go on a final ride," he said, feeling like a creepy vintage movie villain luring a young heroine into a trap.

She crossed her arms, doubt written all over her face.

Guy winced. *Damn, lying to her is not easy. But it's the only way.*

Another revelation struck him. *Dorothy's fond of actual picnics. I'll bring a basket and food. That might help her pretend.*

"Tell you what. We'll do it up right. I'll whip up some nice snacks for the occasion. How's that sound?"

Her expression softened a bit.

But first, some of mother's little helpers. He smoothed two patches onto her upper arm and got her to swallow one of the new pink pills. As he descended the stairs to the kitchen, his thoughts spun with the eerie importance of his deadly mission and the irony of him being both an executioner and sacrificial victim.

Without hesitation, he brushed aside the accumulated clutter on the counter. Out came the bread, salami, pickles, lettuce, and condiments. The comforting everyday task of making lunch provided a temporary distraction from his intended deed. He gulped a swig from his beer and considered the last remnants of mayonnaise at the bottom of a jar. "I should remember to buy more." Then, he sighed. *No need for mayo where you're going, idiot! Focus on the plan!*

After a brief search in the recesses of a hall closet, he found a weathered wicker basket that had lain unused for years. It soon brimmed with wax paper–wrapped sandwiches, juice, and napkins.

He returned upstairs holding the basket in front of himself like a prize he was about to award and discovered Dorothy already sitting up at the edge of the bed.

"Oh, great. You're getting ready. And I made us a lunch," he said with a hopeful grin.

"I see the way you gawk at the women in those newspaper ads, especially the lingerie section," she said with more than a hint of her old sass. "You sure about this? You were supposed to stay alive and chase a bunch of them."

"Yeah, I know," he played along. "I had several dates all lined up, but now . . ."

"You're a dog." She wagged a finger at him. "But tell me again, what's wrong with your pecker?"

"Nothing." Guy recoiled and reached out to straighten the covers on the bed. He couldn't look into Dorothy's eyes. "It's my ancient prostate. Gotta be grapefruit sized by now. The devil got in there. Just like what happened to you. And it's hurting something awful!" He threw the last words in for good measure.

Dorothy fidgeted, lips moving with an unheard conversation. He knew this moment was critical. She at last nodded. "I never dreamed it would end this way. But I guess it's fitting."

Guy helped her finish getting dressed, his fingers fumbling with the blouse buttons. After ten silent minutes of concentrated effort, they headed downstairs.

Pedro padded in through the cat door as Guy and Dorothy entered the kitchen. He headbutted Dorothy's leg, sliding his whole body against her shin. She took a seat at the table, and Pedro immediately jumped onto her lap and gazed up at her with half-lidded eyes. She stared back for a minute, then focused her attention on Guy. "He knows it's time. Let's do this little picnic of yours."

A shiver went up Guy's spine. "Yes." He grimaced and looked

at the door, half expecting Heather to walk in with Alex four hours early. "We'd better get a move-on."

What a horrible thing for them to see. Guy shuddered at the image—the police photographs would be gruesome. But he swallowed hard and repeated the mantra that had kept him going throughout these tough days: *I need to take care of my Dorothy.* He hoped that when the family read the note, they would understand and forgive him.

The note! Oh shit. How could I forget the damn farewell note? He scolded himself and kicked a chair under the table, lamenting his lack of sleep the night before. He chuckled to himself. *They better have my favorite pillow where we're going.*

Guy covered Dorothy's shoulders with a shawl as she started for the door. He didn't dare risk making her wait any longer while he attempted to compose his hasty exodus opus. *I'll do it in the car,* he decided. *It doesn't need to be long. I'll just say we love everybody and I needed to do it. Stuff like that.*

Picnic basket in hand, his lovely wife on his arm, Guy held his head high and proceeded out of the house toward the garage-turned-transcending module, with all the solemn pomp of a funeral procession.

The humid, warm Florida air felt velvety and soothing to him. He inhaled the overgrown and tangled jasmine bouquet covering one side of the building. He didn't call her attention to it; she had lost her sense of smell months ago, a fact that was important to Guy's plan. He figured the intensifying exhaust fumes would not bother her until their heavenly car ride was complete.

Guy opened the side door, closed it behind him, and guided a somewhat frail Dorothy through the dim light into the front seat of the immaculate 1964 Olds 88 convertible. The soft seat's familiar scent brought back fond memories for Guy.

He squeezed around the back of the car, between the rear bumper and the closed double garage door, slipped into the plush bench seat, and chanced a peek at Dorothy. Her glazed expression with a nonde-script smile revealed the familiarity of trust—and the haze of drugs.

"You'll see, honey. Heaven awaits," he squeaked the words out.

"Yeah, but a picnic first, right?" Dorothy frowned, suspicion in her eyes.

The 394 cubic inches of Detroit excess, with a four-barrel dino-saur goo-gobbling carburetor, roared into life. The deep rumbling reverberated in the enclosed space.

Guy chastised himself once again for forgetting the note; the all-important manifesto apologizing, asking forgiveness, explaining everything, and conveying final "I love you"s.

He reached back into the picnic basket, where he had stashed a clipboard with paper and pen, and grabbed a wrapped sandwich.

"Honey, I have to take a minute and write a little note for every-body. Here"—he held out the sandwich—"you can start eating."

After fastening her lap belt, she sniffed at the proffered sandwich as if examining something found on the floor but accepted the food, took a nibble, and craned her neck to check out the garage. The scen-ery was only garden tools and boxes stored in the rafters, but she seemed content for the moment.

Guy turned his back to her as far as possible and began to compose:

> **Dear family and friends** . . . *Should I name everyone? Not enough time!* **I'll bet this is a big shock.** *Duh* . . . **I am very sorry.** *I wonder if they will believe me.* **This wouldn't have happened if I didn't have to.** *Wait, that's bullshit. I didn't have to do this!* **To be honest, I want to do it.** *Oh, that's great! They'll think I'm a sadistic killer.* **Nothing makes a lot of sense to me, but I . . .**

"What are you doing, Guy?" Dorothy's needle-like question poked at him.

"Hang on a minute, honey," Guy said through the thickening smog. *Red alert. Dorothy's got a raised eyebrow.*

He finished with, **I can't write much now. We've got to go. Time's up. This is best for her. Me too, I think. I love her and all of you.** He signed, **Guy,** then wiped his eyes and folded the paper. A second later, he clicked his pen and added, **And Dorothy.**

He refolded the letter once again, put it in an envelope, and slipped it inside the picnic basket. By this time, the fumes were getting dense. His brain swam with a danger message, adding to the nauseous swirl in his stomach. *Yuck! Well, it's happening.* He blinked at Dorothy, who somehow still appeared radiant.

"Where's the picnic? Let's go," she said with a slight edge to her voice.

Guy struggled with his woozy vision and refocused on her. "Yes, honey, don't you remember? You know. Our plan?" He rasped out the words. "Maybe you could just take a nap." He had figured she would be ready to sleep by this point.

Dorothy somehow seemed unfazed as she pointed backward and waved hand signals, directing Guy toward the best route out of the garage. "It's getting stuffy in here. Let's go."

Without warning, the engine coughed and missed a beat, interrupting his smoggy musing. Guy sat in disbelief as the entire car shuddered, shuddered again, and seconds later died with a final quiver. He forced his hazy vision to concentrate on the instrument panel, in particular the gas gauge. Needle pegged on *E*. "Shit. I forgot!" He had intentionally let the gas get low, planning on doing some maintenance on the tank.

His stomach howled. His forehead throbbed.

His wife screamed—"Guy!"

Another detail blown. Oh, God, please just shoot me. Or both of us, that is. He pounded the steering wheel.

Despite his brain's failing fume-soaked synapses, he remembered the red plastic five-gallon gas can that kept the lawnmower alive. Peering through the noxious atmosphere, he spied the object of his desire, the saving grace and holy grail of his life—*and death*—at that moment.

"I got it." He called as he stumbled out and groped his way around the smaller Ford Fairlane. "Aha!" Lofting the can, he estimated it was half full. *That ought to do it.*

Guy backtracked to the Olds's rear end and fumbled with the can's spout. "C'mon, c'mon," he urged the liquid into the gullet of the beast. Much to his chagrin, the fumes were already dissipating. *Gotta hurry.*

"Guy, I want to go now."

Irony punched him in the stomach, and he snapped. "You have *no idea* how much *I* want to go right now!"

He jumped behind the wheel. "Okay, we're back in action. We'll be gone before you know it."

He hit the ignition switch and stabbed the gas pedal with the fury of the damned, but the motor only cranked with a high-pitched, spinning howl. A cough or two, then more of the unwelcome sour engine whine.

Like a dog scratching at fleas, he kept pumping the accelerator. When the first trickle of atomized gasoline ignited in the deep recesses of the V8 block, the Olds finally sputtered to life with a roar.

With the engine revving past 3,000 rpm, Dorothy's woozy eyes focused on Guy. "Evidently, you need help!" she reached over and yanked downward on the steering column–mounted transmission lever.

The metal tortured gears slammed into reverse, and in a magnificent act of performance art, the rear tires broke loose, spinning with billows of burning rubber. Imitating a dyslexic dragster, the Olds lurched backward, bursting through the garage door, splintering it from its hinges. The wide door teetered on the trunk for a second, then flopped down like a welcome mat for reverse-charging convertibles.

Guy's upper lip bounced off the steering wheel as the car squealed and careened in reverse along the driveway.

Through the murk of poison and panic, Guy jabbed at the brake pedal, but his foot slipped and instead floored the accelerator. He swerved over the lawn and out of the Pickerings' yard, taking out a swath of corn stalks. They shot across the street, bounded over the opposite curb, and at last rocked to a halt, up-to-the-fenders deep in Mrs. Tooney's flora.

A silence settled over the scene, the only sound the Olds's low, steady engine idle. Guy's thoughts swirled with fog and pain. "Oh God, honey!" He turned to his wife, fearing the worst.

But Dorothy, despite looking a bit dazed, was unscathed. She swiveled from side to side, blinking in the sunshine, and surveyed the picnic site Guy had chosen for them. "This is not a good spot." She crossed her arms and raised an eyebrow.

While trying to shake off the carbon monoxide miasma, Guy groaned as a car stopped in the street, right in front of the scene. He recognized the driver as Albert Dunley, a local preacher who lived two blocks away. Without doubt or rancor, he and Albert had long ago acknowledged their innate differences and limited their interactions over the years to the barest of pleasantries. In the back seat, Albert's fifteen-year-old daughter, Amy, stared out from a window. Albert gaped at the sight, wonderment written on his face. He and Amy popped out and approached the Olds's driver's side. Albert appeared somewhat translucent, as if he'd seen a ghost.

"Mr. Pickering. Oh my God, is everything alright?"

"Oh yes, Mr. Dunley, thank you. We're just out for a drive. You can keep going."

Amy stood with a huge enigmatic grin and waved a few fingers toward Dorothy.

Albert's mouth opened, but no words came out. He stumbled back, grabbed Amy's arm, and scurried to his own car. Within seconds, they were gone.

Izetta Tooney burst from her house and scuttled up beside Guy's door with wide, glassy soap-bubble eyes.

Guy slowly twisted in her direction. "Hello there. Thought we'd visit."

"Mr. Pickering!" she shrieked. "Oh my Lord! Look at my petunias!"

Guy blinked several times toward the colorful, flattened foliage surrounding his car. He wiped his forehead with the back of his hand and gawked at the flowers. "Yeah, they're beautiful up close. Good job." With slow, deliberate motions, he straightened up and adjusted the rearview mirror to his satisfaction. He pivoted his stiff torso to the side and spoke just above a whisper, "Well, sweetheart, we should get on home now."

With shooting pains sparking like downed wires all over his head and a growing bump on his lip from where it had hit the steering wheel, he shifted the transmission into *D*, gave a polite salute toward Izetta, bounced out of the flower bed, inched across the street, and retreated to his own driveway.

In the review mirror, Guy watched Izetta totter after them, but thankfully, she stopped short, stood slack-jawed, hands on her hips, and clucked at the receding car.

Guy stopped the Olds in front of his splintered and flattened garage door, set the parking brake, and turned to Dorothy. He recognized her expression, a classic combination of raised eyebrow and curled lip. Deep suspicion.

She snorted her disdain. "It's all coming back to me now. Swing and a miss."

Guy winced as her words hit him harder than the Olds had hit the garage door. "Give me a big fat break, will ya?" he pouted. "It's kind of tricky!" *And it's not like I've ever done this before,* he wanted to add.

"You're not good at this, are you?" With a trembling hand, she pointed at her upstairs window. "Right now, I don't feel so great and need to lie down."

Guy switched off the engine and escorted Dorothy into the house. With each of her faltering steps, he was reminded of his failed mission. Her skin was even paler than usual, and Guy had to help her into bed fully dressed. As he leaned down to kiss her forehead, Dorothy's hand rested on his.

"Remember, you promised," she whispered and drifted off to sleep.

His throat caught, and he wiped at a tear that threatened to fall.

"I will," he whispered back.

A clip from the seventies-era television classic *ABC's Wide World of Sports* revolved in his mind—an image of a hapless ski jumper, accompanied by the words spoken by Jim McKay's immortal voice: "And the agony of defeat."

8

When drama spins, the spider delights.

From inside the kitchen, Guy leaned against the sink and peered out at the devastation. Garage door splinters had flown into the tangled bushes, giving them a shape like porcupines. He followed the black line of burnt rubber on the driveway to the yard's torn-up grass littered with fragments of broken taillights, through the bent corn stalks, to the deep ruts in Mrs. Tooney's flower bed. Muddy tire tracks trailed from across the street right up to the wounded Olds, sitting in the driveway like an aging boxer that had just lost a fight.

He gulped down four Advils, along with a Miller High Life to dull his throbbing lip. A police car pulled up across the street. "Great," he said as he watched a policeman's beefy figure walk up the driveway. "That's all I need . . . cops. That's just perfect."

He leaned toward an ancient mirror that hung on a nearby wall space to examine himself. His upper lip had swollen, and his clothes reeked of exhaust fumes. He tensed. *What am I going to say? Some thug hit me in the mouth and tried to steal the car?* He crushed the beer can with one hand. *Nah . . . people saw me behind the wheel. I had an epileptic seizure in my right leg.*

Sighing at the absurdity of his stories, he tossed the bent can into the sink.

Oh shit. Heather. Through the window glare, he spied his daughter marching up to the rotund officer. A troop of three young males slunk along behind her.

God, that must be Alex. Guy hadn't seen his grandson in over a year. He sucked in a breath. This fifteen-year-old from Miami appeared like one of those kids from a reality show about runaway teenagers. Alex held a hand up to his neck, clearly self-conscious about the birthmark Guy knew he was hiding. His hair flopped to one side on top and was cropped short on the sides with purple-tinged stripes. Guy rubbed his chin. *What's with the hair?*

Heather and the officer were now standing in front of Guy's decimated garage, looming wide open like an urban cave. Guy hesitated, nervous about going outside, but stiffened his resolve. "It's time to face the music." He proceeded out of the house with a deliberate but shaky gait.

The policeman swiped a sleeve over his sweaty forehead and kept raising his finger, trying to pause Heather's nonstop inquiries. He spun around to the few remaining curious bystanders and dismissed them with instructions to "move on now."

"Officer, is there anything wrong?" Guy held out his hand to the cop, who ignored the gesture. He then turned his whole stiff body to face Heather and made the mistake of engaging her worried eyes. A wave of guilt engulfed him.

Heather stared. All three kids stared. The police officer stared. From the flower bed, even Pedro stared at Guy.

"Papa, what happened?" A horrified Heather scanned the yard. "Are you all right? Where's Mom? Oh my God, is she okay?"

"Of course. Everything is fine," Guy offered, showing as many teeth as he could through the lump on his lip. The discussion struggled on, laced with excuses and apologies, as he tried to reassure all present that the destroyed garage and battered car were "just a silly accident."

Heather cut in after a minute of Guy's babbling. "I'm going to check on Mom." Directing a withering stare at her father, she jerked her arm upward in a sweeping arc and directed her young charges inside the house.

Alone with the officer, Guy flashed back to a schoolboy afternoon, standing in the principal's office, guilty of cutting class but thankful that he had escaped punishment for his real mischief. Guy glanced at the man's badge identifying him as Officer Hirschcorn and mused that the officer's bodily abundance probably kept him from ever seeing his own belt buckle.

"You know, these things happen," he started. "Throttles get stuck all the time. I can't tell you how many times I've told myself to check that carburetor linkage."

Hirschcorn stopped writing, waiting for him to stop chattering. As soon as Guy realized he was not making any sense, he paused and lamented the carnage in his driveway.

"What a mess," he said, just above a whisper. "I can't even kill myself."

"What did you say?" The cop did a slow swivel.

Uh oh . . . Guy couldn't imagine he had spoken loud enough to be heard. He cleared his throat. "I feel a chill myself. Don't you?" His arms shot up and clutched his torso, as if huddled in a frozen tundra.

Hirschcorn pulled out an already-damp handkerchief and wiped his brow. His raised eyebrow indicated that the odd statement, while standing in full sun on a ninety-degree day in Florida, did not go unnoticed. "You making fun of me?" He leaned closer, wrinkling his nose at the shivering old man.

"Of course not, no, sir! It's just me. I'm funny that way." Guy strained to display even more teeth as a sign of peace, signaling "nothing personal," all the while noticing that in the late morning heat, the officer radiated the reddish tinge of a well-used hibachi.

Guy didn't dare meet the officer's eyes for long. He peeked over the broad shoulders at Mrs. Tooney, standing like a morose victim in her recently deflowered petunia bed. He jerked the overworked cheek muscles up again and waved. She remained motionless and glared back.

"I must inform you I will forward this report to the DMV." Officer Hirschcorn brandished a pen in Guy's face. "They'll want to check your eyesight and driving skills before you can renew your license, Mr. Pickering!" He emphasized his name with an upward verbal jab and thrust a pink sheet of paper at him, suspicion written all over his face.

Guy stuck the paper in his pocket. "Thank you, I guess."

Hirschcorn scanned Guy up and down, smirked one last time, and retreated across the street.

Guy fled back inside, where, from the safety of the kitchen window, he could see Mrs. Tooney waving an animated arm, pointing at Guy's death chariot. He couldn't hear her words, but her angry expression conveyed the message.

A half hour later, Heather descended the squeaky stairs. "She's asleep now. Papa, how many of those morphine patches are you using?" She frowned, studying his face.

"Two or three a day, I think." His attention wandered upward as if the answers to her questions were scrawled on the ceiling.

"Jeez, Father, write everything down and let Dr. Berger know how it's going. Will you do that?"

"Of course. No problem."

Heather drew back and pierced him with a long stare—arms crossed, resembling one more interrogation cop. "Father, dear, you look horrible."

Not as bad as I'd look if the plan had worked. "Thanks, Heather. I do try."

"What the hell went on today? What were you doing? I don't get it." She pointed toward the Olds, a sharpness in her voice.

Guy inwardly winced with the start of another lie. "I'm sorry. We were just going for a ride. Throttle got stuck, I guess. It's my fault. Won't happen again."

"Papa, I worry about you." She lowered herself onto the chair next to him and laid a hand on his shoulder. The weight of her hand brought a flood of tenderness mixed with guilt.

Guy drew a breath. "Thank you, and I can imagine what this must look like, but . . ." He paused and focused on a faraway scene. "I'm taking care of your mom. That is my priority right now. She needs me. Please, I can handle this."

Heather scrutinized him. Guy knew he was treading a thin line. *If she knew the truth, she'd do anything and everything she could to stop me.* An uneasy and unfamiliar silence fell between them.

Heather threw up her hands. "There's been so much going on. You haven't even said hello to Alex and the kids yet. I'll get them!" She darted down the hall, and soon, Guy heard whines and complaints about "their show" and "turning off the TV" coming from the den. One minute later, a reluctant young pack shuffled into the room behind her.

With a blank stare into space, the six-year-old rocked back and forth while fumbling in his pocket for a miniature gaming device. The four-year-old beside him stood still, paying rapt attention to that same pocket. Alex, wearing a ripped black T-shirt detailing Slayer's East Coast touring schedule, slumped a few feet away, unconsciously cupping the side of his neck without any eye contact.

Guy extended his hand. "Good to see you, son."

Alex hesitated but stepped forward and grabbed his grandfather's hand with a firm grip. The six-year-old and the four-year-old stared up at the golf-ball-sized birthmark on Alex's neck, dark brown with an irregular shape. Heather thumped the taller one on the shoulder.

"Alex promised to help you around here, Papa. I know he will." Heather patted the reluctant teenager on the back with implied expectancy. "Won't you, Alex?"

Alex raised his palms in surrender. "Yeah. Sure. Whatever."

"I'm so sorry, I've got to run. Both boys have games, and I'm the chairman of the school fundraiser meeting."

"Of course, sweetie. Go on; we'll be just fine," Guy said. *It will be easier to come up with another plan if she's not here.*

"Bye!" the brothers shouted to no one as they bolted out the screen door. Heather began to follow.

"Hold on a minute," Guy called. "I'll walk you out."

In the driveway, he touched her shoulder. "I only wanted to express how much I love you. And your mom does too, of course."

Heather's eyes narrowed. "Thank you; I know that. I love you too. Is there something specific you want to tell me?"

"No, not at all." He shifted his gaze away from his daughter. "I just wanted to say that."

She glanced toward the impatient whines emanating from the minivan and tapped a finger onto Guy's chest. "I've got to go, but I get the feeling you're not telling me everything."

"What gives you that impression?" Guy's twitchy face did not help his case.

An awkward ten seconds of silence ensued, finally broken by Heather.

"I don't like it. I'll be back soon as I can."

Guy took several deep breaths while standing in the driveway, watching the Toyota disappear around the corner. *Shit. She's on to me.*

Upon returning to the kitchen, Guy found Alex sulking in a corner chair.

Now what? What to say? What to do?

He noticed an upper lip with a shadow of early hair and recalled the late-night phone call he'd gotten from Mitch a few months ago. His only son had been drunk once again, crying about Dorothy's prognosis and probation with his law firm. He hadn't even mentioned Alex. *Damn shame. Miami's a tough place to be left alone.*

Alex's fingers twitched on the table, displaying an inner adolescent tug-of-war. Guy kept a steady gaze on his grandson.

"This is a lot of bullshit." Alex declared and shoved his back into the chair as if digging in for a battle. "You don't know anything."

Guy chortled. "Yeah, and I don't suppose you've met Jack in your neck of the woods."

Alex frowned, silent again.

"Never mind. A lot of people don't know him." Guy lowered himself onto a chair and sighed. "Guess what?" he said in a soft voice, staring at his grandson.

Alex averted his attention, not wanting to connect. Guy waited for any sign of telltale interest.

"Sometimes, I'm pretty out of it. And you're right: There's a lot of bullshit out there in the world."

Alex snorted and jerked his head but said nothing, shifted in his seat, and drummed his fingers with eyes fixated on the ceiling. Guy noticed a weariness in Alex's demeanor. His slumped shoulders spoke of weighty drama. Guy suspected that beneath the hair dye and angst, Alex harbored some sadness and disappointment. He flashed back to images of a younger Alex. Summers filled with county fairs, bass fishing trips, and Dorothy's fresh berry pies. And the Beechcraft Bonanza flights. *He loved those.*

"How's your mom?" Guy couldn't recall any updates and realized it had been close to two years since he'd seen her.

"Right now? Probably in some fancy hotel in Jamaica with the Sleazeoid." Alex took a pocketknife from his jeans pocket and started working on a fingernail. "Not that I care."

Guy kept his face neutral. "And your dad?"

"He's okay, I guess. He's at work a lot."

"Yeah, I suppose he is."

"And school? How's it going for you?"

"How is it? It's a bunch of full-of-shit teachers." He flicked one hand in dismissal and slumped back in his chair.

Guy considered his grandson. "Must be hard when everybody around you is full of shit."

Alex winced. "I mean . . . they're old and try to tell you what you have to do. Can't do this, can't do that."

"I can remember some of that. Well, what do *you* want to do? What do *you* want to be?"

Alex gazed out the window. "Don't know. I've thought about being a pilot. That would be cool. You're one, right?"

Guy shook his head to clear the instant memories, good and bad, that reeled past his vision. "Used to be. Don't have much time for it anymore, though."

"That's fucked up too!"

"Getting old is not for pussies or pilots." Guy snickered. "You think things are terrible because you don't like your teachers? My God, you have no idea how lousy things can get. If you're smart, you'll learn from the example of people who've led a good life. A proper way to be in the world. You've got to take care of yourself right along with others, too." He groaned with the pain in his knee as he rose from the table, then grimaced out the window at the mess in his front yard. "The whole shebang is not about us! And remember the most important thing: You do what you've got to do." Guy said it as much to himself as to Alex; then, he pointed out the window. "Now, think you can cut loose of your discontent and give me a hand out there?"

"Whatever," Alex grumbled but got up and trailed behind his grandfather out to the driveway.

Guy kicked aside a few splintery bits of wood and taillights, positioned himself on one side of the garage door, and motioned Alex toward the other edge. "Right now, we've got to stash this somewhere in the back."

The door was heavier than expected. They pulled and pushed and levered the handle over the driveway perimeter, and after five minutes, they had dragged it around the corner and out of sight. It flopped down in a dust cloud with a satisfying *whomph*.

Guy dusted off his hands. "Thank you, son. Much obliged."

Alex hesitated, then shook off the thanks with a wave and headed for the porch. After collapsing onto a couch, he surveyed his surroundings with the haughty eye of a prospective tenant being shown a hovel. "This place used to look a lot better."

"Thanks for the feedback. I'll get the staff to toss rose petals in front of you!" Guy glared at his grandson, then hobbled into the garage, grabbed a broom, and began a vigorous sweep of the driveway, keeping tabs on his grandson as he worked.

Alex rose and wandered over to a part of broken taillight lying in the grass. He bent, picked up the chunk, and tossed it into the open trash can fifteen feet away, then noticed the upright, splintered wooden remnants of the garage door that remained fastened to the steel mounts on either side of the opening. He tapped his finger on the tip of the shard. About eight inches long, it resembled a sharpened spear. As Guy watched, he grabbed one and yanked it to the side, but the stubborn piece wouldn't budge—the wood was too thick and bolted tight.

"Hey, you got some kind of tool or something to get these pieces of wood off?" Alex yelled, fingering the sharp point as he waited for an answer.

Guy dropped the broom onto the concrete and limped over beside his grandson. He pointed his nose upward and squinted through his bifocals. "Yeah, looks like you need a couple of five-sixteenth wrenches. There's a bunch of sockets and open ends in that lower pullout, right there." He pointed under a workbench at a bright red metal tool cabinet.

After a few minutes of trial and error, Alex found two wrenches that fit the nuts and bolts and started removing the offending oversized splinters. First one side, then the other. With satisfaction beaming from his face, he spiked the shards into the garbage can, then frowned at the tire tracks in the lawn.

"So, Grandpa. What the fuck really happened here?"

Guy stopped dead. He pivoted and, with deliberate steps, marched back to the garage, his concentration trained on his grandson. "Young man, when you're here at this house, I'll take care of my business, and you mind yours—and your mouth, too. Fuck! I'm the only one around here that's allowed to say *that* word!" he sputtered.

Alex stuck out his lower lip and refused to meet the gaze. "Oh yeah? Well, I'll just fucking leave then. Then I can say what I want. I can take care of myself." He glanced toward the street. "I know I was dumped here. No one wants me around."

The dejected tone in Alex's voice slapped Guy across the face, waking him from his ire. He sighed. "You weren't dumped . . . forget that. You're family. That means a lot. It's just a stressful time around here. But it's good to see you. I mean that." He laid a hand on Alex's shoulder. "Let's get something to eat."

Alex brooded for a few seconds, then spun on his heel and followed his grandfather back through the screen door.

Dreams should be embraced and never judged.

The sun had set an hour ago. Upstairs, with the help of morphine and little pink pills, Dorothy tossed and turned with a most remarkable dream.

A magnificent Roman palace celebration: A hundred flickering candles illuminate dark wooden tables piled high with oversized platters of food. Men and women, dripping with jewels and gold, lounge and laugh in their elaborate togas. Wine overflows from ornate goblets. The finest raiment adorns Dorothy. All in attendance love her. Muscular, well-oiled servants stand guard at the foot of her throne. Exotic dancing and shouting abound.

Something is wrong. A still tension fills the air. Menacing shadows grow. Uneasiness grips Princess Dorothy. The princess must flee. She must escape.

In the bedroom's dim light, Dorothy bolted upright. Her haunted eyes snapped open like a mousetrap in reverse. Although sleep was now gone, her dream still clung to her morphine- and pill-soaked reality. The muted window curtains gave off just enough glow and shadow to keep the palace party alive in her mind.

Her feet hit the floor. *I have to run!* She shuffled toward the door, but an inner voice born of moonstruck royal blood and pink pills called to her. She turned her head up to the sky, closed her eyes, and listened. *Princess . . . duty . . . sacred statue . . . Yes! I must endure.* An electric tingle shot through her spine with more energy than she'd had in months.

She tiptoed to a dresser and opened the lowest drawer. From behind a pile of spare togas, she plucked her all-important statue. She clutched the object to her chest and swore an oath into her misty, dream-soaked reality with such ferocity that anyone standing by would have been frightened. "This symbol of our people cannot fall into enemy hands."

Over to the window, the princess scuffled in her flannel slippers. Another morphine patch slipped to the floor. "Ah," she peered down at the vaguely familiar guard inspecting a battered metal chariot. A shorter figure, no doubt a superior officer, watched the worker from the mouth of the curious open cave. "A *centurion*." She hissed the word.

She lifted her gaze to the distant lands of the East. Beyond the cobblestone road, she discerned the faint firelight from her village— the amber-colored beckoning lights from a dozen torches.

"The homeland . . . my destiny." Dorothy swooned under the portent.

The bronzed, bejeweled young princess seeking freedom and glory scanned the room. Needing a disguise to slip by the guards, she glided over to the closet, shed her robe, and rummaged deep into the furthest recesses of half-forgotten attire. She stretched her arms out to a hanger in the farthest corner and selected a musty cloak.

She wrapped a woven focale turban-style around her head. *I'm still missing a water jug to carry! I'll never make it without looking like a slave girl.* She grabbed a nearby urn and dumped the contents onto the floor, then placed the figurine inside and crept toward the bedroom door, steeling herself for the dangerous escape from the palace.

With renewed energy and a willingness to sacrifice it all for the cause, Dorothy crept down the stairs. At the kitchen window, she peeked at the cursed soldiers still milling around the grounds.

She tiptoed out the screen door, down the porch steps, and slipped to the left, skirting the lawn away from the preoccupied soldiers. She saw the older one staring at her own window. *Ha! They'll never capture me!* She rushed toward the village lights, beckoning like a beacon.

She arrived much faster than she had anticipated. Her people had vanished, but undaunted, Princess Dorothy began burying the sanctified statue amid a patch of flowers. "Even if they catch me," she uttered with fierce determination, "they won't get the holy figurine."

She plucked up a nearby trowel and dug and scraped for all she was worth. Alyssums, tulips, daisies, begonias, root balls, and dirt flew over her shoulders.

A noise from the nearby structure distracted her; she saw a dangerous looking female warrior screaming into an object held to her ear. *I have to hurry.*

Guy was leaning against the open garage doorway, deep in thought, when he heard a scream echoing from across the street. "Shit! What now?"

He bolted to attention but couldn't see anything.

"Stop that!" Another shriek issued from Izetta's direction.

Guy craned his neck toward the commotion, then swiveled to the upstairs window. *I can't leave her.*

"Pickering!" came the next howl from across the street.

His body went rigid, and his head darted between the window and Izetta's shadowy yard. "Shit!" He scurried into the street as fast as his knees would allow.

"Should I come with you?" Alex called out.

"No. You stay here!"

Alex didn't listen. Guy heard him running behind him as he quick-stepped toward Izetta's house.

Officer Hirschcorn's police car screeched to a halt with Guy, shielding his eyes, in the headlights.

"You again," the cop scowled as he exited the car.

Mrs. Tooney ran up to them. "She's back there! Hurry."

All four charged ahead, past the solar-powered tiki torches and into the darkened yard, where flowers still arced through the air. A wild-eyed figure suddenly popped up and struggled to rise, then tottered forward into the torch's pulsing glow. All parties stopped dead in their tracks.

Guy's jaw dropped. *Dorothy?*

A few awkward seconds of incredulity mixed with reluctant recognition ensued as Dorothy stood, glaring back at the four. A dank towel headdress sagged to one side of her dirt-smeared face, and she wore a Hawaiian muumuu, a souvenir from a 1976 Waikiki vacation Guy had won as top insurance adjuster of the year. A perforated plastic laundry hamper sat nearby. Her muddy arms held aloft a kitschy eight-inch-tall Norman Rockwell figurine he hadn't seen in a decade or so. With the porcelain figure clasped in her hands, she tottered toward the attackers, shrieking a battle cry, "Ayyyieeyeee! I am the princess, and you will never get it!"

A palpable silence hung in the air, as no one knew what to say or do. Then, in one swift motion, Dorothy slam-dunked the porcelain statue onto a walkway tile, smashing the effigy into what physicists refer to as smithereens.

More silence.

These new pills are something else. With a sigh of resignation, Guy stepped forward. "Honey," he offered in his gentlest tone. "Let's go home."

———

That was all it took. Guy's deep voice penetrated her psyche, leading her like a lighthouse leads a ship out of the fog. Shaking off some of the morphine- and pill-induced psychosis, she cocked her head to the side for a second and squinted at Guy. His deep voice had always been a source of comfort during trying times. At this moment, his simple words served as a link to the road back.

"Guy, it's time to leave," she said with a haughty lilt, as if someone had just insulted her at a party. "Right now, if you please." She smoothed the front of her muddy muumuu and extended a hand to her husband.

———

Guy took a deep breath, glanced at Officer Hirschcorn, stepped forward to take his somewhat-soiled princess on one arm, and proceeded toward the street.

Mrs. Tooney stomped around in a wide circle, holding a clump of damp foliage and clucking and fussing under her breath. "I don't trust that man," she said, loud enough for Guy to hear.

He paused and turned with gritted teeth to take in both Izetta and Hirschcorn.

"Please take better care of your wife!" Mrs. Tooney spat.

"Izetta," Guy began, casting a soulful gaze in her direction. "Dorothy and I have something that, I'm sorry to say, I'll bet you've never experienced in your whole life. And that's a shame. Trust that comes from true love. It brings deep caring." He patted Dorothy's arm and, with head held high, made his way toward the more familiar side of the street. "Let's go, son," he said to Alex.

"Hold on there a minute." Hirschcorn turned to Mrs. Tooney. "Would you like to press charges?"

Guy frowned and wrapped his arm around a sagging Dorothy as she blinked back tears.

For the last few minutes, Alex had stood in silence, gaping at the entire scene in amazement. Now, he closed the distance between himself and the officer and Mrs. Tooney.

Hirschcorn snarled, "And what do *you* want?"

"You need to give my grandma a break," he said, squaring his shoulders. "She's old and sick and gets kind of crazy, but she's still *way* better than *your* fat asses." Alex stared into both adults' eyes, letting the statement hang between them.

Hirschcorn chuffed a few times and crossed his arms. Mrs. Tooney appeared too shocked to speak. Alex spun around and joined Guy and Dorothy. They marched together as a bonded tribe toward the Pickering house lights.

Guy nudged his grandson. "That was blunt but cool what you said back there. Thanks for sticking up for your grandma."

Alex shrugged. "Those two are just more full of shit than you are."

Back in the safety of their own bathroom, Guy spent five minutes holding Dorothy's hand as she vomited up what little she had in her system. The trip to Mrs. Tooney's had sapped much of her limited reserves.

By the time Guy had Dorothy bathed and eased back into bed, her pain had returned. She refused any food and instead reached out and grabbed his sleeve. Her red-rimmed eyes seemed to focus somewhere in the distance.

"I'm so sorry. Dreams take over my head." She swallowed hard. "I'll rest now."

Time for another patch. As he applied the morphine to her thigh, Guy hummed a simple church hymn melody remembered from childhood—he never memorized the words. She soon drifted off to sleep.

Rising from the bed, he went to the window and saw the porch light go off across the street.

He lowered himself onto the chair beside Dorothy and removed his shoes. He sat for a long time, listening to her breath.

"My beautiful problem," he said into the darkness.

PERRYTON, TENNESSEE
MAY 1950

The senior prom is so important,
one remembers it even if they didn't go.

Guy's grass-stained right boot tapped in a nervous pattern on the sidewalk in front of the Bensons' home. His eyes shifted back and forth from the familiar refuge of his parked truck to the alluring, ornate front door. He couldn't budge.

The year before, Dr. Cecil Benson had moved his family into this grand Victorian-style house in town with a generous veranda and a lush, sprawling lawn. Heavy spring rains that season brought an abundance of hollyhocks and fragrant wild honeysuckle to the Tennessee countryside, and tall weeds and grasses burst with green energy inside the Perryton city limits. This suited Guy Pickering just fine. He was almost eighteen years old and full of ambition, leading to arrangements with several households around town to mow lawns after school and on weekends. The time spent doing yard work conflicted with his farm chores, but with extra effort and minimal sleep, he was managing the two jobs. Cattle often got fed in the dark.

While working on other yards in the neighborhood, Guy was always watchful of the Benson grounds, and especially the upstairs windows. He waited, timing that important knock on the door until their yard's vegetation was overgrown, and today was the day. Nevertheless, he couldn't bring himself to approach this most important residence.

He spun around and took a step back toward the truck, feeling the guilt of a challenge postponed, when the front door cracked open. Frieda Benson's fine-featured face peered out. "Is that you, Guy Pickering?"

Guy froze. "Yes, yes. It's me."

"I thought so. Guy. I know who you are. I remember you well, ever since your egg-gathering days. Yes, I remember." Mrs. Benson zeroed in on him. "Do come in."

Mrs. Benson's demeanor conveyed a presumed understanding regarding social elements. She wore a pleated skirt and a pressed white blouse with starched cuffs. Her hair, drawn back in a tight bun, pulled at the corners of a wrinkle-free face that radiated the countenance and essential manners that come from a privileged youth—her family hailed from Boston. "You're here to call on Dorothy, I suppose."

"No, ma'am. You see—"

"Nonsense. She's just upstairs. Do come in."

Guy pointed at the random dandelion sprouts that showed the real reason he was here. The plan was a week or two of meticulous mowing underneath the windows; then, Dorothy might one day venture out to say hello. *That would be more natural.* "Mrs. Benson, I—"

"Dorothy! You have a caller. Come downstairs, dear!"

Mrs. Benson had turned toward the staircase, so she didn't see the horrified look on Guy's face. He glanced down at his grass-stained work boots and then his pickup truck through the front window's lace curtains and yearned for an escape.

Mrs. Benson motioned to a couch in the adjoining parlor. "Please sit a moment, and I'll bring some nice iced tea. You must be thirsty. I see you doing yard work all over the neighborhood. Lord knows we need someone ourselves. There's so much to do." She smacked her lips and straightened her pristine skirt.

Guy saw his chance. "Yes, well, actually—"

"Mr. Benson is so busy at his practice these days. Anyway, I'll get that iced tea . . ." She lifted her chin and disappeared down a hallway.

Guy took off his straw hat, swiped his hair back, and sat on the edge of a velvet-upholstered seat beneath a sepia-hued portrait of a stern-faced man dressed in a tailored suit. A sudden dampness appeared in his armpits. One of his knees bobbed with the disregarded regularity of a piston engine. He noticed the precision of every object in the house. The doilies on the chair's arms were perfectly straight; the polished hardwood floors shone almost like a mirror; a tall ornate vase sprouted a bountiful array of fresh flowers. Guy bit his lower lip and envisioned his own old farmhouse. He had never thought less of it with its smoke-coated stone fireplace and its torn screens. *That's where I belong.*

He glanced at the door. *Maybe I can slip out.*

"Guy Pickering." Dorothy pronounced his name with a touch of amusement and surprise, as if he were a butterfly just landed on her arm. She stood wide-eyed in the doorway.

"Oh, hi, Dorothy. Sorry, I didn't mean to . . . uh. I was looking for your father. He might want me to—"

"Here you are, you two. Fresh mint iced tea." Mrs. Benson burst into the room with a tray holding two tall glasses and a china plate arrayed with cookies. She placed it on the coffee table with a flourish while surveying them with the open smile of a party hostess. "I'll just leave you alone now. Shall I?"

"Thank you, Mrs. Benson. I wondered if Mr. Benson would be—"

"Oh, yes, yes, he'll be back. I'm going to run along to the kitchen. Do be polite to our guest, Dorothy." Guy heard her talking to herself as she vanished into a polished hallway.

"Mom. She tries so hard." Dorothy's eyes followed her mother. She lifted the tray and motioned toward the door. "Let's bring this out to the porch."

Guy, unable to form a coherent sentence, nodded in silence.

"So, what brings you here today? Is it about the lawn, or did you want to see me?" She flopped onto a swaying porch swing.

He couldn't answer right away. His face flushed, witnessing this woman looking like a living jewel in a rocking pendulum. He'd matured to just over six feet this year and, being unaccustomed to his new stature, was prone to a slight stoop to maintain a customary friendliness.

"Sit down, will ya?" Dorothy swept her arm in an arc, indicating any one of several ornate high-back wicker chairs festooned with bright cushions.

Guy pushed back several huge potted plant fronds and gingerly sat down a respectable distance from Dorothy. At the far end of the porch, a woman in a maid's uniform quit sweeping, nodded her head toward them, and disappeared inside.

Dorothy softened her voice. "I heard about your mother."

A stab went through Guy's heart. Three months earlier, Molly had succumbed to pulmonary fibrosis after "a lengthy illness," as the obituary had stated. It had been a hard winter at the Pickering farm, and Lloyd often sat beside the fire with a bottle late into the night.

"Yeah, I miss her." Guy shifted his feet and gazed at the sky to the west. Chirping birds filled the silence. For a brief moment, he fell into a reverie, his mother, Molly, smiling and setting freshly baked biscuits down on the burnished kitchen table. A familiar aching joy flooded his being.

"I can't imagine losing my mom," Dorothy said.

Her words plus the rhythmic squeak of the swing springs brought him back. Guy beheld this other woman in his life, so large in his mind and so removed. He averted his eyes under the weighty specter of loss.

"Who are you taking to the prom?" She riveted him with an expectant glare. "You *are* going to the prom, right?"

Shaken from his daydream, Guy pondered this question and peered down at his grass-stained jeans and T-shirt. "I was thinking maybe . . . I'm not sure." He raised his gaze up to the veranda's ceiling and extended his arm onto a post, leaning against it with fabricated disregard. A mix of girls' faces from school swam in his mind—they were either already taken or too much effort. And besides, the only one he was interested in was sitting right in front of him.

"Guy Pickering! You're going! That's all there is to it." She shot him a scolding smirk and looked away. "Marvin asked me, and, well, I'm going with him. You've just got to go," she said. "Everyone's going to be there, and it will be so much fun."

Guy already knew Marvin had scored the date. Various school-boys had jockeyed for the position, but in the end, they deferred to the varsity football team's star quarterback. Guy was not in the running; he didn't even play football this year.

For five minutes, Dorothy leaned back in the swing and, one by one, ticked off the current social order. Mary had angled for Brad, but he wound up with Laura after John asked Susan because Loreen was simply not going if she couldn't go with Tim.

Guy tried to concentrate on the school hierarchy but soon realized that she was zeroing in on Betty.

Betty Trull? He winced but said nothing. *I don't even know her, and I don't like her.*

"That's settled, then. It's only a week away, you silly. No one's asked Betty, so either you do it, or I'll arrange it for you."

Despite his hesitation about Betty, Guy was amused by this new glimpse of Dorothy. She was formidable when she got a notion.

"Hey, I should go now." Guy shuffled toward the steps.

"Are you going to mow our lawn?"

Guy had almost forgotten the reason he had originally come by. "I don't know. I haven't talked to your dad yet."

"How much? He'll go with whoever I say." She raised an eyebrow.

Guy hesitated for a few seconds and stuck his hands in his back pockets. "The folks around here pay me a dollar and a half. I use your mower and rake it up." He extended his chin and pointed at a trimmed yard down the street.

"Hmm." Dorothy inspected her nails. "Will you do it for a dollar?"

He frowned and blinked a few times, weighing the unfamiliarity of negotiation.

"Oh, I'm just fooling with you." She broke into a huge grin.

Guy blushed again, and they giggled and chatted on the porch for another few minutes before he raced home with mixed emotions. *She seemed comfortable, I think. That was great.* But even so, Guy kept imagining Marvin's smug face spinning Dorothy around the dance floor. *Why him? And Betty Trull?* At least he was going to the prom now. Whether that was good or bad, he didn't know. But then again, when did he ever know anything for sure?

On prom night, dozens of nervous teens showed off their best moves in the packed high school gymnasium. Streamers hung from the ceiling in twisted waves, and balloons and confetti littered the floor. Guy wore his best clothes and had never seen so many fancy dresses in his life.

Betty turned out to be a real ring-a-ding, as they say. She had smuggled a flask of whiskey into the gym, probably hoping to dull the pain of being last invited and winding up with farm boy Guy Pickering.

Guy was unaware of the true depth of Betty's feelings for him until she spun away and glared at him in the middle of the dance floor, during Les Paul's and Mary Ford's "How High the Moon."

"What a loser you are, you loser boy." Her slurred voice cut through the music, and the closest couples to them stared and snickered. Guy stood confused and embarrassed, surrounded by a circle of grinning faces. Betty lurched back and blinked her whiskey-soaked disappointment at him, expecting him to react. When he didn't, she reeled away and stumbled toward the gymnasium doors, looking green in the face.

The song kept playing, and the couples continued dancing, but many had seen the spectacle.

Guy wove his way through the crowd and followed Betty through the double wooden doors. Maybe she needed his help. He didn't know, but going outside seemed like the right choice.

Just as he reached her, two of Betty's girlfriends appeared out of nowhere, turned their noses up at Guy, and whisked her away into the parking lot shadows.

Guy stood alone on the bare pavement with his back to the gymnasium's pale light and muted music. The night air blew across his face, cooling him from the crowded, hot dance floor and from his embarrassment. *Who cares about stupid Betty anyway?* His thoughts drifted to the other women on the dance floor . . . well, one other woman. After checking his watch and kicking all the small rocks in sight, he knew he couldn't go inside and face all the others. He took a few unsure steps toward his pickup truck, parked in the football field.

"Guy, wait!"

Dorothy caught up with him at the edge of the football field's grass and grabbed his sleeve. "Betty, what a dud," she panted with a slight giggle.

Guy could only purse his lips and look away. It was hard to view this vision in a blue dress. He felt the heat in his face despite the cool breeze.

"Sorry about fixing you up with her," she said. "I didn't think she'd be that way."

"That's okay. Not your fault. She's got something against me for some reason." Guy stroked his chin.

They stood in silence for a moment, gazing up at the stars, glancing at each other.

"Is that your pickup over there? Same one?"

"Yeah."

Dorothy sighed and gestured out to the field. "My dad's asking around for someone else to mow our lawn. Did you know?"

Guy felt a sting in his gut. "No. Why? I cut extra careful and everything." He stared at the ground.

She couldn't hold it any longer and burst out laughing. "Oh, Guy, you're so sweet." She punched his shoulder. "I told him to be happy. He's fine as filigree."

Guy grinned, once again disarmed, baffled, and entranced. He couldn't stop his sideways glances at her. The pale illumination emanating from the gym behind her gave her a glowing sheen, as if she were an angel surrounded by light. Her skirt hem lifted with the breeze, and he caught sight of her slender calves and knees all the way up to her lower thigh. He blushed.

Through the open gym doorway, they watched the couples shimmy as the speakers cranked out one more swing song. Another silent minute passed.

"Well, aren't you going to ask me to dance?" She stared up into his face.

The invitation was the last thing Guy expected. Her left eyebrow arched high. He stammered a few words until she reached out and took his hand.

"C'mon." That was all she said.

She tugged, and he obeyed the entire way back to the center of the gymnasium, letting himself be led by the blue angel. They danced not one dance, but three, right there in front of everyone, including Marvin, who sulked in a corner the whole time.

———

After the dance, Guy drove home, and when he entered the farm-house, he saw Lloyd slumped in an easy chair, asleep with a book laying in his lap.

"Dad. Hey, Dad! Wake up. You stayed up to see that I made it home, didn't you?"

Lloyd shifted up in his seat and cleared his throat. "No . . . no, I just wanted to read this here book."

Guy smiled. "Yeah, you did. You didn't have to do that."

"Well, how'd it go, anyway? Your big dance."

A million details flooded Guy's mind, and he wondered where to start. "You know how sometimes, things start out real bad, but then out of the blue, the unexpected happens? All I can say is some people weren't happy. But I sure am."

ORLANDO, FLORIDA

2007

~~MONDAY~~

~~TUESDAY~~

~~WEDNESDAY~~

THURSDAY

When confusion reigns, confused people reign.

Guy awoke at first light to the motion and intermittent moans of Dorothy's labored breathing. He yawned and rolled out of bed as quietly as possible to begin another last day of his life.

With morning coffee in hand, he sat in the kitchen and stared at his cup. *I can still do it. I can.* He pushed away the onus of doubt, as if trying to ignore an outlandish necklace around his neck.

And then there was Alex to consider. With a grandson on board, the captain understood he had one more crew member than he needed for this voyage. The elders need an excuse to slip away and attend to business. Business that a youngster would and could never understand.

Guy leaned forward and looked down the hallway toward the second bedroom. *He's a good kid. Came through last night for us. He deserves better breaks. I'm letting him down, and Heather and Mitch and other people, too.* With rueful insight, Guy knew he would never again be in this position.

He pushed himself up from his chair and poured more water in the coffeemaker. *One more for the road and plan B.*

Heather, with her two young ones, pulled into the driveway before he'd even finished his coffee. They couldn't stay long. The older one had a soccer game, and the younger one was headed to a birthday party.

Much to Guy's chagrin, Alex raced into the kitchen and blurted out the details of last night's foray into the neighbor's yard.

Guy listened in awkward silence. Heather listened in riveted disapproval.

"Papa, I don't like this at all. This is not working for me, for Mom, or you." Her tone was soft, but her eyes shone with ferocity.

She gets that from her mother. His thoughts turned to Dorothy upstairs and his promise. "It's been a hard week," he said, trying to sound reassuring. "She just got a little confused. Trust me. I'll take care of your mother."

The irony bell rang out loud, but only Guy heard it.

Heather continued her suspicious stare at him over her shoulder as she headed upstairs to deliver food and spend a few minutes with her mother.

Upon returning, Heather embraced Guy with a long, firm hug, then held him at arm's length. "I've got to get going, but I'll be back soon. I don't know what, but something's happening here."

She gathered her boys and herded them out the door.

Heather's minivan had only been gone a minute when Guy spun around to Alex. "Oh my gosh!" His words boomed out a bit too loud. "I just remembered. Silly me. Dorothy's got a doctor's appointment today. How could I forget?" He thumped his forehead in fake self-admonition.

Alex stood by the refrigerator and studied his grandfather. "Go right now, you mean?"

"Yeah, real soon." Guy rubbed his neck and glanced warily at his grandson. He did a double take. *Shit, he's got that dang raised eyebrow like his grandmother's.* His thoughts were coming slower, and three at a time. "We'll be back real soon. You can do whatever you want. Do you want money for the store or anything?" The words spilled out rapid-fire.

Alex shook his head. "No, I'm okay."

Guy did not mistake the doubt in his tone.

As Guy headed up the stairs, one concern felt like a lead weight. *Will she still agree to the plan?*

He opened the bedroom door, shocked to see her sitting on the bed, fully clothed, but focused on her feet. She glared at him. "Well, *there* you are. I've been waiting. We *are* going, aren't we? On this damn picnic of yours?"

She blew her nose in a handkerchief and studied her husband.

Hoping for the best, he sat on the mattress edge. "So, you're still up for this final journey?" he said in a voice dripping with apprehension.

Dorothy tilted her head, that old sharpness in her eyes. "You wouldn't lie to me, now would you, Guy Pickering? You don't seem sick to me."

A chill went up his spine. His entire life, he had never hidden anything from Dorothy. His head swirled with the weight of untruths and the pros and cons of coming clean. He opened his mouth to speak, ready to spill all the beans.

"How bad is it?" She interrupted his would-be confession in a soft voice. "Do your nuts hurt?"

Guy suppressed the impulse to chuckle and pushed this river

along. "Sometimes. Oh yeah, a lot. Mostly inside. It snuck up on me, but it's bad. It's so bad. Both of my boys feel like they're in a vise."

Dorothy nodded her understanding. "That sounds terrible. We get old. We die. That's the way it is, I guess. You and me, Guy." Her attention sailed out the open window. "I'm so ready for release, but you shouldn't have to do this. I love you. Thank you for taking care of me and us."

"We'll do what's right for us." He squeezed her hand to bring her attention back to him. She gazed into him with the eyes he loved so much. "But remember, unfortunately, we have to hide all this from everybody, especially Alex. You understand?"

"Alex is not coming." She added the affirmation. "But you are doing up one of your picnic lunches again?"

"Of course."

He wondered about her lucidity—so far, so good—and decided on one spoonful of morphine and one pink pill for the day. He was well aware of morphine's benefits and drawbacks: less pain but more irrationality and mood swings, and the pills were definite wildcards.

A particular problem occurred to him as he helped Dorothy down the stairs—he had anticipated a much longer time frame to get Dorothy ready. The allotted interval to take care of details had vanished. He wanted to rewrite yesterday's cryptic and unsatisfying goodbye note but now didn't think he could accomplish that *and* make fresh sandwiches before Dorothy got too antsy.

After situating Dorothy in a kitchen chair, Guy rushed out the screen door and headed for the Olds, where stashed inside the picnic basket lay the all-important note.

———

Alex sat down across from his grandmother at the table, noting the mismatched buttons on her pink sweater. "So, you've got an appointment with the doctor again, huh?"

She peered at him with no response.

Maybe she had not heard him. He didn't really know what the cancer had done to her other than what he could see, and he certainly didn't want his grandma to die. Death had always been distant and scary. He opened his mouth to repeat the question.

Dorothy burst out, "Guy and I are going." She turned her face away. Alex wished he hadn't said anything. He didn't know what to say now.

She swung her gaze back to him. "Are you hungry?"

"I'm fine," Alex said.

"I . . ." She pursed her lips as her perception seemed to fade. Her voice was barely above a whisper. "We're going on a picnic."

Alex spied Guy through the window as he fumbled in the Olds's rear seat. "A picnic? You're going on a picnic?" *Oh, there's her mind slipping away again.* Alex let the thoughts trail off.

"It's about time too! This is no good. I need to go."

Alex frowned but switched to a heartfelt smile. "I know. It is kind of boring around here. A picnic sounds like fun," he said in a syrupy sounding voice. *Grandpa has to lie to her. Sad.*

———

Guy returned to the kitchen, carrying the basket containing yesterday's squashed food. He yanked the stained note out, stuffed it into his front pocket, and pulled from the refrigerator all the sandwich makings he spotted. He slapped two pieces of bread on a cutting board while his mind raced to find a plausible explanation for everything.

"A picnic, huh? Excellent day for one," Alex said with a hint of sarcasm. He sidled up to his grandfather and leaned over, his purplish hair streak almost touching Guy's shoulder. "I know what you're doing," he whispered.

Horrified, Guy looked wide-eyed at the possible new co-conspirator.

"I want pickles!" Dorothy called out.

Alex held his gaze with that certain eyebrow-furrowed frown that, between men, conveys understanding.

"What? What do you mean?" His voice rose several keys. He stabbed again and again at the bread with a peanut butter–laden knife. Guy's mind juggled questions and pieces of the puzzle. *Oh God. Dorothy must have told him!* With each distracted jab, the intended sandwich morphed into a more indistinguishable lump.

Guy glanced at his wife staring out the window—she seemed so content. Lost for a second, he fumbled his knife, and it clattered to the floor. "Whoa!" he exhaled. Palms spread wide, he took a deep breath and turned to his grandson with a pleading, tired look. *Now what? Is he going to stop me?*

Alex peeked over at his grandmother and shrugged his shoulders. "Hey, it's okay. I won't say anything. You do what you've got to do, right?"

Alex's words exploded in Guy's mind. *He knows! God, how could he be so calm? Does he even care?*

"Really?" Guy searched Alex's face but saw only a blasé teenager. "You understand that I'm going now too? I'm doing it with her." Guy choked on the words while gazing at the Olds.

"Of course you are. You have to. Who else is there to do it? I'll help you get her into the car."

Guy's feet wouldn't move. "Well, I guess so . . . I suppose it's no big deal to some people."

Alex didn't seem to hear him. Guy stood frozen as bulk concepts of family, love, and life spiraled down a mental drain.

A few minutes later, with rationalizations churning and a simmering distress at Alex's nonchalant approval of their death mission, Guy took Dorothy's arm and descended the front steps with his grandson behind him ferrying the mangled sandwiches. Before them, the waiting Olds beckoned, aloof and pretentious like a rolling sacrificial altar.

He dismissed all sorts of myriad dire images and forced his mouth into an improbable grin. *I'll step up to the plate, set my jaw into the wind, and stiffen my upper lip. Ha!* He gingerly explored his still-tender upper lip, cleared his throat, and blinked. *Whoa, boy, stay on track here. It's all new now.*

He settled Dorothy into the passenger seat and slipped behind the wheel. With the only cargo that mattered beside him, the pointless picnic food stashed in the rear seat, and himself ready for destiny, he turned to say a last goodbye. "You should call Mitch. Tell him what we're doing."

"Mitch? He doesn't care. Fuck that!" Alex crossed his arms.

Dorothy swiveled with a pleasant expression on her face. "Fuck that," she repeated in an innocent, soft whisper.

Guy's body jerked. Alex blanched at his gaffe.

"Oh . . . sorry." Alex leaned down to the driver's door and whispered, "I'll see you when you get back. I could walk to the store for something if you want. We need groceries. We're out of a few things. Grandma will drink milk, right? And I could use some Gatorade. Tell me what you need, and I'll go get it. I'd like to help." With a nod toward this grandmother, he drew closer. "I hope the doc has good news for you."

Dumbfounded, Guy stared in wonderment at the smiling young man—the same one who, moments before, had inferred that his grandparents ought to just run off and die. He dropped his gaze down to Alex's T-shirt of the day. Tiny block letters splayed across his torso read, HEY, SHITHEAD! IF YOU CAN READ THIS, BACK OFF! His eyes welled up in understanding. He wanted to slap himself for being so foolish and hug his grandson at the same time.

"Are you okay?" Alex zeroed in on Guy's face with that raised eyebrow again.

A bursting need to say more gripped Guy—to share his true feelings and life's lessons. Instead, he looked away. "Oh sure. I'm fine."

He sighed, hating the lie he was about to tell. "There's money in the top kitchen drawer. Go treat yourself. When we get back, we'll go out for dinner. How'd that be?"

Alex straightened up. "Yeah, cool."

With a poignant lump in his throat, Guy jerked a last salute to his grandson and guided his battered but still-proud convertible out of the driveway and on to her last voyage.

Mrs. Tooney stood in her side yard, grasping a shovel in one hand, the other one resting on her substantial hip. She frowned at the Olds as it sped by.

Guy waved an impassive backhand in her direction. *That's one thing in this world I won't miss.*

Attraction is like honey: sweet but sticky.

Alex viewed the Oldsmobile until it receded from sight, the right taillight bulb shining clear around the shattered red lens. *God, is everybody that weird when they get old?* He kept shaking his head, even after the car had vanished beyond a corner.

"No way. That's not going to happen to me."

He eyed the rocking chair with the bar clamp—it had loosened and slipped to one side. *I could take care of that.* He unwound the remaining threads, set the tool aside, and, after plucking a soda from the refrigerator, settled into his grandfather's favorite chair. He scanned the yard with a restless gaze.

After a moment of indecision, he headed for the downstairs bedroom, burrowed through his suitcase, and pulled out a sketch-pad. After returning to the porch, he contemplated the blank page, checked the pencil's sharpness, and began to draw. The outline of a World War II–era P-38 Lightning fighter took shape on paper. While drawing, his thoughts drifted to times long gone. He'd known this front porch his entire life. *The time Grandma and Grandpa surprised me on my birthday with a chocolate cake and a trip to Walt Disney World. And the time I cried my eyes out when it was time to leave. It's all so different now. Fuck!*

"Hello. What are you doing?" With his face buried in the sketchpad and his mind certainly elsewhere, he hadn't noticed the slender teenage girl approaching up the driveway until she was standing at the foot of the steps. One languid hand rested on her hip while she waited for an answer.

"Oh, uh . . . huh?" Alex jerked to attention and dropped his pencil. "Me? Nothing."

"Yes, you are. You're drawing something. My name is Amy. I live down the street. Can I see?"

He chanced a fleeting glance at the girl and his throat tightened. "This? I . . . well, I was only doodling."

Amy didn't wait for more of an invitation. She stepped up beside the rocking chair and peered at the nearly completed iconic war plane sketch. "Wow, that's cool. What's your name?"

"Alex . . . It's Alex."

"Do you fly in airplanes?"

"Me? Well, with my grandpa. We go up all the time." Alex grinned with bravado he didn't feel. "Yeah, we do," he said with a little less emphasis.

She leaned closer. "What's that on your neck?"

Alex's hand shot up and covered the spot. His face flushed red. "It's just a birthmark. No big deal."

Amy smiled. "Kind of looks like Texas."

"I get that a lot."

"Your grandparents are different." She pointed across the street. "I saw your grandfather, probably your grandmother too, sitting in their car in the flower bed over there. It looked like they crashed backward." One side of her lip curled upward.

"That? I guess it was just an accident. But yeah, strange."

"What are you doing here?"

"What am I doing? Uh, I guess I'm just visiting. I'm supposed to help out."

"Help with what?"

He paused and gauged this new person. She seemed easy to talk to. Her blonde hair hung in a straight cut past her shoulders, and she wore a purple tank top with jean shorts. She looked pretty and kind of cool. He felt he could trust her. "They're old. And my grandma is sick. It's pretty screwed up."

"Sorry to hear that." She twirled her hair between her fingers. "My parents are so boring, they put each other to sleep."

"Family. We're stuck with them." Alex rolled his eyes.

Amy nodded her agreement. Your grandfather's car is a convertible. "Do you drive?"

Alex puffed up his chest. "Well, you know. When I want to."

She broke into a broad smile. "Rad! I've never even sat in a convertible. Take me for a ride someday?"

"Sure, yeah. That would be great."

Amy glanced back at the street. "I've gotta go. My dad always freaks out when I'm gone for two seconds. Did I mention screwy?" She looked him up and down. "I'll see you later."

She wiggled a few fingers in Alex's direction and sauntered down the steps and away. With an unfamiliar nervousness in his gut, he eyed her catlike movements while she sashayed away.

13

When at first you don't succeed, try,
try and . . . oh, give up and go home.

The new plan was off and running. The drive to the mini-mart with two gas pumps took only a couple of minutes. A quick stop for a few gallons, and down the road he and Dorothy sailed, central Florida's heat and humidity blowing across them like a moist furnace. Today was perfect for a top-down ride in the country.

The highway snaked out of town and veered north, toward the nineteen thousand acres of open marshland in Woodruff Refuge. Eventually, the subdivisions thinned out and gave way to scattered houses, then opened up to meadows dotted with only an occasional residence.

For Guy, life's harsh reality eased its relentless crush. His shoulders relaxed and his hands loosened around the steering wheel as the breeze lifted his spirits. The moment took on a rare quality as he allowed nature to nurture his being. The seductive feeling of wind and sun, coupled with the landscape's visual beauty, captivated his attention, and last week's concerns faded away. He eyed Dorothy with her hair being tossed every which way as they barreled down the road. Her face, although concentrated, appeared peaceful.

Fantastic. She looks content. Soon, her suffering will be over, and I won't be worrying about a thing either. It's all sort of . . . good. He reached over and patted Dorothy's knee. "Everything is going to be fine, dear. We're together."

"Yes, you're here . . . I can see you," she said. "But I forget: We're headed for which picnic?"

"Right now, honey, let's just enjoy the ride," he said. "It's a beautiful day." *I better get back to the plan.*

He turned onto a narrow side road and considered several large trees. Graceful sycamores, towering oaks, fragrant pines, and dense bunches of mangroves whizzed past, some with long limbs drooping to the ground. *Not the right one. Not yet.* He checked all of them. *Just find a tree close to the road and mature enough to stop a speeding lump of Detroit steel. God! This is so perfectly terrible!*

"Guy. Where are we going?" Dorothy gathered the shawl around her neck, suddenly seeming confused.

Uh-oh. He looked over as she shifted her body in the seat, wincing in discomfort. *This has to happen while she's having fun.* Concentrating, he picked up the pace, still not seeing the perfect combination of tree and approach.

With a flash of irritation, he remembered the letter in his pocket, crumpled and smeared with mustard and mayonnaise. *The note will have to do, but it should not be in my pants. Easier to find in the basket, and cleaner too.* He bit his lower lip with the vision and plunged his right hand deep into his Levi's, retrieving the envelope. He swiveled, stretching his arm back over the seat, barely reaching the picnic basket. His fingertips fumbled with the lid . . .

A tremendous thump shocked the Olds, and a brown blur flashed by the passenger door. Dorothy let out a soft cry as the car swerved and screeched. Guy fought the wheel with one hand, the other shooting across Dorothy's chest to protect her. He still managed to keep the vehicle going straight.

The Olds slowed, and it took him only a second more to know what had happened. He braked to a stop on the wide shoulder, shoved the transmission into park, and switched off the engine.

"Are you okay, honey?" He scanned Dorothy for signs of injury.

She looked pale and a bit shaken but otherwise fine. Only one fresh pain to add to the list—Guy's knee throbbed from hitting the steering column.

"Did we kill a deer?" Dorothy's tenuous, strained voice cracked through the silence.

"I think so. You wait here. I'll check it out."

He exited the car and limped the hundred feet to the quivering animal. Its head lay on the hot pavement and its haunches on the graveled shoulder. He threw up his hands. "Stupid deer! Why now? Of all times!"

The young buck lay at his feet. Guy watched the slight rib cage rising and falling and heard the sound of the death rattle. *He's not dead yet.* Kneeling beside the fallen animal, he shivered at the contorted way in which its body lay and the blood seeping from the mouth. He flashed on the paradox that he and Dorothy would have looked much worse if the poor thing hadn't jumped out in front of them. *Only got a minute or two to live.*

The deer's fixated black iris seemed to register Guy's presence. He had never meant to become a killer. Well . . . he had. But not to an innocent deer. Unblinking, it gazed back at him. He inched closer, trying not to look threatening.

Guy waited in limbo, somehow fascinated, watching and listening to the dying buck. A blue jay scolded from a nearby treetop. Down the shallow embankment, the wind rustled the dense brush that an eternity ago had hidden this deer.

Like a rogue wave, emotion washed over him. *This is awful.* A stab of pain attacked his knee, and, unbalanced, he fell onto his rear end beside the fading life. Before him lay the raw spectacle of death, which, mere moments before, he had sought for himself. Life's shadow side, with its dark beckoning peace, swept him away in a tide of sorrow. His eyes brimmed, and he broke down and cried for the animal; he cried for his beloved wife; he cried for himself. On the edge of this country road, he let it all out.

Dorothy silently shuffled up from the Olds and stood behind him. Guy snapped to attention, struggled to stand, and finally made it to his feet. He brushed the back of his pants, cleared his throat, and wiped at his tears. She studied his face and took his hand but didn't say a word.

They remained standing together in silence for a minute more, two bent figures watching a final breath. When the deer heaved its last, Dorothy shattered the remnants of Guy's plan. "We're not leaving him here."

Guy knew from many years of hearing it that this particular tone brought finality to any discussion. Even so, full-sized red flags sprung up in his head, and he had to protest. "Honey, we have to leave him. There's nothing we can do for him." To get back on the road was important—already two cars had slowed, then sped away.

"Honey, sweetie pie." He tried one last time with a billboard-worthy grin.

Dorothy shook off Guy's excuses. "He's special. I saw you bonding with him. He deserves a decent burial at least."

"I can't bury him out here," Guy squeaked. "I don't even have a shovel."

"Then we'll take him home. Put him in the ground out by the garden." Her words were a proclamation. "You have to do things proper. You should know that by now. I'm getting back in the car." With that, she turned and made her way back toward the Olds.

Guy felt the battle slipping away and rubbed his temples. Arguing was useless. *This makes no sense. But what does anymore?* The ill-timed, bloody diversion lay at his feet, mocking him. But there was still hope. *If I can somehow get it into the trunk, it's back to the plan.*

Within a minute of backing his car up to the lifeless deer, he caught a break. A small sedan packed with smiling faces slowed and rolled to a stop beside them. The dented compact's cheap speakers blared out smooth Latino crooning. The driver, a local who looked like he had seen many roadside happenings in his native country, leaned out the window and scanned the scene.

The driver and three more men piled out of the tiny car and sur-rounded the motionless deer, nodding their approval of Guy's score.

"*Bueno, señor.*" The driver gave a thumbs-up. "Mouths to feed at home, no?"

Guy's mouth stretched into a grimace, and he gave a reluctant shrug. Using the limited Spanish he'd gleaned from years of living in Florida, Guy managed to half-speak, half-mime his request for help in loading the hefty beast into the Oldsmobile. "*Por favor* . . . please . . . this deer . . . help me into car . . . automobile. *Sí?*" He bent over, grabbed the deer's hindquarters, and jerked his head toward the Olds. Mean-while, the oldest among the men idled up to the Olds's passenger side and tipped his sweaty straw hat at Dorothy. She glared at him with the chill of a captured raptor, and he slunk away embarrassed.

After a semicoherent exchange with Guy, the driver shrugged and spoke in brisk Spanish to the others. As if he had just delivered a killer punchline, the group erupted in laughter with much celebratory back slapping. They gathered around the deer and waited for Guy to open the trunk.

Guy pounded, tugged, wrestled, and grunted, but it soon became obvious that the previous day's carnage had rendered the trunk lid inoperable; it wouldn't budge. He knew his new friends would not wait long, so he swept his arm at the only option left. With total chagrin written all over his face, he clenched his teeth and pointed at the back seat.

The committee studied the classic car's pristine leather interior, looked at each other, and shook their heads no. But an even more horrified Guy kept gnashing his teeth and jabbing a finger at the Olds's interior. After a long beat, the driver spewed a rapid-fire stream of instructions.

The four men jumped to grab different parts of the animal, and with a spirited hoist, the bloody buck dropped into position behind Dorothy. She nodded her approval.

Guy looked on the proceedings with a kind of grateful horror. *Oh well, whatever it takes. But today, if I can pull off the plan, people will forever wonder why there was a dead deer alongside us.*

A buck didn't fit in an Olds 88 like he had imagined. The animal's head, topped by its budding antlers, lolled over the upper edge of the door with its hooves sticking straight up, two feet higher than the seat backs. The unfortunate visual impression was one of a drunken buck getting a ride home—but the most important thing—the deer was literally on board with the plan.

Guy pumped each man's hands. "*Gracias, gracias, mi amigos.* Thank you, thank you."

Within seconds, the four men had piled back into the rusty compact, and with much laughter and waving, they chugged away.

Guy stood and listened to the fading sounds of the tubas and accordions. He stared after them, dazed and numb until they disappeared around a corner.

He slowly turned to survey the damage to his car: a scuffed and dented rear end with broken taillights, a crushed right front fender with a missing headlight, and a dead buck overflowing the backseat and leaking blood all over the upholstery. He blew out a long exhale and glared upward, searching for any sign of a heavenly omnipresence. "What the hell is going on?" He added a quick, "I'm sorry," to the Oldsmobile gods.

Now, back to business! He squared his shoulders and tried to ignore the rising pain in his knee where it had hit the dash. It wouldn't matter for long.

As he slid back behind the wheel, he paused, took a breath, and stared straight ahead. The odds for success today were diminishing by the minute. *One last try.*

The rear tires sprayed gravel as he floored the accelerator. The buck rolled and rocked in the backseat. *It doesn't get any wackier than this.* The buck's head seemed to bounce in agreement.

He glanced over at Dorothy; her face was stiff with alarm.

"Guy, slow down! What are you doing? You're hurting the deer!"

He knew that as her pain increased, so did her irrationality. But the intensity and volume of her voice surprised him. He looked over, straight into her frightened eyes, and knew it couldn't happen this way. He would not tolerate any pain or stress of any sort accompanying her ending, so he took his foot off the gas and slumped in his seat.

We keep on living. What a nightmare. He peered back at his unwelcome carjacker. *How come he gets to die and we don't?*

With a reluctant sigh, he lightened his grip on the steering wheel and cruised at a moderate pace through the now-taunting landscape until pulling a U-turn. They were not out of the woods yet, in any sense. He still had to drive home with an impaired wife and a deceased animal passenger and later conduct a feral funeral.

He reached a numb hand out and switched on the radio. "Please! Let there be some goddamn golden oldies!"

Butterflies at the pearly gates.

Thirty minutes later, Guy, grateful to be home but dreading what was coming next, backed the Olds into the driveway, came to a stop in front of the open garage, and switched off the engine.

For a long minute, he sat motionless, listening to pinging from the Olds's contracting metal. He finally craned his neck around to re-establish his grip on the reality of a deceased deer lazily sprawled in the back seat. Swiveling back to his slumbering wife, he was relieved to see at least both of them were at peace. He leaned his head back against the seat and stared up at the gathering dusk as it swallowed the last light. The television's glow coming from the den's windows gave him an unexpected comfort—Alex was there. *Excellent. I'll need some help.*

As if on cue, Alex's face appeared in the kitchen window. Within seconds, he pushed his way out the screen door and stopped in his tracks at the sight of the young and quite dead deer crammed into the car's rear seat.

Guy waved his grandson forward with encouraging hand signals.

"We've got to get your grandma inside and make her comfortable," he said. "Look at her. She's all done in." He smiled at his wife and spun back to Alex with the face of a grinning beat-up dystopian snake oil salesman. "And then, would you please help me with a funeral for this lucky animal?" Guy jerked a thumb at the buck and stared deadpan into Alex's face. "Nothing fancy. We'll dig a hole, and I suppose some candles and special words. Maybe you could think of something to say?"

"What?" Alex retreated a step, his face contorted with horror at the scene. "No way I'm touching that thing."

"Son, it's plain to see this appears a bit out of the ordinary, but I could really use your help and no comments." Guy waited for an answer.

Alex cast another sour look at the dead buck's lifeless eyes and thrust his hands in his pockets. He exhaled with emphasis. "Okay, okay. Whatever. First time for everything."

"Thanks." Guy rubbed his chin. "Just a warning. I may not be able to explain."

"Hey, why start now?" Alex muttered.

"We need to move her inside first." Guy said as he slid his hands under his wife's torso and legs with great care.

"Honey, we're getting you into the house," he said in a tender voice, just above a whisper. "Hold tight."

Five minutes later, Guy deposited Dorothy near the kitchen in her favorite overstuffed chair. After receiving her blanket, she waved the men off with funeral instructions.

Under a starry sky, Alex and Guy found themselves standing on opposite sides of the Olds, pondering and peering at the lifeless buck. Guy pointed past the herb patch to an area that, after years of Dorothy's vegetable gardening, had the softest soil in the entire yard.

"Sorry, but we gotta bury him," he murmured. "It's important to keep her happy."

Alex looked aghast. "You know, everybody except you just leaves roadkill beside the road."

A silence hung in the air like an apathetic pendulum. Guy kept glaring at his grandson. He knew Alex was too young to understand the depth of Guy and Dorothy's bond.

"Okay, okay," Alex grunted.

Without another word, they each grasped a pair of hooves, and, after a cumbersome and labored pull and tug, they managed to deposit the carcass near the fence.

Guy retrieved two shovels from the garage and held one out. Alex looked at Guy, looked at the ground, looked at the buck, and back to Guy. He gawked at the shovel, then shook his head, grabbed the handle, and sank it a few inches into the earth with one listless hand. He blew out a last meaningful, nonverbal protest and jumped on the shovel with both feet.

The digging went on in silence for a half hour, with Guy taking more breaks than Alex. Finally, Guy judged the hole deep enough. "This'll do it, Alex. Let's get this thing in the ground."

Alex peeked at his grandfather and broke into his first smile of the evening. "Grandpa," he panted, "this is certified nuts."

Guy paused and leaned on his shovel. If he'd had it his way, someone else would be digging his grave by now. *My, how the wheel turns.* "Sure is! And damn, I'm glad you're with me in this parallel universe." He gestured toward the kitchen door. "She's probably asleep already, so we won't have to do any funeral thing. We'll just get him in there and cover him. That will be that."

———

The activity at the Pickering house had not gone unnoticed. Izetta's stepniece Lisa Marie, a vivacious, early-thirties woman, almost spilled the wine she was pouring into a glass as Izetta's head jerked up when the Olds's headlight swept past her front windows. Her eyes narrowed to mere slits. She pressed up against the window and craned her neck a fraction to peer over a shrub. "I wonder why Pickering is backing his car in the driveway. He never does that."

Lisa Marie shook her head at her nutty aunt. "Why does it matter?" She held up the bottle. "Here, let me top you off."

"I don't trust that man." Izetta held out her glass behind her with her forehead still pressed against the windowpane. "No doubt getting ready to make a frontal attack this time," she snorted her disdain. "And oh my God, there's his wife, and she looks just *awful*. Not even moving!"

Lisa Marie peeked over her aunt's head in the direction she was facing. A smallish limp woman was being carried out of the car. The moonlight reflected off her too-pale skin, and her cheeks looked hollow.

Straightening up, Izetta's eyes roamed the room. "Dear, do you happen to see a pair of binoculars lying around here somewhere?"

"Auntie Izetta, forget your silly neighbor." Lisa Marie shrugged off her impatience and held up her glass. "I can't stay long, but today is my uncle Fred's birthday, and I miss him. I thought I'd stop by for a visit and ask if you've had any word from him." She gave her aunt a hopeful look. "It's been—what—three years?"

"Can you believe, after twelve years of marriage, a man just up and runs off?" Izetta flopped onto the couch and downed the remaining wine. "He wrote a letter a few months ago from Nicaragua."

"Oh, what did he say?"

"It wasn't very nice."

"I see . . ." Lisa Marie looked away to the ceiling hoping, but failing, to stave off any further personal details.

After enduring a few nonstop verbal minutes, Lisa Marie got a word in edgewise. "Well, let's toast to a new beginning," she said, refilling their wine glasses.

Izetta didn't wait to clink glasses before taking a gulp. She leaned back on a pillow and then straightened up, pulling her binoculars from underneath. "Oh, yes. Those Pickerings." She rushed to the window, her backside extending behind her and the curtains swallowing her face. "What are they doing now?"

"Izetta . . . Auntie? Come sit down. Let's enjoy the last bit of cheese and crackers I brought." Lisa Marie held up the almost empty plate she had been snacking on as her aunt spoke.

"Poor woman, I think she's not well, and I suspect he just wants to be rid of her. I don't trust him at all. Did I mention that before?"

"Oh, Auntie, that stuff only happens on TV." Lisa Marie took another sip of wine.

"I'm telling you. Yesterday, he crashed his car right into my yard with her in the front seat. You should have seen her. She looked awful."

"Here, give me those binoculars." Lisa Marie trained the lenses out the window. "Hmmm. I think they're digging a hole in their yard. Wouldn't it be just priceless if it were like one of those cop shows and they were actually burying her?"

"Oh my God!" Izetta slapped her forehead. "You might be right. The poor thing must have done an outlandish deed again, and Pickering and that purple-headed hooligan went ahead and killed her."

"Auntie, please. I was just joking. It's probably nothing." Lisa Marie's gaze strayed back across the street. "But . . . you think so?"

"You've always had a good head on you. And a phenomenal sense of intuition."

"Really?" Lisa Marie flung a handful of hair from her shoulder.

"Yes. And listen to this. He told me straight to my face that she would not be here much longer. I think they're really burying her."

"Jeez." Lisa Marie pondered this. She couldn't deny that sounded possible.

"It's also possible they accidentally killed her, and now they're panicking. I saw an episode on TV like that! They can't get away with it! You're a reporter, aren't you?" Izetta blurted the words, more of an accusation than a question.

"Well, yes. For now, all I report is traffic up there in the whirlybird." Lisa Marie gazed upward. "I'm frustrated with my career and hoping that—"

Izetta cut her off. "Well, here's a story for you!" She leaned closer, her voice straining with excitement. "Murder!" She scrutinized Lisa Marie's face. "Someone has to expose them. You're the one," she said, and tossed back the last splash of wine. "I'll help. Follow me."

Lured by the addictive promise of a breaking news report, Lisa Marie, flushed with confusion, excitement, and wine, tiptoed behind her aunt out the front door and into the pitch black.

———

"Have the mourners come?" Dorothy's voice rang from deep inside the house. "I don't care for Susie Babcock and her two-faced sister, Irene. Do not let them sit in front!"

Guy's attention swiveled to the windows. "Oh God, she's awake. No doubt checking to make sure we do the job right." He spun and headed for the garage. "There's candles in here. Nothing like show business."

A few minutes later, the requisite layer of dirt lay heaped up on the newly departed. Since Guy had miscalculated the hole size, a mound now rose a good foot higher than the rest of the garden. In a hasty affirmation of ritual, grandfather and grandson lit the votive candles and settled into a semicomfortable reverence around the impromptu grave.

"Dear Lord, we come here tonight to give back one hell of a stupid buck." Guy glanced at the windows. "I didn't know him long, but—"

Alex stifled a snicker. Guy stared at him.

"I'm sorry," Alex chuckled. "But I'm questioning our family's DNA."

"You want to add something?" Guy's eyes, both perturbed and expectant, bored into the young man.

Alex shrugged and contemplated the garden's new lump. "I have a question."

Guy waited.

"Is there a heaven?"

Guy chuffed. "This is not the time for that kind of talk. We just have to do this."

"Yeah, I get it, but I want to know."

"Get in line, buddy. What do *you* think?"

Alex stared at the candle in his hands. "I'm not sure, but I think there is . . . for people anyway. But what about him? You know, like, for animals." Alex nudged the mound with his foot. "What happens to them? Where do they go?" A flying insect flitted in front of his face, diverting his attention. He waved it aside. "Even butterflies. Do butterflies go to a special heaven?"

"First of all, that was a moth." Guy rolled his eyes skyward. "Yeah, I can just see a bunch of butterflies lined up at the pearly gates. And how am I supposed to know?" *Yeah. Shit. That's a good question.*

Alex frowned at the deer mound, and another moment passed until Guy broke the silence, speaking just above a whisper.

"Okay . . . I figure there's some kind of great big goodness on the other side. Probably beyond anything we can imagine, and everybody and everything goes there." Guy stopped, grunted, and pointed at the guest of honor. "Now get back to saying some lovely words for this dude."

Alex bowed his head. "Well, God . . . these things happen. It wasn't my grandpa's fault. I guess it was this deer's time." He shifted the candle to the other hand. "It's fucked up, but sometimes it's people's time, and they have to go too." He glanced up at his grandfather. Neither moved an inch.

———

Lisa Marie trailed behind Izetta, weaving through the shadows, shrubs, and trees alongside the old wooden fence at the far side of the Pickering driveway, and slowed her pace, experiencing some misgivings.

"Wait, Auntie." Lisa Marie tugged at Izetta's sleeve. "I'm not sure about this. It's a little bizarre."

"They can't get away with murder," Izetta hissed as she pulled Lisa Marie forward. "Not on our watch!"

"Yes, of course. I guess you're right," Lisa Marie's steely eyes focused on the disheveled Pickering yard. *Holy shit show. This could be real news.*

With her heart pounding and her arms flailing at spiderwebs and dangling branches, Lisa Marie crept closer, flanked by her aunt and drawn by flickering candles and murmured words.

No more tentative steps; Lisa Marie felt the rush of an unfolding story and took the lead. She stormed past the Olds and stopped cold, facing her astonished perpetrators. "Aha!" She aimed her cell phone camera at the pair. "Caught ya! I'm a reporter!"

She paused, waiting for their dark confession. Instead, the purple-tinged teen stepped forward.

"You don't look like one," he said.

She brushed the cracker crumbs clinging to her shirt and fought past the wine buzz. Then, Lisa Marie straightened up. "Well, I certainly am one."

Izetta came bustling up beside her. "She's on TV, and we caught you red-handed! We get what you're up to, and you fellas are in big trouble!" She flicked her finger at them. "Lisa Marie, these two are the Pickering murderers."

Just then, the missing, frail-looking old lady Lisa Marie had seen being carried inside threw aside a screen door, limped over to the railing, and scowled at her neighbor. "Hush up, Izetta! Mind your manners!" She shifted her gaze to Lisa Marie. "Who's the bimbo?"

Lisa Marie peeked down at her low-cut blouse and flushed red.

"Guy," the old lady said, "is he in heaven yet?"

"Yes, he is, honey," the older Pickering said. "The funeral is all done. You can go to bed now." He raised his palms up and gave a slight wave.

They all gaped at the woman as she grunted her disapproval and shuffled inside the house.

A few seconds of gilded silence followed.

Lisa Marie slowly lowered her phone. "What's going on here?" she squeaked, feeling her chance at a newsworthy story evaporate in thin air.

The old Pickering glared at Mrs. Tooney. "Izetta, so nice of you to drop by. And you brought a friend." His eyes shifted from the women to the suspect pile of dirt. "Oh, that? That's a nosy neighbor I caught in my yard."

The teenage Pickering raised his hand. "Hold on. Just a dead deer. See?" He strode over to the mound and kicked at the loose soil, exposing a hoof.

"But how? Why?" Lisa Marie blanched.

The teen's arm shot out with a pointed a finger at the battered Olds.

"Fine job of reporting neighborhood crime there, young lady! Way to go!" The old Pickering's words hit her like an out-of-control TV news van.

Batting her eyes repeatedly, she cleared her throat. "What you're doing has got to be against some rules somewhere. You're not supposed to kill animals and bury them in city limits, or something. I'll be checking on you!" To her chagrin, her voice wavered as she delivered her last line.

"Well, how about you do that from a distance? Quite a distance." The old Pickering took a step in their direction. "Huh?"

"Auntie, we're leaving right now." Lisa Marie clamped onto Izetta's elbow.

Izetta let out a final disapproving exhalation as they both retreated across the street.

From the safety of Izetta's living room, Lisa Marie contemplated her silent and bewildered-looking auntie, now collapsed on the sofa.

"I think it's safe to say that didn't turn out the way we envisioned."

Izetta only frowned. "I still don't trust those Pickering men."

"Yeah, I agree." Lisa Marie's face set into a stone-like visage. "I don't like them at all."

Lisa Marie peered through the window. The older Pickering was running his hand over the fenders of that beat-up old car. Then, he waved to the younger one and went inside the house.

She couldn't figure out why, for the longest time, the teen just stood staring up at the sky.

PERRYTON, TENNESSEE
SEPTEMBER 1952

When love breaks a heart, even the flowers weep.

Guy guided an assorted pile of groceries forward, toward the cashier at Simner's market—Dorothy. Back home after a monthlong trip helping out on his uncle's Texas farm, he had planned this shopping trip for days.

"Well, hello, stranger," she grinned.

"Hi, uh . . . you work here?" He faked surprise while shifting from foot to foot.

One hand on the cash register and a can of peas in the other, Dorothy paused and studied his face. "Yeah," she said. "I'm saving up to help with college. I still want to go." She pushed the heavy paper sack across the counter to him and hesitated, taking a moment to weigh her detachment from earlier plans.

Guy fidgeted, distracted by the next man in line, who inched his box of cornflakes forward in an annoying manner.

"My break is in a minute. Wait outside for me," she said, motioning through the windows to the parking lot.

Five minutes later, she pressed through the front doors, sans the blue work apron, chewing on a tuna fish sandwich. She sauntered up to Guy. "Want a bite?" She held up the other half. "And where have you been?"

He chanced a sideways glance at her face—the childhood freckles on her nose were fading, her hair longer. "No, thanks, not hungry. I've been down to Abilene for most of the summer at my aunt and uncle's place." Her body seemed fuller, not so innocent anymore, pushing outward from behind her blouse, new Keds on her feet.

"No wonder I haven't seen you." She dabbed at her mouth with a handkerchief. "That's in Texas?"

"Yeah, they needed me on the ranch. Extra work, you know." Guy slumped against the once-red farm truck and lifted his eyes to the South, hoping to be admired for his travels—at least he'd gotten out of town for a while. "I might go back for another spell."

"I missed you." Dorothy's body tensed, and her voice took on a singular edge. "You're as much a part of this place as any of us, you dummy. Don't just go run off and . . ." The half-eaten sandwich swung toward the outside world. She let her words trail off while maintaining a bantam pout.

Guy struggled, as he always had, to understand Dorothy's message. "Well, how are *you* doing?" He extended the question like a risky poker bet, then, with forced nonchalance, shoved all the chips to the center with, "How's Marvin doing?" He shifted on his feet and propped an arm against the hot fender with exaggerated indifference.

"Oh, he's okay. Busy. You remember: He's working for his dad. Gave him that new car." She shrugged and tossed the uneaten bits of lunch into a bush. "He's nice to me most of the time. I don't know. And heck, you're not around." She scrutinized his face. "Almost a ghost."

"Well, I . . . maybe . . ." Even after months of thinking about things to say to her, Guy couldn't quite get the right words out.

Dorothy grinned, then peered at the interior behind Simner's glass doors. She flicked her hand toward the store. "I've got to get back." She straightened up, turned to him with a flicker in her eyes, and reached out, fingers lingering on Guy's forearm. "Don't be such a stranger, will ya?" She shot him a frown and grabbed a stray grocery cart.

He watched her wheel it to the store's entrance and shove it into a clanging reunion with its steel-wired family. She waved to him before disappearing through the doors.

A week later, Guy rose early on a Sunday morning and sat in his kitchen, reminiscing about the smell of fresh cookies and talk of chores from long ago. Now, with his mom gone, he had only the ceiling's cobwebs and barren jars. Out the window, an abandoned garden patch appeared dry, choked with weeds and shriveled tomatoes.

From the barn came the shrill whine of the grinding wheel. He knew that Lloyd kept his ancient scythe and shears razor sharp, even though they were seldom used anymore. The family farm had become too large for one Pickering and too small to be viable in the postwar years. Something needed to change.

He bolted from the chair. "I think I'll go to church."

It only took a half hour to arrive in town, and now Guy sat drumming his fingers on the farm pickup's steering wheel. From his vantage point in the far corner of the First Baptist Church's parking lot, he contemplated the people coming and going through the tall front doors. Kids chased each other up and down the steps and across the sweeping front lawn. Some families had already come and gone, but Guy stayed put—he was not ready.

Eighteen months had passed since he had last stepped inside this church. A hard rain had pounded the ground that day—Molly

Pickering's memorial service. The pews had overflowed with solemn faces, firm handshakes, and devout adages whispered with unpracticed deliberateness, all designed to convey sympathy for his loss. With time's compassionate balm, the funeral's fresh sting had dulled into an often-remembered ache he carried in the depths of his body—an unseen scar.

But in truth, it wasn't the memory of his mother's passing that brought so much trepidation to him today. It was the certainty that Dorothy Benson was here. The Bensons showed up every month at the Sunday afternoon social. They had a reputation to uphold.

The truck's interior soon grew too hot to remain inside. He wrestled with the passenger window's broken handle one more time, hoping for a miracle—it hadn't rolled down in two years. The church's entrance doors beckoned while Guy's shirt continued to dampen. He gave up on the window and instead cracked open the driver's door, and with the tentativeness of a burglar's first step into a darkened house, he set a polished boot on the pavement.

With a flourish of resolve, he slammed the door shut behind him and marched with deliberate strides toward the church's imposing doorway. "I'm going in there."

"Well, heavens be blessed. It's Guy Pickering," the pulpit-practiced voice boomed from the front steps. "Good to see you, son. The Lord welcomes you again to his house. Let's catch up soon, shall we?" Reverend Meehan, an immense man, seemingly born with a perpetual smile, slapped him on the shoulder. "There's still plenty of food. Help yourself. We love the errant bird that comes back to the nest." The reverend nudged him toward a hallway folding table stationed by gray-haired women and turned to beam his aura onto the next in line.

"So nice to see you, young man." Irene (or Iona—Guy couldn't recall her name) goggled at him as the woman beside her hunched over a stick-on paper label. She struggled to block letter Guy's full name—the *ing* wound up squeezed into the southeast corner. He assured the ladies how wonderful it was to be standing there, pasted the badge of belonging on his chest, sidestepped a group of squealing five-year-olds, and stepped into the fluorescent-lit recreation hall. The low-ceilinged room buzzed with the weekend devout milling around, eating sweets and catching up on all the latest. Children darted in between cloth-draped tables and clumps of elders leaning toward each other and shouting to be heard above the din.

He couldn't miss her. Dorothy stood with her back toward him, talking to a girl on the far side of the room. Beyond the sea of tables and chairs, the late afternoon sun streamed through the nearby windows and illuminated her hair, mesmerizing him like the shimmer of a delicate beacon.

He stared, chewed on his lip, and didn't move a muscle until the voice of the reverend's wife, Myrtle Meehan, cut through the air. "Oh, dear me, if it isn't Guy Pickering! Come. You must say hello." She made a stab at grabbing his arm. A quick glimpse revealed a half dozen matronly women with identical smiles waiting for him opposite a starched white refreshment counter.

"Yes, I'll be back in just a minute." He held up a finger, pretending to recognize someone in the crowd, and weaved his way to a corner table—a round lily pad of gingham in a pond of chattering folk.

After a moment's exaggerated smiling in all directions, he turned his attention to the table's sole other occupant. A freckly, redheaded young woman of around eighteen years of age sat staring at him. Guy inclined his head to the girl and offered a friendly hand wave, then snuck a glance at Dorothy. He drummed his fingers on the tabletop, crossed and uncrossed his long legs, but threw more fleeting glimpses across the room at her.

The silent girl next to him swiveled her gaze in the direction that he had been looking. She pivoted back to Guy, her unblinking stare once again boring into him.

"Go on." She delivered her words in a soft, deliberate directive, untainted by doubt.

Huh? He cocked his head.

"Go!" The voice blew against him like a puff of wind urging him on. Without breaking eye contact, she jerked her head toward Dorothy.

He didn't dare look away from her as he rose from the table and nodded his understanding. *How did she know?*

Guided by renewed inspiration and hope that he was doing the right thing, he wound his way through the random townsfolk, careful not to get snagged in their acknowledgement of his surprise attendance.

As he approached, Dorothy's two girlfriends hugged her, turned, and waved goodbye to the group. Guy sensed his time had come. Dorothy was alone and gathering her purse, preparing to leave. It was now or never. He dug as deep as any farm boy could, summoning an unpracticed but instinctual courage for courtship. He took a couple of steps forward—and, as if averted by detoured tracks, succumbed to the safety of the nearby refreshment table.

I'll get her some punch. Guy's heart raced as he pretended to listen to the chatty women in front of him and poured the drink into two Dixie cups. Nodding and mouthing a lame, "Great to be here," he spun around.

In his haste, he'd failed to notice that Dorothy, sporting a flirty smile, had snuck up behind him. As he swung around, the cups thumped into the soft front of Dorothy's new chiffon dress, splashing the fruity liquid all over her bodice.

She gasped, staring at her purple-blotched torso. Guy's ears pulled back—his entire face stretched outward to the edges in a horrific cringe. In a flustered panic, he grabbed a handful of napkins and, to make it right, dabbed wherever he saw color.

"Hey there! It's customary to take me on a date first!" Dorothy brushed his hand away and shot him a stony pout.

Guy froze, realized what he was doing, and dropped the damp paper to the floor. He couldn't look at her and mumbled an inaudible apology.

Dorothy forced a smile at a few bystanders. "So," she began in a casual tone, "is *that* the way you treat the ladies in your life? You toss punch on them and then wipe them down?"

"No . . . No . . . I don't." He felt the burn in his cheeks. "I'm sorry. I was bringing it to you."

"You were? Well, that's different then, isn't it? Thank you, I guess."

Their eyes met, and he was relieved to see an easy grin on her face. She was teasing him, as usual.

"Come outside with me. I have news." Dorothy hooked his hand and led him to the church's side door.

Guy took one last peek over his shoulder at the redheaded girl, still sitting at the table. She continued to stare at him, but this time, she bore a faint smile.

Tall sycamore trees provided shade to the church's back steps, and a cool breeze blessed Guy's face after the heated embarrassment of moments before. Dorothy motioned for him to sit with her, and they sat in silence for a minute as a family gathered their children and left. Then, she twisted to gain his attention.

"I would like to invite you to my wedding. Marvin has asked me to marry him." She searched his face for a reaction.

An ice pick stab to Guy's heart took his words away. His eyes darted around the churchyard, trying to hide his shock.

"Well, I got tired of waiting for you, sir." Her timid smile faded, along with her words.

He struggled to keep back a bitter, rising tide. "Congratulations," he rasped. His ears pounded with the fresh blood of a wounded dream.

In an apologetic-sounding voice, she added, "It's in two weeks. Will you come?"

Guy could not imagine, under any circumstance, attending Dorothy's wedding. "Why are you marrying him?" The sharpness in his tone was unintended, and he reddened at his reaction.

Dorothy slid her fingers along the pleats of her dress. "Well, you know he's got that job now, running equipment for his father and . . ." Another pause. "He tells me he loves me." She didn't look up.

Guy recoiled. "Is that all it takes?" he said—the ropes of self-doubt tightening around his stomach—a child left behind by a departing bus.

Dorothy's face flushed. She looked away, tears brimming in her eyes. "There's something else. It would be good for us," she said, her voice on edge. "Things just happen."

"What are you saying? I don't . . ."

"He just . . . Oh, never mind."

Guy's body jolted with comprehension. He knew what she was *not* saying. He threw an arm around her shoulder and drew her to him. Dorothy was pregnant.

Guy couldn't speak. He ran his hand over a bruise on her wrist. Her hands were so beautiful to him and so far away. Nothing was said. A type of lucent silence passed between them, but something beyond the scope of words gripped Guy—a tender closeness and a parting at the same time. He wouldn't fully know or understand it until much later.

With the sun fading, Guy knew he would never go to this wedding. In this instant, the hanging indecision regarding the farm and his father was also resolved. He wanted to be gone from this place. But right now, this moment was still here. What he wanted more than anything was to hold Dorothy in his arms, right here, in the back of the First Baptist Church—for this moment to last and last.

He took a hold of her shoulders and gently spun her toward him. "But I love you," he blurted, shocking even himself—pulled by a looming pit of disappearing hope. There was nothing to lose and nothing to gain, and he spoke without thinking. "I never told you."

Dorothy blinked, taken aback. Her lower lip quivered, and she forced a veneer of composure. "Oh, Guy, you're so silly! What am I going to do with you?" She took his hand; he squeezed back. "I have to run now. I do. But I'm going to watch out for you, Guy Pickering." With streaming tears, she leaned into his cheek with a lingering kiss. Hiding her mouth, she fled down the few steps to the lawn and beyond.

She was gone.

"I do love you," Guy whispered into the wind.

———

Two days later, Guy sat in the farm's somber-feeling kitchen with his father. "Well, son, I'll miss ya. I sure as hell will." Lloyd paused and lit his pipe. Silence and smoke added meaning and weight to the moment—the last remnant of a family takes a final departure from home. "The Army's a fine outfit. They're lucky to get you. You do us proud, now." He set his pipe down in a very deliberate manner and, without another word, limped out to the corral to check on a heifer.

Guy had already caught the train out of Perryton for boot camp when Dorothy had her miscarriage. His father wrote him later that the young couple had gone through with the wedding as planned. He crumpled that letter and threw it away, along with his hopes.

ORLANDO, FLORIDA
2007
~~MONDAY~~
~~TUESDAY~~
~~WEDNESDAY~~
~~THURSDAY~~
FRIDAY

An irresistible force. An immovable object.
It's sometimes called family.

Guy sat slumped in a kitchen chair sipping coffee and watching the sun's first light scrape away any darkness clinging to the corners of the room. *We live to see another day. How wonderful that is.* He raised his mug toward the sky in a lazy salute. *Just fantastic. Thanks a lot, whoever's up there.*

Many years ago, Guy had perceived the not-so-gentle guiding hand of God smacking him down. A week before his mother's passing, during the days of fever and pain, Reverend Meehan had called on the Pickering farm. After a closed-door session, he came out to the hallway and embraced seventeen-year-old Guy. "The good Lord knows best, son. It's in his hands now." He remembered the minister's face and countenance—someone confident in their doctrines—and felt torn in half by his heart's desire to believe the words but, in the same moment, anger at life's injustice. This assurance of a divine plan in these matters echoed like a paltry consolation and left him confused and doubtful. "This is God's way?" Guy spat—more of a statement than a question. The reverend didn't answer but bowed his head and whispered a brief prayer. The last moments of the reverend's visit had been hard for Guy to endure.

Today, the only sounds punctuating the silence were snoring and an occasional murmur from upstairs. Dorothy lay in a fitful sleep after a restless night. Alex remained sprawled out on the den's couch like a purple-haired rag doll. Guy had tiptoed downstairs at midnight to turn off the sounds of laughing and bits of conversation from Leno's guests. For a few moments, he studied the slumbering man/boy. *So young. Still innocent.*

Guy filled his cup and drummed his fingers on the countertop. Last night's anxiety-provoking dream lingered—an office scene with endless sorting through page after page of a drama with no end.

Pedro leaped through the pet door, sauntered into the kitchen, and threw his side against Guy's leg, reminding him of his daily promise to fill the bowl.

He contemplated the aging cat. The heavy stone of guilt and the inevitability of further abandonment weighed on him. "Sorry," he whispered.

Needing the fresh brace of outdoors, he pushed through the screen door and strode past the Olds's buckled metal and loosened chrome—a wheeled participation trophy, mocking him. The facts did not lie. Dorothy's suffering was likely to increase, and his call to duty had stalled.

He was back at square one. *Am I doing the right thing? This is so awful for Alex and Heather and—everyone who cares about us.*

From a corner of the garage, he pulled a folding chair from behind a stack of boxes and lowered himself onto the seat facing the driveway. Hunched forward, forearms on his knees, and focused straight ahead, he sat and examined this unfamiliar blemish of ineptitude. *I get things done, even fixed an airplane in the middle of the jungle.* He rubbed his eyes and stared at nothing. *What the hell? Damn! I've turned into an idiot.* With a lifetime of responsibilities met, and a stubborn reluctance to admit defeat, he felt the ground shifting beneath him. *What if I just . . .*

"Oh, didn't see you." From the entrance to the garage, Alex's voice pierced Guy's reverie.

He jerked to attention. "Hey there . . . I'm just resting my bones." Guy forced himself to shake off his gloom and sat upright in his chair. *Time to pretend again.* He cleared his throat and pointed center stage—the Olds. "I sure got plenty of work cut out for me." He waved Alex forward. "Here, grab a seat."

Alex looked around as if there might be something better to do but spied another folding chair and placed it a dutiful distance from his grandfather.

"Do me a favor, will ya? Get a beer out of the fridge and bring it here?"

Alex hesitated, gave a half nod, and reappeared a minute later with the can in his hand. "Now, open it and have a sip," Guy said, keeping a steady gaze on his grandson.

"What?" Alex wrinkled his nose and pulled the beer back a few inches.

"I'm used to talking to a man I can drink with." Guy waited.

Eyes darting around the garage as if someone might catch him in the act and trying to appear as if he'd done it a thousand times, he popped open the can, tipped it to his lips, and coughed twice.

"Now, give it back. That's all you get." Guy reached out and snatched the can. "Have a seat."

The two of them settled in silence inside the shady enclave, the battered but still proud Olds 88 before them.

"Sorry about your car," Alex said.

Guy studied the Olds. Visions of sunny Florida days and Dorothy's hair tossing in the wind raced through his mind. Their trips to the beach. Ice cream on summer days, and that maddening time Dorothy dropped her cone on the floorboards. Ah, the sweet taste of reminiscence. "This is a great automobile. It's not about speed, but it had that style that always appealed to me. I wanted one for a long time before I got my hands on this baby." His face brightened. "Right after I bought it, Dorothy and I took it over to Daytona during race week. We showed it off, up and down the street. Silly, but fun." He spoke in a soft, distant voice while rubbing his knee.

"You hurt?" Alex pointed at Guy's leg.

"Banged it on the dashboard yesterday." Guy pulled his pantleg up to check it out. Beneath the bruised knee, a jagged, discolored scar ran up the inside of the calf. He noticed Alex's shocked expression. "I guess you never saw this before, huh?"

Alex blinked a few times, unsure of this odd new sort of intimacy.

Guy yanked his Levi's down to the ankle. "That happened long ago. I got nicked in Vietnam." He considered his grandson for a moment before shifting his gaze up to the corner shelves. "I want to show you something, son. You interested in peeking at a couple of old folks' lives?"

"Sure, I guess." Alex's hands fidgeted.

"Think you can get that there suitcase down?" He pointed at a midsize tweed case. "There's a ladder right over there."

Several minutes later, Guy opened the battered suitcase and seized a stack of photos. He flipped through them, giving Alex a brief explanation of who, what, when, and where. "Here." He held up a black-and-white portrait of a tall woman dressed in overalls, smiling with an armful of fresh-picked squash. "Your great-grandma died when I was seventeen. She was a beauty, she was. You'd-a liked her." Guy passed the photo to Alex, who raised it up to the light, studying the image with an intense frown.

Guy rifled deeper into the pile and handed over a few more. They showed nameless young soldiers posing with exaggerated bravado, wearing boots, military caps, and blank T-shirts, portrayed only in gray, white, and washed-out color images. Most of them goofy boys, barely old enough to be deemed men, holding weapons in front of tropical palm trees.

Alex zeroed in on one particular photo of a lone soldier standing next to an airplane, a single-prop tail dragger. He inspected it closer.

"That's me and my plane," Guy said, gazing at the now-familiar picture. "They were little Cessna L-19s we called Bird Dogs. Mine was Miss Molly, after your great-grandma."

"What'd you do over there? What was it like?"

Guy took the photograph and stuck it back in the stack, then leaned back in the chair and folded his arms. "It was the early stages of the war. We were so damn wet behind the ears . . . Not for long, though. I was still in my twenties, but it turns out, I was one of the older boys." He shifted in his seat. "I flew reconnaissance for the Army. We'd fly these planes in low over the jungles and map as many roads as we could find. No GPS gizmos to help, plus we dodged bullets every time. A few days later, the helicopters followed, spraying this god-awful Agent Orange. They sprayed tons of that crap for months. It killed pretty much everything it touched. All their trees, foliage, crops turned brown and ugly as death." Guy paused and rubbed his chin. "You can only imagine what it did to people, our boys included. With the jungle cover dead and roads exposed, the jets and helicopters proceeded to shoot or bomb everything that moved. Terrible. By the time I left, I hated every aspect."

He stopped and inhaled a deep breath—the memory of war had thickened the air.

"Got shot up on my last mission. I made it back to base, but not by much. Enemy fire busted up one of my landing gears, and another round took out the oil supply to the engine. Also took a bullet in the leg." He chuckled. "A close one, and by far my most spectacular landing. They patched me up, and I got out of there. My tour of duty was over anyway, and they gave me this medal as a sort of booby prize."

Guy lifted the lid on a small felt-covered box. A pale satin bed held a complicated and often misunderstood military medal. He unfolded the single piece of paper that lay tucked inside and held it up to the light.

The President of the United States of America has awarded the Purple Heart established by General George Washington . . . to Lieutenant Guy Hamlin Pickering, United States Army Air Division, for wounds received in action this 4th day of May, 1964.

Quietly staring at the heart-shaped icon, he refolded the paper and lowered it back into the box.

"I've heard of those medals. You should be proud," Alex said.

"Eh," Guy said with a shrug, but he brightened as he reached into the suitcase and dug out a wedding album. "You want to see more out of the past?" He held up a dog-eared photo, then slipped it to Alex. "Here, check this one. Me and your grandma, a little bit older than you."

"You guys look so young."

They both studied the candid shot of Guy and Dorothy laughing and hugging with a knife held to a traditional multitiered cake. In the background, men and women clapped. A freckled young redheaded woman was the only one staring into the camera.

"Twenty-two years old and on leave from the Army for the big day. Check this out." Guy pointed to newspaper clippings announcing the engagement, the wedding invitation front and back, along with the original envelopes covering the next pages. The entire collection of RSVPs from all the attendees bulged from between the covers. A brochure from a hotel in Miami where they went on their honeymoon and a guide map of the Florida Everglades fell to the floor between Alex's feet.

"This shit is sick, man," Alex muttered in amazement. "Fuckin' A."

"Thank you, son. That's charming to hear." He smirked, but his eyes strayed away as memories from a love-filled life flooded Guy's chest, bringing him a warmth he usually only felt in Dorothy's hugs.

"I remember seeing one photo of my parents' wedding," Alex said. "It was an old faded Polaroid that some Las Vegas minister took of them necking underneath a crazy-colored neon steeple."

Guy only nodded. Still in the suitcase lay several newspapers, a bundle of letters, and, at the bottom, a dry brown Army leather flight jacket. He pulled it out; the folds and creases were deep and stiff with age. He ran his fingers over the insignias sewn on both arms—101st Airborne and Miss Molly. He shook out the thirsty leather, then held it out toward Alex. "Hmm, let's see how it looks on you."

Alex spun away with a frown that Guy construed as embarrassment.

"Why don't you keep it, son? I'm sure it'll fit you fine." He looked Alex up and down. "Maybe give it a couple of years."

"No, I shouldn't have it." Alex spat out the words.

"Why not? I'm giving it to you."

"I don't know. It's not mine."

"That's not right." Guy frowned at Alex's profile. "I mean, you shouldn't feel that way."

"Yeah, well, I do," Alex snapped back.

Guy paused and pondered the history-laden memorabilia before him. It didn't seem right not to personally pass some things on. "Just the same, I'm thinking you could take that Purple Heart with you. It used to be important to me, but . . ."

Alex turned to face his grandfather. "What makes you think I want your old stuff? I'm not some kind of museum." He bolted out of his chair, fists clenched, but stopped dead a few feet away, his backside to Guy. "I don't deserve any of your things, okay?"

Guy gaped at him and started to object but stopped himself, then began again. "Sit for a minute, will you?"

Alex hesitated, his hand lingering on his birthmark, but after a moment, he shuffled back and slumped into the chair beside his grandfather. "What?"

Guy reclined deeper into his chair and sipped his beer. He noted Alex's pouty face, baggy jeans, and the mess his hair was in today.

Several minutes went by before he broke the silence. "None of us are that important."

Alex glanced at him with curiosity and distrust.

Guy crushed his empty can. "Life's not fair. So what? We do what we need to do!"

"Yeah, I've heard you say that. But I've been thinking," Alex began while running his hand along the chair's armrest. "Everything used to be so much fun." He let his voice fade.

Guy tapped his chin, as if trying to remember having fun.

"You know, like when we went up in your plane. And remember the time we went boating on a lake? I fell overboard trying to reel in that stupid fish. You howled, and I was so embarrassed . . . but it was still really awesome."

Guy smiled. "Yeah."

Guy's eyes welled up, and Alex looked away. "I don't want to make you feel bad. But why do things have to be so different now? Those days were so cool. What happened?"

What happened indeed. Guy's mind wandered to the woman upstairs. He pictured her healthy form wasting away into the weakened woman he had carried inside the night before. "Son, everything changes for everybody all the time. Things go along just fine; you think it's always going to be that way. You know, rosy, and then life sneaks up on ya. All of a sudden, you're old, and you gotta deal with hard situations."

"Like Grandma, right?"

Guy studied Alex. *You have no idea.* "Yeah. It's a tough one," Guy said.

Grandfather and grandson sat without words, staring past the dented Olds at Florida's palm trees swaying in the gentle breeze.

17

*When need, ideas, and
opportunity collide, oh boy!*

Fifteen minutes later, Guy was deep into a melancholy daze when Heather's minivan pulled into the driveway. The brakes squeaked to an abrupt halt inside the sidewalk, and Heather wasted no time vaulting from the driver's door.

He sat up straight and held his breath as she marched toward him, then slowed to a saunter as she passed the Olds. Her eyes simmered while running a finger over the crumpled metal on the front right fender.

"More? Really, more? God, look at the back seat." Her lip curled while spotting the blood stains on the upholstery. "Are you okay? Is Mom all right? Where is she?"

Guy winced at the sharpness in her voice. "She's still asleep," he murmured, pointing at the upstairs window while staring at the cement slab. "We're fine. No big deal; nobody's hurt. Only a minor accident. You can ask Alex," he said with a hint of apprehension as the teenager bounded down the porch steps.

"Hey, how you doing?" Alex's tone sounded upbeat and sarcastic. His gaze went from Heather, to Guy, to the Olds, and back to Heather. "You might be wondering, right? Just your commonplace, ordinary night around the Pickering household." He broke into a broad grin. "Like any normal human, Grandpa stuffed a roadkill deer inside the car and hauled it here for a backyard funeral. There wasn't time for cremation. We conducted a beautiful little ceremony. Even the neighbors attended."

"What . . .?" Heather's mouth hung open.

Guy took a deep breath and sighed. "I can explain everything."

Heather kept hands on hips. "You can, huh?" Heather zeroed in on Guy with the suspicious demeanor of an intolerant judge. "I can't wait to hear every last detail." She jerked her head toward the house. "But first, I brought a bunch of groceries. I planned on making breakfast. Let's get inside."

While his aunt cleared the counters and pulled out mixing bowls, pans, and basics for pancakes and eggs and his grandpa headed upstairs to check on his grandma, Alex lounged in front of the television, surfing the channels with minimal attention.

His ever-expanding taste in entertainment had turned up a special news report. A liberal-leaning public television producer had teamed up with a popular commentator to create a feature segment on the current use of medical marijuana. Alex might have surfed right over the channel but for the passing image of an older gentleman in a wheelchair displaying a vegetation-filled baggie to the camera in his thin, bony hands.

"This stuff is saving my life," the wizened old man said into the lens. "Before, I couldn't eat. The pain was horrible. I was depressed. Thank the good Lord for giving me my pot."

Alex waved his aunt forward when Heather poked her head into the den.

"Breakfast will be ready soon. What are you watching?" She directed a wooden spoon at the TV.

"Check it out," Alex said, his eyes fixated on the TV.

"The current administration continues to deny funding for research into the medical uses of marijuana. Doctors find themselves in dangerous territory if they wish to recommend it for their patients. Federal laws still make possession a crime. Let's hear from a cancer patient in Bozeman, Montana, who remains anonymous. She has told our camera crew, if identified, she fears she could not receive her medicine."

"It has been a miracle," said the diminutive figure with a shadowy face. "Now, I can live a normal day. I've gained eight pounds and feel much better."

Heather sank into a seat, concentrating on the screen. "What show is this?" she asked. "Where's this coming from?"

"I don't know. Some news show. Cool though, right?" He wrinkled his nose.

"Hush, I want to see this."

A woman in a doctor's smock spoke with passion into a camera. "Studies from around the world unequivocally show the benefits of medically prescribed marijuana. The problem is . . ." Alex and Heather leaned forward. "It grows in your backyard, so drug companies haven't yet figured out a way to make a profit. Plus, this so-called war on drugs is big business."

"Wow," Alex whispered.

"Well, then," Guy said from the doorway. Alex wasn't sure how much he had seen, but it seemed he'd gotten the gist.

"Mute it, will ya?" Heather sat motionless, with her stony face fixed straight ahead at the screen. She lowered her voice. "Papa, I read an article this week saying the same thing. I've been thinking." She turned to face Guy and glanced over the top of his shoulder toward the upstairs. "I never thought the day would come that I, Heather Pickering-Schlusser, would ever, ever consider my mom smoking pot. But people out there are getting relief." She jumped out of her seat. "I heard Laura Crawford's mother-in-law used it for years while she was in and out of chemo. And by the way, she's alive and doing fine." She crossed her arms and took two steps closer to her father—a long pause. "Daddy, we've got to talk about this."

———

Guy had only revealed his history with marijuana to one person— Dorothy. In Vietnam, many times he'd indulged in smoking along with the soldiers. It helped alleviate the horror of the times. But after coming home, he'd associated getting high with a time in his life that he did not want to revisit. His present buddies had nothing to do with pot, and he hadn't tried it again. Dorothy had never considered trying it.

"Wow, Heather, I'm not sure." Guy crossed his arms. "I've read about this. I even asked Dr. Berger about it once. But in Florida, no doctors will touch the subject, even if they want to. So I didn't pursue it." Guy took two steps back, poker-faced.

The still-muted television displayed the commentator pointing his microphone at various gray-haired men and women in lab coats and people obscured by dim light and clouds of smoke.

Heather leaped to her feet as a burning-eggs smell wafted into the room. "We're going to eat now, but we are going to talk about this," she called out over her shoulder while running for the kitchen.

———

Alex sat uncomfortably, shifting in his seat. The silence around the kitchen table was deafening as Heather glared at him and Guy while they poked at the unappealing yellowish lumps forming a perimeter berm on their plates. A healthy dose of ketchup wasn't helping.

"Okay," Heather began, "they're a bit overdone. And about your escapade last night, we'll set that aside for the moment. There's more important things to discuss." She pointed down the hall toward the TV.

Alex took a moment to assess the situation. *Yeah, grandma smoking pot. Goes right along with escaped princesses in the neighbor's yard and, of course, crashed cars and deer burials.*

Guy held up a finger. "For one thing, it's illegal."

"Oh, Papa, it won't happen, anyway. It's probably too late to think about this, and we don't have any or know what to do and everything." Heather's face summed up her confusion and dejected feelings. "I just want to do something to help her." She slouched back in her chair.

Alex kept an eye on his grandfather and thought hard about his next move. He wasn't sure he wouldn't get in trouble, but this would guaranteed be more entertaining. His fingers drummed on the table, and he decided to rise to the occasion. "There is a way."

"Oh, you mean just go out on the street and find a pusher? Find a webpage for addicts that sell grass?" Heather threw up her hands.

"Yeah, that doesn't happen," Alex chortled, then lowered his voice to a whisper. "There might be some . . . available . . . here." He searched their faces, then dove in. "I have a bag of pot."

"What?" Heather gaped and leaned in toward him.

Guy's eyebrows shot up.

"It's supposed to be good shit." His palms rose in a gesture of surrender. "My mom's asshole boyfriend gave it to me."

Indeed, as Sharon and Sleazoid (as Alex referred to him) were squeezing into his Porsche convertible on their way to their fabulous Jamaican getaway, the handsome greaseball had slipped his girlfriend's kid a slender baggie. Being a former drug-smuggling client of Mitch's, he had reliable connections to a supply. Alex's lasting image of the encounter was his own reflection in a pair of designer sunglasses resting above a set of perfect white teeth. "Hey, man, keep it cool. Have fun." The man's shaved head bobbed to a steady inner beat.

Later, Alex had kicked himself for saying "thanks" to the gutter-licker. But he'd brought the weed along in case he wanted to smoke—an emergency stash if he had to escape the droll reality of grandparents. Since arriving, he hadn't touched it.

Heather began, "Well, that sure is interesting, isn't it?" Her eyes darted back and forth between Alex and Guy. She stood up. "Where is it?"

"Hold on, now," Guy interjected.

"Daddy!" Heather snarled with the voice of someone on a mission. "I am already convinced."

Permission granted. Alex ditched his chair and flew out of the room.

———

A few tense minutes later, Alex reappeared dangling a misshapen plastic baggie and, with a tentative stretched out hand, laid it in the center of the table.

Heather regarded the offering with a wary fascination. "So, Papa, we need to know that you are with us on this. It won't work if you're not." She folded her arms and tossed the challenge to Guy like a basketball.

Guy stared at one and then the other. A middle-aged stay-at-home parent and a purple-haired teenager sat, waiting for his thumbs-up, an important step in getting a seventy-five-year-old woman stoned for the first time.

Guy stood up, grabbed his plate, and turned to the sink. He didn't want them seeing his true feelings: that Dorothy's disease had progressed too far for marijuana to make any difference.

"She's eating next to nothing each time I see her," Heather began. "Maybe this could at least stimulate her appetite."

Guy considered this. Still, doubts lingered, and he had one last card to play. "She can't smoke anything," he said with as much finality as he could muster. "Never has. Won't happen."

Heather slumped on the table, frowned, and patted her fist to her mouth in deep concentration.

Alex shook his head back and forth, sporting a crooked smile. "Brownie time."

PERRYTON, TENNESSEE

JULY 1953

Home is not for the faint of heart.

Dorothy guided the Benson's Chevy around a series of potholes as they rolled past the few scattered farms on the outskirts of town. Dorothy took her right hand off the steering wheel just long enough to wipe a half-dried spot of blood from Guy's lip. He jerked back at the touch but remained silent.

"That's swelling up some. Do you have ice at home?" Her focus continued to dart between the road and Guy's brooding presence.

"Maybe," he monotoned while staring straight ahead.

"I feel so bad about what happened. Marvin's not like this all the time, but he can be such a bully. It's the drinking to blame."

"Bullshit. I can drink and not sucker punch people." Guy turned to face her, his gut tense. "He's hit you too, hasn't he?" Guy remembered the bruising on Dorothy's wrist at the church.

Dorothy slowed the Chevy down, shifted the transmission gear into second, and mumbled something about the ruts in the unpaved road.

"Hasn't he?" he demanded.

"Everybody has faults. No relationship is perfect."

Guy grunted out his displeasure as he looked down at his blood-spattered Army uniform.

Dorothy pointed a finger. "Those will come out if you wash it right away. Use cool water and lots of soap. A bit of hydrogen peroxide if you have it . . ." Her words trailed off. "I'm sorry. This couldn't be the homecoming you had imagined."

"Nope."

"You've been gone almost a year. I missed seeing you. I'd like to hear about your time in the Army. Was it hard?"

"*I'd* like to hear why you're still with that jerk!"

Guy knew Dorothy had miscarried the pregnancy that had led her into marrying her fool husband, but he couldn't understand why she hadn't bolted right afterward.

She bit her lip and guided the car down a dusty driveway. "We're here already. I bet your dad is glad to see you back for a while. How long you here for?"

"Too long. Glad we had this chat!" Guy spat out the words, pointing out the side glass. "I'll get out here."

The car rolled to a creaking stop, fifty yards shy of the farmhouse. For a moment, a silent tension filled the stillness. He opened the door and started to exit but paused. What he saw caught his breath—tears streaming down Dorothy's face. She looked like she was trying to hold back her emotions but losing the battle. Still wearing that pretty flower-patterned dress, she brushed back her hair, cleared her throat, and spoke in a soft, faraway voice. "I remember this place so well. When we were kids . . . so simple and innocent."

Guy swallowed hard, his taut lips relaxed. "We live with our choices. That's the way it is."

"Easy for you to say."

"No, it's not easy. It's the last thing that I ever wanted to say to you." Her tears were still brimming, giving her a very vulnerable look. Guy suddenly lost track of his anger and leaned back into the seat.

Dorothy dabbed away the tears, and her eyes turned to slits as she stared him down. "I'm mad at you!"

"What? What are you talking about?" He jerked to attention and crossed his arms. "I've done nothing to harm you."

"That's the problem. You did nothing! You and your whole damn shy act! I kept thinking, waiting for you to try harder. You could have stepped up, talked more, and swept me off my feet, and all that!" Dorthy choked back sobs as she spoke. "But no, no, you always hung back. Always making doe eyes at me, and then nothing. What's a girl supposed to think? Then, Marvin comes along, and he's strong and really nice in the beginning."

Guy blanched, his mouth open. "I . . . I . . . shit."

"Everything's all wrong," she wailed, collapsing against the steering wheel. "It's all your fault!"

Guy's last resolve started to melt under the weight of her accusations. "I never saw it that way," he said, his head bowed. He almost reached a hand out to grab hers but still held back. He still wasn't sure where he stood, but he knew where he wanted to stand.

"No, you wouldn't, would you? You don't know a damn thing about courtship and women."

"That may be true. But I know you."

"No, you don't."

"I know you're good," Guy said while contemplating Dorothy's profile as she stared out the windshield. Another moment passed.

She shut off the ignition key, and the engine rumbled to a stop. "I'm still mad at you." She shot a quivering look in Guy's direction.

Guy's brain spun with past images and choices to make. Engine off. She wants to stay. *It's now or never, Loverboy. Speak up or forever . . .* He'd missed it before. *Not again.*

Guy's fist pounded the dashboard. "Well, then, I guess we'd better talk about it. So here's what we're gonna do. You're going to come in and sit for a while. We'll have coffee."

Dorothy wiped at her cheeks and blew her nose into a handkerchief. "Okay."

Ten minutes later Guy and Dorothy sat at the burnished kitchen table while Lloyd stood beside the stove waiting for the coffee water to boil. Under his bushy eyebrows, his concentrated gaze considered the pair. Guy held an ice cube wrapped in a small towel up to his lip. He glanced at Dorothy. Her lips were taut and her downcast eyes darted around the room.

"What I don't understand"—Lloyd spoke slowly—"is this. My boy returns from many tough months in the Army without a scratch. He's in town for one day, and you, young lady, drag him back here all beat up. I'm under the impression it has something to do with you."

"Dad, it's not her fault," Guy protested.

"Of course not. I never thought it was. But women bring out the best in a man. And sometimes, we pay the price for it." He brought over two steaming mugs and set them on the table, never taking his eyes off of Dorothy. "He let you slip away, didn't he?"

"Dad!"

Dorothy softened and nodded—a simple gesture, but to Guy, it meant the world to him. *There's a possibility!*

"Anyway, I've got chores to do. It's a pleasure to have visitors in the house. Possibly see you again." With a wave of his hand, Lloyd pushed out the squeaky screen door and limped toward the barn.

Guy and Dorothy shifted in their chairs, playing it safe with aimless chatter—both reticent to embrace the dangerous territory where genuine feelings collide with life's crossroads. Bordering on gossip, she gave updates on old classmates' lives, but an unspoken truth lingered in Guy's mind—their lives were on separate paths, and change was enticing but daunting to embrace.

Guy shifted in his seat and laced and unlaced his fingers. He wasn't so sure anymore, but he knew he could never live with himself if he didn't speak his truth.

After a brief moment of lingering eye contact, Guy's fidgeting exploded. He jumped up and glared at her. "Here's the deal. It's hard to admit, but you scare me. You're the one person in the whole world who can hurt me."

Dorothy's head drooped. "And I'm scared I'll do nothing and always live with regret."

He lowered himself back down onto the chair and gulped the last coffee drops from his mug. "Well, now at least you know how I feel." He cleared his throat a few times as he waited for a response.

Dorothy rose, strode over to the window, and stared at her car. "I better get going. Maybe spend tonight at my parents' house." As the tears began again, she burst out the door, running for the Chevy.

Guy stood for a long time staring out the window and shaking his head after Dorothy's car pulled away.

———

Silence was customary at the Pickering dinner table, but that evening, Guy sensed an unusual scrutiny from his father.

"What?" He slammed his fork on the table, fed up with all the raw feelings he'd been through that day.

"You've got it bad, don't ya?"

His cheeks flushed. "No, I don't. It's all in the past. I'm just wrapping things up, that's all. She used to mean something, but now . . ."

"That sounds like bullshit. Looks and smells like it, too. Take a wild guess what it is."

All the rest of Guy's pent-up energy forced itself out in his next bitter words. "She married the asshole!"

"So you're letting some asshole rule your future?" Lloyd chuffed. "God knows I'm no expert, but I'd bet you a whole herd of heifers that the next twenty-four hours will be the test. Don't let yourself get in the way."

———

Guy tossed and turned that night.

At dawn, he listened to Lloyd bustle around the kitchen, then leave to help fix a tractor at a neighbor's farm. He fell back asleep, but sounds of soft knocking jolted him awake, and he pulled on his jeans and padded up to the front door, opening it a crack.

Dorothy rocked on her heels and wrung her hands with a hopeful smile on her face. His heart swelled. To Guy, she looked like a box under a tree on Christmas morning. Before his brain could pick what to say, Dorothy spoke. "Hello. Got any more of that coffee?" Her gaze shifted across the street to a cornfield that stretched beyond the furthest bend in the road. "And then you want to go for a walk?"

ORLANDO, FLORIDA

2007

~~MONDAY~~

~~TUESDAY~~

~~WEDNESDAY~~

~~THURSDAY~~

FRIDAY

Words! Such a finite way of understanding.

Heather grabbed her purse and sped off to the store in search of brownie mix. Alex searched through the kitchen cabinets for a strainer and a bowl. Guy carried a small meal upstairs on a tray garnished with an array of hollyhocks, pineapple sage, and a red rose poking out of a rinsed juice glass.

I've got to get back to a plan for us that's foolproof. Ha! With me the fool, he thought as he entered the bedroom.

Dorothy opened her eyes but only stared at the food. Guy persisted, and she swallowed a few bites. He set the tray on the floor and ran his hand across the back of her head, through her pillow-flattened hair. Nothing was said between them.

The stillness in the room gave rise to an unspoken recess of uncertainty that gripped him with surprising force. The floodgates of Guy's self-doubt burst open, parading his setbacks. The thoughts he had been shoving aside, the folly of his plans, the awkward failures all descended and hung on him like a damp, ill-fitting suit. Guy was used to accomplishing tasks, getting things done, and these recent failed attempts threw doubt into his center. *What the hell do I know?* He clenched his fists, straining at the delicate threads of an heirloom patchwork quilt. *I think doing us both in is the right thing—but is it? Do I have what it takes?*

Dorothy's attention focused out the window on things unseen. He jumped up and darted to the same glass to see what she saw— maybe outrun his uncertainties.

As far as the Almighty was concerned, he'd take his chances, but with Dorothy, no matter how illogical she was, he needed to fully trust that she was still on board with full knowledge and blessing of his deadly proposal. He struggled to find the words to fit the situation. *Are you okay with me killing both of us?* It sounded so preposterous to him.

"My dear." He sat on the bed and took her hand. "I want to tell you once again that I love you. And by the way, I don't care if God is mad at me, but I need to check with you on our plan."

She turned her face to him and blinked.

"Plan . . . oh yeah. We're supposed to tango into the afterlife together. Right?"

He stopped and wiped the mist from his eyes. "Well, that's sort of it, yes. I'm ready, and I . . . I must make sure you are too." He paused and lowered his head, searching for words, for answers. "Turns out I'm not very talented at this business. But I'm still willing."

She watched his face. After a moment, she coughed and scrutinized him, up and down—then, in a fine sandpapery voice—"You could take lessons."

Guy resisted but couldn't help breaking into a grin.

With a flicker of spirit, her gaze lifted toward the window and the open sky. "Yes, Guy. You and me."

In an instant, everything harmonized in his mind. *That's all I need.*

Life and plans? Oil and water?
We can't help ourselves.

The smell of baking brownies and fine Colombian wafted throughout the house. Heather wasted no time in her quest, and soon, a batch of potent brown squares with a faint iridescent sheen sat on the kitchen table.

"We can't have her eat these on her own," she proclaimed in an unsure voice. "I don't know how strong they are. Do you?" She turned to Alex.

He shrugged. "Not really. How much did you put in?"

"The whole bag," Heather said.

"Is that a lot?" Guy asked.

"No idea," Heather and Alex echoed.

They fell silent and studied the mind-altering mound of chocolate.

"One of us has to try them too," Heather said.

"I will." Alex raised his hand. "I am the most qualified here."

In unison, Guy and Heather protested, vetoing the motion. "You are too young, Alex, but thank you so much for the drugs," she said, and aimed her attention at her father.

Guy frowned and shook his head, dispelling any notion that today he would get high with Dorothy.

Heather bit her lip. "I was the one that encouraged this, and probably a good gauge of how it will affect her, too. After all, I'm a lot like her—that's what you always say, right, Papa?"

Guy grunted his agreement.

"Well, then." She lifted her chin. "I'll do it."

With the magic platter in hand and an uneasy smile on her face, Heather headed upstairs to share unexplored realms with her mom.

Moments later, squirming on a hard kitchen chair and straining to hear, Guy heard the phrases "my favorite" and "mmm" and "oooh." *How odd,* he mused. But after the mind-bending events of the last few days, he could believe anything.

Sharp Spanish chatter and clanging pail sounds broke his spell. Guy peeked out the window and slumped with dismay at the sight of the early-model Mazda sitting in the driveway. He had forgotten that today was the "day of the mop," as he called it.

Seconds later, a short, wide, and weathered-looking woman charged through the door.

Dominga had arrived to do her semimonthly house cleaning.

Guy cringed and drew his lips apart in an uncertain greeting to this familiar force of nature. He'd heard stories of Dominga's youth—walking the entire distance from violence-torn Guatemala to the United States. She was, to him, a five-foot-tall buffalo–volcano mix—powerful, unrelenting, and combustible. But he also knew that she was as dependable as a sunrise, and she had always shown great affection for Dorothy.

"You wreck your cars now, eh?" Her thick black braided ponytail flew aside as she jerked a thumb toward the Olds. She leaned forward, balancing on a fist at the edge of the table, and shook her head.

"*Hombres!*" The proclamation sounded like a curse. Guy figured her husband, Juan, had crossed a line earlier that day. She took one look at the dirty dishes and shooed him away from the kitchen with a wave of her feather duster.

He fled out the door.

Out in the yard, Guy paced around the fresh memorial mound. *Damn deer is dead, and we're still very much alive.* At this point, his failures were just embarrassing. It was getting personal. It was Heather's voice, calling out to him, that broke through his attention-consuming angst.

"Papa!"

He swiveled as she approached, her face taut with concern.

"I don't feel anything. I'm going to eat one more. Unless you think that's not a good idea."

"You should ask Alex. I wouldn't know." Guy stuck his hands in his jeans pockets. *Probably a waste of time.*

"I already did. He said some people aren't affected that much or just take naps." She sighed with a hint of disappointment. "I'll try another."

She trudged back up the steps and disappeared inside the screen door while Guy resumed his pacing around the backyard. The thirsty vegetable garden lay abandoned and choked with weeds. Yet another item jettisoned from his responsibility, like a neglected parking ticket. He picked up a dirt clod and threw it against the fence. *There has to be a way.*

A single-prop airplane buzz sounded overhead, and he stopped between two overgrown zucchinis and looked to the sky.

Sordid inspiration, the kind that scared him, spawned a deadly vision.

Guy's eyes glowed anew. *Maybe . . . hmm . . . yes . . . yes, of course. I should have done this in the first place!* He sauntered over to the garage, leaned a shoulder against the peeling paint, and locked his sight on the heavens. *So, you can't let us just slip away?* He spat and turned his scrutiny to his beaten-up 88. *You're having fun prolonging this, huh? Then we'll do it different, and better.*

He grinned in satisfaction, the warming balm of self-righteousness flowing through his veins. Tapping his chin, he muttered, "I wonder if I can get a hold of Sam today."

Guy beelined for the house while keeping a watch out for Dominga. He slipped through the kitchen to the den, where Alex lay sprawled in front of the television. With a pasted-on smile, he snatched up the cordless phone.

After retreating to the backyard, he dialed.

"Sam? Can you hear me? It's Guy Pickering." He tried to sound casual. "Good, good, fine, thanks, and you? How's Margaret?" He listened to his friend for a moment, then forced the slow words out of his mouth. "Dorothy? Well, she's hanging in there. Say, listen, Sam, I was wondering if anyone has the plane booked for tomorrow. Yeah, it's been a while for me; that's true. Oh no, I've kept my medical certificate current." He winced at the lie and clenched his teeth.

"I just had a hankering to go up and fly around for a while. Just for fun. You know, just for an hour or two. Tomorrow." Rolling his eyes at the awkward inquiry, he crossed his fingers. *I must sound like an idiot.* "It's clear? Nobody's reserved it, huh?" He pumped his fist. "Great, I'd love to have it in the morning then, if that's okay. Fantastic. No, I still have my keys, so I guess that's it. New tires? Excellent! No, I didn't hear that, but I'm glad to hear it. You've been getting my dues, right? Good. No, I'm feeling fine, Sam, thanks for asking. I've got to run, though, so I'll take good care of the Bonanza. By the way, is nosy old Dirk still in charge at the airport? He is? I suppose I'll have to deal with him. You have yourself a good day. Bye now."

He punched the *off* button with a flourish. *Now we're cooking with gas.*

Unbeknownst to Guy, Alex had crouched only a few feet away, underneath an open back bedroom window, while Guy conducted his call. The strange look on his grandfather's face and the lame attempt at hiding the phone had drawn him to eavesdropping.

And now, having overheard the gist of the conversation, he beamed with anticipation. *Cool. He reserved the airplane for tomorrow. I'll bet he wants to surprise me with a ride!*

Two years ago, his summer's highlight had been an extended flight over the coastline with his grandfather. *Grandpa said he didn't go up anymore. He's doing this for me.*

He returned to the couch, smiling all the way.

───────

Guy lingered in the garden for another few minutes, mulling over his mental checklist. *No slipups this time. Insurance is current. My medical expired a year ago. I don't care. Never thought I'd want to pilot the plane again. I'll break old Dirk's check-in rule.* With a smirk, he shoved all remaining concerns aside. *What are they going to do, shoot me? Go ahead! That would be quicker.*

"Wow," he murmured to himself. "A big ending."

Girls just want to have fun.

"Can you hear it, Mom?"

"I sure can, sweetie."

Mother and daughter stood on the porch, their arms entwined, eyes shut, faces basking in the sun. Bright orange and purple sashes wound around their waist and necks. Guy tiptoed closer and bent his ear forward, listening. He couldn't hear a thing.

From behind the screen door, Alex spied Guy and maneuvered over to him.

"Grandma ate a half of one, and Heather had three." Alex held his hand over his mouth, stifling a laugh.

"Is that a lot?" Guy rubbed his whiskers. He wasn't even sure how potent "a lot" was and worried what it would do to each of them.

Alex lifted his shoulders and dropped them. "Could be."

"Did you eat any?" Guy figured he'd better name the sober remnants of the family.

"Nah, it's too much fun watching them." His eyebrows arched up, and his entire face broadened into a grin.

Heather wrapped an arm around Dorothy's waist and led her on an exceedingly slow perimeter stroll through the yard. They maneuvered amid the random gopher mounds and paused to marvel at a clump of semidehydrated marigolds. Spontaneous laughter erupted every time they peeked at the clouds. Guy followed close behind like an anxious parent of toddlers in an antique store.

Heather came to a sudden halt midstride. "Oh no." She exhaled long and low, resembling a tire losing air. She reached down and made a *V* in the blades of grass with her hands and scooped up a gooey blob—she had crushed a snail. "Look, Mom. She was just gliding along, minding her own business, and now see what I've done." Her palm held the hapless gastropod as tears formed in her flaming red eyes. "Why is everything dying around me?" She swiveled to face her mother. "Oh, I'm sorry. I'm so sorry."

Dorothy laid a hand on her daughter's arm. "Don't worry. It would be wonderful if a heavenly foot came down from the sky and crushed me right here and now."

Heather drew back with shock on her face. "What? No. What are you saying?"

Dorothy leaned into her daughter and chuckled. Heather's expression went from astonishment to awe, then broke into a matching smile. Within seconds, both were howling with laughter.

As the giddy couple doubled over, Guy rushed to bolster his wife. Heather had sunk to her knees in a fit of hilarity. Without any pretense, the infectious nature of laughing and the mysterious, unexpected phenomenon of a contact high broadsided his reverie, and he couldn't contain the moment. He snorted, then erupted in a belly laugh like he hadn't had in many months.

For a full minute, the trio roared together. But then some movement across the street caught Guy's attention, and his mirth dried right up. *Shit. There's dang Izetta again.* He whirled his body away, pretending not to notice the neighbor's emergence from her side yard. He could feel the woman's eyes on the back of his head, stickier than suction cups. *We're silly exposed out here, damn it.*

He seized Dorothy's arm and steered her toward the house. "Sandbox time is over. We should go inside now," he said, peeking behind him. Mrs. Tooney stood amid his tire tracks from earlier in the week with a flat of industrial-grade petunias in one hand and a shovel in the other. She frowned and twitched her nose in their direction, looking hungry for drama.

"Tea would be fine," Dorothy said. She took a faltering step. "I'm getting tired."

"I feel fantastic, Papa. You go on," Heather said in a faraway, glassy voice.

Guy cringed at the idea of abandoning his daughter to the harsh judgment of the world, but one look at her blissed-out face, and he chose to let her be.

"Let's get you back to the mother ship, shall we?" he said to Dorothy.

Within minutes, he had two cups of steaming chamomile tea sitting on the kitchen table.

"What's for dinner?" Dorothy said, her face beaming with expectation.

"Well, it's still a bit early. You're hungry, though, huh?" Guy scratched his head. Dorothy seldom expressed a desire to eat in the afternoon. "I could come up with something." He combed through the refrigerator and cupboards while she examined a saltshaker.

———

Dominga stood at the garage side door, dangling a dust-packed vacuum bag over a garbage bin, her fierce glare sweeping the yard. *Algo está pasando. Something is going on.* She had known and cared about the Pickering women for over ten years and considered Heather a worthy daughter, but never had she seen her act *tan estúpida*. For an hour, the leather-tough Guatemalan had stared in disbelief as Heather paraded around the lawn in her outlandish outfit, gathering snails and then delivering them one by one to safety.

"*Mujeres locas.*" Dominga scowled as the sooty vacuum bag thumped to the bottom of the trash can.

Heather now sat cross-legged, serene as a statue, in the center of the flower bed.

Dominga's ever-aware scrutiny landed on the plump lady from across the street who kept pretending to work while staring at Heather over the top of her sunglasses. She knew this woman. She'd once tried to have Dominga's old car towed away because it had stayed overnight on the street when the battery died. Forgiveness from Dominga was rare, and ever since then, she had carried a smoldering coal of resentment for the neighbor.

Today, the rotund gringa marched around her property, paying way too much attention to the activity in the Pickering yard. *Hembra curiosa. What business is it of hers?* Dominga tensed and balled her fists as she watched the woman rise from her petunia patch, slap the dirt from her knees, and start toward the unfortunate and unprotected Pickering daughter. Heather's head, poking just above the hibiscus bushes, faced away from the street. iPod wires hung from her ears.

Dominga glowered at her as the woman tiptoed over the pavement and zeroed in on Heather—a human island amid a sea of flowers. A generations-deep instinct to protect her own kicked in. *Not today, chucha.* She raced across the lawn, reminiscent of a guard dog, and positioned herself on the sidewalk, hands on her hips, three feet in front of the gringa intruder.

An ashen-faced Mrs. Tooney stopped dead with one foot on the curb, like someone who's rammed into a stop sign.

"What you want, fat bitch?"

The glaring brown eyes and words punched with the power of a fist. The neighbor stuttered and staggered backward a step into the street. She opened her mouth to say something, but nothing came out. Dominga finished her off with the back of her hand in a sharp upward slice—an unmistakable wave of banishment. The ashen-faced woman reeled and trotted back to the safety of her own door, not pausing to pick up her tools from the petunia bed.

Dominga didn't move an inch until the woman had disappeared inside her house, then, with utmost care, picked her way through the flower garden to Heather's side. She stood beside the pretty but damaged daughter for a minute and watched the beaming face and arms sweeping high overhead, then lowering to her sides in a slow, graceful arc.

Reassured that the girl was safe enough, Dominga wrung her hands, muttered a brief Mayan prayer, and ambled off to resume her chores.

———

Back in the kitchen, Guy ladled the last spoonful of chicken noodle soup into two bowls, pleased that Dorothy had already finished one portion. *It's nice having this quiet meal*—just the two of them, like they had done countless times. The only sound was the refrigerator's hum.

As if lured by the mechanical drone, he rose and snatched a beer from inside the door, but before he could open it, Dominga barged into the kitchen. Ignoring Guy, she marched directly over to Doro-thy, pulled a well-used plastic brush from the bag tied at her hip, and stroked it through the older woman's hair with the precision and care of a dutiful loved one while murmuring what sounded akin to an urgent storm warning.

Dorothy purred with pleasure and held still as Dominga contin-ued muttering in a dialect that Guy couldn't begin to understand, though the tone was darn clear to him.

He popped the tab on his beer can—the noise sounding outsized in the still room. Dominga froze him with a burrowing stare, frosting the hairs on his neck. He lowered his chin and raised the beer one inch in her direction as an apology. "*Gracias, señora.* Here's to your shining spirit."

Before she could respond, Heather glided by the window with half-lidded eyes fixed on the backyard. The tails of a yellow scarf, à la headband, bobbed up and down in rhythm with her snapping fingers.

Alex strolled into the kitchen and pointed at Heather. "Man, she's in the zone." He pulled a Pepsi from the refrigerator, yawned, scratched his armpit, strode over to the table, and plopped into a seat. "How's Grandma?" He grinned with a confidence likely derived from his newfound usefulness to the family.

Dominga's brush froze midstroke, and an immediate silence fell upon the kitchen. Under her glare, Alex rose and took a tentative step backward. "I'll go, um, to the den." He retreated down the hallway, only glancing back.

Dorothy's eyelids grew heavy. She shifted in her seat, winced, and pushed away the unfinished bowl of cold soup. Time for rest.

Guy helped Dorothy up from her chair and guided her up the stairs to the sanctuary of their bedroom. He had just settled her on the bed and sat on the edge when he heard Richard's voice call out from downstairs.

"Hello? Heather? Guy? Anybody home?"

Guy frowned. "I should go and run interference."

She reached out to him. "Stay for a minute, will you?"

He softened and took her hand. "Of course I will."

No doubt Heather still hovered in the zone. She had quite naturally transformed into a late-blooming flower child and drifted to the backyard far corner. She swooned with joy at finding a special private dais: the flattened garage door. After grabbing two lawn chair cushions and tossing them onto the ready-made deck, she settled in to enjoy the sun and her unprecedented journey of music and visions. With a quick check of the premises and gauging adequate privacy from the outside world, she felt drawn to enhance her absorption of the life-giving solar rays by taking off her top. The bountiful daisy bush just a few feet away had offered a couple of bright yellow floral pasties that covered her nipples. Now she lay on her back, eyes shut, hips bumping and grooving, her arms waving to Ra the Sun God while Sly and the Family Stone blasted in her ears. Her reality had detoured.

———

"Boys, did you find your mother?" Richard yelled from the porch stairs. He thought he could hear them whimpering from somewhere near the backyard fence and strode over to where they were standing.

The younger one stood with his fists bunched up to his mouth, shifting from foot to foot. He and the older one gawked at the person laid out before them who resembled their mother. "Mom . . . Mommy?"

With ecstatic sounds and visions dancing in her head, a writhing Heather belted out the chorus to Sly and the Family Stone's "Dance to the music."

"What the . . ." Richard's jaw flew open in a spontaneous mouth spasm as he grabbed both boys.

Heather didn't hear him, but Guy, Alex, and Dominga did, and they all burst through the doorway.

"Heather!" Richard tried to shove his two sons behind him. "Boys, get in the car right now!" He turned and flicked a finger toward their SUV. They didn't budge and continued hitting each other, fighting for a view from around their father's body.

Alex ran up and perched atop the deer mound. Guy followed, along with Dominga, her broom still in hand. Heather was belting out an off-key harmony to a song no one else heard. The group froze for a few seconds, gape-mouthed in agonized fascination, as if witnessing a family heirloom slip overboard and sink into dark waters. Alex was the only one grinning.

"Heather!" Richard's face bulged.

This time, sheer volume worked. Her eyes fluttered open, and for a moment, she lay motionless, returning to third-dimensional reality.

"Richard?" She pivoted her head toward the unexpected voices.

"Heather?" Richard gaped at his wife.

Bit by bit, her torso rose from the garage door like the slow ascent of a plant seeking sun. Her eyes widened, resembling landing lights on an approaching airliner. She blinked three times at her dumbstruck family, then screamed and snapped her arms around her bare breasts.

Instantly, Dominga thrust the broom into the air, and with the ferocity of a warrior and the grace of an Olympic fencer, she swung it in a menacing arc over her head. "*Vamos, hombres!*"

The stout defender of women stepped forward, slashing the broom like a mighty sword, forcing all the males to scramble away. Richard tried to herd the boys in retreat.

Daisies flew as Heather yanked her ear pods free and grabbed her blouse. She wobbled and struggled to get up on one knee, covering as much of herself as she could. Lowering her head and mimicking an NFL running back, she wove her way through the crowd in a dash to the house with scarves and blouse sleeves trailing behind.

<hr>

Guy and Richard stood in awkward silence on the front porch, and Guy realized that with the show over, he was now the scene spokesman. He sidled up to his son-in-law. "Hey there, Richard, how was work today?" he said while nodding and smiling in a Hail Mary pass effort to bring reassurance.

Richard only glared.

Guy sped up the explanation. "We were watching TV, and it said marijuana would help Dorothy. And then Heather, well—"

"Somebody on TV tells you to get my wife and Dorothy stoned, and you just go ahead and do it? What the hell were you thinking?" He gestured to his kids. "What am I supposed to tell them?"

"What can I say? It was pretty good stuff, I guess. Let's sit down. I'll explain everything."

"I don't think so, Guy, not today." Richard shook his head. "No, I will be getting Heather home now." He marched over to the screen door and yelled through the mesh, "I will be in the car, Heather!" He spun on his heel, and goading his boys in front of him, he strode across the lawn to the leather and metal cocoon of his own SUV.

Guy headed back inside, where a reassembled Heather emerged from the downstairs bathroom.

He put an arm around her. "Wow. Must have been that third brownie."

Heather's expression mixed amusement with embarrassment.

Guy pointed a finger toward the driveway. "I don't suppose *he* thinks our little experiment is very funny."

She blinked up at her dad and broke into an apologetic grin.

"That's better," Guy chuckled.

"Tell Mom I love her, and . . . despite me being so silly, I'm not sorry we did this. I hope it helped her." Heather ducked out the door. Ignoring her own minivan parked to one side, she beelined straight for the SUV and dove through the open passenger door. Richard didn't look at his wife before punching the car into gear and speeding down the street. As they drove away, Guy got a glimpse of Heather huddled in the front seat, head down behind Ray-Bans and a smile still tugging at the corners of her mouth.

I'm not sorry either, Heather. It was great to see you bust out of the ordinary. He watched the SUV fade into the distance. *So sorry about tomorrow's shock.*

Seconds later, Dominga banged out of the kitchen and arranged herself into position on the front porch, arms crossed like belts of bullets. Her laser glare could have burned a hole in Guy's forehead.

Over Dominga's shoulder, Alex's nervous face peered out from behind a window curtain.

Guy cleared his throat and flashed a sheepish grin. *Maybe Alex and I should get out of here for a while.*

Sometimes, the pot just boils over.

"Dominga? We go for groceries, *sí*?" Guy made a slight gesture toward Alex, standing in the kitchen doorway. "Dorothy is sleeping. Keep an eye on her. Yes?" He remained a respectful distance from the simmering woman.

"*Váyanse ahora!*" She gave an almost imperceptible nod and flicked her fingers at the Oldsmobile—a clear dismissal if Guy had ever seen one.

He motioned for Alex to follow him, and they darted down the steps two at a time.

In minutes, they were accelerating onto Highway 42 in the dented Olds. The road signs promised Orlando in a flat, open ten miles.

As Guy eased into traffic, Alex looked toward the rear, drawn to the loose trunk lid's peculiar chatter.

He waved off any concern from his grandson. "It's nothing! Don't worry."

"Okay, no problem," Alex shrugged. He clasped his arms and rocked forward in the seat, a contained expression on his face.

Guy studied his passenger. "You got something to say?"

"Oh, I could say a few things. But let's start with Richard was kind of a dick, wasn't he?"

"Yeah, he can be that way."

Alex leaned back and looked over. "Did you see those kids run for the car? And Aunt Heather? She was ah . . ."

Guy swiveled and caught Alex's devilish raised eyebrow. "It's not funny!" he shouted above the wind.

Alex continued to look straight at his grandfather and held his breath. A snort escaped his lips.

Guy fought to keep from smiling. "I *said* we shouldn't laugh at this!"

"Of course, Grandpa, whatever you say." Alex bit his lip.

"Here we are at the supermarket already." Guy braked and swung into the shopping center.

The Save-Mart was busy as usual. Guy leaned his forearms against the shopping cart handle and frowned at the woman at the head of the checkout line. The impatient customer drummed her fingers on the card reader, waiting for her coupons to be validated.

"I like the way you shop, son. You remind me of myself. Get in, get the goods, and get out."

Alex peered into their cart. "Okay, but I don't see very many goods. Some frozen food, a case of beer, and a gallon of milk. This is not much, and I remember you said we're low on coffee."

Guy blanched. "By golly, you're right." He U-turned the cart and beelined for aisle four with Alex following.

Guy stopped, facing an elaborate gourmet coffee array, and stared at the selection for a minute, then poured a couple inches of beans from a bulk dispenser into a brown bag and chucked it on top of a frozen chicken pie.

Alex stared at the bag's meager quantity. "What's up with that? I drink it too, you know. That's less than a day-and-a-half supply, tops, man."

Guy peered at the limp paper sack as if seeing it for the first time. With any concern beyond tomorrow obliterated by his current plans, he had defaulted to routine practicality. *Oh crap. This looks off. The act goes on.* "You're right, Alex. Guess my mind's elsewhere." He snatched up the bag, returned it to the dispenser, and filled it to the brim. Alex's still-skeptical face evaluated the quantity, so Guy, grinning like a madman, filled another bag to overflowing and placed them in the cart like a peace offering at an altar.

"There's other stuff we're out of too."

"You're right again," Guy said. "We need more stuff. Whatever you want, toss it in." He scanned the opposite shelves and grabbed a familiar-looking bottle of vanilla extract. While beaming approval, he dropped it beside the beer.

They took off down the aisle, and within minutes, the cart was bulging with three boxes of cereal (one for Guy and Dorothy, two for Alex), a twelve-pack of D-cell batteries (Guy figured they seemed practical), a case of soda (all for Alex), assorted candies (Alex picked those), lunch meats, bread, sauces, more mayonnaise (all for more "picnics"), and a giant shrink-wrapped package of toilet paper.

"That should do it," Guy said, proud to have kept up his ruse. "Let's go."

———

The Olds's engine revved to three thousand rpm in quick successions as they sat idling at the intersection that fed to the only exit from the shopping center.

Guy chewed his lip and muttered under his breath, "Goddamn traffic gets worse every year." He raised his voice. "Guess what we're doing at this moment?" He swept his hand in an arc, pointing at the deep line of cars awaiting their turn to proceed. "We're waiting for a stupid electrical box to tell us when to go. You and I can plainly see there's no oncoming cars, and it's an easy decision for a few of us to just go." He tapped his fingers on the steering wheel. "Is this screwy or what? People should be allowed to leave when it makes sense."

"What are you talking about?" Alex raised the eyebrow again.

"I mean, we live by mindless rules, not what's needed to be done," Guy said. "It's a bunch of bull crap."

"That's crazy, Grandpa," Alex protested. "Even I know you can't just drive without rules."

Guy rubbed his temple. "I'm not talking about being reckless. I mean, at times, use your own judgment." The light turned green, and he zoomed past a large arrow with the letters EXIT THIS WAY. He jabbed a finger at the sign. "Yes. That's what I'm trying to do! The point is people have to get things done. Even if it's against some rules." He tapped his chin hard and looked over at his grandson. "Sorry."

The look Alex returned shouted, *You're crazy, old man.* But all he said was, "Whatever."

"Say, you hungry? Want to grab a burger? We've got enough time." Alex nodded. "Yeah, for sure."

A minute later, they pulled into a low-roofed, glass-fronted drive-in with a red sign announcing HAMBURGER HEAVEN in rust-tinged white letters. Guy loved this old place, which still had the same chrome-rimmed booths and vinyl bench seats Heather and Mitch had sat on during their high school days. Not much had changed since then, including the strange and now-iconic mural on the back wall: a life-sized angel resembling an image of Jesus munching a jumbo hamburger.

Today, six extremely modified cruiser motorcycles had positioned themselves in a wide arc near the entrance door. The only space available was a narrow slot next to a chopped Harley with ape-hanger bars and a chrome-plated shrunken skull mounted above the headlight.

Guy hesitated but inched his way up to the tire berm. He'd seen these same bikes around town before and sometimes scowled to himself at their exhaust pipes' ear-shattering volume. He shoved the car into park. "Let's go eat."

Inside the diner, a young woman eased by Guy and Alex's table. "Excuse me," she said as she ushered a child toward the door and flashed a terse smile at them—a nonverbal sign of condolence for those left behind. She and her kid had been beside the two booths filled by the six black-leather-and-denim-clad men who were overpowering all other conversations in the diner with their loud, profane banter. Guy's jaw tightened.

A sixty-something waitress appeared at their table and set their baskets of paper-wrapped burgers down. The woman suffered dark circles under her eyes, appearing like she just woke up from a binge. "Enjoy," she said in a flat monotone.

Guy swiveled his gaze to the woman's name tag. "Hold on there, Dolores. To be clear, you're *telling* me to eat this and like it. It's like you're insisting, right? What if I don't *want* to enjoy it, huh?" The words chilled the air while he drummed his fingers on the table. Dolores stood still with expressionless eyes trained on Guy.

Alex raised his hand. "Forgive my grandpa. He's a little wound up. It's been a weird few days."

She leaned forward, her long gray hair falling forward to form a tunnel around her face, and searched her teeth with a roving tongue while examining Guy, then straightened up. "They tell us to say it. What's your excuse?"

Guy peered up sideways at Dolores. "Sorry," he muttered.

Dolores limped off, and Guy stared at his meal as if conceding a fight. After a minute, he chomped into his hamburger with a fierce deliberateness. On the other side of the table, Alex concentrated on a local advertising handout while he ate, only daring to glance at Guy and the bikers.

Minutes later, all six of the leather-clad clan got up as one and paraded toward the door. They carried their self-importance like a set of hefty luggage. The group's largest member, a tall, heavyset man, bumped Guy's shoulder as he passed with no acknowledgment.

Guy thought about getting up and saying something, but he was supposed to go *with* Dorothy into the afterlife, not beat her there thanks to a few ruffians. Guy dropped the remnants of his burger into the paper-lined red plastic basket. "I'm done. You?"

Alex gave a thumbs-up while swallowing his last bite.

They headed toward the parking lot, where Guy noticed the rude biker who had bumped him straddling an oil-dripping '87 hardtail Harley parked beside the Olds's driver door. The man tied a bandana around his forehead while talking to a skin-and-bones, greasy-haired man wearing dark shades and no expression.

"I gotta say, man, that's low. Even for you, Tiny," the other man said.

"What am I supposed to do?" Tiny spat. "Put up with that shit? What a bitch. She had it comin'."

Guy stopped short at the Olds's front end and laid a hand on the left fender, gauging the tight squeeze into the driver's door. He had overheard the remarks, particularly the last one, and glared at the biker—perhaps a few seconds too long.

At the other end of the choppers arc, a mustachioed, lean, and muscular man with graying temples raised a gloved fist. All the bikes roared to life with a deafening, exhaust-filled thunder. Tiny took a last sip from a thirty-two-ounce plastic cup, extended it midway between himself and the Olds, and in a quasi-ceremonious gesture dropped the drink and ice straight to the pavement.

That did it. Guy had reached his limit. He couldn't contain his ire any longer, and his eyes narrowed into a Clint Eastwood–style squint. "Get in the car," he directed Alex. In three strides, he was bending over the offending trash. He picked up the cup with small pieces of parking lot flotsam stuck to the sides and held it out to Tiny. "I believe you dropped this."

Tiny cocked his head to one side, eyes darting back and forth between Guy and the cup. "What are you doing, you old fart?"

Guy didn't flinch. After the last few days, he was running on a different sort of energy, and all his angst came to rest on this overweight nitwit. He extended the cup out farther and shouted above the thundering exhaust. "Respect. Get some!"

Tiny reached between the handlebars and shut off his bike. One by one, the bikers silenced their engines. He swiped the cup from Guy's hand and hurled it down between them. It clattered on the pavement and rolled away.

Guy stood his ground and crossed his arms. "You know how young kids develop at all different rates and times? Some are just slower. Like you, probably. I'll bet it took extra time for you to learn how to wipe your ass."

"Why, you old bastard." Tiny's face turned a shade of beet red, and he churned his left leg in a frenzied search for his kickstand. The other five bikers broke out chuckling and snickering.

"Grandpa. Grandpa," Alex pleaded from the front seat. "Let's go. C'mon, we've got to get out of here!"

Guy realized his grandson was offering sound advice. He reached for the Olds's door handle just as Tiny sped around the tail of his bike and bumped his considerable girth up against Guy—the black leather tower smelling of grease and gasoline was at least four inches taller.

He grabbed Guy's shirt with one hand, the other a clenched fist. "You want to take that back, you son of a bitch?" He raised his fist higher.

Tiny and Guy both jerked upward as an immense, loud car horn blast startled everyone. Alex leaned on the center of the Olds's steering wheel for a few more seconds. Every person around the parking lot and most of the people behind Hamburger Heaven's grease-clouded windows gawked at the mounting face-off. He pawed the air. "Grandpa! Let's get the hell out of here!"

"Okay, okay. That's enough, Tiny." The order sliced through the tension. It was the man who had held up the glove. The sides of his long mustache led to his jawline, and he wore a cutoff vest that revealed tattoos of women, daggers, and a smiling elephant holding a baby. After swinging a leg off of his motorcycle, he strode over to the confrontation and stood, hands on hips, in front of the two.

"You heard him. He insulted me," Tiny said in a squeaky high voice.

"Let go of him," the man said while pulling his gloves off, one finger at a time. Tiny took his time but released his grip, and Guy fell back against the Olds. The man jabbed one of those fingers into Tiny's chest. "Damn it, your fat ego is twenty pounds heavier than you! You have to work on your issues, man, and those triggers. Losing your cool out in public puts us all in a bad light."

Tiny jerked and snorted.

"Besides . . ." the man spun around to Guy and studied him up and down. "I like this old dude. He's got some balls." The man broke into a huge grin and extended a hand. "They call me the Captain."

Tiny slumped and groaned.

Still taking shallow breaths, Guy reached out and shook. "The name's Guy Pickering." He motioned toward the front seat. "This is my grandson, Alex."

The Captain studied the two, then spun around to the assembled men and proclaimed, "Listen up." He waited until the others quit snickering and he had their full attention. "Mr. Pickering here brings up an important point. I wish to be welcomed back to this fine establishment. But if you animals can't mind your manners, it becomes difficult for me." A collective grumble and complaining circled among the bikers.

He peered into the Olds's bloody interior and gave a brief scan of the crumpled body work. He winked. "I don't want to know."

Guy grimaced and nodded.

The Captain lowered his voice. "Here's the deal. I can only keep these mongrels caged up for so long. I suggest you take your grandson's advice and leave. Now. Let's not meet up anytime soon. Shall we?"

"Yes, yes. I agree. Sorry for any misunderstanding. . . . We're leaving right now." Guy fumbled at the driver's door, opened it, eased behind the wheel, and had the engine started in an instant. Tiny studied every move with a malevolent sneer while the Olds backed out of the parking slot and sped onto the road.

They rode in silence for a full five minutes before Alex even looked over at his grandfather. He shook his head, sending an obvious message. A few miles later, the Olds whizzed past a single-story wood-shingled bar and grill featuring a tilted neon martini glass. Guy didn't notice it at all. His pouty face stared straight ahead, and never could he have imagined that inside were three people who would soon change the Pickerings' lives forever.

THE OUTSKIRTS OF ORLANDO
DINO'S STEAK HOUSE

*When a strange door opens, either enter
or run away, but always pray.*

Today, a sparse crowd attended Dino's happy hour as the three-songs-for-a-dollar jukebox in the background crooned Engelbert Humperdinck.

In the center of the main room, a handsome fifty-something Black man wearing a leather jacket emblazoned with flight patches huddled with two others at the horseshoe-shaped bar. Billy Bellams was a regular here and, like all the others in attendance, didn't know or care about a beat-up Oldsmobile speeding past on the highway. Indeed, he liked Dino's specifically because he and everyone could ignore the outside world.

But as he looked around this legendary hotspot, he couldn't help but notice the stained countertops, a patched window, the holes in several cushions, and the moping teenager he didn't recognize list-lessly sweeping the floor. He missed old Dino, who had died the year before, and chuckled to himself as he remembered the old man's slogan: "Folks here want beef, strong drinks, big bosoms, and another chance."

His view turned back to his companions. In the middle of their group, Lisa Marie, looking like an estrogen factory perched upon high heels, held an oversized margarita. She shook her head and raised her hands, gesturing complete bafflement. "I mean, what's up with that old Bernie, anyway? He's always telling those corny jokes about traffic and stuff." She sipped her drink. "He's got seniority, but I can do better than him. I know it."

She glanced to her left, where a crooked-toothed smile and a face wearing the eagerness of an overzealous Labrador retriever gazed back at her. "Oh yeah. Of course you can," Dirk Rainey gushed. With his hawkish nose and the bent stature of someone accustomed to apologizing for his six-foot, six-inch height, Dirk curved over his drink of choice, root beer, and leaned in as close to Lisa Marie as the rules of social decency allowed.

"Dirk! Would you stop that?" Lisa Marie pushed him away and tugged inward on the edges of her blouse. Turning her attention back to the future, she gazed into her half-empty glass. "I can't be a screwy traffic reporter forever, flying around, looking down at cars all day." She flicked her finger upward and swiveled to her right. "There's a whole bunch of satellites that are going to replace us real soon. No need for chattering away in a helicopter. No offense to your job, Billy."

Billy stroked his three-day-old stubble and tilted back his bottle of Bud Light. "None taken. I'm just the chauffeur. But you're right about being replaced. I hope they'll find other jobs for me and my chopper." He didn't blame Lisa Marie for wanting more. But at fifty-eight, having survived a dozen years of crop dusting, bush piloting, a tumultuous marriage, and a hasty discharge from the Army after punching his commanding officer during a drunken, heated defense of the New York Yankees, he was more than happy to have a steady job as WFYU's helicopter pilot.

Single for six years, he often wondered if his lack of attraction to white women had something to do with his present company. He contemplated his companion.

With long jet-black hair falling straight down between her shoulders, any day of the week, Lisa Marie was damn sexy. The combination of striking good looks and generous cup size always provided an unending stream of suitors. But Billy had watched her dismiss most of these men, their fantasies, and persistent stares in the casual manner of a horse's tail swishing away flies. Except as a plaything, she did not seem to actually want a man.

Billy figured other fantasies engaged her imagination and nagged her unfulfilled ego. He suspected that she wanted to be on the cover of a magazine, to give an autograph, to have people she didn't even know fawn over her daily life.

"Someday, I want to be a real reporter for the news," Lisa Marie said. "And other stuff that's newsy."

Though he had zero interest in her romantically, Billy fostered a begrudging fondness for this woman and thus indulged her particular mix of exaggerated veneer and fanciful expectation. Besides, he had learned the hard way not to disagree with the women in his life. "You could be a reporter. It's bound to happen sooner or later. Could be any day, really," he said.

Dirk seldom contained himself around her. "You're the best, Lisa Marie. You can do anything. You'll always be the best." Dirk panted out the praise. Billy knew his fascination with her ran deep.

"Wipe that silly grin off your face, will ya?" Lisa Marie shot a scolding glance at Dirk, who tried but couldn't comply.

Lisa Marie touched Billy's shoulder. "Don't take this personally."

"I won't. Don't worry."

"But I want something better than the helicopter thing for myself." She folded her hands over her heart. "Like I've told you before—"

"Yes, you've told me before," Billy nodded with eyes rolled to the ceiling. After one margarita, no one could stop her.

"Our family lived in the dirt-poor part of town, and my friends— and most of my mom and dad's friends—were Black and poor, and we were all poor together."

"Uh-huh, I know. And us Black folks were just as good." Billy hurried the conversation along.

"They taught me our playmates were just as good as us." Lisa Marie flashed a genuine smile at her friend.

"That's what they call me, 'Billy Just-as-Good Bellams.'" He grinned and took a swig of beer. "It sounds like your parents were decent people. That's better than a whole lot of others. My ma always said, 'There's blood, and there's turnips, and there's white folks. Don't be expectin' more.'"

"Thank you, Billy. That means a lot to me."

"And I see you're itching to climb that ladder, and I hope you get a chance. That would be fun to watch." Billy threw back the last of his beer.

"Aren't I pretty enough?"

"Of course you are," Dirk burst out.

"I can talk into a camera, like all the others, can't I?"

"I've seen you do it," Billy said.

"Aren't I . . ?" She paused. "I just need a break. A story that gets me noticed. You wait. Something's going to come up, and someday, I'll be famous."

"Stranger things've happened." Billy was losing interest; it was time to pack it in. He rose from the barstool. "Dirk, you've had enough kiddie sauce, and Lisa Marie and I have to work tomorrow. I'll give you a lift back to the airport. Lisa Marie, you want a ride home?"

Lisa Marie scanned the bar, where at the far end, a small group of silver-haired conventioneers were yucking it up and glancing her way. "No, I'll be all right." She raised her eyebrows at Billy. "See you in the morning."

"A word to the wise: The stocky guy with short gray hair sitting over there to your left—no, don't look," Billy whispered in Lisa Marie's ear. "He's nervous and been trying hard not to be noticed, big time. I'm sure as soon as we leave, he'll be over here. Be careful."

"Thank you, but I can take care of myself." Lisa Marie gave him a coy grin and twirled a lock of hair around her finger.

Billy nodded, and with Dirk in tow, they pushed out the front door into the evening dusk.

While Lisa Marie fished deep in her purse for a lipstick, the same stocky individual Billy had warned her about materialized in the seat beside her.

"Whoa!" she said, leaning away from him. "That was quick. You hard up or what?"

The man shushed her through his teeth while staring straight ahead. He tapped a cigarette out of a pack, flicked a lighter to the tip, and blew out a forceful smoke cloud.

Lisa Marie chuckled, "Well, this should be good. My friend Billy told me you'd be over here."

"Shh! We've got to keep this quiet." He glanced around the room. "The Black dude, correct? He's ex-military, for sure. I can spot 'em a mile away. Listen, I don't have much time."

"Neither do I, so you're still in the game. Let's move on to who the hell are you?" Lisa Marie studied her new companion. He appeared scrubbed clean, taut as a barbed wire fence with a scar above his left eye.

"I've seen you on television," he said. "You're a reporter, right?"

That word, that very important word, kissed her ears. She swiveled and regarded this person with renewed interest. "Yes, I am Lisa

Marie, and I'm only doing the traffic stuff while waiting for my preferred position to open up, and when it does—"

"Cut it!" For the first time since he'd sat down, he looked Lisa Marie in the eye. "I've been beating my brains out about how to get my story out. I am not acquainted with any reporters, but if you're interested, I've got a real scoop."

"A real one, huh?" she said, and spun to better inspect him. "Look, mister, just because I have a pretty face doesn't mean I'm not smart. I'll give you original, but that's still a lame pickup line."

"I'm not interested in that, Dollface. Pay attention. I don't believe in hocus-pocus crap, but when you walked in, it struck me. Maybe this was meant to happen. Some kind of lucky fluke thing." He placed both palms on the counter. "I've written a total exposé of the United States military complex. A systematic outline of the outrageous prejudicial treatment of its own officers. This is going to bring the armed forces to its knees." The man grinned and bobbed his head.

"I'm thinking that doesn't sound very nice," Lisa Marie drew out the words.

The man groaned. "You're not supposed to think! I do not expect you to decipher this stuff. All I need you for is to be a messenger. Take it to your boss. I assume he's a man with news experience. He'll understand and see the importance. I want this to make its big splash before my retirement, and I'm almost out of time. When I'm free, which will be soon, I'll come forward and take the glory and the heat. It's my task and my destiny." The man paused, and his eyes wandered off. "Nevertheless, I need someone with media connections." His words popped rapid gunfire. He swiveled his chair and scrutinized Lisa Marie. "You want to be a part of history?"

Lisa Marie looked doubtful. "Maybe." She drummed her fingernails on the counter. "I have no idea who you are. How do I know you're not just a nutcase?"

The man dropped his jaw. "I'll have you know . . . oh, never mind. I can't disclose my entire identity while I'm still on duty. That will come soon. Call me Mr. X in the meantime. Your role is critical to the unmasking." He stubbed out his cigarette, leaning in with a lowered voice. "Are you the one?"

The one? These words did have a definite tickling effect on her imagination. "Okay, okay. I'll have my boss check it out."

Mr. X reached into an inside breast pocket, pulled out a bulging envelope, and pushed it across the counter. "Here's a summary and a list of key details in the report. There's plenty more. My private number is on top. Give me your cell phone number."

Lisa Marie studied the packet as if it were a lump of losing lottery tickets. "I don't give that out to just anybody."

"I'm not just anybody. If you're serious about doing more than traffic reports, I'm handing you your shot on a silver platter." He waited while she rolled her eyes and scribbled her number on a cocktail napkin. Without another word, he shot up next to his seat, placed aviator reflective sunglasses on his face, and bent closer. He whispered, "We'll stay in touch. Let me know when this will hit."

She watched in fascination as Mr. X squinted in all directions before beelining to the exit doors. After he disappeared from view, she sat motionless for a minute, tapping her chin, then dug out her cell phone and dialed.

"Hey, Ted, as you know, I've been wanting to scoop a story. This guy I met might have handed one to me. Kind of a weirdo, but he just might be the real deal. I'm not sure. I thought about throwing this envelope into the trash, but just in case, I'll drop the papers off on your desk."

***

Outside Dino's, Colonel Lance Hooper marched across the parking lot and slipped into his government-issued Ford sedan. Twenty minutes later, he pulled up to the well-fortified entrance of a nondescript military residential complex.

After peering into the sedan's interior, the stern-faced guard saluted and lifted the gate. "Welcome back, Colonel Hooper."

Hooper gave a lazy salute in return and gassed the Ford forward. "I like the Mr. X name," he mused aloud. "It gives me a bit of mystery."

After parking the sedan, he climbed the stairs to an unadorned second-story apartment, where a miniature furry dog greeted him with spinning, barking, and wagging. "Jack! Calm down. It's nice to see you too."

He beelined over to a cupboard, pulled out a bottle, and poured himself a generous shot of bourbon. After plopping in one ice cube, he settled onto his sofa and lit a cigarette. Jack at once jumped into his lap.

"I met a reporter today, Jack. I handed the exposé synopsis over to her." Jack held still and stared back at Hooper. "Don't be so quick to judge me. Yeah, she's a woman, but sometimes, you've got to take a chance. Do I need to remind you this is a goddamn conspiracy? I've got to get this out before my last week is up, and I'm running out of time!"

Jack whined in response.

Hooper studied his cigarette. "And you'll be pleased to hear, as I promised you, I'm going to quit smoking. Not today, but tomorrow."

A knock on the front door interrupted his thoughts. He tiptoed over to the shade-covered window next to the entrance and parted the curtain one inch. Outside, a young soldier stood at attention.

"Oh, for Christ's sake." Hooper opened the door.

"Colonel Hooper, sir!" The cadet snapped a salute. "Your mail, sir!" He stiff-armed two envelopes forward, his stare fixated on the no-eye-contact zone.

"At ease, soldier. How many times have I said I can walk the flight of steps to collect my own mail?"

"Yes, sir! Will that be all?"

"Dismissed," Hooper groaned. He watched the young soldier high-step down the stairs and dive into an Army jeep.

"You see, Jack? Perfect example! Nowadays, our military has nothing better to do than run around in circles, always practicing meaningless procedures and tasks, but still finding time to harass real men like me. *God, I loved Iraq. Blowing shit up every day. That is until the she-wolf Monica ruined everything.* He took a gulp of bourbon. *Unfortunately, I'll be finishing out my assignment without any real action.* "Damn shame for a man of my caliber," he shouted. "What we need is to get out there and kick butt in the world, right?"

Jack leaped over to the window, slipped under the curtain, stood on his hind legs, and did his own survey of how wrong it was out there.

It's never too late to dance under the stars.

Dusk had arrived at Willowside Road. In the upstairs bedroom, Guy bolted upright in a chair, trying to grasp what had awoken him. In his dream—the sound of a struggling wood saw. Dorothy's snoring filled the room. He yawned, stretched, and leaned forward. She lay on her back, mouth gaping open. *She's all right for now. I'll check on things downstairs.*

A half dozen Chinese food containers had arrived while Guy was napping—double the usual order now that Guy fed a growing teenager. The chef-owner of the Wok Man had quit asking for the Pickering address a couple of months ago.

Guy prepared one delicate portioned plate and set it aside before he and Alex ate their portions in silence. Alex offered to do the dishes, and a grateful Guy ascended the steps, once again hoping Dorothy would eat.

She nibbled, sighed, grimaced, and downed a small portion while

Guy praised each bite until she pushed the food away, unwilling to try anymore.

He set the plate down on the nightstand, then picked up a gold-framed picture of Heather, Richard, and their two boys. He rubbed the dust from the flat glass, remembering that the photo had started out as a Christmas card—four merry faces sitting around a fireplace hearth. *Heather's such a good person. What a wonderful spirit.*

Another picture of Mitch, Sharon, and Alex caught his eye, taken years ago at Disney World. Only Mitch smiled at the camera. *I could have done something different with him.* From his internal island, Guy sent his entire family a blessing.

An evening breeze blew through the screen, and the gathering darkness beckoned from beyond the confines of the house. He sat mesmerized, gazing past the fluttering curtain.

"I kept saying 'the best is yet to come.' Ha! I said that for years. Hell, I said it not too long ago. Damn carrot out there looks so tasty. I didn't pay attention to little stuff . . . ordinary everyday life. I see it now." Guy sighed. "We just got dealt a bad hand here at the end, and we're out of time." He buried his face in his hands. The Beechcraft Bonanza appeared in his mind. Hope on the horizon. "We had a good run though, didn't we?" he said in his soft, deep voice. "I'm truly grateful for that."

Dorothy coughed. "Yeah, but now we're all moth-eaten."

He straightened up, considering her words with a wry smirk. "You're right, but . . ." He drew a breath and crossed his arms. "The day's not over, and I'm not beat yet." He rose and parted the thin drape, revealing dusk's shadows and the familiar sidewalk while the streetlight's buzzing halide bulbs blinked into life. He broke out into a crooked, determined smile. "Remember our after-dinner walks?"

Dorothy pursed her lips at him. 'Course I do. I'm not that far gone!"

He clapped his hands together. "Fresh air would be just the ticket. Baby doll, we're going for a stroll."

Ten minutes later, Guy guided Dorothy past Alex—asleep on the couch, looking like a fallen angel—and out to the driveway. He ducked into the garage and returned, guiding the rented wheelchair.

She screwed up her face in distaste. "I hate those things. Makes me look old and sick."

"Then think of yourself as an old and sick important person rolling down a promenade." He crossed his fingers.

Dorothy squinted down the murky street and huffed a sigh. "All right."

"Okay, then. We're off. A little adventure before our everlasting final one."

With no specific destination in his thoughts and a blossoming interest in the present moment, Guy wheeled the chair past house after house, pausing at each corner and choosing the route with which he was less familiar. By the fourth block, his bruised knee was beginning to ache, but onward he pushed.

The clicking of wheels over sidewalk cracks, the soft breeze, the muted lights from behind drawn shades, the steady rhythm of his tennis shoes on concrete, the balmy Florida evening against his skin—Guy embraced these sensations, experiencing them as fresh and losing his sense of self. He stopped in front of a darkened house with a FOR SALE sign and sun-yellowed newspapers scattered on the lawn. The sight broke into his reverie. *I suppose our place will look similar.*

This impromptu journey, deliberate as it was, began to take on an outsized importance. He didn't want to stare for long; instead, he listened. Each home they passed revealed, for a few seconds, a unique story—a living diorama. Laughter in one—the next, abrasive with sharp quarreling—another, only blaring television commercials.

"We're all so isolated in our own little lives. It's a shame it works that way. Why haven't I at least met these people?" Guy posed the question to a silent sky.

Dorothy craned her neck around to see his face. "Probably because they don't drink beer."

He turned right at the next corner, heading down a lane marked DEAD END. *Well, that fits, doesn't it?* The furthest residence on the cul-de-sac had scattered bright multicolored plastic toys and an upturned tricycle lying amid the fallen leaves. It was dimmer here, only the pale glow from windows and patio lights. Overhead, the trees obscured most of the stars, except between a gap in the overhanging limbs, where a half-moon shone.

A wailing cry, protesting the unacceptable fate of having to go to bed, came from behind a tall hedge. Guy maneuvered Dorothy's chair a few steps until they were near the driveway entrance. A pickup truck with a construction company logo on the door blocked a full view, but over the hood, he saw a young mother and child rocking in a swing set on the front porch. She stroked her child's head and murmured a song into the child's ear.

"Remember all the trouble with Mitch at bedtime?" he asked. "That boy never wanted to go to bed."

Dorothy stirred in the wheelchair and wiped her eyes. "I remember."

"You're crying. What's wrong, honey?" A stunned Guy dropped down to his good knee to stare into her eyes. She couldn't meet his gaze.

"I'm scared about dying. It's stupid of me to say. Especially after asking for it. But . . . I thought things would be different," she spoke between soft sobs.

"None of this is fair," Guy's voice trembled.

She at last looked into his face. "I recall that passage in our vows: *Till death do us part.* I always wondered about that. Will we be together? Afterward, I mean."

"I think so. I hope so."

"You don't sound very convinced."

Guy bit his lip. "The truth is nobody knows for sure. But I'm sure I want to be with you now, and at the end. Or the beginning, whatever it turns out to be."

Dorothy sat in silence for a moment. "It's my time. But you . . ." her voice trembled. "You're supposed to hang around and remember me. Be sad, sing my praises and all that." She blew her nose in a tissue.

Guy blinked back a tear and the urge to confess his deception.

She cleared her throat. "We're both old and sick enough. I guess we're doing this."

"Yes. We are." He let out a sigh of relief.

"What are you going to do?"

He hesitated, unsure about sharing his plan. "I'll tell you soon. Just trust me."

She patted his hand. "Always have. So, what are we doing here, staring like stalkers at these folks?"

Guy chuckled. "All right, let's go home." He spun the wheelchair around and started back.

A block later, he scanned the street's pavement and judged it a smoother path than the buckled sidewalk for a wheelchair. There had been no traffic; moving to the street seemed safe.

The sleek, lowered Nissan sedan came out of nowhere. Guy heard the escalating engine whine and jerked his head around, squinting into the fast-approaching high beams. He tripped, losing his grip on the wheelchair's handles, and landed on his hands and knees. Dorothy wheeled away, stopping only after bumping into the door of a nearby parked car. The Nissan screeched to a halt with blue rubber smoke from the tires and exhaust wafting across the headlight's beam. The driver sounded a long angry horn. Guy struggled to his feet, cursing and shielding his eyes, and rushed over to the wheelchair, hobbling on his knee, even more bruised than before. The driver took advantage of the clear path and, with another tire-spinning squeal, lurched forward, veering past the two elders.

"Goddamn punk!" Guy shook his fist at the receding taillights. "Dorothy, are you okay?"

She clung to the armrests—her mouth held in a tight-lipped grimace. She looked up at him and nodded.

"I'm sorry, honey. Damn kid." He laid a hand on her shoulder. "My fault. Let's get you out of the road." He pulled the chair back and guided it across the sidewalk and into the driveway of the nearest house. "Why don't we sit for a minute?" His legs and hands trembled as he lowered himself onto a short brick wall that marked the entrance to the residence.

"Christ almighty. You can't even walk around here anymore!"

"For a second, I thought you hired someone as part of your new genius plan," Dorothy said.

Guy stuck his tongue out at her.

At last, his pulse returned to normal, and he swiveled to face the house. *I didn't recognize it at first. This is Frank Hancock's place.* Surprised to feel a twinge of resentment in his gut, he couldn't quite remember why he felt this way. "Oh, that's it," he muttered, "the stupid weed trimmer." Long ago, Guy loaned Frank the tool and waited for it to be returned. He asked about it once when they ran into each other at a local hardware store, but Frank did not get back to him. From then on, he avoided Frank, and their fledgling friendship never recovered. "What a shame." He observed Frank's hunched figure shuffle behind the muted curtains in a living room window. "I rather liked the man. I think he wanted to repair it and then just forgot."

From a wicker basket sitting on the porch, a collie sniffed the air and contemplated the two arrivals in her driveway. She got up on all fours and limped across the pavement toward the visitors, her tail wagging a welcome. The dog ambled up to the foot of the wheelchair, leaned forward, and ran her nose up the length of Dorothy's leg. The tail stopped.

Guy reached down and stroked the dog's head. "I remember you. Your name is Betsy. Tell Frank I said hi. Okay, old gal?"

He stood and resumed his station behind Dorothy.

Despite the cracked surface, Guy stayed on the sidewalk, rolling along at a careful pace the entire way home.

Dorothy slumped to one side of the chair, sound asleep as they arrived at the front steps. Guy stopped and listened. The far-off traffic hum from town, the buzzing insects, the chirping birds, a television show's jingle, the bark of an unseen dog—it all blended into a perfect symphony.

Guy leaned close to her ear. "Time for bed, sweetie. Tomorrow, there's a sunset like no other." He straightened up and felt the knot in his stomach. *Dying is the goal. The only marker of success. Crazy.*

25

FLORIDA

DECEMBER 1999

*What mysterious glue keeps
families sticking together?*

"C'mon, Dad, it's millennium New Year's. This one's a big deal. You know, Y2K. The entire world is going to crash," Mitch Pickering chuckled into the phone. "Wouldn't it be great for the whole family to be together? Besides, we haven't been camping in forever."

Guy searched for excuses. "Listen, son, we've never been the camping sort. We don't have any equipment or anything."

"Leave it to me, Pops," Mitch said in his smoothest voice. "I'll take care of everything. Hey, sorry, but I have to run. Talk to ya later. Bye."

"What's got into that boy?" Guy returned the phone to the cradle and muttered to Dorothy. "We haven't heard from him for three months, and all of a sudden, he wants to throw us in the woods up in Okefenokee on New Year's Eve." Guy shot an arm out, pointing north. "Remember when we drove through there? Big dank swamp, that's what it is."

"We should go," Dorothy said at once. "Why not? Yes, we're not real campers, but we can do it. We're sixty-eight years old, and how many more chances do we get with the family? I'll bet that's what Mitch is thinking."

"Nah, it was some other lawyer in his office that got his pants all afire." Guy rolled his eyes. "Told him he had this hard-to-get camping reservation for the millennium New Year's Eve and now he can't go. Dorothy, there are snakes and alligators up there, and God knows what else. What about little Alex?" He tilted his head toward her and stared for emphasis.

Dorothy sat in her chair, arms crossed, and stared back at her husband.

Guy made one last attempt. "And remember, Heather's pregnant." He folded and refolded the kitchen towel. Dorothy continued her silent, passive observation. Bunching it up, he threw it on the counter. "Oh, all right." He looked out the window, fretting about what might go wrong.

Twelve days later, under scattered clouds, an uncertain and reluctant two-thirds of the Pickering family waited at Guy and Dorothy's house. Studying their faces, Guy could see apprehensive hopes that ranged from magnificent fun to mere survival. Guy rummaged through the garage for extra batteries while Richard sulked in the driveway.

A horn blasted away the silence. Guy jolted to attention and scurried down the driveway where Richard stood, gawking at a giant glossy thirty-six-foot-long RV bus rolling up to the curb. The brakes gave off a final *chuff* as it rocked to a halt. From behind the wheel, Mitch honked three more times, grinning from ear to ear. Richard covered his own. Dorothy peered from the front porch and commented about a stylish, painted toaster.

Guy and Richard approached the camper just as the side door opened with a *whoosh* and Mitch swung out, hanging onto the massive rearview mirror.

Richard frowned at his brother-in-law. "Wait a minute, I thought we were going camping. Tents and all that."

"Hey, fellas, how ya doing?" Mitch slapped his brother-in-law on the back. "Somebody has to bring the toilet . . . just in case." He winked and arched his eyebrows high. Richard bunched his own into an arrow point. "And besides, this rig has a kitchen for cooking and all the pots and pans and stuff. Don't worry about a thing. I've got super tents for you guys." He aimed a thumb toward the rear. "C'mon, it'll be a blast."

Guy hadn't liked the sound of tent camping, but this behemoth didn't seem right either. Things were already going off plan, but Guy remembered his promise to be relaxed about it.

Mitch shifted his focus to a side window in the RV—where his wife sat holding a small mirror to her face. "Sharon, baby! Come on out and say hi to the fam!" Sharon canted her head to the side, flashed a coy smile and tucked away her lipstick.

She glided down the RV's steps and set one perfectly manicured foot on the curb. "Hello there," she said in her deep New Orleans drawl.

Richard waggled a few fingers. "Hello, Sharon. Great to see you again." His voice rose, hinting at a long-simmering attraction to his sister-in-law.

Guy snorted with disdain at his son-in-law's fascination. *He looks like he's in awe of another man's big-bore pistol.* He approached and kissed Sharon's cheek. "You *do* know how to make an entrance."

"Everybody ready? Wagons ho!" Mitch circled his hands overhead and leaped back into the RV.

Richard snagged Guy's arm. "This is already going sideways."

Guy didn't disagree, but he decided to act like a faithful member of the pack. Maybe things would turn around.

———

After an unscheduled grocery stop, the RV and the van full of Pickerings eventually made it out of town and onto the highway heading north. The one-hundred-seventy-mile trip took over five hours after several wrong turns and two pregnancy-driven bathroom breaks for Heather.

The sun hung low in the sky just over the treetops when they pulled into their designated campsite at Stephen C. Foster State Park in the Okefenokee National Wildlife Refuge. Their cleared space, carved out from the surrounding bushes, had only one wooden table and a fire ring.

It took several tries and a few hand signals and muttered obscene remarks from Richard to help Mitch back the RV into the designated parking spot, but they were finally there. Guy stretched his back from the long drive and contemplated what on earth they would do now.

"This senior partner in my law firm kind of likes me." Mitch took a drag off his cigarette and let it dangle from his lips while reaching deep into the RV's belly. He tossed two tent bags on the table, each one still bearing brand-new tags.

After much trial and error, Guy and Richard managed to snap enough poles and Velcro enough fabric together to erect both synthetic-smelling tents—each designed to withstand high winds and subzero weather. "Perfect! I knew we could do it," Mitch said.

Guy peered hard at the glowing cigarette silhouetted against the last remnants of daylight. "Yeah, good work, Mitch." He pointed and smirked at the small but sturdy tents. "These seem gator proof, too."

Mitch pumped a fist. "Only the best."

"Hey, Mitchy baby!" Sharon called from the RV. "Could you come here? We can't get the stove to work. It won't light."

"Gotta go, fellas. Help out the little ladies." Mitch's tone dropped, slipping into his John Wayne imitation as he sauntered toward the RV.

A minute later, he came back. "Oh, uh, Dad, Richard, do you know how to turn on the propane gas?" He hesitated and jerked his thumb at two seven-gallon tanks. "I thought you just twisted these knobs. Counterclockwise, right?" Mitch spun the knobby brass circles once again.

Guy stepped up and thumped the tank on the left with a fist-sized rock. He did the same with the other. Hollow rings revealed the bad news. He sighed and stared at Mitch with a joyless face. "These tanks are dead empty."

Mitch tapped his chin. His eyes scanned the campground as if searching for an excuse. "He didn't tell me I had to fill them up . . . Wait, I've got an idea. There's a fire ring over there. See? So there's gotta be wood lying around here somewhere. We can cook over a real fire. It'll be even better."

Mitch was on a roll again. He snatched a flashlight and charged into the trees, the light beam swaying to the left and right. "Hey, Alex, help me!"

It was a somber crowd inside the RV when Guy broke the news—dinner was delayed at best and maybe shot to hell. But then Sharon stood up.

"I have something to say. We all know tonight is a great big, huge-type major happening. They say our computers are pooping out at midnight, planes are going to fall out of the sky, and all kinds of crazy stuff, right? This could be our last night to have a good time." She paused, all ten painted fingernails fanned out in a *What can you do?* gesture.

Guy aimed a bewildered glance at Dorothy.

"Just kidding, c'mon," Sharon giggled. "Hey, we brought a friggin' cartload of tequila and limes, and enough beer and wine to keep us happy well into next year. What do you say we party? We have cheese and bread and other stuff that doesn't need cooking if y'all don't want to drink your dinner like me." She waved a svelte arm toward the RV's refrigerator, indicating her immediate preference for libation over sustenance.

At that moment, Dorothy's stomach growled just loud enough for everyone to hear. She snickered in embarrassment, and everyone laughed. "Okay!" she proclaimed. "When Mitch gets a fire going, we'll cook us some dinner. But in the meantime, you've got tequila, huh?"

Guy did a double take. He'd only seen her drink Mexican liquor once. She lifted an eyebrow at him and gave him a devilish wink.

In short order, the gloomy, hunger-dreading group all raised shot glasses (including Heather, though hers contained ginger ale) and toasted the last thousand years of existence.

Twenty minutes later, as the Rolling Stones blasted "Brown Sugar" through the RV's speakers, Mitch, with Alex skipping along behind him, struggled into the campsite, pushing a wheelbarrow full of shrink-wrapped firewood cubes.

Soon after, a heavy pot of hearty stew sat simmering on the fire ring grill. The potato chips bowl had only crumbs, and a new beef jerky bag was disappearing fast.

A teary-eyed Heather reclined away from the smoke with her head resting on Sharon's shoulder. Guy recognized the inexplicable prenatal emotions that engulf women and bond them together when the subject turns to babies.

Dorothy and their grandson were standing at the firelight's far edge, peering out between the other campsites into the gloom of Okefenokee. Guy sidled over to eavesdrop on their conversation.

"Did you hear that, Grandma? Was that an alligator?" Alex tugged on her sleeve and edged closer to her.

"Yes, Alex, you're right." She hugged him tighter and squinted into the shadows. "They get sleepy in the wintertime. But don't wander off by yourself."

Alex gripped her hand and gawked at the shadowy bushes. Guy smiled to himself, then frowned at Mitch hovering over the stew pot. "Dorothy, we better supervise."

"Okey dokey. This stew's gotta be done by now. Let me check it out." Mitch teetered over the glowing embers and tossed aside an empty beer bottle.

"No, no. Leave it alone. It's ready, and I can manage by myself." Dorothy stood up and reached for the potholders. Heather passed out soup spoons to everyone.

"Hey, I'm an old cowhand," Mitch slurred and danced a clumsy imitation of a Western-style jig. Alex giggled at his dad. "I'd make an excellent camp cook. Let's take a peek." He picked up a large wooden spoon and aimed it at the loop in the pot's heavy lid.

"Mitch! Don't!" The warning came too late. Four shots of tequila took their toll on Mitch's sense of balance, and he stumbled forward. The spoon skipped off the pot's broadside, shoving it to the very edge of the half grill. Everyone gasped as the precious kettle teetered directly over the center of the flames. Despite a chorus of warnings and protestations, Mitch wobbled headlong, trying to correct his gaffe, and grabbed the pot handles with his bare hands. The hot blast and burning fingers jerked him upright—he snapped his hands away, but not before tipping the balance. A heart-wrenching crackle and cloud of savory ash steam rose in the air as the main dish toppled upside down in the center of the fiery coals. Amid the fire's glow, a dark lump snapped and popped.

Mitch gasped and jumped back, lost his footing, and landed on his butt. All present shouted or groaned in unison at the sad finality of the stew's fate.

"Oh, shit," He uttered as he struggled to stand. He jerked his arms up in a sign of surrender. "Whoops! I'm sorry."

In an instant, the evening's fleeting camaraderie evaporated. Guy felt the moment stop, as brittle as an icicle.

"Goddammit! You asshole!" Richard jumped up and grabbed a fistful of Mitch's jacket.

"Hey, lay off," Mitch slurred.

Guy forced himself between the two men as they shot liquor-laden glares at each other. "Now, boys, let's take it easy."

Never taking his eyes off of Mitch, Richard shoved Guy backward with his free hand.

"Richard!" Dorothy snapped. "You don't treat your father-in-law that way." She brushed past her husband. "He's just trying to keep you from losing a tooth, you drunken fool!" She reached up, seized Richard's left ear, and tugged downward. In seconds, his six-foot frame was on its knees, head sideways to the heavens. Guy drew back, amazed to see Dorothy's signature move from Mitch and Heather's childhood in action again.

"And you, Mitch, of all the dang idiot moves!" She glowered at her son. He grimaced and raised his hands to ward off the attack. "You owe us, big time!" She let go of Richard's ear. "This is bad enough without the two of you making it worse." Dorothy crossed her arms as Richard staggered back to his feet. Lit by the flickering firelight, Guy imagined her as a fierce peacemaking angel. She always could take charge of a situation.

After a long, uneasy moment, Mitch looked around at the group, their dour faces illuminated by the flickering fire. He held up a finger. "Can I say something?" He waited for approval; after receiving none, he continued. "I've been holding out on all of you." He gave a wan smile and gestured at the RV. "I've got sparklers."

"Cool!" Alex yelled out. "Let's do it now!"

Guy complained and muttered along with the rest of the family, but within minutes, Alex was racing in circles, a lit sparkler in each hand.

Meanwhile, Sharon rummaged in the cooler. "We still have the bread and cheese, and look!" She hoisted two tubs of delicatessen potato salad aloft.

Soon, fresh wood crackled in the fire, apologies were accepted, promises were made, and snack foods were praised. In a short time, the charisma of Okefenokee's new millennium celebration evaporated most of the lingering resentment. The entire Pickering family was on a camping trip. It was New Year's Eve, and they would not starve to death.

Guy uncorked a wine bottle, grabbed two plastic cups and a bag of honey-roasted peanuts, and motioned for Dorothy to follow him. Beyond earshot of the campsite, a fallen tree trunk looked perfect to him.

"I thought a pretty woman such as yourself ought to have a quiet moment and a glass of wine with one of your admirers." Guy handed her the cup, smiling a dopey grin.

"Very well," Dorothy replied. "Don't mind if I do."

They sipped their wine and looked up through the tree canopy at the brilliant stars.

"You really stuck up for me." He glanced over at her and straightened his back. "For the record, I could have handled that myself."

"Yes, I'm sure you could have, but you're my husband, and nobody treats you that way in front of me. That's all there is to it." Dorothy took his hand.

"Dorothy," he began—a hiccup interrupting him—"I love you."

She leaned into him. They embraced, balancing on the log for several more minutes. Thousands of chirping crickets added to the music and revelry from other campsites, and they sat in silence, listening to the medley.

"Guy, we need to talk about something." Dorothy paused and drew a deep breath. Guy tensed, recognizing her tone as one that usually accompanied some serious topic. "I've been thinking. We're getting up there. Someday, you and I are going to kick the bucket, right?" He groaned. She held up a finger and pursed her lips. "And . . . I went to see Francis a week ago in that care facility." She waited until he met her eyes. "She lay there hooked up to tubes and stared straight at me for the longest time. Then, she drooled and asked who I was. Imagine that! My friend for forty years. I broke down and cried. She didn't even notice." Dorothy turned and focused on a faraway image. "One thing became crystal clear to me. I'm not winding up like that. No way!" Her voice took on an edge. "If I end up with some awful condition . . . you may have to help me. I don't want to linger in that state. Remember: I'm your old mare, and we know what they do to horses. And we know why."

Guy recoiled, speechless at the portent of the words. "Honey, that's terrible." He snorted and covered his mouth. "I couldn't do that. No way." He stared off into space for a moment. "And what about the other way around? You'd do that to me?"

"Look at me." She grabbed his face and brought it center to her own. "Hell yes." Her eyebrow went up. "You're all used up in body and mind and suffering something awful? We'd drink one of those expensive French champagnes we could never afford and dance a tango like we did that night in Miami. At the end, that would be good. Then, I'd throw you off a cliff." She tilted her head onto his shoulder. "You always liked to fly, right?" A moment of silence fell between them. "Anyway, that won't happen to us. But just in case it does . . ." She looked up at the stars. "I want you to promise you'll respect my wishes and give me that boost into heaven, or whatever's beyond."

Guy could only stutter incomprehensible words. Dying wasn't a subject he wished to contemplate just then, and Dorothy's request was beyond anything he could imagine.

"People are so afraid of dying. I'm not, and I'm only talking about when it's close and inevitable and I'm in pain and, you know . . . when it makes sense, and it's up to me."

"Dorothy! I can't do that!" Guy's mind reeled, and his eyes brimmed with tears.

"Yes, you can. If you love me, you'll promise me right now. In the end, I want to be in control."

Guy blew out a long breath and studied Dorothy's face, her steady gaze. He wiped at his eyes. "I'm going to go before you anyway." He kicked a rock with his foot and puffed his cheeks out. "Damn it. I promise, if that's what you want."

"That'll do. Now, let's be happy we're alive."

They kissed and hugged each other. But despite the crackling campfire blazing nearby and the sounds of the new millennium's celebration, Guy couldn't shake the daunting glimpse of a potential future.

26

ORLANDO, FLORIDA

2007

~~MONDAY~~

~~TUESDAY~~

~~WEDNESDAY~~

~~THURSDAY~~

~~FRIDAY~~

SATURDAY

The final and last end it all day.

Alex arose early, put on clean clothes, and dug a light jacket out of his suitcase, remembering that in an airplane, it got cooler at higher altitudes. He bounded downstairs to an empty kitchen and decided he'd wait on the front porch for the day's adventure to unfold. *I've got to remember to act surprised when he tells me.* The morning air was still and muggy, with a few high, fluffy clouds overhead. Coffee added to the anticipation.

A few minutes later, an unfamiliar sensation in his chest gripped him as he noticed a familiar figure approaching up the driveway.

"Hiya. Whatcha doing?" Amy said.

Alex sat up with an embarrassed grin. "I was just hanging out. What're you up to?"

She shrugged. "I prefer to walk instead of being cooped up in the house. Where're your grandparents?"

"They're not up yet, I guess."

Amy crossed over to the forlorn Olds and stroked the wrinkled fender. An abundance of hair fell across her profile. Alex took the opportunity to glance at her long tanned legs. He bit his lip at the sight.

"Today would be a decent day to take me on a ride," she said with a coy smile.

"I would, of course, but Grandpa and I are going up in his plane." Alex grinned stupidly.

"Wow, that's awesome. I can't compete with that. He must be a pretty cool grandpa. Mine just sits around complaining about his church and everything else."

"Well, mine's still sort of a dweeb." Alex flayed his hands out in a surrender gesture.

"Yeah, but a flying dweeb? That's awesome."

Alex grinned. "I guess so. . . ."

"Hey, if you're back in time, we're driving to the beach down by Cape Canaveral to watch the shuttle launch. You could come with us if you want."

"Shuttle launch? I didn't know."

"It's a big deal around here. Maybe I'll see ya."

"I'm thinking there's no way I can go flying and also be at the beach, but thanks for the invite."

"Okay, till later."

He watched her until she disappeared around the corner.

Upstairs, Guy bolted awake, erasing the remnants of a disturbing dream and leaving only a lingering aura of dread. Dorothy snored into her pillow, a brief rest after a restless night. At two o'clock, he had awakened and found her gazing and mumbling at the ceiling. He couldn't understand the words and wondered if she was speaking with an angel. He'd slept only in brief fitful spells after that.

Rubbing the sleep from his eyes, he swung his legs over the edge of the bed and walked the few steps to the window. He flung open the drapes and spied young Amy Dunley strolling down the driveway. *Well, look at that. Alex has a friend.*

He brushed away the thought and returned to more immediate matters. *I must get back on track.* Heather would be in the doghouse with Richard, likely staying home that morning. A wave of loss gripped his heart. *I'll never see her again. I love you, my girl.* He gazed toward the south. *And you too, Mitch. Take care of yourself, son.*

Guy wiped away a few tears. He had to keep it together, bury his doubts, and continue reminding himself of the greater good for Dorothy. With rueful irony, he realized sadness was for those left behind. He and Dorothy would soon be beyond all sorrow.

The morning sun peeked through the trees, and amid the soft sounds of Dorothy's sleep, he sank down into his favorite bedside chair, overcome with myriad unaddressed details.

Like Pedro. The cat squeezed through the gap in the bedroom door and jumped up on Guy's lap. He stroked Pedro's head and studied his feline companion. *What's going to happen to you? Damn.* "Pedro, you're a great kitty, but . . ." He hesitated, feeling foolish. "Someone will take you in, I'm sure." Pedro meowed, demanding his breakfast, then dashed through the door.

"I give up. Can't solve everything."

"Is this the last farewell day?" Dorothy said as she rose upright on the bed. "Or another practice run?" She raised her eyebrow.

Surprised at her sudden aliveness, he bolted up in the chair and shook off his complicated daydream. "Give me a break, will ya? There's no manual for this. And frankly, I'm getting a little tired of being the only one trying to kill us." He rose, shook off his sudden crankiness, and sat on the bed. "But I'm glad you're up. Let's get ready."

She started by rejecting or nodding at selected pants and sweaters as Guy pulled them from a drawer or closet—choosing only the fanciest garments. "Today, I want to appear elegant." Her eyes glinted with a renewed light.

After ten minutes of deliberation, she indicated her approval, and Guy stepped back. "As usual, you look beautiful, honey."

"Of course. I'm a regular cover girl." She gripped his hand and, after a brief coughing spell, said in a subdued tone, "Think of poor Alex when he hears. He'll feel betrayed."

Guy drew a deep breath. "He will. This is terrible for him, for you and me, for everybody. There's no easy way anymore." Guy dared to hope that today's plan would be easy enough. More obstacles were the last thing he needed right now.

"I wonder if we'll turn into ghosts," she said with a grin. "Wouldn't it be fun to appear across the street and haunt that Tooney lady? Maybe we could ruin more of her yard."

"Over my already-dead body!" Guy snickered. "Forget about her."

He guessed about a medicinal formula that would bring both pain relief and lucidity—two doses of morphine but no more of those "cutting-edge" pink pills. *Those things make her too unpredictable.*

He kissed her on the forehead and pointed at the staircase. "Here we go with our last day."

As soon as they entered the kitchen, Alex appeared from the porch, striding like an enthusiastic salesman, and beelined for the coffeemaker. After filling his mug for the second time, he slid into the chair at the table beside Dorothy, beaming with keen eagerness. Dorothy's expression softened, but her lips grew taut.

"Hey, Grandma. What's up?" Alex said.

She averted her gaze.

Showtime, Guy thought. He gulped and launched into what he hoped would be a passable story. "Uh . . . so . . . Dorothy, did I forget to tell you I ran into Doug Baumgartner?" (Guy did bump into Doug at a gas station a year ago.) "You remember his wife, Millie? You and she were always so close. So, they invited us over to their house for lunch. Isn't that nice? Huh?" He forced himself to smile.

Dorothy frowned.

Desperate to sound plausible, he recalled Millie Baumgartner's cooking. "Remember those special lemon meringue pies you used to love so much?"

Dorothy raised her head. "Oh yeah, her pie." She nodded. "So what about it?"

"That's where we're going today. On the picnic."

"Right, right," Dorothy mouthed.

"Okay, then." He wasted no forward motion or time. "We'll just put a few things together and go." He glanced at his grandson. "Uh, sorry, Alex. You wouldn't enjoy these people. They're really old, like us, but worse. But we'll bring you a piece of pie. That'd be okay, right?"

Alex rose and leaned on the counter, watching Guy search through the cupboards. "Man, I . . . I thought you wanted to, like, surprise me with an airplane ride. You and me. Now, instead of flying, you're going to lunch?" His voice rang like an accusation.

"I-I don't know what you're talking about," Guy stammered. *How the hell does he know about the plane?*

"But I heard you . . . I thought . . ." Alex's cheeks flushed with disappointment. "Fuck it, never mind."

"Well, things have changed. Millie's a great baker but not such a good cook, so I said we'd bring sandwiches." Made-up excuses swirled in Guy's mind as he slid the open wicker basket closer beside him. "We all love a nice picnic, don't we?" He dared not look up and instead slathered a huge glob of mayonnaise on a piece of bread.

Alex edged up next to Guy and whispered into his grandfather's ear, "What the fuck? You're acting all weird."

Guy only jerked upright in response. Guy followed Alex's eyes into the picnic basket—at the bottom lay the crumpled envelope, smeared with mustard-colored blotches. Alex reached in and pulled it out. "What's this?"

"Oh!" Guy sprang forward, jabbed his arm out like a fencer, and snatched it from Alex's hand. "Ah, yes! What a fine day for a picnic!" He shouted the words with a flushed face. "I think we're done here, ready to go." He tossed in a half-wrapped, mayo-only sandwich and slammed the lid shut.

Alex folded his arms. "What's up with you?"

Guy spun around. "There's nothing wrong."

Alex eyed the envelope clutched in Guy's hand and, in one swift motion, swiped it back. "And what's so important about *this*?"

"Give that to me!" Guy lurched forward.

Alex dodged him and held the envelope out behind him. He glared at his grandfather and slipped to the far side of the kitchen table while ripping it open. Guy protested, but Alex needed only seconds to scan the mustard-stained note.

His jaw dropped. His eyes darted between his grandparents. They all stood still—complete silence.

Alex's voice cracked. "You want to kill yourself and grandma too? That's what you've been trying to do?"

Guy sighed. "Let's sit down. I need to explain everything."

For the next ten minutes, the smiling-sun wall clock ticked the seconds with merciless indifference, adding the only sound of normality to the Pickering kitchen. Guy poured his heart out with solemn details of a grim, prolonged demise. He confessed to a grand plan to release both of them from suffering. Alex fidgeted in his seat, shaking his head in disbelief. Guy made sure to elaborate on his own fictitious diagnosis.

After a silence, Dorothy grabbed Alex's forearm. She stuttered, searching for words. "I . . . I . . . made him promise," she rasped. "It's no good for me. I want to go."

"I wanted to help your grandma, and it turns out, I've only got a month or two as well," Guy pleaded. "I'm in the same boat. It makes sense for us, son. You have to realize, by law, because of stupid rules, we're not allowed to have control over our own lives. This is the only way."

Alex directed his gaze at his grandfather. "You don't seem sick at all."

"Yeah, but the doctor was clear, plus I hide my symptoms. Maybe that's why I act crazy." Guy forced a grin. "You're young and don't think about it, but everybody's got it coming someday. But cancer takes folks too early. It's a bitch."

"I can't believe this. This is nuts." Alex jumped up from the table and gazed out the window. "You were just going to off yourselves and leave me here?"

"Please forgive me." Guy hung his head. "I . . . I couldn't imagine having this conversation with you."

"*You* couldn't imagine!" Alex threw up his hands and paced around the kitchen. "Well, let me tell you. Of course it was the first thing I realized when I got here! I knew right away my grandparents were planning to run off and kill themselves and I'd just hang out for a while!" He jumped to the refrigerator, yanked out a beer, pulled the tab on it, and stared wild-eyed at Guy. "I was just pretending to be in the dark about the whole thing!"

A stillness descended upon the room. An impossible vise squeezed Guy's heart as he beheld his grandson. Dorothy sat in silence and wiped tears from her eyes.

Alex lowered the beer to the counter and started to cry. "You *have* been acting weird, but this!" he gasped through his tears. "What am I supposed to do?"

Guy struggled to pull up the needed resolve. "Let us go," he said evenly. A plane was waiting.

"No! I can't do that!"

Guy put his hands on Dorothy's shoulders. "Son, you want to see your grandma endure more suffering?" *Shit, I hate this lie.* "And then watch me mope around, grieving and declining for maybe a couple more months by myself? The news about my health was the final straw. Sometimes, you can't put the pieces back together. This way, it will be quick. I figure quick's not so unacceptable."

Dorothy pointed her finger at Guy. "You're terrible at this, though." She swiveled back to Alex. "You know any decent hit men?"

With his face brimming with tears, Alex burst out with a choking laugh. "Grandma, you're something else. I don't know what to say. Unbelievable!"

More minutes passed without a word spoken. At last, Guy broke the silence. He held out a hand to Dorothy. "We should do this now. Say goodbye to Alex, dear."

Dorothy teetered to her feet and hobbled a couple of steps toward her grandson with obvious difficulty. She cupped her hands on his cheeks like she used to do when he was younger. Her right hand gently lowered to Alex's birthmark and lingered there, as if exploring it. "I love you. Goodbye," she whispered.

Alex turned to Guy. "This is all . . . so *much*. Are you sure?"

Guy struggled to speak, but an involuntary gasp came out instead. "I'm sorry," was all he could say. He grabbed the basket and Dorothy's arm and swung through the screen door.

He cast one final glance backward. Alex had slumped into a chair, glowering and staring into space.

In the garage, Guy led Dorothy to the modest Fairlane. For today's ten-mile journey to the Torvis Airport, he deemed the Olds still drivable, but it looked terrible, and he ran the chance of getting stopped for broken headlights and taillights. *Besides, my luck in that car hasn't been great.*

After settling Dorothy into the front seat and tossing the picnic basket in the back, Guy patted the fender on the classic 88 with a wistful sigh before circling around to the Fairlane's driver side and sliding in behind the wheel.

He started the engine; blue exhaust spewed from the tailpipe. Dorothy turned to him with a tight, tear-streaked face. Guilt punched him in the gut. He had lied—to her, to Alex, to everyone. *It's the only way.* He set his jaw and backed out of the garage as fast as he could, as if even the slightest delay could throw another monkey wrench into his plan.

"We're knockin' on heaven's door now, sweetheart," he croaked as they sped away.

Alex moped over to the kitchen window and wiped tears from his cheeks as he watched his elders disappear down the street. *I should call Aunt Heather.* But before he could reach for his cell phone, the house telephone rang.

After a morose stare at it for a few rings, he snapped it up and pressed it to his ear. "Hello?"

"Is Guy Pickering available?"

"No, he's definitely not." *And he never will be.*

"This is Dr. Berger from the Orlando clinic. Are you related?"

"I'm his grandson. Now's not a good time—"

"I won't keep you long. Just give him a message. I thought a bit of good news might benefit your family. But first, I'm so sorry about what's happening with your grandmother. Guy's biopsy came back clear as a whistle. No sign anywhere of cancer and a clean bill of health. There's minor arthritis in some joints. That will bring aches and pains a bit. His triglycerides could be better, but not bad. Over-all, he's doing okay. . . . Hello? Are you there?"

The house phone dangled by his side while Alex screamed into his cell phone. "Aunt Heather! Get over here right now! I mean *right now*!"

Use caution upon opening.
Contents under pressure.

Dirk Rainey awoke at sunrise in his cramped studio bedroom on the first floor of a modest two-story building situated on the edge of Torvis Airfield's runway. Staring at his bed, he wondered for the umpteenth time whether to make it, an especially important question, the answer to which often depended on Lisa Marie's schedule. Today, he decided to make the bed. *Just in case . . .* He climbed the stairs, threw open a flimsy door, and blinked at the rays of sun fighting their way through the streaked wall of windows.

He flipped a few switches on an ancient radio, flipped the air conditioner on to medium, and settled into an office chair that tilted to one side—due to a broken caster replaced by a square piece of two-by-four. He was going to fix that soon. Another ordinary day in the control tower.

For over a decade, Dirk had been *the* man at Torvis Airfield. He surveyed his kingdom, a single landing strip. The sunbaked airport had been in decline for the past few years, after a new private airport had opened twelve miles away with two much-longer runways. Dirk eyed the subdivision just beyond the other side of the fence. Orlando's ever-expanding sprawl had encroached upon the airport's borders. Despite the aging enterprise suffering in its perceived relevance to society, to Dirk, it was still his domain and one he would continue to watch over like a mother hen. He had to admit, though, his current responsibilities had dwindled to logging the occasional flight, sweeping the parking lot, spraying weed killer on the runway, and locking the gates in the evening. When the phone rang, he answered. It's not that he didn't recognize the inevitable march of progress; he just didn't want to live in that world.

But at times, even he had to admit that the airport struggled to be profitable. Offering tie-downs and easy access for a dozen small airplanes provided the primary source of income, but that barely covered the bills and didn't result in much air traffic to control. The single remaining point of regular activity was a thriving enterprise run by a pair of resourceful young aircraft mechanics. They had leased an older but adequate hangar at the far end of the grounds and had wrenched an assortment of private planes into shape. Their best client kept them in steady business: WFYU Channel Seven News. The two performed all routine maintenance on the television station's new Bell 407 helicopter.

Every Tuesday, Dirk's job was to wash and vacuum the chopper—the only instance where he ever cared to be inside any aircraft. Despite loving airplanes of all sorts, he himself had only piloted for a short time. He always flinched at the memory of his near-miss landing eighteen years before. The experience had robbed him of his nerve to fly. What remained of his piloting days was an envy-laden aloofness toward pilots. He made an exception for his friend Billy.

"Quirky Dirky, how the hell are you?" Billy Bellams burst through the door, took three strides over to Dirk, and punched him on the shoulder.

"Ouch, doggone it. Give me a break. I'm busy here." Dirk concentrated on the papers arrayed in front of him and pushed a pile of magazines to the side.

Billy winked. "Sure you are, buddy."

Dirk's cheeks heated. He didn't like seeming useless in front of anyone, much less what might be his lone friend.

Billy poured himself a cup of coffee from a brown-stained carafe and plopped down on a faded velour couch that hugged one wall beneath an enormous picture of an F-22 Raptor in a steep ascent. "My God, this stuff is awful. Tastes like something died in that pot."

Dirk smirked. Yesterday's reheated coffee was good enough for him.

Billy set the mug on an upended crate and pulled a soda from a half-sized refrigerator. "By the way, any big plans for the weekend?" He stretched his legs and picked up June's issue of *Plane and Pilot*.

Dirk's eyes darted up and to the left. "Plans? No . . . Lisa Marie's working today, right?" He tried to sound nonchalant.

Billy crossed his arms and relaxed into the old couch. "Yeah, she'll be here." He wrinkled his nose. "Man, you're rotting away in this place. You need some excitement in your life."

———

Lisa Marie steered her SUV through the intersection marked TORVIS ROAD, threw her dead cigarette out the window, and barked into the cell phone at her ear, "Ted, I'm sorry. I should have read through it first before giving it to you. You've got a better take on news stuff, so I just handed it over."

"Listen to me," Ted barked over the phone. "Just in case I was wrong, which I wasn't, I called in a guy from downstairs that does fact-checking for us. This whole thing is crap. An amateurish bunch of tabloid headlines mixed in with a lame defense of sexual harassment, a whining protest of promotion denials, and 'conduct unbecoming of an officer' accusations! Who is this joker, and why are you playing footsie with him?"

Lisa Marie blanched. "That's not what . . . sorry. At first, I thought he might have something. Looks like I wasted your time."

"Yup," Ted snorted. "So get off his bandwagon and do your job!" He hung up.

Lisa Marie glowered at the phone for a few seconds before narrowing her mascaraed eyes and curling a lip. "That jerk! Now Ted is even less likely to promote me. Son of a bitch!" she snarled while swerving and dialing. She waited for the call to be picked up. "Mr. X man? Is this you? Your *one* is calling."

"Reporter woman!" a raspy voice answered. "I've been expecting your call. What's the good news?"

"Oh yeah, the release. I want you to know, I had my boss and staff go over it, and guess what? You have a big fat *nothing*. Nothing! And now the man who holds the keys to my promotions thinks I'm an idiot."

"No surprise there!" Mr. X grumbled. "I can see I've made a serious error in judgment and created a security breach. This must be your fault. You bungled it. I can't believe I trusted you. I demand that you return those documents immediately!"

"Oh sure, no problem. I'll check the trash bin as soon as I get back to the office." She stabbed the phone's *off* button and tossed it onto the passenger seat. She tried to shake a cigarette out of her pack, but her wheels hit the roadside gravel, and she fishtailed, sending the cigarettes flying across the seats and onto the floor.

Lisa Marie contemplated this minor setback with her boss. It was time to default to her strong suit: not letting her lack of experience and sophistication interfere with innate cunning and the power of seduction. "Just one decent break. Is that too much to ask?"

Her focus far away, she floored the SUV's accelerator, swerved past an old Ford Fairlane, and sped through the open gates of Torvis Airfield.

———

From behind the Fairlane's windshield, Guy watched a bulky SUV zip by them and skid to a halt in the gravel beside the control tower. *Dang, I didn't want a lot of people here. I guess it doesn't matter. I'm going for it anyway.*

Stealth was his MO today; he took a sharp right turn and headed for a dilapidated hangar. The long structure paralleled the runway, with airplane fragments and overflowing bins of worn-out parts lining a narrow backside passage.

Knowing this route would shield him from view, he steered the Fairlane between a corrugated wall and a rusty chain-link fence. The club's Beechcraft Bonanza sat a hundred yards beyond the far edge of the hangar.

With a last look around, he coasted the remaining silent stretch and pulled up beside the airplane. He hummed in satisfaction as he surveyed the scene. "I'm sure nobody's spotted us yet."

Guy switched off the Ford's engine and peeked at Dorothy, who had ridden the entire way in contemplative silence. Now, she turned to him with a perturbed sneer.

He snatched her hand and smiled as broadly as he could. "Honey, we're headed up one more time. Just like old times." She stiffened and studied him like a serving of spoiled meat—the storm clouds of doubt in her eyes.

Damn, I should have prepped her better than this.

"What exactly is the new plan?" she demanded. "Are we jumping out? Hold on." She paused and scrutinized him. "You're going to crash it, aren't you? That seems a bit much. And what about the Bonanza? It doesn't belong to you."

"A portion of it does."

"Is that so?" She curled her lip at him. "Well, which portion are you crashing?"

Guy grunted. He truly hadn't cared about the aftermath of the plane's fate, only his and Dorothy's. "It's all insured, and think about it." He swept his arm in a wide overhead arc. "We're going out in grand style."

"Style, my ass. This is scary."

"But only for a minute! Here's the deal." He lowered his voice and cast a nervous glance in all directions, instinct dictating that he keep this conversation private although not a soul was in sight. "We're taking her up and . . . diving real quick into the ocean. Nothing will be harmed."

"Except us."

He sighed. "Well, yeah. That's the whole idea. It'll be over in an instant, and I'll try to make it fun. Think of a roller coaster."

"Oh sure, dying in an airplane wreck is exactly like a carnival ride. Sounds delightful."

Guy swiped his hair back. He couldn't let another plan slip away and fail. "I'm evidently bad at this sort of thing. We both can see that, and I confess, I'm nervous about it. It *is* scary, but there's no perfect way to do it, and not many options left." He gazed at the floorboards. "It's what you wanted . . . the best I can do."

"You silly old goat. I love you." Dorothy grasped Guy's hand. "I *still* think it's a little over the top—but all right, let's do this. One last ride in the sky. You and me, Guy."

Dorothy's smile warmed Guy's heart and loosened the squeeze on his lungs. *The plan is on.* "All right, then." He reached into a pocket and pulled out a small bottle of morphine. "Here, honey. Take a last nip."

"Nah, it makes me too loopy and drowsy." She flicked a dismissive hand at the bottle. "I'm feeling okay right now, and flying into the ocean is so outrageous. I want to be awake for this."

Dirk pressed up against the control tower's windows and watched as Lisa Marie exited her SUV. With three undone buttons on her blouse, pants that looked painted on, and heels high enough to mandate experience, she strutted like a pro across the tarmac toward the tower.

Dirk lit up at the sight of her. "Here she comes," he whispered with childlike delight.

Billy winced. "Face it, dude. That gal will *never* boink you."

Dirk recoiled, heat reddening his cheeks. "How do you know? Sometimes, people just click," he sputtered. "I think she likes me." His voice rose along with his eyebrows.

"What are you goofballs doing?" She had arrived. Lisa Marie headed straight for the compact refrigerator and yanked out a Mountain Dew. "Okay, Billy. Once again, Ted has indeed stuck me in that hot tin can with you. I suggest we get going." She popped the pull tab and tossed back a swig of soda.

"Lisa Marie, you're a real piece of work." Billy reclined further into the sofa. "I happen to be ready, willing, and able . . . but we've got time. Relax." He pointed at his watch.

Dirk leaned against a wall with exaggerated casualness. "Would you care for another Mountain Dew, Lisa Marie?" he asked in his most polite voice.

"I just started this one, *Dirk!*" She shot a pouty look at both the men. "C'mon, Billy, Let's go."

Billy peered over the top of his Ray-Bans at her. "There's a shuttle launch today, you know. We could swing out in that direction and check out the traffic out there. Tons of people will be driving out to the beaches for a good view."

"Oh yeah," she smirked. "What's the big deal? They do them all the time."

"No, they don't. And have you ever seen a friggin' rocket blast off into space? It's awesome." He drained his soda, turned, and squinted out the front window facing the airstrip. The empty can dangled from his fingertips while he gestured toward the line of airplanes tied down in a row off to the east side of the airfield. "Who's that?"

Dirk glared at two diminutive figures exiting a parked car. He jumped up and stomped one boot. "What the hell?"

"Hey, buddy," Billy said. "They're getting in that Bonanza."

Lisa Marie lowered herself onto a metal chair, focusing on a problematic fingernail.

Dirk mumbled curses and dove into a cabinet. "Gol-dang, where's my binoculars? Ah, here!" His frantic fingers seesawed across the binocular's focus wheel. "Hold on, that's the Timeworn Airborne Beechcraft plane." He paused and looked over at Lisa Marie. "That's what they call themselves. Group of retired airmen and a couple of old doctors."

"Hmm," Lisa Marie said, continuing to stare at her splayed hand.

Dirk's face brightened. "The new rule is they have to check in with me ever since this one member forgot to let anybody know he'd be gone overnight. Everybody thought he had crashed." He suppressed a chuckle and winked. "The guy radioed in, all hung over, after waking up in Jamaica beside some tattooed babe." He spun back to the window with a taut face and stomped his foot. "This is not supposed to happen. Dang it, they're even leaving their stupid car right there in the way!"

An instant later, the landline phone's irritating bell pierced the room.

28

What happens when you start out on the wrong foot?

The phone rang a fourth time—a fifth time. Dirk groaned but picked up and spoke in an automatic monotone. "Torvis Airfield, Dirk speaking."

Lisa Marie stood and jerked her head toward the door. "Let's go, Billy." But she stopped cold, distracted by Dirk's contorted face.

"What? Who? Wait a minute, say that again. What?" Dirk squeaked while gawking at the mystery figures. His knuckles went white under a fierce grip, and his eyebrows shot up. "What are you saying? I don't understand, lady."

"What's going on?" Lisa Marie zeroed in on Dirk's rattled expression as the sharp smell of *something's gone wrong* froze her in place. She pursed her lips and took a step closer—always drawn by crazy-shit drama. "Give me the phone." She snapped open a hand.

As usual, Dirk did as she said.

She put the cordless to her ear.

"They're going to crash the plane! You've got to stop them! You have to! Are they there? Have they taken off? Oh, God! They're going to die!" the unknown woman sobbed.

Lisa Marie heard someone yell in the background, and the line went dead.

———

"Look out!" Alex screamed.

Heather yanked the wheel to the right, stomped on the brakes, and skidded sideways to a stop two yards from a skinny young boy holding a watermelon-sized rubber ball. Her cell phone clattered against the dashboard and fell to the floor under her feet. A shrieking woman with large pink curlers in her hair dashed into the street and snatched up the child in her arms.

Heather wore the face of a conqueror leading an invasion. "Get your fucking kid out of the road," she screamed out the window.

Alex cringed and gave a tentative wave to the horrified woman as she herded her child back to the sidewalk.

Heather crushed the accelerator pedal, and the minivan squealed and fishtailed forward. "Forget the phone," she ordered. "We're almost there!"

———

As if in a trance and without saying a word, Lisa Marie held the phone out to Dirk, only to let it drop to the desk before he could grab it.

"That woman was real upset," Dirk gulped out. "She said they're crashing the plane on purpose! Said we should stop them." He turned to the window. "You think we ought to run out there and arrest them?"

"How we gonna do that, Wonder Boy?" Billy said. "Too late!"

They crowded together and watched the innocent-looking little craft, bearing the portent of an unidentified threat, gathering speed on the runway—seconds from liftoff.

Reality took a brief intermission while she dove into a personal mental vacuum chamber. All outside sounds and concerns ceased as Lisa Marie weighed this unexpected moment. She lowered herself onto Dirk's chair. *Planes crashing? People dying? A prank? Suicide? A kidnapping? Terrorists? It sounds crazy, but that freaky woman sounded real.*

Opportunity was slapping Lisa Marie in the face, and she loved the pain. Deep within her cerebral cortex, pleasurable neural hormones flowed. The Big Boat of Life had delivered bait, and her instincts reeled in the catch. *Oh my God. This is fantastic!*

Her half-full soda can went skittering across the floor. "Billy, how many on board?"

"I'm not sure. I saw two, but could be more." Billy's voice sounded hesitant under the possibility of importance.

Lisa Marie sprang from the chair and zeroed in on Dirk. "Who was that woman? She *did* say plain and clear whoever's in that plane wants to crash it, right?" She grabbed his shirt. "Did you hear that? This *might* be a terrorist attack! Can we say for sure they didn't kidnap the pilot? They could aim that thing into a big building, or a mall, or something else real important!" Sensing breaking news, worst-case scenarios cascaded in her mind. And *she* was right here at the beginning.

"Really? You think?" Dirk staggered back.

"Dirk, you have to do the right thing. This could be another 9/11 attack." She stared deep into his solemn eyes, jabbed a finger in his chest, and went for the gold. "Call the Pentagon." Majestic movie music swirled in Lisa Marie's head.

"Oh, Lordy!" Dirk swooned and stumbled back a step.

Billy gaped at Lisa Marie for a moment, then snapped into action. "Lisa Marie, you don't call no Pentagon. Just call 911. They'll know what to do."

Guy thrust the throttle forward, sending the Bonanza rumbling down the airstrip. He pulled back on the yoke, and with a final bump, into the air they rose. Amid the noise and buffeting, he checked Dorothy's profile and put his hand on her knee. He had done this bonding ritual every time they flew together.

As the wheels left the ground, she let out a "whoop!"

The trio in the control tower watched the Bonanza lift off and bank toward the ocean.

Billy skidded to a halt at the door. "Let's get in our chopper and chase 'em! This is exciting!"

Those words targeted Lisa Marie's heart. She clutched her hands to her chest. "If that is our calling," she said solemnly, "then let us go."

Dirk stared, open-mouthed, as the pair dashed out the door.

"Make that call to 911!" Lisa Marie barked before bounding down the stairs.

That ought to bring enough attention to this. She couldn't help but grin.

"Damn it. How could he do this to us?" Heather honked her horn as she sped past one more car. "Torvis Airport is right there." She blinked through her tears and pointed through the windshield. Her heart was racing as horrific images paraded through her mind.

Alex gripped the handrest as they screeched around the last corner and blew through the stop sign.

They zipped through the open entrance gates and past the control tower before veering to a rocking halt in front of a gate in a chain-link fence separating the parking lot from the runway.

She scanned the grounds—to the right, the Ford Fairlane sat abandoned next to an empty tie-down slot. *Bingo. But where's the Bonanza?*

Alex pointed at a diminishing spot in the sky. "Oh my God! Is that their plane?" Heather sat horror-struck for a split second before her brain kicked into high gear. *Oh no they don't.*

She could see two hundred yards directly ahead a Channel Seven helicopter preparing for liftoff—the blades spun, and the engine whine rose in intensity. Heather's eyes bore through the windshield glare. The pilot's and a passenger's silhouettes were clearly visible seated in the cockpit, adjusting his headset.

"We're getting on that chopper!" she said, fixating on the gate's dull chrome padlock. "I don't care!" With adrenaline coursing through her, she ground the minivan's transmission into reverse. She stabbed the gas again and rocketed backward, swerving to a halt fifty feet directly in front of the barrier.

"Whoa!" Alex cried. "What are you doing?"

"No time to lose!" The chopper's blades were now a spinning blur. Heather bared her teeth and clenched her jaw.

"Aunt Heather! No!" She only glowered at the gate and yanked the transmission lever into low.

"Hang on!" She buried her right foot into the gas pedal, and the Toyota careened forward.

Three seconds later, both of them howling at full volume, they hit the gate with a wrenching clang, ripping it from its hinges and scraping it over the car's hood and top. The back of the van kicked out sideways, but Heather corrected and straightened out.

In all, six sections of fencing tore loose and lay twisted on the tarmac behind them as they sped forward with the left front bumper dragging on the pavement, its bolts torn from the frame. All the lights in front and the passenger-side windshield shattered.

"Woo! Yes!" Alex yelled. They hurtled toward the helicopter and exchanged wide-eyed glances at each other.

———

Billy jolted against his seat straps. A van, its bumper showering sparks underneath it, was careening toward the chopper like a beat-up torpedo. Lisa Marie clapped a hand on Billy's shoulder. She spied the distraught woman behind the wheel as it raced closer. *The crazy caller! Probably family. Perfect human angle.*

The Toyota skidded to a rasping halt beside the helicopter.

"Billy, let them in." Her tone sounded more like an order than a request.

Billy gave her a sharp look. "That's the lady on the phone, right?" He wiped his brow. "Okay, why not?"

Lisa Marie signaled to the pair, encouraging them to get on board.

Without hesitation, the two bounded from the van and headed for the chopper as Billy slid the side door open. The fierce prop blast battered the woman's hair in all directions and obliterated all her attempts to talk, so instead, she pointed at the tiny Bonanza disappearing fast. Lisa Marie nodded and gestured to the rear seats.

The two exchanged bewildered looks and scrambled through the door.

As the pair slipped into the seats, Lisa Marie locked eyes with the teenager—recognition dawning on her. "You're the kid from across the street!"

The boy blanched. Then his arm shot up and also pointed after the Pickering plane.

"We know. We know!" Lisa Marie shouted.

"Buckle up, everyone!" Billy ordered. He eyed the little Bonanza, now a receding dot in the sky. "It looks like they're just putting along. This is a fast chopper. I'm sure I can catch 'em."

The craft's engines surged, and the Bell 407 lifted off, banking northeast toward the open ocean.

*Ignorance may not be bliss,
but it dodges bothersome reality.*

"Holy crapola! No!" Dirk yelled through the dirty glass. "You can't do that. You just damaged private property, lady." He threw up his hands. Sixty feet of flattened chain-link fence lay on the ground, and now this culprit and some freakish kid were boarding the news copter.

"Wait, you're not supposed to leave!" he called out in the empty room with as much authority as he could muster. He stomped his boot again and dialed the phone.

"911 dispatch, what is the nature of your emergency? 911 dispatch, can you respond?"

"Oh, hello." Dirk swallowed. Recalling his duty according to Lisa Marie, he tried his best to assume a calm telephone demeanor. There was also the vandalism and property damage; he didn't know where to begin. He sputtered into the phone, tentative as a schoolboy at his first performance. "There's at least two people in an airplane who are definitely going to kill themselves. They've taken off with no permission *at all* from *my* airport, and they intend to crash into something. Nobody knows what." He pounded the side of his head in exasperation. The Bonanza and the chopper were fast disappearing from view. "And then this wild lady smashed through my fence, and they all got on the friggin' helicopter and just took off!"

"Sir," the dispatcher cut in, "what is your name and exact location?"

Remembering the alarming possibility Lisa Marie had wisely uncovered, Dirk lowered his voice and added with a conspiratorial flourish, "This could be kidnapping by terrorists. We don't know that, ma'am, but we suspect it."

"Sir, are you reporting a terrorist threat involving an airplane flight currently in progress?"

"Yes, I think so. We're not sure. Some crazy woman called and seemed quite upset about this suicide thing, and—"

"Sir, are you in personal danger? At what time did these events occur?"

Dirk answered as many questions as he could, giving the dispatcher all the information he could remember about the call and what he'd seen.

"Please stay on the line," the voice droned with an official crispness. "I will notify the appropriate authorities."

"Okay, I'll hold," Dirk said, scowling at the carnage on his airfield.

Dirk *did* hold. He held on and fielded a series of phone calls, one after another, for the rest of the afternoon.

"Honey." Guy peeked over at Dorothy, her headphones hanging lopsided on her head. He thought it looked comical and sweet and reached over to adjust them. "Sweetheart, I want to tell you I love you. You have been the best wife and partner a man could ever ask for. You have been there for me countless times when I've needed you, and I know it." In these last moments on earth, he picked his words with care, imagining they would connect with a never-before-experienced form of magical, spiritual intimacy.

"You're a crazy old nincompoop," Dorothy muttered.

"Well . . . okay." *So much for magical. Just like Dorothy to bring it back to the concrete.* "But back to my point—you understand this is it. We're flying into the great beyond . . . or heaven . . . or the Almighty."

"That sounds delightful and tidy," she said. "But I thought you didn't like God."

"It's not that I don't like him," he said. "I just don't trust him, or her, or whatever, to do the right thing for us."

Dorothy paused and scratched her chin. "I hadn't given it much thought, but just in case, I'm thinking now would be a good time to get clear on all that stuff. We should introduce ourselves." She raised her gaze upward. "If you're there, if you're listening, we'll see you soon if this time my husband can pull off his plan." She landed a soft punch on Guy's shoulder. "I'm Dorothy; this is Guy. You probably already knew that. I'm not afraid to go. Heaven sounds wonderful, even if it's only half as good as some folks say, but I need to ask for a favor. I loved my daddy, but we had our differences. So could we change up that bit about family for all eternity? That's an awful long time. I'd like to have Guy with me and visits from everybody else. That's all—and an expensive bottle of wine once in a while."

Guy beamed at her. "I think that will do the trick."

He glanced out the window, into the blue sky, searching for strength. He crossed his fingers—still juggling his beliefs and doubts. *Bearded man in the sky? I don't think so. Sit on a cloud or burn in hell for all eternity? Too simplistic. Some karma-type reconning? That could happen. Ah, there's probably just a big nothing . . . I really don't know. But I'll soon find out.*

———

Lisa Marie hunched down in the helicopter's front seat and articulated into her microphone, trying to keep her conversation with her boss private.

"Yes, that's right, Ted. Two people, maybe more, confirmed on a suicide mission. We are currently in pursuit, have corroborating witnesses on board, and have the suspects in sight."

She knew skinny old Ted—with his nuisance beard and rumpled clothes that always appeared slept in—bore the heart of a true newsman. Despite the looming budget cuts threatening early retirement, he would be in his office handling daily duties with the dedication of a faithful dog. *He needs a big story just as much as I do.*

"What are you saying?" Ted said.

"Well . . . there's no *confirmation* of a kidnapping or terrorist connection. But something is happening, and we are right here! Onboard cameras are operational." She held her breath.

"Kidnapping? Terrorists?" Ted sputtered. "What the hell?"

Lisa Marie focused on the Bonanza ahead of them. They were gaining on it. A sudden epiphany hit—a vision every bit as glorious as the Tabernacle Choir on Christmas Eve. *It's the same as O. J.'s chase!*

"Lisa Marie!" Ted's voice shrieked through the headphones. "I've got to know if this is real. You're sticking your neck out here. Mine too."

She snapped back to attention as vague, unrelated dots connected in her brain. She searched for the right words—the right angle to take with her boss. "Mr. Melden, sir, there's a shuttle launch scheduled for today. They're headed in that direction, and it might be their target. I request permission to dog this one out." She had once overheard a seasoned news reporter use this slang.

Ted grunted. She recognized that familiar sound and could imagine his face; she'd often seen the contorted scowl.

"I need approval to abandon normal traffic duties. No matter how this ends up"—she lowered her voice—"this could be *very* good for you and me, if you know what I mean."

Ted paused, and Lisa Marie knew he smelled the opportunity. He was always going on about how these first-on-the-scene nuggets were rare and they needed to be ahead of the game.

"Billy, can you hear me? Get the cameras swiveled out to catch the plane! Are your zooms working? Lisa Marie, give me everything you've got!"

For the next few minutes, Lisa Marie listened and obeyed while Ted peppered her and Billy with orders for specific camera shots and angles and broadcast dialogue. She was more than ready. *No more traffic chopper. They'll give me a raise and beg me to go primetime.*

Lisa Marie held her breath when he gave the full go-ahead to preempt the current programming on Channel Seven and live stream these unprecedented developments.

She could hear the prerecorded message: "We interrupt your regularly scheduled programming for a special breaking news report."

"Okay, here we go. Live in . . . three, two, one, you're on." Ted went quiet, and Lisa Marie put on her best "this is serious news" face.

"This is Lisa Marie, reporting live from our Channel Seven helicopter. At this moment, we are in pursuit of an unauthorized flight that is reported to be on a desperate suicide mission near Orlando. There are unconfirmed reports of a possible kidnapping with terrorist connections. We have eyewitnesses who are telling us the identities of the pilot and at least one passenger. We will release the names of the occupants as soon as we obtain confirmation. Lisa Marie reporting. Stay tuned to WFYU Channel Seven News for continuing coverage of this unfolding drama."

The camera switched to a rear shot of Guy and Dorothy's Bonanza, heading out to sea.

Lisa Marie knew, or at least hoped, what was coming next. Across the south, a news buzz shockwave would spread from the epicenter to other media networks. Identical orders to tie into WYFU's feed would spread throughout other newsrooms, and in a matter of minutes, television stations throughout the southeast would scramble to report this developing tragedy.

Some are called to duty; some are called names.

Inside a deep underground bunker, in a nameless location that did not show up on any map, a stocky young soldier in a starched uniform slipped through the door of a glass-walled enclosure and placed a single sheet of paper upon a desk.

Colonel Lance Hooper brushed aside the sheet before him and continued to thumb through the latest issue of *Guns and Ammo* magazine. He had risen early this morning, given Jack a stern warning not to lie on the bed, and arrived ready for his last week of military service.

Five days a week for three years, he had sat in this stark fluorescent-lit office, growing more and more frustrated by rubber-stamping the same protocols and inconsequential notifications. With battlefield experience in Desert Storm and Iraq, he itched for more field operations, but during his last deployment, a three-weeks-long affair with a young lady soldier had led to harassment charges, plus what was deemed "an overly aggressive leadership style" had nearly culminated in a court-martial. The most convenient way of avoiding consequences led to accepting a hasty reassignment in this underground monitoring station. He still ground his teeth thinking about the lost opportunity for any real engagement and now considered himself a mere glorified rent-a-cop. After years of no genuine threats or even a decent low-level crisis, he now only tolerated his cursed desk job. A bored Colonel Hooper looked forward to his imminent retirement.

He had five more days to go, but this morning's phone call gave the week a disappointing twist. That blundering bimbo and his own misjudgment had sullied the long-anticipated release of his epic exposé. For months he had worked on his treatise detailing his simmering feud with Army hierarchy, and now he sat stewing over the quandary like a smoldering tree stump.

Hooper ignored the soldier standing at attention before him.

"Sir, you might want to read this one, sir," Corporal Baker said in his usual formal tone, eyes trained on the far wall.

Hooper's gaze strayed from the magazine page. "What is it?" Hooper snapped. "Just tell me."

"Yes, sir. An alleged suicide flight due east of Orlando. It came in less than a minute ago. We're tracking it on the main screens."

Hooper snatched up the page, scanned it, and slammed his taut spine against the chairback. "This is in our quadrant. Show me!"

Pouncing on the suicidal airplane report like an emaciated tiger, he bolted up and charged around the corner of his desk. *Could this finally be some real action?* In the adjacent room, he barreled up behind a row of uniformed men and women glued to their computers. His eyes locked onto a large display screen. Florida's outlined coast glowed green, with dozens of pinpoints monitoring the positions of everything that moved.

Baker stepped forward and pointed at a blip in the center. "That's the one, sir."

"What's the intel on this, soldier?" Hooper barked.

"Sir!" Baker shouted. Hooper hated when he yelled so close to his ear. He stepped back and let the corporal continue. "Information has been very sketchy so far. What we have is the name Pickering, from this TV reporter who's observing them from a news station helicopter." He pointed to a screen on an opposite wall.

Hooper spun around to a larger-than-life-sized face staring back at him, mouthing words he didn't want to hear. His voice rose to a squeak. "What the hell is *she* doing there?"

"Do you know her, sir?" Baker peered at his superior officer.

"What? No, of course not!" Hooper rapidly crossed his arms, whirled around and began pacing. "I don't like this. That's real close to Cape Canaveral, and the *Atlantis* shuttle launch is in a few hours. We can't take chances here. A high-profile target! It might be some freaking crazies, trying to get their cause in the headlines. My God, this could be another big one."

He paced up and down the line of seated soldiers. "I'm calling a Code Yellow. Get a Navy chopper in the air immediately. Establish visual and radio contact ASAP! Put a couple of F-22s on alert. Have them stand by in ready status." He leaned forward within inches of the radar screen. *Not letting this one get by me.* "Let's find out who the devil is up there."

31

Exit this way. ↓

Five thousand feet above the Atlantic, Guy was having a moment. Yesterday, he had expected nostalgia and anxiety to overwhelm his last minutes on earth—he was giving it all up: his concepts of life, his loved one, his own body! But today surprised him. The sheer pleasure of cruising once more in the Bonanza's familiar cockpit satisfied like a hot bath on a wintry day. Gazing at faraway nothing, he accepted the engine's vibrations throbbing in his hands and the beckoning blue-green horizon.

He turned to Dorothy, overwhelmed by a mystical blend of this all-important present moment and fond visions of bygone days. A parade of visual memories flooded in: Dorothy's pigtails in first grade; Dorothy on their fateful cornfield walk; Dorothy's glowing face on their wedding day. "Ah, what a grand life!" he beamed.

Her hand reached out and settled on his thigh.

The faithful Bonanza droned on out to sea.

———

"Intercept time for the Seahawk—six minutes." The message rang out above the general buzz inside the underground bunker. Hooper stopped pacing, rubbed the back of his neck, and marched into his office. Standing over his desk, he withdrew an unopened pack of cigarettes from the top drawer and regarded them as he would an enemy who had strolled into his camp. He tossed them back in the drawer.

———

Lisa Marie pulled a compact mirror from her purse and swabbed at her made-up face with a powder brush. *I wish I'd been more prepared for this. Oh, and this top.* She eyed her blouse in disgust. *It's all wrong. At least the cut is flattering.*

She glanced over her shoulder at the woman strapped in the backseat waving, vying for her attention—Heather. She had announced her name after she'd put on headphones.

Billy tapped Lisa Marie's shoulder and flicked the button that blocked their conversation from being heard in the back. "Hey, this is fun, huh? But you know, if this chick and the teen freak are for real, then this whole thing ain't no terrorist attack. It's just two old-timers up to something—probably doin' themselves in, right?" He lowered his Ray-Bans for extra emphasis. "Nothin' more."

"Billy, we don't know that for sure." Lisa Marie paused, trying to rank the sensational scenarios swirling in her mind. She took a different tack.

"I didn't mention it before, but two days ago, I had a run-in with this Pickering guy."

"You did?"

"Get this! I was at my aunt's house, who lives across the street from him, and we caught him"—at this point, Lisa Marie rolled her eyes toward the back—"and this teen freak burying an enormous animal in his yard a few days ago. Who does that? He may be crazy and capable of awful things. My aunt suspects he abuses his wife." Lisa Marie's feigned disgust hid an inner surge of excitement. "Let's run with it for a while. This is a great story either way."

"All the more reason to talk to our guests." Billy motioned toward the rear. "You've got to do it."

She frowned but recovered, turned in her seat, and flashed a girly grin at the back-seat occupants as Billy toggled on the headsets. "Hi there," she began with the friendly tone of a cupcake salesperson. "So tell me: What's up?"

Alex and Heather jumped as Lisa Marie's loud and clear voice streamed in their ears, then shouted back at the same time.

"It's my grandfather and grandmother. I think he's just giving up. Something stupid, for sure!" Alex wailed.

"Can't you stop them? Oh, please, catch them, please, and get them to land. Please!" Heather grasped both sides of her red, swollen face, trying to yell over the copter's thrumming vibrations. Lisa Marie detected that Heather's distressed complexion would play well on camera when she eventually interviewed her and decided to not offer her any makeup.

"What are you saying on the news? What's going on? I need to speak to my dad! Can't you reach him on your radio?"

Billy broke in. "Listen, lady, I've tried all the broadcast channels, and if that's your old man, he doesn't want to talk to you or anybody else!" He looked over his shoulder at Heather and shook his head. "He must have his radio off. And we need to keep our distance here, where it's safe. No saying what he might do."

Heather's face clouded. A second later, she fumbled through her pocket and retrieved a cell phone. After checking the caller ID, she ripped off her headphones, punched a button, and resumed her yelling, this time into the phone. "Richard! Goddammit! You've got to help us . . . I don't care if you had to pick the boys up . . . I know it's loud. Shut the fuck up!" Lisa Marie drew back with a shocked expression. "My parents are killing themselves, and I'm in a helicopter! Fuck! Richard! Do something!" Heather screamed.

She stabbed the *off* button.

Heather held her phone in front of her as if it were an empty pistol and, with a scowl, shoved it back into her pocket, then continued her rant at Lisa Marie, who listened to thirty seconds more. *This woman is a little too much.* Lisa Marie pointed at Alex, who recited the core details of his grandmother's health and the note he'd discovered that morning. Now the puzzle pieces were coming together, but it wasn't a picture Lisa Marie wanted to hear. She studied the two passengers as Billy concentrated on the chase. Heather crumpled into a morose lump, staring out the side window, and Alex kept repeating that his grandfather was a good man but "kind of nuts."

This bothersome evidence *did* tug at Lisa Marie's conscience. The information at hand indicated the most likely outcome: The Beechcraft Bonanza carried plain old run-of-the-mill elderly folks taking a last flight into the sunset.

She weighed her options. *Suicide is one thing. A sexy kidnapping angle would be better, but the terrorist threat—that is awesome. Uncle Fred always said anything is possible.* She was not about to let minor details get in her way—not yet.

I've got news to report.

"This is your moment, Lisa Marie." Ted's words in her headset rang like a message from heaven. "Here we go. In five, four, three, you're on with CNN national."

"Lisa Marie, this is Fred Augustine, CNN, New York. We understand you are in pursuit of an alleged suicide plane and have identified who's piloting the craft." Augustine's voice resonated with media-groomed authority.

Lisa Marie could hear her heartbeat. "Fred, we have reliable sources claiming that the occupants of the airplane are local residents Guy Pickering and his wife Dorothy, from the Orlando area. And I can say with complete confidence that in recent days, he was observed exhibiting extremely unstable behaviors."

For the next thirty-two seconds, Lisa Marie stared into the onboard camera, pouring her best efforts into the performance. She ended with, "Since their course points toward Cape Canaveral, the hope is this does not involve the space shuttle launch."

The shot switched to the diminutive Bonanza, flying lazily over the ocean.

Dorothy squeezed Guy's leg and announced loud enough to be heard over the engine, "I'm hungry!" She reached over and rummaged through the picnic basket tucked behind the pilot's seat.

Guy smiled. *It's nice to see her enjoying herself.*

Dorothy pulled out a square bundle wrapped in aluminum foil and peeled back the top layer, revealing the leftover brownies from psychedelic Friday. She offered the potent chocolate to him.

When'd she sneak those in there? Guy did a double take. Even now, still surprising him. "No thanks, honey. You like those things, huh?"

"They're fun." She showed a mischievous grin. "I'm going to have just a nibble."

He reached into the basket, got out a sandwich and a beer, and reclined in his seat. Wispy clouds ahead, the hum of the motor. Despite his readiness for it to all be over and to keep his promise, Guy felt no sense of hurry. A timeless peace cocooned them.

Dorothy tilted forward, straining against the seatbelt, seeking something far below. She turned back to Guy, a red spot on her forehead marking where she had pressed it against the window. "Where's our picnic?"

He frowned at his sandwich, remembering that all he had slathered on was some mayo before Alex had interrupted him.

She giggled. "No, you know—the *picnic*. When are you going to kill us?"

Guy shifted in his seat. "Jeez, hon. You make it sound so terrible. Like murder."

"Hate to break it to you, but that is what they call it." She gave Guy's arm a soft punch. "Hey, lighten up. Here at the end, we have to laugh."

"I guess so." He gulped, not feeling as cheerful. "Last chance. Are you absolutely sure you want out?" Guy held his breath knowing this moment was her or his last chance to stop the plan.

"Oh yeah, no doubt for me. My body is useless, and it hurts." Dorothy winced and blinked back a tear. "It's my time. You're the one who should be questioning your end."

He brushed it off. As long as Dorothy said she was ready, so was he. "I just don't want to be alone without you." He reached over to hold her hand, but she pulled away.

"But you're sick too, right?" Her eyes narrowed. "Right?"

Guy felt a twinge of guilt—he had never kept secrets from Dorothy. He just wanted to grab hold of her and jump off Luke's rock. *She'll forgive me in the afterlife, right? It's time.*

The steely, sharp blade of intention skewered him to the core. He took a deep breath, cut the throttle back, and pushed forward on the steering yoke—the plane's nose dipped. The vast blue-green waters of the Atlantic lay beneath them, awaiting their arrival.

32

PERRYTON, TENNESSEE
LUCKY ACES BAR

Meanwhile . . .

Marvin Bailey sat head bowed on his usual stool but, after a minute, glanced up at a huge man standing behind the bar. Bud Whorton, owner and proprietor of the Lucky Aces, only glared back. Shaking his head, he pounded a beer bottle on the counter and slid it across to Marvin.

"I'm not sorry. I *had* to throw you out yesterday," he said.

Marvin only grunted in response.

Bud, whose handlebar mustache was long enough to need special care, polished a glass with a dishcloth. "Listen to me. We had a coupla nice ladies in here, and it's not even preseason yet, and you're already screaming at the TV whenever any sports announcer talks about the Titans. Give it a rest, man."

Marvin glowered at his beer. Bud moved down the bar.

Not much had changed at the Lucky Aces with the passage of

time. It had stayed a favorite of Marvin's since he had been old enough to drink.

 Situated on the edge of town, the same giant oak tree hung over the same gravel-packed parking lot and aged building. Only one brief episode in the early eighties had interrupted the years of sameness. A recent Italian immigrant named Augustino Delatorini had bought the run-down establishment after the death of its longtime owner.

The young restaurateur and dreamer struggled with English but completed a budget facelift to the front façade, painted the interior with pastel colors, installed a variety of indoor plants, and renamed it Friendly Spot. Marvin had hated the name and those pastels.

And apparently so did everyone else. Visitors didn't materialize, and locals avoided the place. After six months of empty afternoons, the Friendly Spot tavern went up for sale.

Bud Whorton had snapped it up. Marvin cheered when he saw that Bud had given away all the potted plants and gold-framed panoramas of the Mediterranean coastlines and removed the unfortunate outdoor marquee. To everyone's delight, Bud had touched up the original faded metal logo with fresh paint and remounted the revered LUCKY ACES sign.

Now Marvin felt at home along with the steady regulars—mainly working men with scruffy beards and diesel-spotted denim who clutched a series of beers, argued sports, cussed at politicians, and longed for the good old days. Marvin's people.

Every afternoon, he shuffled the half mile from his apartment to the Lucky Aces and sat on the same stool, often regaling anyone who would listen to come-from-behind victories and general nostalgia regarding a certain glory era of high school sports. A black-and-white dog-eared photo of Marvin, down on one knee with a football under an arm, hung near the men's room door. Bud had thrown it away once, but Marvin found it in the garbage bin and rehung it. These memory scraps sustained a meager thread to his former life.

After the divorce with Dorothy, he had taken over management duties in his father's construction business but soon ran it into the ground. Marvin wound up as a heavy equipment operator for the former competition. On a blustery winter morning, he had showed up for work on the heels of a drunken night, slipped off his backhoe, and landed on his head, qualifying him for a lifetime of modest disability checks.

Today, Bud's forgiveness came bit by bit—he continued to stare at Marvin.

Marvin raised his beer to him. "I'm sorry, man, it won't happen again." He took a swig and bowed in submission.

"Wouldn't that be marvelous?" Bud smirked.

One of the television screens above a row of half-empty liquor bottles aired CNN news. Something the news anchor said—just a few words, including a name— jerked Marvin to attention. He leaned forward, concentrating on the screen, and barked, "Bud, dial up the sound on this here TV." He pointed a bent finger up at the Toshiba in the middle. The volume rose, and to everyone in the room's astonishment, a piece of hometown history was playing center stage on national television.

Marvin sat motionless, hypnotized until the station went to commercial. "Can you believe it? That's my ex-wife up there in that plane." He turned and beer-breathed on the man next to him. "My Lord, she's up there in that stupid-looking airplane with that son-of-a-bitch Pickering guy!" His blurred eyes glazed over and roamed up to the ceiling. "What was his first name, anyway?"

A crowd gathered behind Marvin, staring at the screen and nodding their approval. "Hey, there's that lady reporter again. Hot damn!"

Bud scratched his chin. "I remember Pickering. And Dorothy too. Well, I'll be dipped," he muttered, and reached for his phone. "I'll call some of the old gang."

Mankind aspires for order but settles for chaos.

"Can you hear me?" Billy winced at Ted Melden's voice blaring in his earphones. He visualized his caffeine-hyped boss pacing up and down the newsroom.

"Get up beside that plane, goddammit! These shots are getting boring, Billy Boy!"

"Okay, Chief," Billy said, trying to hide his excitement. "I'll do what I can. But the Navy just radioed me to keep my distance, so I can't get too close. I'll stay above and behind them at about four o'clock. It's the best position for the cameras, anyway." He realized that with the US military and the news world watching him, he was treading the fine line between observer and intruder. He wiped the sweat from his forehead and jumped when Heather's scream pierced his headset.

"Oh no, look! The plane! Daddy, don't!" Her fists pounded the window.

"Damn, he's doing it!" Billy cried.

"They're going down!" Lisa Marie spoke rapid-fire as WFYU's camera image captured Guy's Bonanza tracking a definite steep descent. "Is this a tragic ending to a murder–suicide? Are the Pickerings being forced into something even more deadly? There's no way of knowing what's happening inside that plane." With a voice lowered to a more seductive tone, she lowered her chin and leaned in toward the lens. "Stay tuned for more!"

Billy winced at Lisa Marie's theatrics and thought about reeling her in, but before he could say anything, a fast-moving object streaking up toward the Bonanza caught his attention. "Oh God, it's getting real! Here comes the Navy."

<hr>

The Navy Seahawk sped upward from behind and below, popping up next to the Pickerings at four thousand feet elevation. They maneuvered to an aggressive position, a hundred yards to the left.

"Shit! What the—" Guy screamed and jumped in his seat. "Where did they come from? Why are they here?" He leveled off his descent and banked right, away from the intruder.

The chopper also banked right, correcting their heading to regain their menacing proximity to the Bonanza.

The helicopter's windows showed only men's stern faces, motioning to him. Sweat dripped from Guy's forehead. *What did I do? I better find out.* Only wanting to talk to Dorothy, he had intentionally left the radio off all day. He now flicked it on and instantly recoiled at the blaring voice coming from the helicopter.

"November Niner Niner Seven Zero Two, do you read me? Niner Niner Seven Zero Two, come in!" The Navy's fingernails-on-a-blackboard message came through loud and clear. Guy had no idea how to respond, so in deer-like fashion, he froze in the virtual headlights.

Guy's arm jerked forward and fumbled with the radio switch—and snapped it off. "Some kind of mistake. What do I say? Maybe we just ignore them."

"Sweetie, one escort wasn't enough for you?"

"What? Where?" Horrified, Guy looked back over the right wing at the until-now-unnoticed second helicopter, trailing by two hundred yards. It was the Channel Seven Bell 407, the circular side window framing two people's screaming faces.

He squinted, and even at this distance, he recognized his daughter and his grandson. No need to hear their words—Guy already knew the message.

"Shit!" he groaned. "You've got to be kidding me."

Dorothy reached over and laid a hand on Guy's thigh. Her eyes shone with a curious blend of trust, hope, and suspicion.

His own gaze wandered to the horizon and could only linger there.

"As you can see on our camera shot, a Navy helicopter has intercepted the airplane and is flying *very* close to them." Lisa Marie was on a roll. "There's still no confirmation of communication." She tossed her hair behind her shoulder. "I should mention at this point that a close contact of mine has recently monitored the Pickerings, and I have personally witnessed unusual behavior. More details later." She flashed her signature coy smile.

Upon hearing Lisa Marie's cry of "going down," the assembled patrons of the Lucky Aces bar let out a collective gasp. The same jolt sent waves around the country. Thousands of TV sets, internet sites, and radios throughout the nation fixated on the drama, and more tuned in with each passing minute.

Izetta Tooney sat on her couch with a plate of cookies in her lap. It was time for her soaps to begin. An annoying news bulletin flashed on the screen, but when the name Pickering spiked her ear, she snapped to attention. Like a bird of prey, she swiveled her head to see out the front window and surveyed the house across the street. Nobody there.

"Oh, dear me." She held a hankie to her mouth and dialed her phone.

"Could you put me in touch with Officer Charles Hirschcorn, please?"

"I believe he is off duty today, ma'am," the station attendant responded. "Are you reporting an emergency? Is there someone else who could help you?"

"No, no one else. Please contact him and tell him it's Izetta Tooney. Ask if he's watching TV," she said, hoping her pleasant manner still conveyed urgency.

"Could you repeat that?"

———

Deep in his underground headquarters, Hooper paced in circles behind a row of men and women hunched over their computers like hungry prisoners at mealtime. The enormous bank of monitors covering one wall displayed data from all over the world—several featured Lisa Marie's face. Two women sat with headphones, recording and transcribing her words.

"Can someone tell me why the hell we are getting our intel from this high-heeled nitwit? What has this country come to?" Hooper's incredulous voice boomed through the room. "Pickering!" Hooper spit out the name. He narrowed his eyes. The threat was getting more serious by the moment. "Sounds like code for an operation."

"Visual and radar confirmation. The subject aircraft has changed course due south," Corporal Baker pointed at a screen.

Over the loudspeaker, the crackling voice of the Navy helicopter's pilot brought everyone in the bunker to a standstill. "We've engaged the subject. Visual verification—two occupants. The pilot is refusing to acknowledge our communication. If I had to judge, I'd say he looks pretty distraught."

Hooper whirled around. "Not talking, huh? And now he's headed straight for the shuttle launch. Get me the president's security chief. And for God's sake, what else have we got on this guy?" His heart raced with combat adrenaline.

Baker flourished a sheet of paper. "Very little, sir. Vietnam vet pilot. Wounded, Purple Heart, and completed his tour of duty with an honorable discharge. Married, pays his taxes, not so much as a parking ticket. Clean as they come." He gestured toward the screen emblazoned with Lisa Marie's face. "Plus whatever she says."

"Yeah, yeah, yeah. Whatever our top agent says," Hooper said in a mimicked whine. "I've seen this before. Good men with PTSD go cuckoo, just like that!" He snapped his fingers for emphasis.

He bolted into his office, cursing as he went, and slammed a phone to his ear. As he waited for connection, he fumbled in his shirt pocket for a nonexistent cigarette, then fished the brand-new pack of cigarettes from the desk. With one trembling hand, he mashed them into a misshapen lump and pitched them against the wall.

After a brief, tense conversation, he hung up and leaned over a built-in microphone. His booming voice echoed throughout the tense chamber. "We are Code Orange! Repeat. We are now Code Orange!"

34

There must be some way outta here.

Lisa Marie's added punch of a "maybe" terrorist attack on American soil brought up all-too-recent anxious memories of airplanes and unprecedented disasters. Media outlets around the world pounced on the opportunity to provide a developing catastrophe to an audience that feasted on train-wreck entertainment. The steady stream of video penetrated into other continents, and everywhere, imaginations went wild. A Toronto-based network tied into the digital feed, followed by the BBC in England within minutes of Al-Jazeera broadcasting the account throughout the Mideast. Dozens of news anchors as far away as Argentina vied for interviews and live coverage. The eager-for-drama world was eating up anything and everything Pickerings.

"Lisa Marie, has the plane altered its trajectory?" The retired Air Force pilot-turned-consultant came through loud and clear in Lisa Marie's earphones.

"Yes, Robert," she answered, begging Billy with her eyes for updated information. "Since the naval helicopter's arrival, the Pickering aircraft has changed its direction. . . ."

"Two degrees," Billy offered through the headset. "It's now paralleling the coastline, heading south-southeast off the Florida coast."

"Correct me if I'm wrong: Doesn't that put them on a course headed for Cape Canaveral?" The consultant's voice hesitated.

"Yes, sir. It does indeed," Lisa Marie confirmed.

By now, Lisa Marie had talked to a variety of off-the-shelf TV news personalities from around the country. It occurred to her she could express her opinion about who would merit live access to her domain—and a few other things. "Hey, Ted . . . Ted, are you listening?"

Ted's voice crackled over the headphones. "Yeah, what do you want? You should get up closer. Tell Billy to—"

Lisa Marie interrupted, "I'm thinking that when I arrive back at Torvis, could you arrange a camera crew to interview me? Round up all the locals—I'd like a food truck, too. I'm starving."

Ted lowered his voice. "Lisa Marie . . . Lisa Marie. Do you know the fable of the fisherman's wife?"

"No."

"Well, I can't remember the details either. But I'll bet you're just like her! So shut the hell up and report this story! That's it." Ted hung up.

Lisa Marie pouted at Billy.

He at least tried to hide his grin.

Charles Hirschcorn loved his days off—a sausage and cheese sandwich, a glass of milk, and flipping through the channels while loafing in a spaghetti-stained La-Z-Boy recliner. Today was no different. Ensconced behind a TV tray, remote control in hand, he sat back and pushed the *on* button.

One minute later, the uneaten half of a perfectly good sandwich lay abandoned as Officer Hirschcorn rushed out the door.

———

It only took Guy a minute to put the pieces of the puzzle together. *Alex knew about the plan before we left and called Heather. They somehow got on that news chopper. Shit! But why the Navy?*

"So, Guy! A flying parade. You keep surprising me." Dorothy leaned back from the glass. "What now?"

She waited. He didn't have an answer.

"Well, dear, I'm so glad you're in complete control of things," she said in that mild caustic tone that always tightened his jaw. She pulled the shawl tighter around her shoulders.

Guy swiped the sweat from his forehead. "Don't worry. I got this. . . ."

He stared straight ahead at nothing as his personal realm wobbled—a house of cards on the edge of collapse. Speechless, he drew a sharp inhale, and with an unsure hand, he reached out but hesitated over the radio. *What the hell am I going to say?* Looking like a kid without an answer when called on in class, he faked a painted-on smile for Dorothy.

She swept a pointed finger through the air. "This is turning into quite a show. A kind of public execution."

"Dorothy!"

"Except this time, the killers are the victims." With a somber eyes, she gazed out the window.

"Come on," he pleaded, while bands of fear tightened around his gut. "We're in a pickle here, and I need to concentrate." *This is all-time bad. I've got to figure this out.*

He ordered himself to calm down.

Dorothy leaned closer to his ear. "I want to go home." Her voice sounded raspy and unfocused.

Guy jolted upright and swiveled to look at her. "What did you say?"

She cleared her throat. "Honey, I want to go home. It doesn't matter what happened. Again, for some reason, things didn't work out. It's okay . . . it was a good thought. A good try. But this is not our time."

Her words hit Guy with sledgehammer force. He was nine years old again under an old oak by the river; frozen in place as he beheld uncomplicated, pure innocence. Dorothy sank a bit into her seat and pulled the shawl around her shoulders. *Is she serious?* He gaped at her. This was *not* in the plan. All his hard work (failures though they had turned out to be) flashed in Guy's mind. A heat rose in his cheeks.

"But what about your pain, your suffering? Everything!" He tried to hold back, but his voice raised a few notches. "It's all my fault the plan didn't happen. I'm so sorry. But it could still happen." He looked mournfully out the windows at the helicopters. "I could . . ." He swiveled back to Dorothy.

Her eyes held his, and he saw only love and trust. She shook her head. "No. Don't worry. I changed my mind. I'm a woman, and I'm allowed to do that. I feel different about it now. We can just wait it out in our little house that I love. Yeah, the morphine and pot make me loopy, but they help a lot with the pain. That part's not so bad anymore." She shrugged. "Natural is better for me. And you too, I think."

Guy inhaled—his cheeks puffed out as he exhaled, emptying himself of concepts along with his breath. Only seconds passed, but in this life-altering moment, it seemed like an hour. High over the Atlantic, the plan's last dregs melted away, and he burst into tears. "I will, honey. I will take you home," he spoke as best he could between choked sobs. His chin dropped to his chest, and he swiped at a tear.

Dorothy placed her hand on his thigh. "Thank you, dear."

Guy leaned his head against the cockpit window and raised his eyes skyward. Well, now it's a new ball game. *Thanks, universe or whoever's up there, for giving this old fool another chance. I'll land this airplane with my queen aboard, and whenever nature brings the end, I'll be there.* He blew out a breath of relief. *Somehow, sometime, it would be fantastic to fit in a real picnic.*

He reached over and brushed away a lock of gray hair from Dorothy's forehead. "Okay, baby, let's head on home."

He glanced to the right at the news chopper that carried his family and asked a silent forgiveness. While rolling up his sleeves, he focused his attention on the Navy helicopter. *What a damn pain in the ass these guys are. Talk about a waste of time.* He hated the overkill escort, but realizing communication was overdue, he glared daggers at the helicopter and switched on the radio. *I'll just tell them I'm headed back to Torvis and apologize for any inconvenience.* He knew consequences would come when they landed, but that mattered little to him.

"This is Niner Niner Seven Zero Two. Do you copy? Hello over there. Sorry, everything's changed," he implored into the radio waves, hoping for friendly acknowledgement. "Guess what? We want to live. How about that? Do you copy? Do you—"

"Niner Niner Seven Zero Two, this is Seahawk Four Four Three," a blaring message cut him off. "Be advised, you must change course. You are in restricted airspace. Immediate response is required!"

"Okay, fellas, I get the point. I'll take her back, nice and gentle . . . oh my God!" He stopped midsentence as the chopper swerved even closer to the Bonanza—a hostile move that narrowed the already-slim gap between the crafts.

Guy jerked in his seat. "Hey! What the hell's your problem?"

"Respond immediately!" the demand hissed in Guy's ears.

All of Guy's sadness, his anger, his shock erupted in the cockpit. "What are you doing here, anyway? This is none of your business!" he wailed, and strangled the steering yoke. "We have a right to die! But . . . turns out, we've changed our minds. So, you want a response? Here it is!" Guy pounded his extended middle finger to the side window. "I have a duty, and I aim to fulfill it! Go away, and leave us alone, you assholes!"

A full high-definition video of Guy Pickering's gestures, complete with several very discernable "fuck you"s, dominated every one of the mounted screens on the wall in front of Hooper and all the assembled soldiers.

A tangible silence hung in the bunker.

Hooper was the first to speak in his icy monotone. "We have a certified lunatic on our hands. And he's on a mission."

Shots across the bow.

Soon after Bud's phone call, word spread like rabbits on the run among the long-time locals of the Perryton community. The Lucky Aces turned into ground zero for the Pickering event, with cars soon filling the parking lot. All screens displayed live coverage, the volume blaring over the din of the excited crowd.

The deluge of customers kept coming, exceeding in numbers and noise any earlier event in Marvin's memory. He'd already witnessed a man in a jumpsuit carting in an emergency beer delivery. When people at the bar reached three deep, Bud hoisted himself on a chair and yelled into the crush that he needed to hire a couple of regulars to help out. Then, in a moment of altruistic abandon, he declared a round of half-price drinks.

Marvin was already drunk; everyone who came through the door wanted to buy him a beer. During a commercial break, he jumped on a table, scattering bottles onto the floor and bellowed over the cheering throng, "I married that woman!" He turned to the Toshiba and raised a beer bottle. "Damn fickle woman dumped me for that Pickering fella! Can you believe that? Should have stuck with me, honey. We wouldn't be flying around and crashing into shit."

It was impossible to hear the TV commentary anymore. There was no more room inside for everyone, so arriving folks gathered outside, using lawn chairs wherever they could find space. In the shade of the enormous old oak tree, a local band, the Grassy Blues, began tuning up.

———

Back in the cramped cockpit, bursting with frustration and driven by a brand-new objective, Guy shouted to no one, "I don't need any help or chaperones, damn it! I'm taking her to Torvis, so I wish they'd just leave me alone!" He'd had enough of the Navy's unnecessary intrusion and again banked the plane right. "Hang in there, Dorothy. We'll be home soon, my dear."

Despite his attempted brush-off, the Seahawk followed, maintaining an annoying close proximity. The WFYU chopper also changed course, paralleling the Bonanza at a respectful distance.

"I'm back in the saddle, honey. I'm in trouble, but I'll take the licks as they come." Guy slapped his cheek and scanned his instrument panel—a basic function of any and every flight, except today's. Comprehension jolted through his body. The cruel fuel gauge needle pointed at E.

Guy's forehead beaded up in a cold sweat. *Shit, shit, shit! I didn't think I'd need much today.* His mind raced as he calculated the fuel consumption to the Torvis Airport. The ominous feeling intensified. This did not look good.

"I'm exhausted." Dorothy's voice grew louder. "Can we land now?" To Guy, her words hung in the air like a sweet, innocent flower lei.

He checked out the distance to the gray-green waters. "Honey, it would be a very wet landing right now." *I've blown it again.* Deep inside him, the mounting pressure of the last few days grew into a tornado of self-inflicted foibles. *Is there a record for Stupidest Human on Earth?* He slumped down in his seat—the immense weight of guilt and self-loathing taking turns punching his heart.

In that moment, all hope for a just ending crashed and burned before his eyes, but just then, Dorothy's hand came to rest on his leg. He looked down at the gentle weight. *No. I'm not done. I can do this.*

His survival instincts fired up to full alert and zeroed in on the coastline, weighing his remaining options. If he attempted to make it to Torvis, he'd probably face an emergency landing somewhere. *There's always traffic on the roads. Unacceptable. No, better to play it safe. Kennedy Space Center has the closest airstrip.*

Squinting through the haze, he could just discern the Cape Canaveral compound. Launch complex thirty-nine-A was dead ahead. The space shuttle *Atlantis*, impressive on any day, stood upright and piggybacked on the enormous external fuel tank and solid rocket boosters, ready to spit fire like no other machine in the history of mankind.

More puzzle pieces fell into place. "Shit, I forgot the launch is today. But I have no choice."

He steered the yoke back to direct a course for Cape Canaveral and began a gradual descent. Guy pressed the mic talk button. "Canaveral Control Center, if you can hear me, this is Niner Niner Seven Zero Two. We need permission to land on your runway—"

"Niner Niner Seven Zero Two! Request denied!" The helicopter copilot's intense voice rattled Guy. "You are in restricted airspace. Change course immediately. That's an order!"

Oooh, that man sounds pissed. Guy ran his fingers through his hair. "Easy now, fellas. I bet you're a bit confused about me, aren't ya? Sorry about that. You'd have to know Dorothy to understand." He tried to sound friendly and casual, like old friends running into each other on the street. "It's just ol' me and the wife—no threat. Anyway,

I really am on my last drops of fuel, and I could surely use any old airstrip that you're not using. Please."

"Niner Niner Seven Zero Two. Repeat. Change course immediately! You are in danger of being eliminated."

He twisted the volume knob, lowering the Navy's rant. *Better to ask forgiveness than permission. They can bawl me out later.*

The Seahawk once again swerved close to the Bonanza.

"Would you stop with the bullshit!" Guy's shout exploded out of him. "This has been one hell of a day, and all I want to do is set this plane on the ground! Got it, buckos?"

A wave of chatter swept through the bunker. Hooper stared in disbelief at the screens. "This lunatic's on a direct course. Goddamn minutes away from the shuttle site! And we're supposed to believe him when he says he's out of gas? We can't take that chance." He fled to his glassed-in station and, with great care, punched a series of buttons on the phone, waited, and entered another series. After a few seconds, he spoke in a powdery, cloaked voice. "Inform the president and the war room. Code Red. Repeat. We are now Code Red."

Hooper slowly lowered the phone to its cradle and stared into space. *It's finally here. Goddamn. My last week, and now it comes! What a shit show of a test. This is where my legacy is tested. The innocent sometimes pay the price. I can't be weak.*

He bounded to the wall, bent over, and grabbed the crushed cigarette pack from the floor. Holding it up to his nose, he took a deep inhale and glared at Corporal Baker standing in the doorway. He straightened up. "Do you have a dog, Corporal? Do you?"

Baker gave a tentative nod, his face pale.

"Well, don't ever fucking promise him anything!"

"Guy, where are they going?"

Dorothy's inquiry reeled him back from his personal brink. He followed her finger past the window and saw the Navy Seahawk pulling down and away from Guy's plane. On the right side, the Channel Seven Bell also dropped back at a rapid pace.

"Hmm . . ." Guy said. He craned his stiff neck around to see more. "They're finally leaving us alone. It's about time."

———

A few hundred yards away, Lisa Marie projected her best grim face at the camera while delivering the latest updates. Without warning, the WFYU helicopter jerked to the right, changing speed and course and sending her makeup kit spilling to the floorboards.

"What the hell? Billy, we got news to report here. What's going on?"

"You need to get closer!" Ted demanded through the headset.

"Not now, people," Billy broke in. "All I know is we're out of here for a while. I got a direct order from the Navy helicopter to withdraw and get out of the way, and pronto. They don't care about your coverage and your shots!" Billy scanned the sky as he maneuvered the controls.

Deep out over the Atlantic, he saw two black dots low over the horizon. They were growing fast. Seconds later, he put it together. "Holy crap!"

———

The massive sound of an amplified earthquake—the deafening roar of godlike thunder—descended from above and rocked the tiny Bonanza in a sonic shockwave. Two Air Force F-22s, the world's most advanced fighter jets, flew a tight pattern over the Pickerings' aging aircraft at six hundred miles per hour in a too-close-for-comfort warning pass—a speeding Hummer passing inches away from a donkey cart.

Guy and Dorothy screamed and bounced in their seats. Within seconds, the jets were far out in front, banking tight left to circle back.

"For Christ's sake, why are they doing this?" Guy grappled with the yoke amid the wake turbulence. Dorothy gripped his shirt, watery pools filling her eyes.

He managed to right the Bonanza's flight path, and the little plane droned on toward the Cape—the comforting hum of the engine becoming a dwindling link with life.

You roll the dice; you take your chances.

"Control, this is Intercept Five Eleven. Colonel Hooper, sir, we've just buzzed the subject and must have scared the bejeezus out of them, but they have not changed course. Please advise."

The F-22's squawking message pierced the somber room, loud and clear. The assembled men and women hunched before their radar screens shot nervous glances at each other and confirmed the information in short bursts.

Hooper held up his hand for silence. All awaited his response.

He gave a small smirk. These tech-driven slackers had never seen combat or even a serious situation. The self-assuredness of rank swelled in his chest.

"Intercept Five Eleven, do you read? Subject is confirmed on course for the launch site. We are Code Red, weapons-ready status. Stay in formation, tight radius. Fire upon my order."

Inside the cockpit, a frantic Guy picked up the mic and swiveled his head in all directions, screaming into the handset, "Navy Chopper Four Four Three, or anybody for that matter! What the hell's going on? What are you doing?"

The response was immediate and bone-chilling. "Your airplane will be terminated. Do you copy? Repeat. Change course, or your craft will be terminated. Do you copy?"

Within seconds of the flyby warning, Guy realized the high price he was paying for bumbling into a no-fly zone and maintaining minimal radio contact. This was unprecedented deep doo-doo and talking more would probably be useless. His grim choices read like a menu from hell: Continue flying to the nearest landing strip, but risk going down in a fireball; or change course, run out of gas, and likely crash land on a crowded Florida highway.

Should I jump off the cliff, or shoot myself first, then over the cliff?

The Bonanza kept nosing toward the Cape. Each second could be their last.

When the F-22s soared past, Lisa Marie's head had bounded off the side window, rendering her temporarily mute. Inside the WFYU copter's backseat, an awestruck Heather and Alex also fell silent.

Billy kick-started Lisa Marie into action, feeding her information streaming into his headset from the military.

She blinked into the camera, visibly unnerved. "This is getting super bad, folks. Those poor Pickerings are in big trouble. Two really scary jets might shoot them down."

Billy cringed at her words but knew she was not faking emotion. To add authenticity, a tuft of Lisa Marie's hair now sprouted out sideways from under her headset. *This is scary, but I'm into it.* Billy hadn't been this excited since his Middle East military missions.

———

Marvin had reached his tipping point with beer, and despite the drunken fuzziness, he started concentrating on the television. News stations had begun interspersing video segments of the 9/11 attack along with the Pickering coverage, further stoking public fear and anxiety. Was a horrible event about to happen? Guy and Dorothy Pickering—victims—perpetrators? Were they going to die on television, in front of everyone?

Marvin bowed his head. What had seemed like a novel event half an hour ago had quickly turned his stomach sour with dread. Sure, he wasn't Dorothy or Guy's biggest fan. But ending this way?

"Hey, ya want in on the action?" A patron Marvin didn't know had grabbed his elbow. "Ten-dollar entry. It's five-to-one odds they croak today."

Marvin pushed the man away and barreled through the crowd to get some air.

———

Hooper paced up and down the row behind the soldiers huddled in the chilly underground bunker. They knew better than to take their eyes off their glowing screens while Hooper wielded such authority.

"What we have, people, is an airplane that has blocked all contact until within striking distance of a fully fueled shuttle rocket!" He pounded on a nearby desk, and a young recruit fainted, toppling off his seat onto the tiles. Two others rushed to help. *Sissy.* Hooper ignored them and continued speaking toward the ceiling, "Now, all of a sudden, the suspect radios he's out of gas and he wants to land nice and gentle! Beside a ready-to-launch rocket!" He paused. No one clacked on their keyboard.

"How do we know we're not being tricked into giving this freak a red-carpet welcome right into the side of our space program? For Christ's sake! Who does that?" He expected silence. No one responded.

"Pickering!" Everyone in the room jumped. "This nut job is headed straight for half a million gallons of liquid hydrogen and oxygen! We can't let him get close to that! This is just the kind of show crazies love to pull off. Damn them!" He spun and glared at Lisa Marie's face, mocking him from several screens. He pointed a finger and machine-gunned his next words. "And why the hell are we still getting our best intel from *this* twit?"

The upturned faces of the group waited for the virtual smoke to clear. Hooper let out an enormous roar, raced back into his glass-enclosed office, and slammed the door behind him.

He pinched the bridge of his nose. Then, from a vest pocket, he pulled out a cell phone and checked the contacts. He pressed *call*.

In the WFYU chopper, Billy grabbed Lisa Marie's upper arm. "This is getting real serious. We should do what we can to defuse this situation—"

Lisa Marie cut Billy off with her upheld finger as she dug in her purse for a buzzing phone.

She held it up to her ear. "Who is this?"

"You call me Mr. X, and I need information."

A surprised Lisa Marie jerked back. "Mr. X? You're kidding. I can't talk right now. I'm busy here—"

"Listen, I'm about to blow up that plane you're following!"

Lisa Marie hesitated. "What do you mean? Who *are* you?"

"Never mind that," he snapped. "We're out of time, and I need to know who's onboard that aircraft and what they're up to!"

"I don't like you."

For a few beats, all she heard were choking sounds.

"I'm . . . sorry I was unpleasant with you." Mr. X seemed to fight for a civil tone. "Can we move on before we have some extreme fireworks and whoever is on that plane gets barbecued? I want the facts on this Pickering guy."

"Yeah, that's him. But, for real?"

"For real."

"Hang on." Lisa Marie looked at Alex straining against his seatbelt, put the phone on speaker, and offered it to him. "Here, talk to this man. He wants to shoot down your grandparents."

An astounded Alex hesitated but took the phone.

"Who is this?" A pause.

"My name is Alex Pickering, and it's only my grandpa and grandma. Grandma's very sick, and he was only trying to end her suffering and die with her. Please don't. They wouldn't hurt anybody . . . Hello?"

Alex held the phone out at arm's length, gaped in dismay, and tossed it to Lisa Marie. "Dropped call."

———

Deep underground, Hooper frowned at his phone, then let it slip through his fingers to the desk. His eyes darted around the room and landed on Baker, rocking on his heels outside the glass door. He threw the door open and grabbed the young corporal by the lapels. "My God, this Pickering might be just an innocent old fool." He studied Baker's face. "My last week. Can you believe it?"

"Yes, sir," Baker squeaked. "I mean, no, sir."

"But, then again, he could be tricking us. The stakes are so high! It's too big a chance! This is not happening on my final watch!" Spinning around, he pressed a button. "Intercept Five Eleven. No change in the subject speed and course; we have less than five minutes to stop them. Arm your missiles, circle another pass, and lock on target. Be prepared to fire upon my order!"

He turned back to Baker and said in a voice just above a whisper, "He *did* say they wanted to die, right?"

In football, pile-ons are penalized.
In life, troubles do it all the time.

A compelling thirst for land consumed Guy. *Gotta set this baby on the ground.* He could make out the seductive landing strip just beyond the launch tower—it beckoned like a shimmering mirage in the desert. *It's the closest thing . . . my best chance. They wouldn't hurt a couple of old folks, would they?*

He glanced over at Dorothy. Her lips were taut, tension written all over her face. He leaned into the windshield, urging the Bonanza on while crossing his fingers and mumbling a faint "please."

———

Billy turned to Lisa Marie. "Why the hell is he headed for the Space Center? They're telling me I can't follow anymore. Gotta drop back even further."

Alex's face grew red as he overheard this from the back. He threw aside his seatbelt, flashed a thumbs up at Heather, and jumped forward.

Lisa Marie was responding to yet another question from the BBC—her countenance lacked the confidence it had shown an hour earlier. "Yes, George, we have followed this story from the start, and it doesn't look good for the Pickerings. The military is threatening in a really awful way. We may never understand the full reasons behind—"

Alex leaped over Lisa Marie's seat, landing on her lap.

"Hey!" he demanded. "What are you telling people? Tell the truth—right now!"

Billy grabbed Alex's sleeve. "Kid, Mr. Pickering turned his radio on, and I'll bet he can hear the emergency channel. We got nothin' to lose, so take a crack. I'll engage the mic on your headset. We're still broadcasting too."

"Grandpa? Can you hear me?" Alex's voice wavered while Lisa Marie's flailing hands and hairdo poked up behind him. He looked over at Billy, who only bit his lip and shook his head.

"Grandpa!" Alex repeated, louder this time. "I love you, and I'm so sorry I didn't say it." He paused, listening for a response.

"You know more than I do about life," he blurted out. "But I want you and Grandma to come home. She needs to be home, and you don't have to die now. You're still healthy, and we can go flying and stuff together. You have to live. And to the man who wants to shoot them down, if you can hear me, don't! I'm telling you, he won't hurt anybody!"

Dorothy's faint voice came crackling over the radio. "Let me talk to that boy. Listen, my dear grandson. I'm sorry, but the fact is we're none of your business. We told you: We're both sick, and it was our decision to get on with it. You get home. We might be back. Maybe not."

Upon hearing her mother's voice, an overamped Heather also bounded in between the two seats. Billy leaned to his left as far as he could. Lisa Marie squeaked and flailed behind the new bodies.

"But, Mom," Heather pleaded, "that doesn't make sense. Alex talked to Dr. Berger this morning. He said Papa's in good health."

"Down, boys and girls," Billy broke in. "Lisa Marie, you gotta tell 'em. There's no threat. No kidnapping. No terrorists. C'mon, tell 'em!" He aimed his finger at the camera.

Lisa Marie, blinking back tears, straightened up—her tousled hair and smeared mascara added authenticity. "Okay," she nodded a quick affirmation. Her message and frantic, unglued image—including Alex and Heather on her lap—began transmitting out to the world. "There's no terrorists on board! It's just two innocent old people!" She struggled to be heard over Heather's wailing. "Mr. X, don't blow up that plane!"

***

In the underground bunker, Lisa Marie's words hung in the air. Baker shot a questioning glance at his superior officer as Hooper's eyes darted between WFYU's wild drama and the radar screens.

"Goddamn circus up there!"

"Control, Intercept Five Eleven reporting. All weapons operational." The F-22's message resonated throughout the room.

Hooper dabbed at the sweat from his brow, then glared at the ceiling. "We're out of time. Green light! Fire when ready!" He slumped against a nearby desk, emotionally drained. *I hope I'm doing the right thing.*

The grim subterranean group drew a collective breath.

Baker lowered his head. "God help them."

***

People all over the globe dropped what they were doing, mesmerized by potential disaster.

In India, a couple sitting cross-legged on their apartment's floor stared, fixated, on the late-night newscast.

In Ireland, a bearded man in overalls admonished his drinking mates to settle down as he pointed to a screen in a crowded pub.

On a Hawaiian shoreline, a kanaka man sipped morning coffee

on his lanai as his wife leaned on his shoulder. A TV blared in front of them.

At the Lucky Aces, even Marvin shut up as the din of the crowd hushed, every face glued to the screens.

———

Guy's grip strangled the steering yoke. A tight-lipped Dorothy sat motionless, her focus riveted straight ahead. She put both hands on the instrument panel and cocked her head, suspicion dawning on her face.

"What's this about you being healthy?" She reached over with all her strength and grasped Guy's forearm. "Maybe no cancer." Her eyes hardened. "Tell me the truth, Guy Pickering. Do you have a month or two to live? Are you sick, or did you lie to me?"

Guy could only stare at the gray clouds around him. His voice cracked. "I've got to land somewhere. Take you home."

"Guy!" Dorothy stared at him. "How terrible. You lying old goat!" She punched him on the shoulder. "This little self-sacrificing plan of yours? You're afraid of spending time alone? You wussy! What about your son, your daughter, and grandkids? You didn't need to die now. I can't believe this."

Guy shot a quick glance at Dorothy. His mind scrambled for an excuse. "But—"

"But nothing! I asked you to end my suffering, not drag you with me into a premature grave." She huffed and turned to the window. "I always thought I'd want to be with you afterward, but now . . . you know what? I might spend a lot of time by myself. Like, all eternity." She pressed a bony finger against the glass. "Stop this plane. I'm getting out!"

Three things happened at once: The fast-approaching F-22 on the left opened its weapons bay door and lowered a single air-to-air AIM-9 Sidewinder missile. Dorothy sighted a strip of sand and cried out, "Guy, land now!" And the Bonanza engine hiccupped.

"Okay. Okay! A beach landing!" Guy howled and yanked the yoke to the right. "Shit, and I'm out of fuel."

———

"Ten, nine, eight . . ." Deep underground, the ominous voice of the pilot echoed over the speakers. Hooper froze, facing the four screens tuned to Channel Seven's helicopter broadcasts. He had seen and heard Alex and Lisa Marie's pleas. What if it was a trap? A ruse? He couldn't let something like this happen on his last week. He'd go out in disgrace. *I can't take the chance. I can't take the chance.* His eyes bulged to saucer proportions.

From somewhere deep in the bunker, an urgent voice rang out, "Radar shows directional change!"

A short, stocky man sprang up, knocking over his chair. "Visual confirmation from the Navy chopper. They veered off!"

Hooper's arm shot out and stabbed a button. "Abort mission! Repeat! Intercept Five Eleven, abort mission! Stand down!"

"Four, three, two . . ." The fighter pilot's ominous countdown and Hooper's orders collided in the still air. No one in the room breathed.

———

Like hungry lions, the F-22s charged the little Pickering craft. At the last second, the astonishing flying machines pulled up in a steep vertical climb, leaving behind a thunderous roar.

The rumble and wake from the jets again rocked the Bonanza—a life raft in a hurricane.

"Stop that, Guy!" Dorothy slapped Guy's shoulder and frowned at her obviously inconsiderate pilot. "That's enough of that."

———

"Roger, Control," the pilot's voice at last crackled over the room's loudspeakers. "Mission aborted."

As if one body, every person in the still air exhaled together.

Relief flooded Hooper. He slumped gape-mouthed into an empty chair and stared with glazed eyes at Lisa Marie's continued broadcast.

"Oh, fantastic, they missed!" Lisa Marie shouted into the camera lens over Alex's head. Aboard the news chopper, the collective screams changed to cheers as the jets performed an impossible-looking turn and ascent.

"No, no! They must have called it off." Billy grinned at Lisa Marie and pumped his fist.

"The Pickerings won't be shot out of the sky as we feared. This is great news, everybody!" Lisa Marie's raw, unpracticed narrative conveyed the message. She frowned at Alex. "Can you please get off my lap now?"

A grand, thunderous applause erupted from the Lucky Aces. Bud declared a round of drinks on the house as regulars slapped backs and hugged strangers. The crowd pressed closer to the blaring TV sets, admonishing the truly drunk to shut up in a vain attempt to discern any details. Marvin's best buddies hoisted him onto the bar, where he shouted insults to Guy Pickering.

All over the world, crowds raised glasses and cheered to cheated death.

Guy wiped his brow and scanned the beaches stretching out to the north, gauging what he could from this distance. "If I find a smooth stretch, without people on it, I think I can do it." *Never done a beach landing. If the sand is too soft, I'll flip forward. Too steep, it'll be pulled sideways. Hard pack above the water's edge—that's the key.* He squinted up to the heavens. "Now would be a helpful time to give me a break."

Just as the words left his lips, the engine coughed, sputtered, gave a last burst, and died. The propeller blade rotated to a standstill, straight up in Guy's view like an extended middle finger. With his jaw hung open, he gaped at the symbolic reminder of his continued folly. The only sound was the wind shuddering the airplane's thin metal body.

Dorothy cleared her throat. "Your plan might work out after all."

Bull horns to the rescue.

Billy pointed at the descending Bonanza. "Look, his prop is still. His engine died! I'll bet that sucker ran out of gas!" He eyed the distance to the nearest beach. "Damn, he's got a ways to go."

Alex and Heather jumped to the windows. Billy could only imagine what they were feeling, watching the star-crossed airplane carry their loved ones over the ocean on a silent, fateful descent.

Heather dabbed at her tears but said nothing. Alex put his arm around her shoulder.

"Keep them informed, Lisa Marie." Billy turned back and motioned to the camera.

Lisa Marie gave a thumbs-up and swiped the hair out of her eyes. "Oh my God, there is a dangerous new development in Guy and Dorothy Pickering's ongoing dramatic flight. After they were denied access to Kennedy Space Center's airfield, their aircraft has now developed mechanical difficulty while still over the ocean. It appears their only option is to attempt an emergency landing on a local beach. The Navy helicopter is tracking behind them. We are too."

In sight lay the only close stretch of sandy coastline free from mangrove trees and just wide enough to land a plane. *That's where he'll try.* Billy could tell the Bonanza was losing altitude at a steady rate and might not make it to shore. Even if it did, he spotted another potential disaster that awaited them on the sand. He made a quick decision. *I could catch hell for this, but if it works, it'll help.*

He switched on the intercom so all three of his passengers could hear what he was radioing on the guard channel. "This is Billy Bellams, pilot of the WFYU helicopter. We are currently close to Beechcraft Bonanza Niner Niner Seven Zero Two and near to what I believe is their intended landing spot." He glanced around at the other occupants.

"Mr. Pickering, if you can hear me, there's people all over that beach in front of you. I'll go in low, buzz it, and scare 'em off. Follow me in!"

Billy dropped his chopper into a deep, downward bank and thrust the throttles at full speed, angling toward the shore.

"Woo! Yes!" Lisa Marie pumped an imaginary train horn. "Way to go, Billy!"

———

"Right there. Do it, Guy!" Dorothy squinted through the windshield at the beach ahead of them. "Looks like a picnic there already."

"Yes, dear," Guy mumbled, half listening to his wife while concentrating on Billy's voice over the radio. He pressed the mic button. "Roger that, Mr. Bellams."

It was hard ignoring the stink eye coming from Dorothy, but Guy focused on keeping his nerves steady and the Bonanza aloft long enough to make it to the targeted strip of sand. The Bonanza drifted onward and down, with only the sound of wind whipping past the cockpit.

Izetta sat on the edge of her sofa with her bug eyes glued to a television. At the window, Charles Hirschcorn cast nervous glances out at the street, where boom-box radios and small battery-operated televisions blared the latest developments to a growing crowd.

The patrons at the Lucky Aces pushed forward, straining to hear and see the screens.

Millions of people from the far corners of the planet held a collective breath.

At this exact moment, Mitch Pickering, while scratching his behind, wandered from his bedroom into the kitchen. A heavy dullness pounded in his head, a leftover reminder of last night's party. An unlit cigarette dangled from his lips as he frowned at the two dozen missed-call notifications on his phone. With a sneer, he tossed it aside, picked up a remote, and flicked on a wall-mounted television, hoping to get an update on a college football game he had money on.

Lisa Marie's face dominated the enormous screen. He watched and listened for not even a minute before his glass of get-me-through-the-day Alka-Seltzer slipped from his hand and shattered on the tiles. The water still fizzed on the floor as he snatched his car keys from the table and dashed out the door.

Send in the clowns.

The Canaveral National Seashore ran for miles north of the base. With its sandy beaches and ever-present mangrove trees, the park on launch days lured tourists and locals alike wanting to see the awesome power and spectacle of humankind's largest rockets blasting off for outer space.

Albert Dunley, along with his wife, Marsha, and daughter, Amy, had arrived at the site twenty minutes earlier, expecting a fun-filled afternoon. But he struggled to follow his girls (as he called them) through the soft sand while carrying a heavy cooler. Marsha, often unsatisfied with life, continued with her discontent and all at once reversed her direction, pointing the entourage back to where they had just come from. Albert tried to suppress his four-letter words.

The ice chest thudded in front of him. "No way! No further!" His dry throat half croaked, half yelled his demand as he pulled out a Gatorade from the cooler. "This is it! We're staying right here!" With his hearing aids forgotten at home and all his concentration focused on twisting open the drink, he failed to hear the helicopter bearing down behind him.

Amy screamed at the fast-approaching chopper. "Dad!"

Albert's face twisted in confusion and dismay as the Dunley girls sprinted away.

"Okay, okay, we can go back. Please give me a minute—"

———

Saturday's park ranger stood in the shade of a mangrove tree at the parking lot's upper edge. Tony Medeiros was twenty-one, tall, and handsome, with a perfect bronze tan. A young woman in a skimpy bikini lingered near him, chatting about a party in town tonight. Tony loved his job.

The walkie-talkie at his hip interrupted them, screeching a frantic message—something about an airplane. "Boss, what did you say? Could you repeat that?"

"Look!" The young woman's outstretched arm pointed south.

Tony spun and saw a colorful helicopter flying up the surf line only a few yards above the sand. He didn't have time to listen to his walkie-talkie or respond to the message—he ran toward the water.

Tony skidded to a halt at the top edge of the beach just as the chopper zoomed past from right to left. Panicked people scattered in all directions, fleeing the noise and sand blast. The helicopter pulled up, then hovered a hundred yards off shore. He recognized the news channel logos. "What the hell are you doing?" he screamed into the wind and clamor. A determined crowd still struggled up through the trees, seeking the relative safety of the parking lot. Then, he spotted it: the Bonanza dropping out of the sky and heading on a course for his strip of sand. "He's gonna land that thing here?"

Tony Medeiros sprinted forward at full speed. To his left, a hovering helicopter; to his right, a silent airplane gliding steadily toward his beach; dead ahead, one heedless bozo tilting a Gatorade to his lips. Tony never broke stride. With no warning, clue, or chance, the former first-string linebacker for the Union High School Gatorbacks took out the first-time visitor.

Tony jumped up and dragged the thrashing and coughing man the shortest distance away from danger—down the short slope and into the waves.

The bikinied young woman later recounted to Tony that the physical encounter had resulted in a fascinating confluence of colors: a streak of horizontal brown ranger, the arcing spray of orange drink against the blue sky, and a pale pink man going down hard on the warm, white sand.

Confessions written in sand.

"Good job!" Guy clapped his hands together. With the last obstacle removed and flopping in the water, he leaned forward. "Let's bring her in." He finessed the rudder pedals while his mind blazed with memories. *Just like Miss Molly. Shit!*

He chanced a quick glance over at Dorothy. Her hands gripped the sides of her shawl, pulled tight around her shoulders. Her eyes were closed—a beacon of calm in a raging torrent of mishaps. *It looks like she's ready for anything.*

The beach is steep, but I won't get a second chance. He gripped the yoke hard. *Tide's out; that helps. Aim right at the top of the surf line.*

One decisive pull back on the yoke. *Now!*

The left wheel bit first, biting deeper into the sand and jerking the craft to the side. They bounced upward, corrected, and bounced again, this time both wheels catching traction.

"Yes!" he roared. The Bonanza slowed rapidly on the damp sand, and while coming to a stop, the tail end rose, then sank down to the shore with the grace of a ballet dancer's leg.

"They've landed! The Pickerings have landed!" Lisa Marie's hoarse voice resounded all over the world. The camera zoomed in on the little Bonanza, with its right wing tilting toward the waves.

"Fantastic!" Billy announced. "There's a clear spot further up the beach. I'm setting her down."

Across the globe, raucous cheers erupted, rivaling in volume the wildest Super Bowl victories. While beer steins rose in Munich and beer bottles clinked in the Australian outback, a few drunken Lucky Ace locals, having exhausted all other forms of endearment, poured beer after beer over Marvin's head.

And in a side room adjacent to the Miami Dolphins training facility, an alert NFL scout picked up a pen and pad and scribbled a reminder to find out the name of that young ranger kid.

Shaking with relief, Guy turned to face Dorothy. Behind her gray hair, the sunlight glittered off the waters of the Atlantic Ocean. A wall of stillness hit him, and he sat mesmerized by the abrupt calm in the cabin.

She blinked and scrutinized the unfamiliar landscape. Guy held his breath.

"Well, at least you pulled off a plan B," she said. A moment of silence passed before she crossed her arms and pinned him to his seat with her gaze. "You lied to me, didn't you?"

Really, right now? Right after I . . . He surrendered any hope of praise for his piloting and hung his head. She was right. "Yeah, I suppose I did."

"Why? Why did you do that?" She pointed a finger at his chest.

"The promise. I couldn't do it. I just couldn't." His gut tensed as days and weeks of worried, anxious fretting flashed in his memory.

"You . . . you *poohead*! It wouldn't have taken much. Maybe kiss me and then push me down some stairs or give me rat poison or something."

"Dorothy! Stop that. I'm telling you the truth. I thought about the options plenty, but . . ." His voice softened. "I couldn't bring myself to do it. I had to go with you. That's all there is to say, and I'm sticking to it."

He thrust out his lower lip and chanced a look out the window at several dozen displaced beachgoers, inching out of the mangroves and murmuring with excitement. A man in the crowd with a handheld radio shouted the now-iconic name, "Pickering!"

"I guess we've created quite a stir."

Several voices rang out, "It's only the Pickerings!" Guy wasn't sure who they were shouting at. Then, he saw them. Anonymous behind their reflective sunglasses, the Navy men from the Seahawk ran up and surrounded the plane in a battle-ready stance, their weapons aimed at the cockpit.

"Shit!" Guy gaped out the window. "For Christ's sake, don't these guys ever let up?" Overwhelmed by the business end of four gun barrels, he opted to remain still.

Dorothy punched him in the shoulder. "Evidently, you need help. Maybe *they* can do the job!"

"Dorothy!" Guy stared at her. "Is that what you want?"

She studied him for a few seconds and shook her head. "No . . . no. I'm only teasing. Your whole plan with the lying to me and all . . . it was awful, dumb, and wrong." She laid a hand on Guy's thigh. The warmth of her touch melted his heart. He misted up again. *What a day this has been.*

"But it's just like you to do something terribly faithful, and in a weird way, sweet. The truth is, I made a mistake from the beginning asking you to do me in and expecting you to follow through. It wasn't fair. It was me being scared and selfish. I want to make this very clear. I have loved my life, and I will accept my ending whenever it comes."

Guy wiped at his eyes and exhaled a long moan. "I . . . uh . . . whoa . . . I—"

"Don't say anything," Dorothy said. "You have been a perfect partner. And . . ." Her eyes flashed. "I'm still mad at you."

Guy blinked at her, overwhelmed by wrung out emotions. His mind was on overdrive with the day's events. "Okay. What now?"

"Deal with those fools out there. Then, get me home."

*Innocence provides more paths
to heaven than knowledge.*

"Hands up so I can see them!" the ranking Navy lieutenant shouted at the Bonanza. "Exit the airplane now!"

"Goddamn idiots. It's just us." Guy reached down to undo his seatbelt.

"Keep your hands in the air!" came the immediate response.

Guy reacted to authority—his hands flew back up.

"I said get out of the aircraft!" The lieutenant aimed his pistol through the windshield at Guy's head.

"Okay, okay, no problem." Guy hoped his pacifying voice had a calming effect and again lowered his arms to unlatch his seatbelt.

"Keep them up!"

"Well, you can't have it both ways. What the hell do you want, soldier?" Guy wagged his fingertips.

Dorothy frowned out the window at the uniformed men now surrounding her. In one swift motion, she unbuckled her seatbelt and popped open the door.

"Dorothy, no . . . wait!" Guy cried.

Not in time.

She slithered to the sand and teetered toward the loud lieutenant.

A helmeted soldier with a gadget-laden olive-colored uniform leaped forward in a vain effort at controlling her. "Ma'am, you'll have to stay back." Guy had seen this determined walk before. Fueled by the energy of an unprecedented afternoon, residual pink pills, morphine, and a nibble of brownie, Dorothy rolled like the shriveled personification of a battle-seasoned tank. The standoff between Guy and the Navy faded from importance as Dorothy tottered up to the astonished lieutenant.

"Can't you see we're having a moment here, young man? I don't like your manners." She hobbled one more step, poked a bent finger in the soldier's chest, and pushed away the barrel of his suddenly flaccid pistol. "I've had enough for one day, so you can stuff that thing up your you-know-what. I need a place to rest." She pointed at a bench under a mangrove tree. "I'll be over there."

"Ma'am, you must remain here."

"Oh, eat soup and die," Dorothy snapped.

That was it for Guy. He undid his belt, hopped out of the plane, and raced over to his plucky wife. "Now, Dorothy," he said, putting both hands on her shoulders, "we want to be civil to the nice men here." His exaggerated smile filled the reflection in the soldier's dark glasses.

Dorothy snorted in disgust.

"Check the cockpit!" The lieutenant jerked his head toward the Bonanza.

A few seconds later, he got the all clear.

"Pickering?" He leaned toward Guy's face.

"Yes, sir, I am Guy Pickering. This here is my wife, Dorothy." He wrapped his arm around Dorothy's waist. The soldier, still holding his gun in a ready position, examined them up and down but said nothing.

The lieutenant cocked his head to one side, scrutinizing Guy. He pulled out a piece of paper and ordered Guy to answer a list of questions, including his address, social security number, family names, and other details only Guy would know. One by one, he checked the boxes. He kept looking back at his helicopter while glancing at the paper and spoke into a microphone clipped to his collar, "It checks out. It's him, all right."

"You guys don't take chances, do you? Is my blood type on that list?"

———

The blades of WFYU's chopper had barely stopped spinning when Lisa Marie threw off her headphones and grabbed Billy's sleeve. "You've got the handheld on board, right? We've got to get over there and interview them." She spun around to Alex. "Hey there, how ya' doin'? Once again, we find ourselves in a kind of unusual situation. How about that? But will you please introduce me to your grandparents?"

Alex and Heather cast dubious glances at each other.

"I'm sure they would love to see you . . . and I could just tag along." Her face lit up with hopefulness.

"Yeah, let's go!" Alex half scowled and unbuckled himself.

They jumped from the chopper.

Lisa Marie grimaced at her tall heels—one of her favorite pairs, but not beachwear by any stretch. She eyed a nearby woman about her size, stripped them off, and tossed them to her with a wink.

The four raced up the beach.

———

Guy watched, uncomfortable, as dozens of displaced beachgoers filtered out of the mangroves, trying to hear and see. They now packed themselves around the tense scene. He spotted Alex, Heather, Billy, and Lisa Marie worming their way to the front of the crowd.

"Stay back, everyone!" The lieutenant swept his arm in an arc, a weapon in his other hand.

The orders, plus the uniforms and guns, froze everyone in place— a dam about to burst. Heather emitted little whimpers and trembled like a racehorse penned behind a starting gate. Guy pointed. "They're family. Let them through." The lieutenant gave a quick nod, and daughter and grandson raced forward.

Lisa Marie and Billy flashed their MEDIA lanyards at a soldier who frowned but waved them through as well.

"Mom, oh, Mom," Heather sobbed and threw her arms around her mother. "Are you okay? I love you so much. Oh my God. Oh my God." The words poured from her mouth in a rivulet of tears and slobber.

Alex sprinted past his babbling aunt and smacked into Guy. He clenched his grandfather hard.

"Whoa there, son." Guy laughed. After a moment, with a firm grip on both shoulders, he pushed Alex out to arm's length. "Damn crazy, how all this happened. But I heard you out there. I love you too. You know that, right?"

Alex nodded and held his grandfather's gaze. They both broke out in smiles. Guy glanced over at Dorothy and Alex followed his eyes. They wove over to her side.

"Grandma, I'm so glad you're okay!"

A pinpoint of smoldering light shone out from her pale blue eyes. "What were you thinking, chasing us like that?"

"I found out the truth."

They both looked at Guy, who could only shrug and grimace.

"Can you believe that man?" She smacked her lips. "Wonderful old knucklehead."

———

"I'm going in, Billy." Lisa Marie tapped her in-ear receiver and whispered into a microphone, "Check, check."

Billy adjusted his camera. "I'll make it work. Ted will be thrilled."

As they got closer, she noticed Guy staring at her with narrowed eyes and detoured over to target Dorothy. *Not ready for him.*

Alex looked annoyed while listening to her plea for an interview with reassurances of necessity and brevity. She gave a final flip to her hair, aimed a perfect smile at the camera, and nodded at Billy. He signaled a countdown with his fingers.

"We're here now with Dorothy Pickering, the captive on today's airplane journey," Lisa Marie launched in. "And what an incredible journey it has been! Dorothy, in your own words, were you afraid for your own life today? Is it true that this was a flight to end it all?" She swiveled the microphone into Dorothy's face.

An awkward silence lingered. Lisa Marie opened her mouth to urge the conversation on when Dorothy squinted at her. "That's a real nice blouse you have on, but who the heck are you?" she said with one raised eyebrow.

"Oh, why thank you. I am Lisa Marie, WFYU Channel Seven News." She peered into the lens and batted her eyelashes a few times for good measure.

Dorothy continued to study her face. "Say, weren't you in our front yard the other night?"

Lisa Marie blushed underneath her heavy makeup and choked down a lump in her throat. "That's a long story. I happened to be visiting my auntie across the street, and—"

"Don't worry. We all make mistakes. Some more than others." Dorothy's face held a wry smile that offered Lisa Marie a degree of forgiveness.

"Yeah, I guess so . . ." Lisa Marie trailed off.

Dorothy turned to Alex and whispered something in his ear. He spun around and ran.

Lisa Marie cleared her throat and refocused on her work. "But anyway, how do you feel about becoming such a worldwide news story?"

Dorothy squinted up at Lisa Marie. "What do you mean?"

"People all over the world were concerned for your survival."

"Well, that's kind of silly, isn't it? *We* weren't."

Alex reappeared at Dorothy's side, and as if by magic, a foil-wrapped platter appeared in her hands. She peeled back the aluminum and offered up the innocent-looking brownies to Lisa Marie. "Would you care for one, dearie? They're homemade."

This is not ordinary TV, but it will play great. Human angle. Lisa Marie debated for one half second. Despite years of hard-fought battle with a sweet tooth, she succumbed to the universal allure of chocolate and defaulted to yes. *And I'm starving.* Her painted nails plucked up the biggest square. "Thank you very much. There you have it, people, the real Dorothy Pickering, safe and sound, and sharing home-baked goods with me. As soon as Mr. Pickering is available, we'll be interviewing him as well. Were there others involved? How did this incredible day begin, and what's the true story behind today's flight? We'll find out and be right back to you. Lisa Marie reporting for WFYU News."

She turned toward the camera, held out the treat, and took a big bite.

42

To err is human, to transform a mistake is divine.

Police cars, fire trucks, drab military vehicles, and television news vans choked the beach's parking lot, lending an emergency vibe to the afternoon, but several hundred well-wishing beachgoers thought otherwise and kicked off party time. Guy stood in amazement as generosity ruled and people by the dozens shared sandwiches, chips, dips, bowls of potato salad, tubs of iced drinks, and more. Hamburgers and hot dogs flamed on every barbeque pit. Music thumped in the air, and hundreds of cameras clicked thousands of times.

Today's unexpected commotion had transformed into a fine public picnic. Dorothy sat in the shade thanking strangers and nodding her approval of the festivities. But as the afternoon progressed, all the excitement and activity took its toll. Guy saw in her face the growing fatigue and asked the police to keep the crowd away from her. Moments later, her head slumped sideways in a gape-mouthed stupor. As a breeze blew in from the ocean, a kind woman tucked her shawl back over her shoulders.

Guy stood off to one side, ducking reporters, muttering apologies, and refusing to autograph scraps of paper. Every few minutes, he craned his neck to check on Dorothy and then toward the beach, past the mangrove trees, keeping an eye on the Bonanza. A tow truck at the top edge of the sand had run a cable out to the airplane and pulled it farther up, beyond the reach of any waves.

One determined young woman reporter with a shiny new lanyard squirmed around a cop and made it to Guy's side. "There's widespread speculation that you were trying to commit suicide with your wife. Is that true?" she said, and thrust a microphone in his face.

Guy sighed and swallowed. "When you're about to lose someone so close, you can't feel the difference between them and you. . . . Rules don't matter. There was nobody else to help. I did what I thought was best." He straightened up his shoulders.

"What made you change your mind?"

"I didn't change my mind." Guy turned toward his wife. "She did. She realized something . . . something inside her." He paused, staring at the waves. "I don't know shit about how these things are supposed to go." Guy zeroed in on the young woman. "And here's the thing. One minute, everything's just fine, and all of a sudden, there's pain and suffering, and the damn grim reaper is knocking on the door. And we're just supposed to accept that's all there is at the end? Misery and no choices? Shit!"

The reporter studied him, pulled a phone out of her purse, and shook her head. "Mr. Pickering, you sure thumped a wasp's nest of controversy. A lot of people are talking about this. Many support your self-determination rights, but there are groups that vehemently denounce your actions. For some, it's a religious issue; for others, it's a moral issue."

"Well, I have an issue with those issues," Guy huffed.

"And of course it's illegal."

Guy raised his eyebrows, now amused. "I'd be in trouble, huh? Throw my dead body in jail?" He smiled at the woman. "Now, if you'll excuse me."

He headed for the nearest policeman and leaned close. "Say there, got any ideas on how we can make our way out of here? I've got to get her home."

The officer looked over at his colleagues. "They're still doing their investigation and paperwork. You're not flying. That's the only thing I know."

———

Alex stood fifty feet away, also surrounded by a few reporters. One moved in closer with a microphone. "Quite a few people around the world heard you and your plea. Can you describe your feelings at that moment? Did you think it would work?"

Alex became aware his hand covered his birthmark. He let it drop and met the reporter's eyes. "I was scared and pissed at the same time. You do what you've got to do." Through a gap in the throng, he saw something and did a double take. "I gotta go."

He maneuvered through the crowd and stopped before a familiar face. "Amy," he said.

"Thanks for making such an effort to meet up," she said, with a sparkle in her eye.

———

"Okay, Ted, got it." Billy spoke into his cell phone. "Lisa Marie! The boss wants us to interview the ranger dude who saved that white whale."

She stood under a mangrove tree, gazing at the waves and swaying to an inner beat.

"Lisa Marie! Are you listening? I see him over by that crowd."

She swung around. "Oh my God, this day has really been full of surprises, hasn't it? I feel so different. Yes. Yes. Let's go talk to that cute man. I can do it."

Billy strode ahead and pulled the ranger aside. "Hey, buddy, what's your name?"

"Tony Medeiros." He flashed white teeth.

"I'm Billy Bellams, the pilot of the chopper that swept in on your beach. Sorry, I had to do it."

"You? That was awesome, man! I get it." Tony punched Billy on the shoulder.

"If it's okay with you, my station would like to do a brief interview."

"Sure, fire away." He shot a thumbs-up at a nearby throng of young women and men.

Billy tilted his head toward the bikini-clad group. "Friends of yours?"

"They are now," Tony winked.

Billy maneuvered him with a better background—a view of the surf. "So here's the deal. My reporter seems a bit overwhelmed. She's had an unusual day." He then waved Lisa Marie over. "You ready?" he called out to her. "Let's do this. Here we go . . . three, two, one."

Lisa Marie sauntered over and swung a microphone near the ranger's face. "How does it feel to be a hero, Mister Ranger Man? Tony, is it?"

Behind the camera, Billy frowned but kept on filming.

"Hey, it's just what you do." Tony shrugged, and his Hollywood-style smile filled the screen.

"And what brings you out here today?" Lisa Marie grinned. "Do you come here often?"

Billy winced.

"Well, you know, I've worked at the park for almost two years now. Nothing like this has ever happened before, that's for sure." Tony beamed and laughed.

Lisa Marie tilted her head at him; her bloodshot eyes couldn't hide the dreamy gaze. "Never, huh? That's wild." She leaned in closer. The camera now showed only half of her face. "Wow, you really *are* something, aren't you?"

Tony hesitated. "Well, I saw this plane coming in and this dude right out there in the middle . . ." He hovered a flattened hand at shoulder height, approximating a descending airplane. Billy watched her eyes rove to Tony's hand, then his tanned muscular arms, then his chiseled cheek bones, and she swooned toward him.

In her hands, the forgotten microphone wavered, resembling an inconsequential toy. "Want to see my helicopter? I've got one, you know," she purred.

Billy lunged forward. "Cut!"

Unlikely friends. Discovered gold.

Marvin relished being the center of attention with all the folks still arriving at the Lucky Aces, but he needed air and stumbled outside. He saw cars parked for a hundred yards up and down the highway. Spotlights were tacked up and leftover Christmas lights strung on the building's exterior so the action would not stop at dusk. The band rocked a medley of country hits, and dancers raised a cloud of dust in the back lot. The liquor distributor's truck got trapped behind a swarm of cars, and after a series of futile attempts at negotiations, the driver, who Marvin had known all his life, locked the cab and joined the celebration.

Marvin felt elated and lightheaded with a pang of long-ago sadness. He shook off the feeling and retreated through the doors to a round of raucous cheers. Bud bustled through the throng, alternating between a nervous scowl and a huge smile while shaking hands and tossing empty bottles into a pile of bulging plastic sacks. A couple of regulars manned the bar. Marvin settled on a stool and started swaying back and forth, pointing up at the TV screen. "I coulda done better," he mumbled. No one heard him.

———

Billy hadn't seen Lisa Marie for almost half an hour when he spied her seated against a mangrove tree at the far end of the beach. "There you are. Where have you been? What the heck *was* that back there? What's going on with you?"

Her red-tinged eyes wandered for a second, then took him in. "Oh, Billy, I've been a bad girl. The Pickerings came so close to being cooked in the sky. It was all my fault." She paused and wiped at her smeared mascara.

Billy sat cross-legged beside her and laid a hand on her shoulder. "Yeah, well . . . that's arguably true. But hey, look at it from another angle: If we hadn't intervened, I doubt they'd be alive right now."

"Something's come over me. Everything is so fantastic." Lisa Marie let a handful of sand run down on her knee. "Feel this. It's so beautiful and warm. Wait, what did you say?"

"I said they were on a one-way mission, and if we hadn't been along for the ride . . . think about it, I'm sure they'd be at the bottom of the ocean. At least now there's a chance for a more natural ending. The kids are happy about that."

"Huh . . . I guess it's not so terrible that I blew it all out of proportion."

"No, that *was* terrible." He gave her a hard look. "But you lucked out. Hell, I was a part of it, so I'm responsible too." He patted her knee. "Come on, let's get you a cup of coffee. We've still got to cover the Pickerings' exit out of here."

———

Dorothy heard an overwhelming bell ringing in her head, somehow strange but familiar at the same time. A slight backward vacuum tugged at her from somewhere deep. A jolt. Her body seemed to meld into her chair as naturally as the fabric. All sounds from every source funneled through an electric tube. A bigger jolt. The left side of her body drooped and trembled. Her twitching vibrated her off the chair, and she landed prone on the sand. With her face contorted with pain and confusion, her left arm drew up in a quivering spasm.

What's this ringing? Where's Guy?

"Call an ambulance! Call an ambulance! She's having a stroke," a voice rang out.

As soon as Billy heard the shouting, he pushed through the bystanders and positioned his camera on his shoulder, vying for a clear shot. Surrounded by commotion, he only got a partial view, but it was enough to see Guy kneeling, holding Dorothy's hand and speaking in her ear.

He flicked the *on* button.

Heather stood nearby with a phone pressed to her ear, projecting her frantic, pleading voice to someone on the other end. Guy hovered a few inches over Dorothy's struggling mouth. Guy only nodded in response to her, and Billy couldn't tell if this man was agreeing to a murmured request or simply accepting this overwhelming event. A drop fell from Guy's chin and landed on Dorothy's breast. *So here you are. I knew all along you weren't no terrorist. You're just a lovesick puppy, you old son of a bitch.*

A thirty-something man with an intense face, clad only in a bathing suit and T-shirt, pushed by Billy, bustled up beside Guy, and said, "I'm a doctor. Stand aside, and let me see what I can do."

Guy stared at the stranger with an exasperated face. He didn't move. Dorothy's grip on his hand felt weak.

"Sir, please. You need to shift back a bit. Let me check her vitals, and we'll get her to a hospital right away." The doctor put an insistent hand on Guy's shoulder and pulled him backward.

Guy lost his balance and took an awkward tumble onto his butt, astonishment on his face. "No! No. That's not what she wants. We want to go home." He struggled to get to his feet as an ambulance siren pierced the air.

"Sir, if you please, we'll take good care of her. Trust me." The young doctor tried his best to convey assurance.

Guy glanced at Dorothy and around at the crowd. "Trust?" he spat the word out. He was breathing hard, panting his message. "No, you trust me when I say this woman does not need more of your hospitals and your futile, grasping efforts. She needs me to get my shit together and take her home. That's where this should end." Guy's bloodshot red eyes blazed at the dumbfounded doctor.

"If you'll just calm down, I'm trying to save her life!" The doctor's voice took on an edge. He waved his hand over the gathered onlookers' heads and signaled to the ambulance attendants pushing forward with a gurney. He grabbed Guy's arm, attempting to maneuver him aside. "Please move, sir. She needs immediate medical attention, and you're standing in the way."

Guy whipped his arm back. "Don't you dare tell me I'm standing in your fucking way!" He trembled, his teary gaze brimming with tears.

As if dismissing the protests of a child, the doctor pushed against Guy's torso and motioned the attendants forward. "Believe me, I understand your concern, and we'll do everything in our power to—"

"Understand *this*!" Guy's body twisted around, one fist arcing upward in a swinging roundhouse. His direct hit on the doctor's chin sounded like the pop of a small balloon, and the doctor staggered backward against two in the crowd, sending all down in a squawking heap.

A second later, the gurney nudged its way into the combat zone, and the confused attendants stared at the prone, moaning bodies, trying to determine which of them their designated casualty was. An eager stranger jostled Heather to one side, and now her phone dangled from a limp arm, her face a portrait of disbelief with lips that moved but uttered no words.

In a soundless bubble amid the chaos, Billy stood mesmerized by the moment's intensity, not bothering to check whether his camera was in focus as the news-driven job slipped away like an unremembered dream. Billy's camera slumped, then went dark. Billy ignored the well-intentioned but pushy physician and studied this distraught, gray-haired mystery man who, in a strange new way, pulled at strings deep inside him.

"What's happening?" Lisa Marie appeared by his side.

"Shit just got even more real—and I've got an idea," he said. "Are you with me?"

"I guess so. Yes. What are we going to do?" She squeezed his arm.

"We're going to make things right."

Without second-guessing his plan, he stepped over the profanity-sputtering doctor and closed the short distance between himself and Guy. He saw the defiance seeping from Guy's face as he hovered over Dorothy's contorted mouth still trying to convey an unintelligible message.

"Mr. Pickering, I'm Billy Bellams, the pilot of that chopper over there." He jerked his head to the north end of the beach, where the Bell 407 sat, looking out of place but important. "When it comes to trust, I can't expect any from you. I understand that." Billy leaned closer. "But I *did* clear the way for you." He waited for a spark of recognition, then whispered, "It's got plenty of gas and ready to go. Let's get her home."

Guy drew back, skepticism written on his face, then frowned when he saw Lisa Marie standing nearby. She scrunched up her nose and waved two fingers back at him.

"Don't worry," Billy said. "She's embarrassed but wants to help." The two men met each other's gaze, and in a meaning-laden gesture, Billy bowed his chin. "We can do this."

Guy blinked. Then, as comprehension spread across his face, he nodded.

That was all the encouragement Billy needed. He spied Alex in the surrounding throng, motioned him forward, and passed him the camera. "Hold this for me, would ya?" He evaluated the young man for a second and made a quick decision. "And come with us. Plan B."

He spun around and pointed at Dorothy. "Hurry, you two!" he bellowed at the ambulance attendants. "Get her into the chopper. The hospital's too far. It's quicker to medivac her."

Guy tensed and grabbed Billy's arm, but Billy shot him a private wink. Again the nod, and Guy let go.

The attendants hesitated. One of them cast a nervous glance over at the whirling red lights atop their ambulance. "But we're supposed to—"

"Hurry up, you shitheads!" Billy pointed at the Bell 407. "These are the Pickerings! What are you waiting for?"

That did the trick. They leaped into action, scissored the stretcher down to its lowest level, and placed Dorothy like filigreed glass upon the padded surface.

Guy grimaced, and Billy followed his gaze to the would-be-Samaritan doctor still splayed on the sand, blinking his crossed eyes.

"Sorry," Guy murmured.

"Forget him," Billy said. "We've got a flight to catch." He slipped behind the gurney. "Get her on that helicopter!" He waved Lisa Marie closer. "You too. Come on!"

The attendants started toward the Bell 407, but before Billy could follow, the ranking navy lieutenant charged up the bank and caught him by the arm. "Halt! What's your authorization and destination?"

The officer trained his gaze on Guy, whose blank and guilt-ridden look didn't help the ambient confidence level.

Billy straightened up and pointed back at Dorothy. "That's my charge. My responsibility." He swirled and stabbed a finger at the Bell 407. "And that's my chopper. Time is of the essence. We've got to medivac this patient!" He knew that sounding and looking confident was important, so he planted his feet in a battle-ready stance, slapped his hands on his hips, and glared at the soldier.

Lisa Marie stepped up to the lieutenant with Alex holding Billy's camera, pointing at them all. "You need to understand we're broadcasting this event, with our camera catching every detail." She glared at the officer's dark glasses. "There's no time to waste! With the world watching, do you want to be the one responsible for an old lady dying right here?"

Billy held his breath; this was *some* bluff.

The lieutenant looked both of them up and down for an eternal moment, then whirled around to the disorganized phalanx struggling behind them. "Thompson! Smith! Rodriguez! Move those people back, and get that damn gurney on board! Now!"

Turning to Guy, the lieutenant gave an apologetic bow. A dazed Guy half raised a hand in response.

Billy and Alex shot relieved glances at each other, and with a quick nod of gratitude to the lieutenant, they resumed their lumbering sprint toward the WFYU Channel Seven News chopper.

Dorothy's life hung by a thin thread.

The biggest thing in life is death.

Dorothy's head swam with a commotion of voices—ringing coming from every direction and making no sense. The sun, though low in the sky, hurt her eyes. The earlier sharp pain now subsided into an unfamiliar, muddy, and heavy numbness. In a frightening realization, she found she couldn't call out or even speak. Amid a jostling, a blur of mangrove trees passed overhead.

Her only thought was, *Where's Guy?*

Billy reached the chopper first. He slid the wide side door open and brushed away the jackets and flight bags on the floor, making room for the gurney. Within seconds, Dorothy's stainless steel and vinyl palanquin arrived, carried by four Navy men who had muscled aside the still-reticent ambulance attendants.

Billy wasted no time buckling himself into the pilot seat as the soldiers gently strapped their cargo onto a secure spot in the passenger area. Guy jumped into the seat by Dorothy's head and stroked back a tuft of her hair. Her panicked eyes darted about.

Lisa Marie, Heather, and Alex broke free from the crowd and stopped near the helicopter's open doorway.

"Stay back!" Billy shouted, and flipped the switch on the chopper's mighty motor.

He called out to Alex and pointed to Tony Madeiros. "Hand that camera to the ranger over there." Alex sprinted the ten yards to a very surprised Tony and thrust the sophisticated device into his hands.

As the din of the engine whine grew louder, Billy focused on Lisa Marie. "I'm taking the family! Hey! You're Lisa Marie. Wrap it up. This is your moment!" He gestured toward Tony. "He's your new cameraman. You know what to do. Give 'em hell!"

Billy winked, and she nodded her understanding.

Heather squirmed like she was ready to burst. "You don't need a ticket, lady!" Billy yelled at her, waving her in and pointing at the front seat beside him.

The rotor blades spun faster and faster.

"Alex, hurry! Get your ass onboard. I need you!" Billy pawed the air with his left hand.

Alex hesitated for a second, grabbed an astonished young girl by the arm, and pulled her to the helicopter door. He looked up at Billy with a silly grin.

"Damn it, bring her!" He jerked his thumb toward the open space. "Might as well make this a party," he said to no one.

The two teens scrambled inside, but before Alex slid the door shut, Amy waved with a half-apologetic, half-gleeful smile toward the crowd. The plump, pale man who had been tackled earlier and the woman beside him waved back with open mouths.

The blades revved higher; people scattered from the sand blast to the safety of the mangroves. With a steady, growling roar, the Bell 407 lifted off and banked west and north toward Orlando.

"Point this at me," Lisa Marie instructed Tony. "Spin the focus wheel until I look good, here," she showed the viewfinder. "And press this button. Can you do that for me?"

"I can do anything," Tony smiled.

"I thought so," she said with a flip of her hair.

It was time to check in with Ted. She hadn't appeared on camera since her interview with Tony, but she was feeling much more clearheaded after the coffee and a bottle of water. She turned on her earpiece, cringing as she heard Ted's voice.

"What the hell? Where's Billy? Where's Lisa Marie? Damn! This is a disaster!"

"Ted! Can you hear me?" Lisa Marie's words broke through.

"God, it's about time." His voice came over the earpiece in heavy grunts. "What is this? Your picture's all blurry and off center!"

"So what? Let's do this." She flashed a genuine smile into the lens. "This is Lisa Marie reporting for WFYU News. What an incredible day, folks. Hard to believe this stuff. Whew! Oh my God, am I blown away!"

"Down, girl. Take it easy," Ted panted in her ear.

She ignored him, feeling a newfound, easy green light flourishing through her veins. "In what began as a report that maybe . . . possibly . . . we were witnessing a terrorist attack or something really awful, turns out that was a hell of a screwup. Ha! The Pickerings are just these darling old people who wanted to kill themselves. Or maybe only one of them did? I don't know, but I gotta say, we *so* stretched it. Sorry."

Ted burst through the connection. "Don't admit that we stretched anything, you idiot!"

Lisa Marie pursed her lips as Ted's rant grated in her ear. She knew he was seeing her on screen in the newsroom. "Go stretch yours,

Ted," she shot back. But then her gaze caught on a vision beyond Tony. "Look!" She aimed a finger, and the camera swiveled down the beach toward Cape Canaveral at the very moment the *Atlantis*'s main rockets lifted the majestic missile above the treetops, filling the sky with red-orange flame and smoke. "Oh my God, that is so cool! Have you ever seen anything like it?"

"Lisa Marie," Ted mumbled. "Lisa Marie, please come home."

———

"Check out behind us, Mr. Pickering."

As the helicopter rose and tilted forward, Billy pointed out a side window. Guy and Alex bent their heads into the glass and watched in amazement as the regal *Atlantis* rocket, spewing immense crimson clouds, soared into the sky. "And to think you almost spoiled the party."

45

There's no place like home,
unless it's a castle under siege.

By the time Billy's helicopter approached 7501 Willowside Road, only sunset's remnants remained, as street lamps blinked on to illuminate the roadways. Conversation had been minimal during the flight. He'd heard a shouted address after taking off and plugged that into his GPS. When he looked back, he saw Guy stroking Dorothy's forehead and Heather cradling her feet.

Billy said nothing, but he fretted about two things: *Number one, I wonder if I'll have a job tomorrow. And number two, I hope to hell I don't get arrested for stealing this thing.* When he broke the silence over the headset, announcing that they were close, Alex leaned into the forward cockpit area.

"This is, like, awesome that you're doing this."

Billy hid a schoolboy grin, checked the scene below him, and whistled his astonishment. "Whew," he said. "Would you look at that? I didn't expect a big welcoming party."

"This isn't our place. Couldn't be," Guy said while studying the neighborhood below.

All aboard strained to see out the windows.

"There's the Olds in the driveway!" Heather said. "But why all the people?"

———

Indeed, Willowside Road teemed with a crowd over five hundred strong, stretching for two blocks in both directions. An hour earlier, the well-behaved crowd had swelled beyond Hirschcorn's comfort level, and he'd called for backup. He watched the men, women, and children sitting in the middle of the street. Some carried candles, and some had signs proclaiming, LONG LIVE THE PICKERINGS and WE LOVE YOU DOROTHY AND GUY. A woman dressed like a Sunday school teacher and two sallow-faced gentlemen wearing suits and ties bounced other signs above their heads that read, THOU SHALT NOT KILL and SINNERS REPENT. A lady clown had set up a free face-painting chair on the sidewalk for the kids, and a few people clustered around a long-haired young man strumming a guitar. He belted out improvised songs about the day but was having a hard time coming up with rhymes for the word Pickering.

Seven police cars had showed up at Hirschcorn's call, but they had to park blocks away because of the packed bodies. The officers now circulated through the widening throng, with Hirschcorn occasionally bellowing commands to vacate the neighboring lawns. Every half hour or so, he made a run to the familiar Tooney nest for cookies and soda, bringing along a variety of news crews. A thrilled Izetta fed them all with colorful Pickering stories.

When the helicopter's *chop-chop* sound arrived, everyone lifted their eyes skyward and "They're coming home!" cheers erupted.

Reporters and paparazzi pushed forward, vying for position and screaming orders at each other. Hirschcorn raced to the middle of the street, holding his arms out in a vain attempt to corral the crowd. All the officers went full throttle at his command, but the sheer number of excited people hampered their efforts to control this mob. The shouting throng surged in all directions, overwhelming the unprepared police.

———

Billy shouted over his shoulder at Guy. "Well, damn it, Mr. Pickering, I can't set this chopper down anywhere near here. They aren't clearing a spot for me to land."

Guy's jaw hung open. He had never seen this many people in his neighborhood, much less holding signs with his name and face. "This is crazy! What are they all doing here?"

"They're here because you're famous now," Amy said. "And Alex is too."

"Famous?" Guy snorted. But the crowd didn't seem deterred by the chopper's proximity. "Shit! What can we do?"

"I see a field over there." Billy pointed at a junior high school baseball diamond.

"That's a half mile away. No," Guy said. "It'll take too long to get Dorothy home."

Billy tapped his chin. "Maybe this wasn't such a good idea."

Guy leaned in to Dorothy. "Hang on, honey . . . please." Her eyes were closed, her face still. Guy's heart clenched until he confirmed the slow rise and fall of her chest.

The helicopter blade's hammering filled the sky over the street—inside the chopper, only silence.

Guy's world narrowed down to a single focus. Dorothy's face appeared calm and pale but emanated a knowingness that mesmerized Guy. He had never seen this look on her face: content, strong, distant. A shiver ran down Guy's spine. *Oh my God. It's close. We've got to hurry.*

"Wait, check it out!" Alex's cry jolted Guy out of his reverie. Alex pressed both hands on the window. "It's like a motorcycle parade."

All five of them peered down on Willowside Road in amazement as a dozen chopped, chromed, and minimally muffled cruiser-style bikes rolled through the throng's upper edge in a tight *V* formation, fanning bodies out like the wake from a ship's bow.

Alex squinted at the motorcycles. "Grandpa! We know that guy!"

Guy looked doubtful as he surveyed the lead biker, who had a stubby cigar hanging between his gritted teeth. "The biker that saved my ass? Captain, was it?"

"Seems he's doing it again." Billy paused and shot a sly glance at Guy. "You know, I've never landed with celebrities aboard. You seem to be making a habit of this grand entrance stuff."

Guy frowned and opened his mouth to object—but stopped. Unfortunately, he thought the man was right.

Guy turned back to the window and watched as the formation rumbled forward, the Captain scanning each driveway. When they reached the battered Olds in the Pickering driveway, he raised a gloved hand and circled it overhead. The bikes peeled off, alternating left and right with ear-splitting blips of the throttle, prodding many people back onto Izetta's petunias.

After the motorcycles formed a clear wide circle opposite the Pickering house, the Captain swung a leg over the Harley's seat, cocked his head skyward, and waved a come-on-down signal to the hovering chopper.

"I'll be damned," Billy grinned. Within one minute, he set the Bell 407 down in the perfect position facing the Pickering household. Billy cut the motors and turned to the passengers. "Stay here until I get some help." With the blades still rotating, he jumped out and raced over to the closest police officer.

Him again? Guy groaned as he slid the chopper door open and recognized Hirschcorn.

"I need two officers to carry a gurney!" Billy shouted.

To Guy's surprise, Hirschcorn didn't hesitate and ordered several policemen to be ready next to the helicopter. He conferred a few words with the Captain, who at once snapped the cigar from his mouth and swept an arm toward the crowd. The assembled bikers began clearing a path. Billy helped Heather, Alex, Amy, and Guy jump out to a round of cheers. Four uniformed officers aided in unstrapping and pulling out the gurney. Guy and Heather were right behind as the men hurried their cargo through the crowd and up the steps to the front door.

In seconds, Dorothy's gurney disappeared inside.

Guy hesitated at the doorway and dared a glimpse back at the incredible swarm gathered in his front yard. For a brief moment, he remained there, dumbfounded by the immensity of the scene—the intense shouts and the bright camera lights. A thousand eyes stared back at him.

He shaded his eyes from the glare and saw the Captain flash a powerful thumbs-up. Tiny's tall bulk stood next to him, struggling with a forced grin. He managed a slight reluctant wave.

His down-home manners kicked in, and Guy raised the other hand up shoulder height to acknowledge the cheering visitors in his yard before ducking through the door.

———

Amy laid a hand on Alex's arm. She spoke loud enough to cut through all the commotion.

"Hey, you. Thanks for the lift. Wow. I never saw this coming."

"This morning seems like a week ago," Alex grinned.

"And I'm real sorry about your grandma. I'll bet she's one of the good ones."

He just sighed, unable to think of any words.

"I better get on home," Amy said. She pointed a finger up the street. "It's crazy, but I worry about my dorky parents. They've got to be losing it by now. Maybe see you around the neighborhood? The convertible would be a little calmer ride next time. I'd like that." She hugged him, and he watched her disappear beyond the swarm.

Billy tapped him on the shoulder. "You did good out there, big guy."

"You're the one who did good." Alex reached out to shake hands.

Billy ignored the hand and embraced him with both arms—a solid hug. He released him and took a step back, looking chagrined. "I've got to fly this tin can out of here before somebody stops me. You take care, all right?"

"Really?" Alex said. "After all that's happened, it ends so quick?"

"Everything ends." Billy said. He shrugged his shoulders. "Sometimes fast."

Alex eyed the house. "Yeah, I guess so."

A shout rang out. "There's the kid." Heads spun and cameras panned to capture another sighting.

"Whoa. Look out. Incoming!" Billy said as a gaggle of reporters approached them. "I'm outta here."

Alex froze, Billy's departing wink lingering in his mind as he was swallowed by the crowd. Sudden finality.

The news crews descended like vultures, shouting for attention, peppering Alex with questions. A teenage girl squirmed her way through the crush and held out her right forearm, bound in a cast up to the elbow. Her eyes glowed with expectation—in her other hand, a magic marker.

"Can you comment on today's events?" a man bellowed into his ear.

Alex held up his hands. "Okay, listen everybody." A cluster of microphones appeared before him. "My grandfather loves my grandmother," he said, glancing into the surrounding faces. "He loved her so much, he wanted to die with her. That's it. Grandpa did what he thought was best. He's a good man, and I'm *really* glad it all turned out like it did."

One news reporter pressed ahead. "Throughout the afternoon, there was widespread fear about a deliberate attack on the Kennedy Space Center. Were there ever any intentions of such a strike from anyone involved in today's events?"

"Grandpa a terrorist? He fought for this country. He's got a Purple Heart! And I've even seen him carry spiders outside," Alex chuckled. "No way! That was a bunch of crap. Some things get blown out of proportion and—" He stopped midsentence and looked around at the faces. "All I can say is that it was all a huge mistake. I guess there's a lot of paranoia out there. I'm tired and I should go. So, that's all."

After a minute more of autographs and shaking hands, Alex waved goodbye, squeezed through the tight circle, and made his way up to the front steps.

The remaining throng scattered again as Billy's chopper took off, but the balladeer on the curb stubbornly held his place amid the wind blast and strummed a new song about a young purple-haired hero. Alex gave one last acknowledgement to the spectators, slipped inside, and bolted the door behind him.

7501 WILLOWSIDE ROAD

~~MONDAY~~

~~TUESDAY~~

~~WEDNESDAY~~

~~THURSDAY~~

~~FRIDAY~~

~~SATURDAY~~

SUNDAY 4:00 A.M.

The crossing.

Heather's eyes fluttered open. She yawned, stretched out her arms, and looked over at Alex, still passed out beside her on the living room couch and emanating a soft snore. For a few seconds, waking in this unusual circumstance disoriented her, and all she felt was a kind of detached confusion. But quickly, yesterday's images mixed with leftover adrenaline and her center flooded with a blend of dread and relief. The family was back in the house.

She rose and peeked out the front window. Like party animals not willing to leave after a bash, a few stragglers wandered the street, no doubt gambling on the chance that some fresh development might yet be forthcoming. Two neighbors, intent on restoring order, ignored the stragglers and carried garbage bags, picking up bits of paper and cans left behind. Quiet had returned to Willowside Road.

She took exhausted, shaky steps into the kitchen and squinted from the bright blazing lights. Mitch, Richard, Dr. Berger, and a matronly woman with a kind but tired face sat around the table, murmuring in hushed tones. She'd met the woman who worked at a nearby home hospice center. Dr. Berger had brought her; he knew it was time. Half-eaten casserole dishes, pots of soup, and drinks, all dropped off by well-wishers, crowded the countertops.

Heather pulled up a nearby chair and joined the group. Other than mumbled "good mornings," not much was said. A knowingness pervaded her body and mind. All present understood and embraced this moment with its inevitable outcome.

In the silent, darkened upstairs bedroom, Dorothy's eyelids half opened as a gentle, permeating hum swathed her body, bringing an awareness of light and wondrous understanding. A rich luminescence stretched outward and connected her to a web of all things. In the periphery of her consciousness, she sensed the faint conversation from downstairs and knew the doctor and others had come and gone from her room. She heard shuffling downstairs—a muffled "let me know" remark and "goodbye" from Dr. Berger.

Her eyes slowly shifted to Guy sitting next to her, slumped into his chair, head drooping to his chest. *There he is.* She tried to smile, but nothing moved. Soft snores resonated from him like strums from a harp.

His breath caught in his throat, and he snorted and coughed.

Once again alert, he reached over and stroked her forehead. She let her eyes close, bathing in the heat of his palm.

"Whoa, I guess I drifted off there, honey." Guy took his time looking around the room before returning his gaze to her. A lone candle burned low. "Can you hear me?" He leaned in. "I'm betting you can."

Yes, you wonderful nincompoop.

He pulled the chair closer and kissed her forehead, his breath brushing Dorothy's face with its gentle touch. "I want to say some things." She waited, as still as a flower welcoming the morning sun. "Sorry about lying, but I didn't know what else to do. I tried my best." He rose and went to the window. "I'm such an idiot," he muttered, bit his lip, and sat back down. "It's a damn shit job, ending it all. But you know what? I'd do it again for you if you asked. That's how much you mean to me."

You and me, Guy Pickering.

He bent forward and grasped her hand. "And now it's come to this. Like you said, it's more natural," he said, wiping away a tear. "You'll go first."

Her eyes felt heavier and could barely move, but she held his gaze. Her mind teetered between desired things to say and the pull of the great beyond. She could only lay in pure silence.

"Forgive my saying, but sometimes, I think God is a real asshole. But we're at this point despite me not liking the suffering. It's what is." His gaze wandered upward. "I suppose it's possible that God knows more than I do."

Dorothy could see the candle sputter and go out with a wisp of smoke.

In the light of the moon filtering through the curtains, Dorothy beheld Guy's face. She took in the wonder of him. Thoughts became visions. All her love blossomed. *Unimaginable love.* The totality of an entire life, compressed into an overwhelming feeling, floated her upward. The light grew, flooded, and lifted.

With eyes opening wide, she drew a deep, rumbling breath and exhaled into the tunnel.

———

Guy brought his face near hers, listening, searching . . .

She was gone.

He drew back, overwhelmed, and slowly lowered his head against her breast. He let it lie there for a long time.

Epilogue

A SATURDAY MORNING
ONE YEAR LATER

It's a wrap.

Hawaii's warm, fragrant air wafted throughout the entire condo complex and out by the pool, where a wide assortment of races, ages, and body types basked in the sun. A graceful dark-haired woman dressed in a summer sari, wearing a hibiscus flower above her left ear and carrying a round tray in one hand, sashayed up to Lance Hooper as he reclined above the wet concrete on a towel-draped lounge chair. White wires protruded from both his ears, with Jack the dog sprawled beside him.

"Aloha, sir. Would you care for another mai tai?" She bent forward with a smile that could melt lava rock.

From behind mirrored sunglasses, Hooper snatched up a glass and wobbled the half-melted ice cubes before his eyes. Deeming it empty, he passed it to the waitress and checked his wristwatch. "Bring it in ten minutes," he said. She gave a polite nod and sauntered away.

Two children ran past him, their feet splashing chlorine-scented pool water onto Hooper's pale legs. He lurched upright. "No running!"

Jack jumped up and, seeing nothing to bark at, shot a reproachful stare at his master and settled back down.

Hooper soon refocused on his preferred stream of fair and balanced news verbiage. "Damn politicians," he muttered, slathering more sunblock on his belly.

───────

Park ranger Tony Medeiros laced up his cleats amid a chaotic bustle of shouts and ill-fitting uniforms. The Miami Dolphins locker room teemed with fresh, grim faces, all hoping to make it through another day of tryouts and survive the next round of roster cuts. Yesterday went well for Tony; the coaches commented on his good instincts.

He whispered a quick prayer before jogging into the practice field's bright sunlight.

───────

"Hey, Bud, you coming or what? The boys went on ahead." A skinny, weathered man with a bald head named Leonard stood with one arm propping open the wide wooden front door to the Lucky Aces.

"Yes, yes, I am. Just a minute," Bud grumbled and slipped a finger under his collar, tugging at a new-bought tie. "Damn these things." He took a last swipe at the already-clean bar surface and tossed the towel into a bin. To the left of the Toshiba flatscreen, above the half-empty bottles, hung a framed snapshot of Marvin. Bud paused, straightened the picture frame, and strode to the door, locking behind him. At eye level, a tacked sheet of paper read, CLOSED UNTIL FIVE O'CLOCK TODAY.

They climbed into Leonard's twenty-year-old Ford truck and bounced their way out of the potholed driveway and onto the highway. Leonard glanced over at Bud. "Nice of you to pay for the stone."

"Yeah, yeah. Somebody's got to do something."

"You didn't have to. I mean, you shouldn't feel guilty or anything. Shit, you must have kicked him out of the Aces a hundred times."

"Probably more," Bud grunted. "Still, what was he thinking?"

"I . . . I . . . kind of miss him already," Leonard stammered. The two men drove at a slow, deliberate pace through town, staring straight ahead.

Bud pulled his cap off and brushed his hair back. "Yeah, me too."

———

Billy leaned up against the Channel Seven News helicopter and gestured at the open door. "Dirk, you always said someday you would go up in a chopper. Today's the day, huh, buddy? C'mon, let's go."

"I don't know. It's not important . . . you know." Dirk readjusted his cap, edged up to Billy, and whispered, "You're not supposed to take people up with you. I heard that. And what about Sally? What will she say?"

"Sally's new, and she wouldn't dare snitch on me." Billy flicked his hand up in dismissal. "Remember? I'm a big shot around the station nowadays." He straightened the lapel of his jacket. "There's no more helicopter traffic stuff. Today, we're doing a feature on the Everglades. C'mon, it'll be fun."

"She's not the same," Dirk said while kicking a small rock to the side.

Sally, the fresh-faced new reporter, leaned out from her seat, straining against her seatbelt straps. "Come, Dirk. Keep us company?"

Billy watched Sally's smile hit home. Dirk gave one last look back at his control tower before heaving a sigh and taking a step toward his first-ever ride in a helicopter.

The Captain adjusted the reading glasses perched on his nose and pulled a stack of papers a little closer. He bit his lip and scrutinized the printing while a very tattooed woman to his left stared at him and a man in a tired suit sitting across a desk drummed his fingers.

"Honey," the woman broke the silence. "You've gone over this contract for three days now, right? So are you going to sign or what?"

"As you can see, our business loans are straightforward. All the conditions have been met, and we're set to go." The man leaned forward from his chair. "After signing, the docs go to final review, and it will fund by Tuesday. The next day, the place is yours."

The woman and the behind-the-desk man leaned forward as the Captain drew a deep breath and reached for a pen. "I've wanted this forever," he said. "I can't believe it." With misty eyes, he handed the signed papers to the loan agent. "My very own Harley dealership."

Alex watched as his dad dried the last of the dishes and placed his dish towel on a hook.

"We have to get going pretty soon," Mitch said. "Everyone will be there."

Shawna, a tanned, slender woman in workout clothes, tapped her chin. "I'm nervous about meeting your family."

"You don't have to worry about a thing. They're going to love you."

Shawna pulled a wicker basket brimming with an assortment of capped bottles from a nearby shelf and held it out to Mitch with expectation on her face. "We're not leaving until you take your vitamins."

"Dad, between the tofu and the yoga, Shawna is bending you in ways I never thought possible." Alex shot his father a wicked smile. "I called Grandpa," he said. "He's hoping I'll stay over and go up in the plane with him. He even promised to teach me how to pilot."

"I thought they took his license away," Mitch said with a frown. "And I don't suppose Amy has anything to do with you wanting to stay for a few days, right?"

Alex jumped up from the couch, his face turning pink. "Dad, that's none of your business. And his buddy Sam will be the official pilot." He composed himself before continuing. "One more thing. I need your permission for something . . . I want to get a tattoo." Alex fingered the birthmark on his neck. "Remember Captain, the biker guy? His wife is really cool, a tattoo artist, and she told me she could turn this into something awesome. She mentioned Texas," he grinned.

"Have her email me a sketch first," Mitch said. "We'll go from there."

"Thanks!" Alex bounded down the hallway and brushed through his bedroom door, adorned with a hand-lettered sign warning of instant death to any trespassers. He picked his way over piles of discarded magazines and electronic gear and sat down at a cluttered desk. For the thousandth time, he stared at the polished wooden frame hanging among his posters of girls and cars—a real Purple Heart.

"Did he answer the phone this time?" Richard stood leaning against the kitchen doorframe.

"Yes, he did. It's all set for tomorrow. We're gathering at his house at noon. And I want everyone together." Heather buried her head in the hall closet, searching for her baseball cap, and called out to her sons, "Come on, boys! Little League games do not wait for you!"

"I know," Richard said. "I get it. Mitch and Alex are coming too, yeah?"

"Yes." Heather paused, her focus on Richard as she waited for yet another intonation-drenched remark.

Richard clapped his hands together. "It'll be great to see them. I mean it."

Heather regarded her husband with an amused look. "Can you believe it's been one whole year? I mean, that day was so . . . so big! It seems like yesterday sometimes." She twirled a lock of hair in her fingers, lost in thought. "I really miss her."

"I know you do. I get it. I miss her too. And that big day? Wow, what can you say? And all the changes since then."

We've all changed, haven't we? Heather looked at her boys down the hallway, close to two inches taller now. *I love my family. And somehow, I feel stronger now too. Life!*

With two baseball mitts tucked under one arm, she blew a kiss to Richard and herded her young ones out the door.

———

A spotless Mercedes with a MUCH BETTER HOMES REALTY placard pasted on the doors pulled up in front of Izetta Tooney's house. A woman with an outsized smile and too much makeup jumped out the driver's side and flipped through a stapled sheaf of printouts. She had a pale young couple in tow and an appointment to show Mrs. Tooney's home.

Izetta drew her nose back from the curtains. "They're here, Charles. Let's go."

Soon after Izetta had received her check from a tabloid newspaper for her "Across the Street from the Pickerings" article, she and Charles had decided he needed to vacate "that dreadful apartment" and move in with her. Within a few weeks, he had opted for early retirement. The nine months since then seemed to have flown by. They were in escrow on a Miami two-bedroom condo.

"Where we going?" Charles grumbled.

"Don't you remember, dear? The mall. I need a sun hat for *Jamaica*." She sang the words and flicked her wrist above her head in an inexperienced imitation of a Caribbean folk dance.

"And listen to this. I found out that our travel agent from Miami that I used was actually a Pickering! Well, actually an ex-Pickering. Sharon used to be married to the son! I remember she told me that she's been to the same resort we're going to." Izetta lowered her voice. "Evidently with one of her boyfriends," she added with a chuckle.

Huey, a pudgy pipeline worker, sat on the stool next to Lisa Marie, emanating a deep oil-and-beer scent. He leaned closer. "I get Saturdays off. Dental too." Neil Diamond crooned a hit in the background. "Hey, you doin' somethin' later? A buddy of mine's got a party going." Huey's eyes roamed up and down Lisa Marie's profile. "Yo! Bartender, two cold ones here, huh?"

Lisa Marie stubbed out her cigarette and stared at the man's face for a moment, as if searching for some inner meaning she was missing. Her gaze drifted to the ceiling but soon settled on the scene out the window. The snowdrifts had melted down to a few stubborn dirty gray mounds. An enormous truck rumbled by and rattled the drinks on the tables. She lit another cigarette, stood up, and blew the smoke toward her hopeful beau. "I'm busy," she said, and grabbed her coat. *So much for being a big fish in a small pond.* She knew it would all change; she'd sent out a dozen more résumés last week.

"Excuse me, I have to make a call," Lisa Marie said as she headed for the door. Standing outside, she drew a phone from her purse and contemplated the dial. After an entire minute, she stuck out her lower lip and punched in a number.

Guy reclined into his chair with a cup of coffee in hand, his feet up on the railing beside Pedro. He waved at Charles and Izetta as they sped down the street and turned to his cat. "Cute, aren't they? Who would have thought?"

He rubbed the three-day stubble on his chin and focused his attention on the front yard. "Will you look at that? They're at it." He petted Pedro, uncurled a finger from his mug, and pointed at the dirt and grass spurting up from a fresh earthen mound in the Pickering lawn.

Pedro yawned, showing no interest in the rodent show.

The once-fought-over lawn, although trimmed, lay pockmarked with brown spots. In contrast, the flower bed burst with a profusion of blooms—marigolds, snapdragons, azaleas, roses, gardenias, and jasmine vines.

Guy sipped his java. He was satisfied with the new peace treaty. A family of insistent gophers got the lawn, but Dominga's son, Eduardo, guarded the flower garden border with diligence. Months ago, Guy traded the Ford Fairlane for gardening work, and today, the polished car sat in the driveway as Eduardo pulled weeds. He'd grown fond of Dominga and her son's company, along with her homemade tamales.

On a table across the porch, the cordless phone rang. He rose, picked up, and answered. "Hello?" There was silence on the other end. "Hello?" he repeated. He almost hung up when—

"Is this Guy Pickering?" a cautious caller began.

"Yes." He let out a derisive snort. Unwanted calls from the uninvited curious had trailed off in recent months, but here appeared to be another one.

"This is Lisa Marie. I wanted to reach out and talk for a minute. Is that okay?"

Guy sank down into the rocking chair, surprised by this voice and a flood of memories. *Why the hell is she calling?* "Well, sure, I suppose so," he said, suspicious of what she had to say. More silence—he waited for a response.

"It's been a year," Lisa Marie offered in a tentative, unsure voice. "Unbelievable, right?"

"Yes, it has been. What is it that you want?"

"I'm not entirely sure. I just knew I had to reach out."

Guy considered this. "Well, um, ah, how are you doing these days?" he asked out of sheer politeness.

"Me? Oh, I'm fine. Everything's great. Keeping busy. Got a new job up in Alaska. And how are you?"

"I'm okay. I miss my Dorothy. But I decided that I'd stick around and give young Alex a flying lesson or two. They issued me a probationary license."

"That's sweet." She paused, and another awkward silence hung in the air. "So we haven't spoken to each other since that day."

"Yeah, I know."

"I haven't had the guts to call you until now . . . I should have done it sooner." She drew a breath, exhaled into the receiver. "Listen, I owe you an apology, big time, for throwing you into that cruel spotlight. I was thinking only of myself, and I feel terrible about it. I'm sorry."

Guy did not answer right away. "Yes, that day was very stressful. I could have done without some of that." His gaze lifted to the sky. "But, okay, apology accepted. And there's something else. I owe *you* a thank you."

"What on earth for?"

"For throwing me into that cruel spotlight." Guy grinned to himself.

"Oh, w-well . . . you're welcome, I guess," Lisa Marie said.

They spent the following fifteen minutes chatting and updating each other on their lives, signing off with a promise to have lunch the next time she was in Florida. *Ha! That was unexpected,* Guy thought as he hung up. *But these days, a lot of things are.*

An hour later, Guy sat and watched several goldfinches splash in the bird bath. He grabbed a pair of binoculars as a northern cardinal landed on the edge and chased off all the other birds. He held still and listened. An image of Dorothy with a hose spraying out the birdbath swept away all other thoughts. He tapped his chest, remembering her timeless expression and feeling the warmth of fond memories.

He hoisted himself from the chair and made his way down the steps to the garage, its new door wide open. With a cloth in hand and cheek pressed to smooth metal, he sighted down the line of the Olds's fender, seeking any imperfection. He and Sam had worked for several weekends pounding all the dents out, filling any remaining depressions with Bondo and sanding for hours. Next week, a completely new paint job. He'd already mailed in an entry form to an upcoming Daytona classic car rally. Dorothy would have loved that.

Out of the corner of his eye, Guy noticed a bit of motion. At the bottom of the driveway, a bent figure with a dog on a leash shuffled along the sidewalk. He searched his memories and in a flash recognized Frank Hancock, the man who'd never returned his weed trimmer. "And that's got to be Betsy," he murmured.

A swarm of thoughts engulfed him, but he stood motionless in the shadows. He recognized the twinge of old weed trimmer resentment—but also something new. Dorothy wanted him to live, to have a good life.

His old friend was almost out of sight when—

"Frank! Hey, Frank!" Guy's shout popped from his body. He dropped the rag onto the hood.

Betsy thumped her tail against Frank's leg. He hesitated, then stopped walking.

Guy strode up to the pair. Betsy barked twice in greeting, straining at the leash.

"Hello, girl. How you doing?" Guy bent down and petted the collie. She ran her nose up and down his leg. Then, needing a rest, she sat on her haunches.

Guy straightened up and extended a hand. "Hello, Frank. Been a while."

"Yeah," Frank coughed, cleared his throat, and shook the hand. "Just out taking a walk." They both nodded, and nothing was said.

"A while back, I read something about planting trees. Take a look at this." Guy pointed a few yards behind them at a thin sapling, secured to a wooden pole, with rich fresh-packed mulch at its base. He and Eduardo had planted it a month ago. "Southern magnolia. Beautiful tree. Hard to imagine it will be sixty or even eighty feet tall someday."

Following Guy's eyes, Frank tilted his gaze up. For just a moment, Guy knew they both glimpsed a future filled with immense, broad branches.

"Ha! We're never gonna see it." Guy beamed. "You thirsty? Why don't you come on up to the house? I have good lemonade. Beer too."

THE END

About the Author

JOHN GRAYSON HEIDE (pronounced HY-dee) has written one previous novel, *The Flight of the Pickerings*, as well as numerous short stories, and a few screenplays. When not fussing over his house plants in Sun Valley, Idaho, he spends time in Panama, Hawaii, and pubs around the world.

In 2008, while residing in Hawaii and stewing about losing his life's savings in a real estate venture gone sideways, he awoke one morning with the gift of a most engaging dream. The Pickerings' story was born. Directing his attention to writing lifted John from depression. *The Flight of the Pickerings* was published in 2016 and garnered a small but loyal fan base. *The Pickerings' Last Tango* is an extensively rewritten version.

Over the years editors and numerous friends and beta readers helped to refine and polish the story with encouragement and feedback. I am grateful to all.

Contact the author at johngraysonheide@gmail.com.

If you or someone you know is experiencing
suicidal thoughts, help is available.
Call or text the National Suicide and Crisis Lifeline at 988.

For more information about assistance at the end of
life, resources are available from World Federation
Right to Die Societies (wfrtds.org), Death With Dignity
(deathwithdignity.org), and Final Exit Network
(finalexitnetwork.org).